HEROES OF THE SPACE MARINES

THE SPACE MARINES are super-human warriors created by the Emperor of Mankind, and the ultimate defenders of humanity. They are fearless, devoted and bestowed with unsurpassed physical and mental strength.

But even these warriors are not infallible, and some have turned away from the light of the Emperor and pledged allegiance to the dark forces of Chaos. Now they wage war against their former brothers, Space Marine against Space Marine, in their quest to destroy the False Emperor.

With war engulfing the galaxy, the scene is set for heroes on both sides to emerge and for names to live on in legend. These are the stories of some of those heroes.

WARHAMMER 40,000 STORIES

HEROES OF THE SPACE MARINES

Edited by
Nick Kyme
& Lindsey Priestley

A BLACK LIBRARY PUBLICATION

First published in Great Britain in 2009 by
BL Publishing,
Games Workshop Ltd.,
Willow Road, Nottingham,
NG7 2WS, UK.

10 9 8 7 6 5 4 3 2 1

Cover illustration by Hardy Fowler.

A CIP record for this book is available from the British Library.

ISBN13: 978 1 84416 731 9
ISBN10: 1 84416 731 3

Distributed in the US by Simon & Schuster
1230 Avenue of the Americas, New York, NY 10020, US.

Printed and bound in the US.

IT IS THE 41st millennium. For more than a hundred centuries the Emperor has sat immobile on the Golden Throne of Earth. He is the master of mankind by the will of the gods, and master of a million worlds by the might of his inexhaustible armies. He is a rotting carcass writhing invisibly with power from the Dark Age of Technology. He is the Carrion Lord of the Imperium for whom a thousand souls are sacrificed every day, so that he may never truly die.

YET EVEN IN his deathless state, the Emperor continues his eternal vigilance. Mighty battlefleets cross the daemon-infested miasma of the warp, the only route between distant stars, their way lit by the Astronomican, the psychic manifestation of the Emperor's will. Vast armies give battle in His name on uncounted worlds. Greatest amongst his soldiers are the Adeptus Astartes, the Space Marines, bio-engineered super-warriors. Their comrades in arms are legion: the Imperial Guard and countless planetary defence forces, the ever-vigilant Inquisition and the tech-priests of the Adeptus Mechanicus to name only a few. But for all their multitudes, they are barely enough to hold off the ever-present threat from aliens, heretics, mutants – and worse.

TO BE A man in such times is to be one amongst untold billions. It is to live in the cruellest and most bloody regime imaginable. These are the tales of those times. Forget the power of technology and science, for so much has been forgotten, never to be re-learned. Forget the promise of progress and understanding, for in the grim dark future there is only war. There is no peace amongst the stars, only an eternity of carnage and slaughter, and the laughter of thirsting gods.

CONTENTS

THE SKULL HARVEST

Graham McNeill

DEAD, GLASSY EYES stared up at the bar patrons from the floor as the rolling head finally came to a halt. It had been a swift blow, the edge of the killer's palm like a blade, and the snarling warrior's head was ripped from his neck before the last words of his challenge were out of his mouth.

The body still stood, its murderer grasping the edge of its crimson-stained breastplate in one gnarled grey fist. Blood pooled beneath the head and squirted upwards from the stump of neck. The body's legs began to twitch, as though it sought to escape its fate even in death. The killer released his grip and turned away as the body crashed to the dirty, ash- and dust-streaked floor in a clatter of steel and dead meat.

The excitement over, the patrons of the darkened bar returned to their drinks and plotting, for no one came to a place like this without schemes of revenge, murder, pillage and destruction in mind.

Honsou of the Iron Warriors was no exception, and his champion's bloody display of lethal prowess was just the first step in his own grand design.

The air was thick with intrigue, grease and smoke, the latter curling around heavy rafters that looked as though they had once been part of a spaceship. Irregular clay bricks supported a roof formed from sheets of corrugated iron, and thin slats of harsh light, like the burning white sky of Medrengard, shone through bullet holes and gaps in the construction.

The killer of the now headless body licked the blood from the edge of its hand, and Honsou grinned as he saw the urge to continue killing in his champion's all too familiar grey eyes and taut posture. It called itself the Newborn, and was clad in tarnished power armour the colour of wrought iron. Its shoulder guards were edged in yellow and black, and a rough cloak of ochre was draped around its wide shoulders. It was every inch an Iron Warrior but for its face; a slack fleshmask of stolen skin that was the image of a man Honsou would one day kill. Stitched together from the skins of dead prisoners, the Newborn's face was that of the killer in the dark, the terror of the night and the lurker in the shadows that haunts the dreams of the fearful.

It turned towards Honsou and he felt a delicious shiver of vicarious excitement as he glanced at the dead body on the floor.

'Nicely done,' said Honsou. 'Poor bastard didn't even get to finish insulting me.'

The Newborn shrugged as it sat across the table from him. 'He was nothing, just a slave warrior.'

'True, but he died just as bloodily as the next man.'

'Killing this one might make you the "next man" to his master,' said the Newborn.

'Better he dies now than we end up recruiting him and he fails in battle,' said Cadaras Grendel from across the table as he finished a tin mug of harsh liquor. 'Don't want any damn wasters next to me if we have to fight anything tough in the next few days.'

Grendel was a brute, an armoured killer who delighted in slaughter and the misery of others. Once, he had fought for a rival Warsmith on Medrengard, though in defeat he had transferred his allegiance to Honsou. Despite that switch, Honsou knew Grendel's continued service was bought with the promise of carnage and that his loyalty was that of a starving wolf on a short leash. The warrior's face was a scarred and pitted nightmare of battered flesh, his cruel features topped with a close-cropped mohican.

'Trust me,' said the warrior next to Grendel, 'the Skull Harvest weeds out the chaff early on. Only the strongest and most vicious will survive to the end.'

Honsou nodded and said, 'You should know, Vaanes. You've been here before.'

Clad in the midnight-black armour of the Raven Guard, Ardaric Vaanes was the polar opposite of Cadaras Grendel; lithe, elegant and handsome. His long dark hair was bound in a tight scalp-lock and his hooded eyes were set in a face that was aquiline and which bore ritual scars on each cheek.

The former Raven Guard had changed since Honsou had first recruited him to train the Newborn. Honsou had never fully believed that a warrior once loyal to the False Emperor could completely throw off the shackles of his former master, but from what Cadaras Grendel had told him of Vaanes's actions on the orbital battery above Tarsis Ultra, it seemed such concerns were groundless.

'Indeed,' agreed Vaanes. 'And I can't say I'm happy to be back. This isn't a place to come to unless you're prepared for the worst. Especially during the Skull Harvest.'

'We're prepared for the worst,' said Honsou, leaning over and lifting the severed head from the floor and depositing it on their table. The dead man's expression was frozen in surprise, and Honsou wondered if he'd lived long enough to see the bar spinning around as his head rolled across the floor. The skin was waxy and moist, the iconic mark of a red skull branded into its forehead over a tattoo of an eight-pointed star. 'After all, that's why we're here and why I had the Newborn kill this one.'

Like his warriors, Honsou had changed a great deal since his rise to prominence had begun on Hydra Cordatus. His unique silver arm was new and a bolt-round had pulverised the left side of his face, leaving it a burned and bloody ruin and making a glutinous, fused mess of his eye. That eye had been replaced with an augmetic implant and as much as he had changed physically, Honsou knew that it was nothing compared to the changes wrought within him.

Vaanes reached over and lifted the head, turning it over and allowing the blood to drip down his gauntlets. Honsou saw Vaanes's eyes widen as he touched the head, his nostrils flaring as he took in the scents of the dead man, while running his fingers over the cold flesh.

'This was one of Pashtoq Uluvent's fighters,' said Vaanes.

'Who?'

'A follower of the Blood God,' said Vaanes, turning the head around and tapping the sigil branded on its forehead. 'That's his mark.'

'Is he powerful?' asked Grendel.

'Very powerful,' said Vaanes. 'He has come to the Skull Harvest many times to recruit fighters for his warband.'

'And he's won?'

'Champions that don't win the Skull Harvest end up dead,' said Vaanes.

'Killing one of his men ought to get his attention,' said Honsou.

'I think it just did,' said Grendel, nodding towards the bar's door with a wide grin of anticipation.

A towering warrior in armour that had once been black and yellow, but which was now so stained with blood that it resembled a deep, rusted burgundy, marched towards their table.

Grendel reached for his weapon, but Honsou shook his head.

The warrior's helm was horned and two long tusks sprouted from beneath the visor of his helmet. Honsou couldn't tell whether they were part of his armour or his flesh. The same symbol branded into the head was cut into the warrior's breastplate, and his breath was a rasping growl, like that of a ravenous beast. He carried an axe with a bronze blade that dripped blood and shone with the dull fire of a smouldering forge.

The warrior planted his axe, blade down, on the floor and banged his fist against his breastplate. 'I am Vosok Dall, servant of the Skull Throne, and I have come to take your life.'

Honsou took the measure of the warrior in a heartbeat.

Vosok Dall was former Astartes, Scythes of the Emperor by the crossed-scythe heraldry on his shoulder guard, but a warrior who now killed in the name of a blood-drenched god that revelled in murder and battle. He would be strong and capable, with a hunger for glory and martial honour unmatched even by those who still fought for the Imperium.

'I thought your Chapter was dead,' said Honsou, pushing himself to his feet. 'Didn't the swarm fleets turn your world into an airless rock?'

'You speak of events that do not concern you, maggot,' barked Dall. 'I am here to kill you, so ready your weapon.'

'You see,' said Honsou, shaking his head. 'That's what you followers of the Blood God always get wrong. You always talk too much.'

'No more talk then,' said Dall. 'Fight.'

Honsou didn't answer, simply sweeping his axe from beside the table. The blade of the weapon was glossy and black, its sheened surface featureless and seeming to swallow any light unfortunate enough to touch it.

Honsou was fast, but Dall was faster and brought his own axe up to block the strike. The warrior spun the axe and slashed it around in a bifurcating sweep. Honsou ducked and rammed the haft of his weapon into Dall's gut, spinning away from his opponent's reverse stroke. The blade passed millimetres from his head and he felt the angry heat that burned within the warp-forged weapon.

He took a double-handed grip on his axe and widened his stance as Dall came at him. The warrior of the Blood God was fast and his roar of hatred shook the very walls, but Honsou had faced down more terrifying foes than Vosok Dall and lived.

Honsou stepped to meet the attack, throwing his arm up to block the blow. The axe slashed down and bit deeply, the blade stuck fast into Honsou's forearm. Like the Newborn and Cadaras Grendel, Honsou wore the naked metal colours of the Iron Warriors, but the arm struck by Vosok Dall's axe appeared to be incongruously fashioned from the purest, gleaming silver.

Dall grunted in shock, and Honsou knew this warrior would expect anything he hit with his axe to go down and stay down.

That shock cost him his life.

The warrior tugged at his weapon, but the blade was stuck fast and Honsou swung his axe in a mighty downward arc, hammering the glossy black blade through the top of his foe's skull. The axe smashed through Dall's helmet, skull and neck before finally lodging in the centre of his sternum.

Vosok Dall dropped to his knees and toppled onto his side, his dead weight dragging Honsou with him. Dall's entire body convulsed as the malevolent warp beast bound to Honsou's axe ripped his soul apart for sport.

Blood fanned from the cloven skull in a flood of crimson, and even as Dall's soul was devoured, his grip remained strong on his weapon.

A bright orange line, like that of a welder's acetylene torch hissed around the edge of where Dall's axe was buried in Honsou's arm and the weapon fell free with a crescent-shaped bite taken from it. Even as Honsou watched, the fiery lustre of the blade faded as its power passed into Honsou's weapon.

Where Dall's blade had penetrated Honsou's arm was unblemished and smooth, as though it had come straight from the silversmith's workbench. Honsou neither knew nor cared about the source of the arm's power to heal itself, it was enough that it had saved him once again.

He rose to his full height, standing triumphant over the dead body of Vosok Dall as the patrons of the bar stared in amazement at him.

'I am Honsou of the Iron Warriors!' he bellowed, lifting his axe high over his head. 'I am here for the Skull Harvest and I am afraid of no man. Any warrior who thinks he is worthy of joining me should make himself known at my camp. Look for the banner of the Iron Skull on the northern promontory.'

A man in a battered flak vest with a long rifle slung over his shoulder and a battered Guardsman's helmet jammed onto his rugged features stood up as Honsou made his way to the door.

'Every warlord that comes in here thinks he's got a big plan,' said the man. 'What's so special about yours? Most of them never come back, so why should I fight for you?'

'What's your name?'

'Pettar. Hain Pettar.'

'Because I'm going to win, Hain Pettar.'

'They all say that,' said Pettar.

Honsou shouldered his axe and said, 'The difference is I mean it.'

'So, who you planning to fight if you live through the Skull Harvest?'

Honsou grinned. 'The worlds of Ultramar are going to burn in the fires of my crusade.'

'Ultramar?' said Pettar. 'Now I know you're crazy; that fight's suicide.'

'Maybe,' said Honsou. 'But maybe not, and if it's not a fight worth making, then this galaxy has run out of things to live for.'

THE MOUNTAIN CITY simmered with tension and threat. Warriors of all size and description thronged the paths, squares and narrow alleys that twisted between the city's ramshackle structures of brick and junk. This close to the Skull Harvest, the city's inhabitants were on edge, hands hovering near the contoured handles of pistols and skin-wrapped sword grips. Honsou could read the currents of threat as clearly as the transformed magos, Adept Cycerin, could read the currents of the empyrean and knew violence was ready to erupt at any second.

Which was just as it should be.

The sky was the colour of a smeared borealis, swirling with unnatural hues known only to the insane. Lightning flashed in aerial whirlpools and Honsou tore his gaze from the pleasing spectacle. Only the unwary dared stare into the abyss of such skies and he grinned as he remembered his flesh playing host to one of the creatures that dwelled beyond the lurid colours.

The streets were sloping thoroughfares of hard-packed earth, and Honsou scanned the crowds around them for an old enemy, a new rival or simply a warrior looking to make a name for himself by killing someone like him.

Hawkers and charlatans lined the streets, filling the air with strange aromas, chants and promises, each offering pleasures and wares that could only be found in a place this deep in the Maelstrom; nightmare-flects, blades of daemon-forged steel, carnal delights with warp-altered courtesans, opiates concocted from the immaterial substance of void-creatures and promises of eternal youth.

In addition to the swaggering pirate bands, mercenary kin-broods and random outcasts, lone warriors stood at street corners, boasting of their prowess while demonstrating their skills. A grey-skinned loxatl climbed the brickwork of a dark tower, its armature weapons flexing and aiming without apparent need for hands. A robed Scythian distilled venom before a gathered audience, while a band of men and women in heavy armour demonstrated sword and axe skills. Others spun firearms, took shots at hurled targets and displayed yet more impressive feats of exceptional marksmanship.

'Any of them taking your fancy?' asked Cadaras Grendel, nodding towards the martial displays.

Honsou shook his head. 'No, these are the chaff. The real warriors of skill won't show their hand so early.'

'Like we just did?' said Vaanes.

'We're new here,' explained Honsou. 'I needed to get my name into circulation, but I'll let Pashtoq Uluvent build it for me when he comes against us.'

'You had me kill that man to provoke an attack on us?' queried the Newborn.

'Absolutely,' said Honsou. 'I need the warriors gathered here to know me and respect me, but I can't go around like these fools telling people how powerful I am. I'll get others to do that for me.'

'Assuming we survive Uluvent's retaliation.'

'There's always that,' agreed Honsou. 'But I never said this venture wouldn't be without some risk.'

THEY MADE THEIR way through the streets of the city, following a path that took them through areas of bleak night, searing sunlight and voids of deadened sound where every step seemed to take a lifetime. Coming from Medrengard, a world deep in the Eye of Terror, Honsou was no stranger to the chaotic flux of worlds touched by the warp, but the capricious nature of the environment around the mountain was unsettling.

He looked towards the mountain's summit, where the mighty citadel of this world's ruler squatted like a vast crown of black stone. Hewn from the rock of the mountain, the entire peak had been hollowed out and reshaped into a colossal fortress from which its master plotted his sector-wide carnage.

Curved redoubts and precisely angled bastions cut into the rock dominated the upper reaches of the mountain and coils of razor wire, like an endless field of thorns, carpeted every approach to its great, iron-spiked barbican.

Honsou's Iron Warrior soul swelled with pleasure at the sight of so formidable a fortress.

Mighty defensive turrets protected the fortress, armed with guns capable of bringing down the heaviest spaceship and smashing any armada that dared come against this place.

Even in its prime, Khalan-Ghol could not have boasted so fearsome an array of weapons.

Ardaric Vaanes leaned in close and pointed to a nearby gun emplacement aimed at the heavens. 'Big guns never tire, isn't that what he always says?'

'So it's said,' agreed Honsou, 'but if what happened on Medrengard taught me anything, it's that fortresses are static and it's only a matter of time until someone attacks you. This place is impressive, right enough, but my days of fortress building are over.'

'I never thought I'd hear an Iron Warrior say he was tired of fortresses.'

'I'm not tired of fortresses, Vaanes,' said Honsou with a grin. 'I'm just directing my energies in bringing them to ruin.'

HONSOU HAD BASED his warriors on a northern promontory of the mountain, a site that offered natural protection in the form of sheer cliffs on three sides that dropped thousands of metres to the valley floor. Under normal circumstances, it would have been a poor site for a fortress, as it could easily be blockaded, but Honsou had no intention of staying for any length of time and his warband had cleared the promontory of its former occupants in a brutal firefight that had seen them hurling their captives to their doom as an offering to the gods.

The Iron Skull flew over Honsou's temporary fortress, a graceless collection of gabions fashioned from linked sections of thick wire mesh lined with heavy-duty fabric and filled with sand, earth, rocks and gravel. A line of these blocky gabions stretched across the width of the promontory, and yet more had been stacked to form towers where heavy weapons could be mounted.

In truth, it was more of a defensive wall than a fortress and wasn't a patch on even the lowliest Warsmith's citadel on Medrengard, but it was as strong as he could make it and should suffice for the length of the Skull Harvest.

An adamantine gate swung outwards as Honsou and the others approached, the guns mounted on the blocky towers either side of it tracking them until they passed inside. Two dozen Iron Warriors manned the walls, their armour dusty and scored by the planet's harshly unpredictable climate. The remainder of Honsou's force was spread throughout the camp or aboard the *Warbreed*, the venerable ship that had brought them here and which now moored uneasily among the fleets in orbit around this world.

Honsou marched directly to an iron-sheeted pavilion at the centre of his camp, itself protected by more of the blocky, earth-filled gabions. His banner snapped and fluttered in the wind, the Iron Skull seeming to grin with a mocking sneer, as though daring the world to attack. Grendel, Vaanes and the Newborn followed him past the two hulking warriors in Terminator armour guarding the entrance to the pavilion. Each of the giant praetorians was armed with a long, hook-bladed pike and looked like graven metal statues, their bodies as inflexible as their hearts.

Inside the pavilion, the walls were hung with maps depicting arcs of the galaxy, planetary orbits, system diagrams and a variety of mystical sigils scrawled on pale sheets of skin, both human and alien. An iron-framed bed sat in the centre of the space, surrounded by bare metal footlockers filled with books and scrolls. A trio of smoking braziers filled the pavilion with the heady scent of burning oils said to draw the eyes of the gods.

Honsou set his axe upon a rack of weapons and poured himself a goblet of water from a copper ewer. He didn't offer any to his champions and took a long draught before turning to face them.

'So,' he began, 'What do you make of our first foray?'

Grendel helped himself to a goblet of water and said, 'Not bad, though I didn't get to kill anything. If this Pashtoq Uluvent is as mad as all the other followers of the Blood God I've met, then we shouldn't have to wait too long for his response.'

'Vaanes? What do you think? You've fought in one of these before, what happens next?'

'First you'll be summoned to the citadel to pay homage,' said Vaanes, idly lifting a book from the footlocker nearest the bed. 'Then there will be a day of sacrifices before the contests begin.'

'Homage,' spat Honsou. 'I detest the word. I give homage to no man.'

'That's as may be,' said Vaanes. 'But you're not so powerful you can break the rules.'

Honsou nodded, though it sat ill with him to bow and scrape before another, even one as infamous as the master of this world. He snatched the book Vaanes held and set it down on the bed.

'And after all this homage and sacrifice, what happens after that?'

'Then the killings begin,' said Vaanes, looking in puzzlement at him. 'The leaders of the various warbands challenge one another for the right to take their warriors. Mostly their champions answer these challenges, for only when the stakes are highest do the leaders enter the fray.'

'These challenges, are they straight up fights?' asked Honsou.

'Sometimes,' said Vaanes. 'The last one usually is, but they can take any form before that. You almost never know until you set foot in the arena what you'll be up against. I've seen clashes of tanks, bare-knuckle fighting to the death, battles with xenos monsters and psychic duels. You never know.'

'That mean I'll maybe get to kill something?' said Grendel with undisguised relish.

'I can as good as guarantee it,' replied Vaanes.

'Then we need to know what we're up against,' said Honsou. 'If we're going to get ourselves an army, we need to know who we're taking it from.'

'How do you propose we do that?' said Grendel.

'Go through the city. Explore it and find out who's here. Learn their strengths and weaknesses. Make no secret of where your allegiance lies and if you need to crack some heads open, then that's fine too. Grendel, you know what to do?'

'Aye,' agreed Grendel, with a gleam of anticipation in his eye. 'I do indeed.'

Honsou caught the look that passed between the Newborn and Ardaric Vaanes, relishing their confusion. It never did to have your underlings *too* familiar with your plans.

'Now get out, I have research to do,' said Honsou, lifting the book he had taken off Vaanes from the bed. 'Amuse yourselves as you see fit until morning.'

'Sounds like a plan to me,' said Grendel, drawing a long-bladed knife.

Honsou was about to turn away from his subordinates when he saw the Newborn cock its head to one side and the inner light that lurked just beneath its borrowed skin pulse with a shimmering heartbeat. In the months they had fought together, Honsou recognised the warning.

'Enemies are approaching,' said the Newborn, answering Honsou's unasked question.

'What? How do you know?' demanded Grendel.

'I can smell the blood,' said the Newborn.

THE GROUND BEFORE Honsou's defensive wall was littered with bodies. Gunfire flashed from the towers and ramparts, a brutal curtain of fire that sawed through the ranks of flak-armoured warriors who hurled themselves without fear at the gates. Sudden darkness had fallen, as though a shroud of night had been cast over the promontory, and stuttering tongues of flame lit the night as the two forces tore at one another.

The Newborn's warning had come not a second too soon and Honsou had massed his warriors on the crude walls in time to see a host of screaming men emerge from the darkness towards them. They were an unlikely storming force, a ragged mix of human renegades of all shapes and sizes. Most wore iron masks or skull-faced helmets and their uniforms – such as they were – were little more than bloodstained rags stitched together like the Newborn's skin.

They came on in a howling mass, firing a bizarre mix of weapons at the defenders. Las-bolts and solid rounds smacked into the walls or from the ceramite plates of the Iron Warriors. What the attackers lacked in skill and tactical acumen, they made up for in sheer, visceral ferocity.

It wasn't nearly enough.

Disciplined volleys barked again and again from the Iron Warriors and line after line of attackers was cut down. Their primitive armour was no match for the mass-reactive bolts of the defenders, each a miniature rocket that exploded within the chest cavity of its target.

Heavy weapons on the towers carved bloody gouges in the attacking horde, but the carnage only seemed to spur them to new heights of fanaticism, as though the bloodshed were an end in itself.

'Don't these fools realise they'll never get in?' said Ardaric Vaanes as he calmly snapped off a shot that detonated within the bronze mask of a flag-waving maniac as he ran at the gate without even a weapon unsheathed.

'They don't seem to care,' said Honsou, reloading his bolter. 'This isn't about getting in, it's about letting us know that we're being challenged.'

'You reckon these are Uluvent's men?' said Grendel, clearly enjoying this one-sided slaughter. Grendel had allowed the enemy to reach his section of the walls before ordering his men to open fire, and Honsou saw the relish he took in such close-range killing.

'Without a doubt,' said Honsou.

'He must have known they'd all get killed,' pointed out Vaanes.

'He didn't care,' said the Newborn, standing just behind Honsou's right shoulder. Its unnatural flesh was still glowing and there was a hungry light in its eyes. 'His god cares not from where the blood flows and neither does he. By throwing away the lives of these men, Pashtoq Uluvent is showing us how powerful he is. That he can afford to lose so many men and not care.'

'Getting clever in your old age,' said Grendel with a grin and slapped the arm of the Newborn. His champion flinched at Grendel's touch and Honsou knew it detested the mohicaned warrior. Something to bear in mind if Grendel became a problem.

The slaughter – it could not be called a battle – continued for another hour before the last shots faded. The attackers had not retreated and had fought to the last, their bodies spread like a carpet of ruptured flesh and blood before the Iron Warriors compound.

The strange darkness that had come with the attack now lifted like the dawn and Honsou saw a lone figure threading his way through the field of corpses towards the fortress.

Cadaras Grendel raised his bolter, but Vaanes reached out and lowered the weapon's barrel.

'What the hell do you think you're doing, Vaanes?' snarled Grendel.

'That's not one of Uluvent's men,' said Vaanes. 'You don't want to kill this one.'

'Shows what *you* know,' said the scarred warrior, turning to Honsou for acknowledgement. Honsou gave a brief nod and turned to watch as the newcomer approached the gate without apparent fear of the many guns aimed at him.

'Who is he?' said Honsou. 'Do you recognise him?'

'No, but I know who he represents,' said Vaanes, gesturing to the looming citadel that dominated the skyline.

'Open the gates,' ordered Honsou. 'Let's hear what he has to say.'

DESPITE HIS EARLIER confidence, Honsou couldn't help but feel apprehensive as he climbed the twisting, corkscrew stairs carved into the sheer sides of the rock face that led towards the mountainous citadel. The emissary led them, his sandaled feet seeking out the steps as surely as if he had trod them daily for a thousand years. For all Honsou knew, perhaps he had.

Honsou had met the emissary, a nameless peon in the robes of a scribe, at the gate of his makeshift fortress where he was handed a scroll case of ebony inlaid with golden thorns. He removed the scroll, a single sheet of cartridge paper instead of the more melodramatic human skin he'd expected, and read the tight, mechanical-looking script written upon it before passing the scroll to Ardaric Vaanes.

'Well?' he'd said when Vaanes had read its contents.

'We go,' said Vaanes instantly. 'When this world's master summons you, it is death to refuse.'

His message delivered, the emissary turned and led them through the squalid streets of the city towards the tallest peak, climbing steep stairs cut into the rocky flanks of the mountain. Honsou had brought Vaanes and the Newborn with him, leaving Grendel to finish the execution of the wounded attackers and keep the compound safe against further assaults.

The climb was arduous, even to one whose muscles were enhanced with power armour, and many times Honsou thought he was set to plummet to his death until the Newborn helped steady him. Their route took them across treacherous chain bridges, along narrow ledges and though snaking tunnels that wound a labyrinthine passage through the depths of the mountain and avoided the fields of razor wire. Though he tried to memorise the route, Honsou soon found himself confounded by occluded passageways, switchbacks and the strange angles within the bowels of the fortress.

On the few occasions they emerged onto the side of the mountain, Honsou saw how high they had climbed. Below them, the city shone like a bruised diamond, torches and cookfires dotting the mountainside like sunlight on quartz as the skies darkened to a sickly purple. Thousands upon thousands of warriors were gathered in makeshift camps throughout the city and Honsou knew that if he made the right moves, they could be his.

Any army gathered from this place would be a patchwork force of differing fighting styles, races and temperaments, but it would be large and, above all, it would be powerful enough to achieve its objective. And if the books he had taken from the chained libraries of Khalan-Ghol gave up their secrets, he would have something of even greater value than mere warriors to drown the worlds of Ultramar in blood.

The higher they climbed, the more Honsou felt his appreciation for the design of this fortress shift from grudging admiration to awe. It was constructed with all the cunning of the most devious military architect, yet eschewed the brutal functionality common to the Iron Warriors for a malicious spite in some of the more deadly traps.

At last, they emerged within an enclosed esplanade lined with pillars and crowned with what could only be the outer hull plates of a spaceship. The metal was buckled and scored from multiple impacts, the sheeting blackened and curved where the intense heat of laser batteries had pounded the armour to destruction.

A great, thorn-patterned gate stood open at the end of the esplanade and a hundred warriors in power armour lined the route they must take through it. Each of the warriors was armoured differently, a multitude of colours and designs, some so old they were the image of that worn by Honsou. Only one thing unified these warriors, a jagged red cross painted through the Chapter insignia worn on their left shoulder guard.

The emissary led them down this gauntlet of warriors, and Honsou saw Salamanders, Night Lords, Space Wolves, Dark Angels, Flesh Tearers, Iron Hands and a dozen other Chapters. He noted with grim amusement that no Ultramarines made up these warriors' numbers and doubted that any of Macragge's finest would be found in this garrison.

Beyond the gateway, the fortress became a gaudy palace, a golden wonder of fabulous, soaring design that was completely at odds with the external solemnity of its design. Honsou found the interior garish and vulgar, its ostentation the antithesis of his tastes, such as they were. This was not the palace of a warlord; it was the domain of a decadent egotist. Then again, he should not have been surprised, after all, wasn't it his monstrous ego and megalomania that had brought the citadel's builder low in the first place?

At last they came to a set of gilded doors, taller than a warlord titan, which swung open in a smooth arc to reveal a grand throne room of milky white marble and gold. The sounds of voices and armoured bodies came from beyond and, as Honsou and his retinue followed the emissary through, they saw the towering form of a daemonic Battle Titan serving as the backdrop to a tall throne that sat on a raised dais at the far end of the chamber.

A hundred captured battle flags hung from the vaulted ceiling and the chamber was thick with warriors of all sizes and descriptions.

'I thought this summons was just for us,' said Honsou.

'What made you think that?' replied Vaanes. 'Did you think you were a special case?'

Honsou ignored the venomous relish in Vaanes's words and didn't reply. He *had* thought the summons was for him and him alone, but saw how foolish that belief had been. This was the Skull Harvest and every warrior gathered here would be thinking that he alone would be the victor.

He saw a profusion of horns, crimson helms, glittering axes and swords, alien creatures in segmented armour and a riotous profusion of standards, many depicting one of the glorious sigils of the Dark Gods.

'Should we have brought a standard?' hissed Honsou, leaning close to Ardaric Vaanes.

'We could have, but it wouldn't have impressed him.'

'There is fear in this room,' said the Newborn. 'I can sense it flowing through this place like the currents of the warp.'

Honsou nodded. Even he could sense the lurking undercurrent of unease that permeated the throne room. The throne itself was empty, a carved block of thorn-wrapped onyx that would surely dwarf any man who sat upon it, even a Space Marine.

He turned as his instincts for danger warned him of threat and his hand snatched to his sword hilt as a looming shadow enveloped him.

'You are Honsou?' said a booming voice like the sound of tombstones colliding.

'I am,' he said, looking up into the furnace eyes of a warrior clad in vivid red battle plate that was scarred and burned with the fires of battle and which resembled the lined texture of exposed muscle. His shoulder guards were formed from an agglomerated mass of bones, upon which was carved the icon of a planet being devoured between a set of fanged jaws.

Upon a heavily scored breastplate of fused ribs, Honsou saw a red skull branded over the insignia of an eight-pointed star and knew who stood before him. The warrior's blazing eyes were set deep within a helmet fashioned from a skull surely taken from the largest greenskin imaginable, and they were fixed on Honsou in an expression of controlled rage.

'Pashtoq Uluvent, I presume,' said Honsou.

'I am the Butcher of Formund, the bloodstorm of the night that takes the skulls of the blessed ones for the Master of the Brazen Throne,' said the giant and Honsou smelled the odour of spoiled blood upon Uluvent's armour.

'What do you want?' said Honsou. 'Didn't you lose enough men attacking my compound?'

'Simple blood sacrifices,' said Uluvent. 'A statement of challenge.'

'You let your men die just to issue a challenge?' said Honsou, impressed despite himself.

'They were nothing, fodder to show my displeasure. But Vosok Dall was a chosen warrior of my warband and his death must be avenged with yours.'

'Many have tried to kill me,' said Honsou, squaring his shoulders before the champion of the Blood God, 'but none have succeeded, and they were a lot tougher than you.'

Uluvent chuckled, the mirthless noise sounding as though it issued from a benighted cavern at the end of the world, and reached up to tap Honsou's forehead. 'When the Harvest begins, you and I shall meet on the field of battle and your mongrel skull will be mounted on my armour.'

Before Honsou could reply, Pashtoq Uluvent turned and marched away. Honsou felt his anger threaten to get the better of him, and only quelled the urge to shoot Uluvent in the back with conscious effort.

'It'll be a cold day in the warp before *that* happens,' he hissed as the Battle Titan's warhorn let out a discordant bray of noise; part fanfare, part roar of belligerence. The harsh wall of noise echoed around the chamber, reverberating from the pillars and reaching into every warrior's bones with its static-laced scrapcode.

Honsou blinked as he saw that the throne at the foot of the Battle Titan was now occupied. Had it been occupied a moment ago? He would have sworn that it had been empty, but sat like a great king of old upon the onyx throne was a towering warrior in crimson armour edged in gold. A halo of blades wreathed his pallid, ashen face and his right arm was a monstrous claw with unsheathed blades that shimmered with dark energies.

A great axe was clasped in this mighty king's other hand and his merciless eyes swept the warriors assembled before him with a searching gaze that left no secret unknown to him. At his shoulder squatted a chittering, reptilian beast that wrapped its slimy flesh around the vents of the warrior's backpack.

The howl of the titan's warhorn ceased abruptly and all eyes turned to the warrior king upon the onyx throne. Every champion in the room dropped to one knee at the sight of so mighty a warlord.

Huron Blackheart.

The Tyrant of Badab.

AT LENGTH THE Tyrant spoke, his voice booming and powerful. A voice used to command. A voice that had convinced three Chapters of the Adeptus Astartes to side with him against their brothers. A voice belonging to a warrior who had survived the death of half his body and not only lived, but returned stronger and more deadly than ever.

Though he tried not to be, Honsou couldn't help but be impressed.

'I see many hungry faces before me,' said the Tyrant. 'I see warlords and corsairs, mercenaries and outcasts, renegades and traitors. What you were before you came here does not interest me, all that matters in the Skull Harvest is who is the strongest.'

Huron Blackheart rose to his feet and stepped from the dais to move amongst those who came before him. The loathsome creature at his shoulder hissed and spat, the pigments of its mottled hide running from spotted to scaled and back again in a heartbeat. Its eyes were black gems, devoid of expression, yet Honsou sensed malignant intelligence behind them.

A warrior in the armour of the Astral Claws, the Tyrant's former Chapter, followed behind Huron Blackheart and Honsou sensed a darkly radiant power within him, as though what lurked beneath the ceramite plates was something no longer wholly human.

Accompanying this warrior was a tall woman of startling appearance, with features so thin as to be emaciated. Her dark hair was pulled severely back from her face and cascaded to her ankles. Golden flecks danced in her eyes and her emerald robes hung from her thin frame as though intended for someone more generously proportioned. She carried a heavy ebony staff topped with a horned skull. Honsou recognised a sorceress when he saw one.

As Huron Blackheart made his way through the crowds of warriors, Honsou saw that the size of the man's throne was not simply an exercise in vanity; he dwarfed even the mightiest of his supplicants.

No wonder the piratical fleets that raided the shipping lanes around New Badab were the terror of the Imperium's shipmasters. Blackheart's reavers plagued the worlds of the Corpse-Emperor from the Tyrant's bases scattered around the Maelstrom, bringing him plunder, slaves, weapons and, most importantly, ships.

The Tyrant and his bodyguards moved through his throne room and the warriors gathered before him bowed and scraped. Honsou felt his lip curl in distaste.

'They worship him like he was a god,' he said.

'On New Badab he might as well be,' said Vaanes. 'He has the power of life and death over everyone here.'

'Not me, he doesn't.'

'Even you,' promised Vaanes.

'Then I'll be sure to keep my thoughts to myself.'

Vaanes chuckled. 'That'll be a first, but it doesn't matter. That creature on his shoulder, the Hamadrya, is said to be able to see into the hearts of men and whisper their darkest thoughts in the Tyrant's ear. Imperial assassins have tried to slay Blackheart for decades, but none have ever come close, the Hamadrya senses their thoughts long before they get near.'

Honsou nodded at Vaanes's words, watching the unseemly displays of fealty and obeisance made by the various warlords and corsair chieftains. He looked across the throne room and saw that Pashtoq Uluvent also kept himself aloof from such toadying, and his respect for the warrior went up a notch.

Then the Tyrant turned his gaze on Honsou and he felt the blood drain from his face and a chill touch of fear run the length of his spine. It was a sensation new to Honsou and he liked it not at all. The Tyrant of Badab's thin, lipless mouth smiled, exposing teeth sharpened to razor points, and Honsou found himself helpless before the warrior's gimlet gaze.

The warriors parted before the Tyrant as he strode towards Honsou, the claws of his huge gauntlet alive with baleful energies and the Hamadrya hissing in animal rage.

Huron Blackheart was a giant of a warrior, his already formidable physique boosted by cybernetic augmentation and the blessings of the Dark Gods. Honsou's head came to the centre of the Tyrant's chest plate and though it galled him to do so, he was forced to look up to the lord of New Badab.

He felt as though he were a morsel held helpless before some enormous predator or a particularly rare specimen about to be pinned to the board of a collector. The Tyrant stared at him until Honsou felt he could stand no more, then transferred his gaze to the Newborn and Ardaric Vaanes.

'This one is touched by the raw power of the warp,' said the Tyrant, lifting the Newborn's head with the tips of his claws. 'Powerful and unpredictable, but very dangerous. And you...'

This last comment was addressed to Ardaric Vaanes and with the Newborn forgotten, the Tyrant turned Vaanes's shoulder guard with the blade of his axe, nodding as he saw the red cross of the Red Corsairs.

'I know you,' said the Tyrant. 'Vaanes. Late of the Raven Guard. You fight for another now?'

'I do, my lord,' said Vaanes, bowing before his former master.

'This half-breed?'

'The last person who called me that ended up dead,' snarled Honsou.

Without seeming to move, the Tyrant's claw shot out and punched into Honsou's breastplate, lifting him from his feet. Honsou could feel the cold, dark metal of the claws digging at the flesh of his chest, the force of the Tyrant's blow precisely measured.

'And the last person who failed to show me respect in my own throne room suffers now at the hands of my most skilled daemonic torturers. They tear his soul apart each day then reclaim its soiled fragments from the warp and the process begins anew. He has suffered this agony for eight decades and I have no inclination to end his torments. You wish a similar fate?'

Honsou's life hung by a thread, yet he still managed defiance in his tone. 'No, my lord, I do not, but I am no longer the half-breed. I am a Warsmith of the Iron Warriors.'

'I know who you are, warrior,' said the Tyrant. 'The immaterium gibbers with your slaughters and the corruption you have wrought. I know why you are here and have seen the path of your fate. You will wreak havoc in the realm of the Corpse-Emperor's worshippers, but those you have wronged will shake the heavens to see you dead. Yet for all your arrogance and bitterness, you have something most others lack.'

'And what's that?' spat Honsou.

'You have a grand vision of revenge and the chance that you might succeed is all that stays my hand.'

Huron Blackheart then turned his attention back to Vaanes and said, 'You wear my marking upon your armour, Ardaric Vaanes, but I sense that you serve a power greater than this half-breed. Just remember that the Dark Prince is a jealous lord and suffers no other masters but he.'

Blackheart sheathed his blades and Honsou dropped to the floor of the throne room, breathless and chilled to the bone from the touch of the Tyrant's claws. The breath heaved in his chest and he felt the nearness of death as a cold shroud upon his heart. He looked up, but the Tyrant had already moved away.

As Honsou picked himself up, he saw the Tyrant's sorceress stare with naked interest at the Newborn, her eyes lingering long over the stitched nightmare of its dead fleshmask. Blackheart climbed the dais to his throne and turned to address the gathered champions with his axe and claw raised above his head.

'Any warrior who dares to bare his neck in the Skull Harvest should present his blade upon the Arena of Thorns when the Great Eye opens. Blood will be spilled, the weak will die and the victor shall benefit greatly from my patronage.'

The Tyrant lowered his voice, yet its power was still palpable and Honsou felt as though the words were spoken just for him. 'But know this: the gods are watching and they will rend the souls of the unworthy for all eternity.'

IN DAYS THAT followed, Honsou's warriors explored the city on the flanks of the Tyrant's mountain, learning all they could in preparation for the violence to come. Warbands were identified and their warriors observed, for each warlord was keen to display the prowess of his fighters and champions.

Ardaric Vaanes watched the sensual slaughters of Notha Etassay's blade dancers, a troupe of decadent warrior priests to whom no sensation of the blade was unknown and whose every kill was performed with the utmost grace and enjoyment. Notha Etassay, an androgynous beauty of uncertain sex, bade Vaanes spar with them and, upon tasting his blood, immediately offered him a place within the troupe.

With every battle he fought, Vaanes felt the vicarious thrill of the kill as every sensation of the graceful ballet of blades was channelled through every warrior priest. It was only with great regret that Vaanes declined Etassay's offer of a bond ritual with the troupe.

Unimpressed with the delicate bladework of Notha Etassay, Cadaras Grendel left Vaanes and the Newborn to their sport and spent his days watching the blood games of Pashtoq Uluvent's warriors as they hacked their way through naked slave gangs. Their victims were armed with little more than knives and raw terror, and such brutal murders were more to Grendel's liking. Soon he found himself wetting his blades with blood in Uluvent's arena. Such was his bloodlust that within the hour he was granted an audience upon the killing floor by Pashtoq Uluvent himself.

Those battle machines of Votheer Tark that could be brought up the mountain roared and rampaged, their engines howling like trapped souls as they crushed prisoners beneath their tracks or tore them limb from limb with clawed pincer arms. Kaarja Salombar's corsairs staged flamboyant displays of marksmanship and sword mastery, but Vaanes was unimpressed, having seen the exquisite bladework of Notha Etassay's devotees.

Honsou himself ventured little from behind his walls, his every waking moment spent in contemplation of the ancient tomes he had brought from Khalan-Ghol. What he sought within their damned pages he would not reveal, but as the days passed, his obsession with the secrets contained in the mad ravings committed to the page grew ever deeper.

The Newborn stayed close to Ardaric Vaanes, watching the killings and displays of martial ability with a dispassionate eye. It was stronger and more skilful than the majority of the warriors here, yet only recently had it begun to take pleasure in the infliction of pain and death. Differing angels warred within its mind; the teachings of its creator and the buried instincts and memories of the gene-heritage bequeathed to it by Uriel Ventris.

Of all the warrior bands gathered for the Skull Harvest, the Newborn was most fascinated by the loxatl, a band of alien mercenaries that laired in burrows hollowed from the sides of the mountain. Vaanes and the Newborn watched the fighting drills of the loxatl on a patch of open ground before these caves.

The leader of this brood-group was a kin leader who went by the name of Xaneant. Whether this was the creature's true name or one foisted upon it by human tongues was unclear, but the Newborn was impressed by the alien mercenaries, liking their fluid, sinuous movements and utter devotion to the members of their brood.

Something in that kin-bond was achingly familiar and the Newborn wondered where the sense of belonging it felt came from. Was it responding to a memory buried deep within its altered brain or was this a fragment of the psyche the Daemonculaba had stamped upon it?

'They are all related,' said the Newborn, watching as the loxatl spun like fireflies through a series of lightning fast manoeuvres designed to showcase their speed and agility. 'Would that not hinder them in battle?'

'In what way?' asked Vaanes.

'Would there not be grief or horror if a kin-member died?'

'I don't think the loxatl think that way,' said Vaanes. 'It sounds obvious, but they're not like humans. It's a good observation though. I remember reading that in ancient wars, kings would sometimes raise regiments formed by men and women from the same towns, thinking it would create a bond of loyalty that would make them stronger.'

'And did it?'

'Before the killing started, yes, but when battle was joined and people began to die, the sight of friends and loved ones torn up by shellfire or cut to pieces by swords and axes destroyed any fighting spirit they might have had.'

'So why do the loxatl do it?' asked the Newborn. 'If such groupings are so brittle, why do it? Surely it is better to fight alone or alongside those you do not care about.'

'Yes and no,' said Vaanes, slipping back into the role of mentor and instructor. 'What keeps many fighting units together is the warrior next to him and the desire not to let your battle-brothers down. Shared camaraderie gives a fighting unit cohesion, but that needs to be alloyed to an unbreakable fighting spirit in order to avoid being broken when the killing starts.'

'Like the Adeptus Astartes?'

'Not all of them,' said Vaanes bitterly.

'The Ultramarines?'

'Yes, the Ultramarines,' sighed Vaanes. 'You get that from Ventris?'

'I think so,' said the Newborn. 'I have a desire for brotherhood with those I fight alongside, but I don't feel it.'

Vaanes laughed. 'No, you won't in Honsou's warband. It's said the Iron Warriors were never ones for easy camaraderie, even before they followed Horus into rebellion.'

'Is that a weakness?'

'I don't know yet. Time will tell, I suppose,' said Vaanes. 'Some warbands fight for money, some for revenge, some for honour and some for the slaughter, but it all ends up the same way.'

'What way is that?'

'In death,' said a voice behind them and both the Newborn and Vaanes turned to see Huron Blackheart's emaciated sorceress. The woman's gaunt features were even more skeletal in the daylight, the brightness of the sky imparting an unhealthy translucence to her skin and reflecting from the gold in her eyes. Her robes shimmered and her hair whipped and twisted like a dark snake with the motion of her head.

'Yes,' said Vaanes. 'In death.'

The sorceress smiled, exposing stumps of yellowed teeth, and Vaanes grimaced. The woman appeared young, yet the price she had paid for her powers was rotting her away from the inside out. 'The Lost Child and the Blind Warrior, fitting I should find you observing the displays of an alien species whose thought processes are utterly inimical to humanity.'

Vaanes felt his skin crawl at the nearness of the sorceress. Within the seething cauldron of the Maelstrom, the terrifying power of the immaterium was a constant, gnawing presence on the edge of perception, but her proximity seemed to act as a locus for warp entities gathering like vultures around a corpse. Vaanes could feel their astral claws scratching at the lid of his mind.

He glanced over at the Newborn, seeing it twitch and flinch as though there was an invisible host of buzzing, stinging insects swarming around its face, but which it was trying to ignore.

'What do you want?' said Vaanes, gripping the Newborn's arm and dragging it away from her loathsome presence. 'I detest your kind and wish to hear nothing you have to say.'

'Do not be so quick to dismiss what I have to offer, warrior of Corax,' hissed the sorceress, reaching out and placing a hand on the Newborn's chest.

'Never speak that name again,' snarled Vaanes. 'It means nothing to me now.'

'Not now, but one day it will again,' promised the sorceress.

'You see the future?' asked the Newborn. 'You know what is to happen? All of it?'

'Not all of it,' admitted the sorceress, 'but those whose lives stir the currents of the warp are bright lights in the darkness. A measure of their path is illuminated for those with the sight to see it.'

'Do you see mine?' said the Newborn eagerly.

The sorceress laughed, a shrill bite on the air that caused the loxatl to halt their martial display and screech in rage. Shimmering patterns danced over their glistening hides and they vanished in a blur of motion, slithering and skittering across the mountainside to boltholes carved in the rocks.

'The destiny of the Lost Child cleaves into the future like a fiery speartip,' said the sorceress. 'His destiny is woven into the tapestry of a great hero's death, the fall of a star and the rise of an evil thought long dead.'

'You speak in meaningless riddles,' said Vaanes, dragging the Newborn away.

'Wait!' cried the Newborn. 'I want more.'

'Trust me, you don't,' warned Vaanes, seeing Cadaras Grendel marching towards them, his armour splashed with blood. 'Nothing good can come of it.'

'The Lost Child wishes to hear what I have to say,' screeched the sorceress, barring their way with her skull-topped staff.

Vaanes unsheathed the caged lightning of his gauntlet-mounted claws and rammed the foot-long blades up into the sorceress's chest, tearing up through her heart and lungs. She died without a sound, the breath ghosting from her lips in a sparkling, iridescent cloud and the golden light fading from her eyes. Vaanes sucked in her dying breath, revelling in the sensations of fear, horror and pain it contained. His entire body shook with the deliciousness of her soul and all thought of consequence fled from his thoughts at the ecstasy of the kill.

Vaanes lowered his arm and let her skeletal frame slide from the blades of his gauntlet. Her corpse flopped to the ground and he set off towards Cadaras Grendel with the Newborn in tow.

'What was that about?' said Grendel, looking over at the shrivelled body of the sorceress. Whatever force had animated her wasted frame had fled her body, leaving a desiccated husk of shrivelled flesh and dried bone.

'Nothing,' replied Vaanes, drawing a deep breath. 'Forget it.'

'Fine,' said Grendel, gesturing towards the sky. 'Honsou wants you back at the compound. The Skull Harvest is about to begin.'

Vaanes looked up, seeing the swirling colours gathering around a toxic swirl of amber, like a cancerous epicentre of a diseased whirlpool.

'The Great Eye...it's opening,' he whispered as Grendel made his way past him in the opposite direction. 'Are you coming back too?'

Grendel nodded, grinning with feral anticipation. 'Don't worry about it. I'll see you in the arena.'

Vaanes didn't like the sound of that, but let it go, wondering whose blood stained Grendel's breastplate. The Iron Warrior looked down at the withered remains of the sorceress.

'Did she try and tell your fortune?' said Grendel, kneeling beside the sagging cloth of the sorceress's robes.

'Something like that,' agreed Vaanes.

'And you killed her for it?'

'Yes.'

'Too bad for her she didn't see *that* coming.'

THE SKULL HARVEST got underway, as all such gatherings do, with sacrifice. Framed by the towering majesty of a growling Battle Titan, the Tyrant of Badab tore the heart from a captured warrior of the Howling Griffons and hurled it into the arena, where it pulsed bright arterial blood onto the gritty sand until it was emptied.

The first day was taken up with the various champions' warbands announcing themselves to the Tyrant, who sat upon a grand throne of bronze and amber, and the allocation of challenges. Blood feuds would be settled first and a number of champions bellowed the names of those they wished to fight in the name of avenging an insult to their honour.

Honsou expected Pashtoq Uluvent to issue such a challenge, but the red-armoured warrior had yet to appear.

'I expected Uluvent to be here,' noted Vaanes, as though reading his mind. 'Champions of the Blood God are usually the first to arrive and begin the killing.'

'No, Uluvent's smarter than that,' said Honsou.

'What do you mean?'

'I think he wants to wait until further into the Harvest before trying to kill me. It'll be more of a triumph for him if he slays me after we've taken other warbands with our own killings. He'll have his blood feud resolved *and* he'll take all my warriors.'

'Then he's more cunning than most champions of the Blood God.'

'Maybe,' agreed Honsou with a smile. 'We'll see how that works out for him.'

'And Grendel, where's he?' asked Vaanes. 'I haven't seen him since yesterday. He said he'd be here. The other champions will know that one of our inner circle hasn't appeared for the beginning of the death games.'

'Forget Grendel,' said Honsou. 'We don't need him.'

'I see him,' said the Newborn, gesturing with a nod of his helmet to the opposite side of the arena. 'Over there.'

Honsou looked over and saw the ranks of gathered champions part as Pashtoq Uluvent took his place on the circumference of the arena. The red-armoured warrior with the ork-skull helmet raised his red-bladed sword and a raucous cheer was torn from thousands of throats as his skull rune banner was unfurled.

Standing beside Uluvent was Cadaras Grendel, his armour streaked with fresh blood and his chainsword unsheathed. The Iron Warrior shrugged and raised his sword to lick wet blood from the blade.

'Grendel's betrayed us?' said Vaanes, his voice thick with anger.

'It was only a matter of time,' said Honsou. 'To be honest I expected it sooner.'

'I'll kill him,' snarled Vaanes.

'No,' said Honsou. 'Grendel and I will have a reckoning, but it won't be here. Do you understand me?'

Vaanes said nothing, but Honsou could see the anger in the warrior's eyes and just hoped the former Raven Guard would be able to restrain the urge to strike down Grendel for now.

'I don't understand you, Honsou,' said Vaanes eventually.

'Not many people do,' replied Honsou. 'And that's the way I like it.'

* * *

A WARRIOR IN bronze armour emblazoned with the skull rune of the Blood God made the first kill of the day, disembowelling a champion in spiked armour who Honsou saw was hopelessly outmatched in the first moments of the duel. The slain warrior's head was mounted upon a spike of black iron beneath the Tyrant's throne.

The warband of the defeated warrior now belonged to his killer, their loyalty won through the display of greater strength and skill. Such loyalty could be a fragile thing, but few gathered here cared for whom they fought, simply that they fought for the strongest, most powerful champion of the Skull Harvest.

Ranebra Corr's sword-champion slew the hearthguard of Yeruel Mzax, a clan warrior of the Cothax stars. The clan-laws forbade Mzax to fight under the leadership of another and he hacked his own head off with an energised claw attached to the upper edge of his gauntlet.

Votheer Tark's battle engine was a hulking monster that had once been a Dreadnought, but which had been altered by Tark's Dark Mechanicum adepts into the housing for a shrieking entity brought forth from the warp. It tore through the warbands of three champions before finally being brought low by one of Pashtoq Uluvent's berserk warriors who fought through the loss of an arm to detonate a melta bomb against its sarcophagus.

The daemon was torn screaming back to the warp and the lower half of the berserker was immolated in the blast. Even with his legs vaporised, the berserker crawled towards Huron Blackheart's throne to deposit the defeated engine's skull-mount.

The Newborn won two duels on the first day of killing; crushing the skull of Kaarja Salombar's corsair pistolier before he could loose a single shot, and eventually defeating the loxatl kin-champion of Xaneant's brood group. This last battle was fought for nearly an hour, with the loxatl unable to put the Newborn down, despite exhausting its supply of flechettes into its opponent.

A daemonic creation of Khalan-Ghol's birth chambers, the Newborn's powers of regeneration were stronger in the warp-saturated Maelstrom and each wound, though agonising, was healed within moments of its infliction.

Exhausted and without ammunition, the loxatl eventually pounced on the Newborn, using its dewclaws to tear at its armour, but even its speed was no match for the Newborn's resilience. At last, the hissing, panting beast was defeated, drained and unable to defend itself when the Newborn crushed its neck and tore its head from its shoulders.

As the fighting and killing went on, warbands began to agglomerate as their champions were slain and armies formed as the most powerful warlords drew more and more fighters to their banner.

Cadaras Grendel fought with his customary brutal remorselessness, winning several bouts for Pashtoq Uluvent, and Honsou could see Ardaric Vaanes's fury at this betrayal simmering ever closer to the surface. To dilute that anger, Honsou sent the former Raven Guard into the arena while the Newborn healed and Vaanes eagerly slaughtered warriors from three warbands, one after the other, bringing yet more blood-bonded fighters into Honsou's growing army.

Honsou himself took to the field of battle twice; once to slay a pirate chieftain armed with two razor-edged tulwars, and once to break a kroot warrior leader who fought with a long, twin-bladed stave he wielded with preternatural speed and precision.

As the Newborn strangled a towering ogre creature with its own energy whip, winning a hundred of the brutish monsters to Honsou's banner, the fourth day of killing drew to an end.

The armies of three champions were all that remained.

Pashtoq Uluvent's force of blood-hungry skull-takers, Notha Etassay's blade-dancers.

And Honsou's Iron Warriors.

With the victories he and his champions had won, Honsou's force had grown exponentially in size, numbering somewhere in the region of five thousand soldiers. Scores of armoured units and fighting machines, as well as all manner of xenos and corsair warbands were now his to command. The swords of seventeen warbands now belonged to Honsou and, by any measure of reckoning, he had a fearsome force with which to wreak havoc on his enemies.

Pashtoq Uluvent had amassed a force in the region of six thousand fighters, while Notha Etassay had procured five thousand through his exquisite slaughters. Any one of these forces was powerful enough to carve itself a fearsome slice of Imperial space and enjoy a period of slaughter unmatched in its previous history.

But the Skull Harvest was not yet over and the Tyrant's rule decreed that there could be only one champion left standing at its end.

Darkness closed in as the three warriors stepped into the arena, clad in their armour and each armed with their weapon of choice. Honsou's arm glittered in the torchlight that surrounded the arena as baying crowds of warriors cheered for their respective champions.

The three warriors marched to stand facing one another in the centre of the arena and Honsou took the opportunity to study his opponents, knowing his life would depend on knowing them better than they knew themselves.

Notha Etassay wore a light, form-fitting bodyglove of rippling black leather with buckled straps holding strategically situated elements of flexible plate. The androgynous champion sashayed into the arena and performed a scintillating pre-battle ritual of acrobatic twists and leaps while spinning twin swords of velvety darkness through the air. Etassay's face was concealed by a studded leather mask with scar-like zippers and tinted glass orbs that glittered with wry amusement, as though this were a meeting of comrades instead of a duel to the death.

Pashtoq Uluvent planted his sword in the bloody earth of the arena and roared a wordless, inchoate bellow of ferocity to the heavens. His armour dripped with the blood of sacrifices and the flesh-texture of his armour seemed to swell and pulse with the beat of his heart. His eyes were like smouldering pools of blood within his helmet and he reached up with a serrated dagger to cut into the meat of his neck.

The champion of the brazen god of battle hurled the dagger away as blood began leaking from the open wound.

Honsou narrowed his eyes. 'Giving up already, Uluvent?'

'If I cannot kill you before my life bleeds out, then I am not worthy of victory and my death will honour the Skull Throne,' said Uluvent.

'Don't expect me to do anything like that,' said Honsou.

'I don't,' replied Uluvent. 'You are the mongrel by-blow of melded genes wrought in desperate times. You are a creature without honour that should never have been brought into existence.'

Honsou controlled his anger as Uluvent continued. 'One of your champions has already sworn himself to me, but I will kill you quickly if you submit to my dominance.'

'I don't submit to anyone,' Honsou warned his enemy.

Notha Etassay laughed, a high, musical sound of rich amusement. 'Whereas it's something I do rather well, though I prefer to be the dominant one in any intercourse.'

'You both disgust me,' snarled Uluvent. 'It insults my honour that I must fight you.'

The howl of the Battle Titan's warhorn echoed across the arena and the cheering warriors fell silent as the Tyrant of Badab rose from his throne to address the gathered champions, the Hamadrya curled around his thigh like a vile leech.

'Tonight the Skull Harvest ends!' said Huron Blackheart, his voice carried around the arena to the furthest reaches of the mountain. 'One champion will be victorious and his enemies will be broken upon the sands of this arena. Fight well and you will go forth to bring terror and death to those who betrayed our trust in them.'

The Tyrant of Badab locked eyes with each of the three champions in turn and raised his mighty clawed gauntlet. 'Now fight!'

Honsou sprang back from a decapitating sweep of Pashtoq Uluvent's axe, swaying aside as Etassay's black sword licked out and sliced into his shoulder guard. Honsou's black-bladed axe lashed out in a wide arc, forcing both opponents back and the three champions broke from the centre of the arena.

Etassay danced away from Honsou, swords twirling and face unreadable behind the leather mask, while Uluvent hefted his sword in a tight grip, watching warily for any movement from his opponents. Honsou knew Uluvent was the stronger of his foes, but Etassay's speed was ferocious, and who knew what power rested in his dark blades.

Honsou's axe was hungry for killing and he felt its insatiable lust to wreak harm running along the length of its haft and into his limbs. Or at least one of them. The power residing in the silver arm he had taken from the Ultramarines sergeant was anathema to the creature bound to his weapon.

This stage of a battle would be where each warrior sought to gauge the measure of the other, searching for signs of weakness or fear to be exploited. Honsou knew he would find neither in these two opponents, warriors hardened by decades of war and devotion to their gods.

Every fibre of Uluvent's being would be dedicated to killing in the Blood God's name, while Etassay would seek to wring every sensation from this bout. Winning would be secondary to the desire to experience the furthest excesses of violence, pain and pleasure.

Honsou cared nothing for the thrill of the fight, nor the honour of the kill. This entire endeavour was a means to an end. He cared nothing for the piratical schemes of the Tyrant, nor honouring any one of the ancient gods of the warp.

Etassay made the first move, leaping in close to Uluvent, his dark swords singing for the red-armoured champion. Uluvent moved swiftly, swinging his own sword up to block the blows and spinning on his heel to slash at Etassay's back. But the champion of the Dark Prince was no longer there, vaulting up and over the blade in a looping backwards somersault.

Honsou charged in, swinging his axe for Etassay, but the warrior dropped beneath the blow and smoothly pivoted onto his elbow, swinging his body out like a blade to take Honsou's legs out from under him.

Uluvent leapt towards Honsou as he fell, the red-bladed sword thrust downwards at his chest, but Honsou scrambled aside and the weapon plunged into the earth. Etassay's boot thundered against Uluvent's helmet and the roaring champion of the Blood God fell back, leaving his sword jammed in the ground.

Honsou pushed himself to his feet and furiously blocked and parried as Etassay spun away from his attack on Uluvent and came at him with a dizzying series of sword strikes. The champion of the Dark Prince was unimaginably fast and it was all Honsou could do to keep himself from being sliced into ribbons. His armour was scored and sliced numerous times and he realised that Etassay was playing with him, prolonging the battle to better enjoy the sense of superiority.

Honsou's bitterness flared, but he fought against it, knowing that Etassay would punish him for even the smallest lapse in concentration. Instead he forced himself to concentrate on exploiting the warrior's arrogance. Etassay thought he was better than Honsou and that would be his downfall.

Out of the corner of his eye, Honsou saw Uluvent circling them, waiting on a chance to reclaim his sword with a patience the Blood God's warriors were not known for. Honsou kept himself close to the weapon, forcing Uluvent to keep his distance. One opponent he could handle. Two? Probably not.

At last Etassay seemed to tire of Honsou and said, 'Let the other one have his blade. This contest is tiresome without his colourful rages.'

Honsou did not reply, instead turning towards the sword embedded in the sand and hacking his daemon axe through the blade. Uluvent's sword shattered into a thousand fragments and Honsou sensed Etassay's petulant displeasure through the studded mask.

Etassay leapt towards him, but Honsou had banked on such a manoeuvre and was ready for it. He hammered the pommel of his axe into Etassay's sternum and the champion dropped to the ground with a strangled, breathless cry.

Honsou heard Uluvent make his move and turned as he stamped down hard on Etassay's chest, hearing a brittle crack of bone. Uluvent slammed into Honsou and they tumbled to the sand. Honsou lost his grip on his axe as Uluvent's gauntlets fastened on his throat. The two warriors grappled in the bloody sand, pummelling one another with iron-hard fists.

Uluvent spat into Honsou's face. 'Now you die!'

Honsou rammed his knee into Uluvent's stomach, but the warrior's grip was unbreakable. Again and again he slammed his knee upwards until at last he felt the grip on his throat loosen. He managed to free one arm and slammed the heel of his palm into Uluvent's skull-faced helmet. Bone shattered and the bleeding wound in Uluvent's neck was exposed, spattering Honsou's helmet in blood.

Honsou slammed his fist into the wound, digging his fingers into Uluvent's neck and tearing the cut wider. His foe bellowed in pain and rolled off Honsou, rising unsteadily to his feet and lurching over to his followers to retrieve another weapon with one hand pressed to the ruin of his neck.

Honsou stood, groggy and battered, and set off after Uluvent, snatching his axe up from the ground next to the groaning figure of Etassay. He ignored the Dark Prince's champion, the warrior was beaten and probably in throes of ecstasy at the pain coursing along every nerve ending.

Honsou felt new strength in his limbs as he followed Uluvent. The warrior had torn off his shattered helmet and Honsou saw his face was hideously scarred and burned. Blood squirted from where Honsou had torn his neck wound further open, but the pain only seemed to galvanise Uluvent as he bellowed for a fresh blade.

Neck wound or no, Uluvent was still a fearsome opponent and armed with a fresh weapon, could still easily kill Honsou.

Cadaras Grendel held a wide-bladed sword out towards Pashtoq Uluvent and Honsou held his breath...

Pashtoq Uluvent reached for the weapon, but at the last moment, Cadaras Grendel reversed his grip and rammed the blade into the champion's chest. The tip of the weapon ripped out through the back of Uluvent's armour and the mighty warrior staggered as Grendel twisted the blade deeper into his chest.

Uluvent roared in pain and spun away from Grendel, wrenching the sword from his grip and dropped to his knees. Honsou gave him no chance to recover from his shock and pain, and brought his axe down upon the warrior's shoulder. The dark blade smashed Uluvent's shoulder guard to splinters and clove the champion of the Blood God from collarbone to pelvis.

Stunned silence swept over the gathered crowds, for none had ever expected to see Pashtoq Uluvent brought low. Cadaras Grendel stepped from the ranks of the Blood God's warriors to stand next to Honsou as the blazing fire of Pashtoq Uluvent's eyes began to fade.

'Sorry,' said Grendel with a grin. 'Honsou may be a mongrel half-breed, and even though I know you'll lead me to a bloodier fight, I think he'll lead me to one I'll live through.'

Uluvent looked up at Honsou with hate and pain misting his vision. 'Give... me... a blade.'

Honsou was loath to indulge the champion's request, but knew he would need to if there were to be any shred of loyalty in the warriors he would win from Uluvent.

'Give it to him,' ordered Honsou.

Grendel nodded and reached down to drag the sword from the defeated champion's chest in a froth of bright blood. He held the weapon towards Uluvent, who took the proffered sword in a slack grip.

'And... my skull,' gasped Uluvent with the last of his strength. 'You... have... to take... it.'

'My pleasure,' said Honsou, raising his axe and honouring Pashtoq Uluvent's last request.

WITH PASHTOQ ULUVENT's head mounted on the spikes below Huron Blackheart's throne, the Skull Harvest was over. Hundreds had died upon the sands of the Tyrant's arena, but such deaths were meaningless in the grand scheme of things, serving only to feed Blackheart's ego and amuse the Dark Gods of the warp.

At the final tally, Honsou left New Badab with close to seventeen thousand warriors sworn in blood to his cause. Pashtoq Uluvent's warriors, and those he had won, were now Honsou's, their banners now bearing the Iron Skull device.

Notha Etassay had survived the final battle and had willingly sworn allegiance to Honsou after hoarsely thanking him for the exquisite sensations of bone shards through the lungs.

Huron Blackheart had been true to his word, and the victor of the Skull Harvest had indeed benefited greatly from his patronage. As the *Warbreed* broke orbit, numerous other vessels accompanied it, gifts from the Tyrant of Badab to be used for the express purpose of dealing death to the forces of the Imperium. In addition to these vessels, the ships of the defeated champions formed up around Honsou's flagship to form a ragtag, yet powerful, fleet of corsairs and renegades.

Battered warships, ugly bulk carriers, planetary gunboats, warp-capable system monitors and captured cruisers followed the *Warbreed* as it plotted a careful route through the Maelstrom, away from the domain of Huron Blackheart.

The sickly yellow orb of New Badab was swallowed in striated clouds of nebulous dust and polluted immaterial effluent vomited from the wound in real space as the fleet pulled away, and Honsou recalled the final words the mighty Tyrant had said to him.

Blackheart had pointed his dark-bladed claw towards Ardaric Vaanes, Cadaras Grendel and the Newborn as they boarded the battered Stormbirds ahead of Honsou.

'Kill them when they are of no more use to you,' said the Tyrant. 'Otherwise they will only betray you.'

'They wouldn't dare,' Honsou had said, though a seed of doubt had been planted.

'Always remember,' said Huron Blackheart. 'The strong are strongest alone.'

GAUNTLET RUN

Chris Roberson

THE RISING SUN was just cresting the mountaintops, barely visible on the eastern horizon, fat and red like an overripe fruit. The morning sunlight lanced across the alkaline flats, every stone and promontory casting long shadows that stretched over the bone-dry remains of an ancient seabed that had dried up long before man's ancestors on Terra had first descended from the trees. Nothing lived in that dead and dry place, the only movement the dust devils kicked up by the hot winds that blew from north to south and back again. These tiny brief-lived tornadoes fed on the thin layer of dust atop the salt flats dried hard as rockcrete, with no sound to be heard but the plaintive whistle of the winds.

Then the Scout bike squadron thundered in from the west, their mighty engines deafening, the treads of their fat tyres tearing up the dry ground, sending up great plumes of dust churning in their wake.

The Imperial Fists had arrived.

The squad of bike Scouts raced east across the desert in a tight vanguard formation. At the forward point of their chevron was Veteran Sergeant Hilts, on his left flank Scouts Zatori and s'Tonan, on his right flank Scouts du Queste and Kelso.

Zatori continued to glance behind. As left flank outrider, it fell to him to watch their left rear, just as Kelso covered their right rear as right flank outrider, while s'Tonan and du Queste scanned the approaches before them, and Hilts set the pace and marked their course.

They had been running through the night, zigzagging north-east and south-east, but while they had yet to unsheathe their blades and the barrels of their bikes' twin-linked bolters were idling and cool, this was no pleasure drive. The stakes for their current mission were dire, with the life of every human on Tunis in the balance. If they were not able to locate enemy forces – and enemy forces of a very particular kind – then they would fail in their duty, and millions would pay the price. But as the morning dawned, they had still found no sign of the enemy.

Until now.

'Sergeant,' Zatori voxed over the shared channel, for all the squad to hear, 'we have picked up a tail.'

Zatori concentrated, employing the enhanced vision of the Astartes to peer farther than an unaugmented human would have dreamed possible.

'It's the greenskins,' he added in confirmation. 'And they've spotted us.'

'Acknowledged,' Veteran Sergeant Hilts voxed in reply, gunning his engine and putting on speed. He motioned forward with his massive power fist. 'Throttle up, squad. The race is on.'

IT HAD BEEN only a few weeks since an ork space hulk had appeared in orbit above the planet Tunis without warning, spat out by a random rift in the fabric of space itself.

The human inhabitants below had scarcely noticed the hulk overhead before countless landers began dropping from the skies, disgorging warriors and war-machines alike.

The first encounters between the human inhabitants and the ork invaders had been brutal and short. The easternmost settlements, ringing the western edge of the salt flats, had been obliterated by orks mounted on bikes, buggies, and battlewagons, gangs of greenskins addicted to movement and murder, ranging as outriders while the main force of the orks entrenched somewhere in the endless caverns and subterranean passages that burrowed under the mountains to the east. The Space Marines knew the orks had a hidden base somewhere beneath those peaks, and if the Fists were unable to locate it, they had little chance of preventing a full-scale invasion. It was only a matter of time before the main body of the ork invaders completed work on their siege-machines and attacked the human inhabitants en masse, but until that time the ork outriders would find their entertainment and excitement where they could.

A SPEED FREEK never stops, never sleeps, never hesitates. For him, there is only motion.

Rotgrim Skab knew that better than anyone. Since the moment the landers had touched down on the surface of this world, he and his crew had been up and running. As Nob of a speed freek warband of the Evil Sunz clan, it was Rotgrim's responsibility to get the bikeboyz fired up and rolling, to pick a point on the horizon and head out, and then kill every living thing they encountered along the way.

He raced at the head of the pack, massive legs wrapped around the casing of his warbike's supercharged engine, its throaty roar the only sound in his ears, exhaust and dust filling his flaring nostrils. Behind him ranged supercharged trucks and battlewagons, bikes and buggies, more than a dozen in all; bikeboyz of the Evil Sunz clan, decked out in leathers, chains and harnesses, with massive steel-toed boots on their feet and metal studs screwed directly into the bones of their foreheads. And all of them had red somewhere on them, whether cloth or stain, paint or spattered blood.

As leader of the warband, the Nob himself, Rotgrim was decked out in red from head to toe, with an axe in one hand and a dakkagun holstered at his side. His ride was painted blood red from grille to ground, as was only fitting – as the old ork adage went, the colour red makes things go faster. On a stanchion mounted behind him hung the banner of the Evil Sunz, a blood-red ork face grimacing from the heart of a starburst.

Rotgrim's warband had been going on raiding forays ever since they touched down on this dry, dusty world, impatient with the preparations being carried out in the tunnels and caverns below the mountains to the east. When the word was given, the full body of the ork army would be unleashed on the humans cowering in their settlements across the desert, and when the army moved out, the Evil Sunz would be in the vanguard.

There'd be work enough for them all to do, when the word was given, but there was no point in sitting around on their thumbs, just waiting, while they could be out and moving.

When Rotgrim spotted the five humans tooling across the desert on their little bikes, he decided to have a little fun before taking them down. It had been too long since he and the rest of the boyz'd had moving targets to practice on.

It had been lucky for the locals that the Imperial Fists transport had been in the area at all, Scout Zatori knew. When the planetary governor of Tunis had sent out his distress call, just as the ork landers first started dropping from the sky on the far side of the planet, the Imperial

Fists had been near the system, returning from a previous undertaking to the *Phalanx*, the Chapter's fortress-monastery, currently at anchor at a few weeks' distance.

Of course, the transport had been a Gladius-class frigate, carrying only a single squad of Veterans of the First Company, accompanied by a Scout squad of the Tenth. But the planetary governor had not been in any position to complain about the size of the force that responded to his desperate calls for aid.

Like the others in the bike squad commanded by Veteran Sergeant Hilts, Zatori was just a novice, not yet a full battle-brother of the Imperial Fists, lacking the black carapace that would allow him to wear and control the powered ceramite armour of a full-fledged Adeptus Astartes. But the years he had spent on the *Phalanx* being transformed from a boy into a post-human son of Dorn had already set him apart from the rank and file of humanity. When the landing party had quit their drop-pods and been received by the planetary governor, Zatori and his fellow Scouts had towered over the locals, who quavered in their shadows, nearly as frightened of the Astartes – Space Marine and Scout alike – as they were of the greenskins who threatened to overrun them from the east.

Aside from Chapter serfs, like those who crewed the Gladius frigate in orbit overhead, or those who served onboard the *Phalanx*, Zatori had had precious little dealing with normal humans these last few years. But looking into the faces of the planetary governor and those who sheltered with him in the strongholds to the west, Zatori could not help but be reminded of the first time he'd seen a Space Marine himself, on the battlefields of Eokaroe, on his far distant home of Triandr. They had seemed the legends of his ancestors given flesh, giant warrior-knights stepping from the realm of myths into the world of men.

Now, years later, Zatori was one of them, at least in the eyes of normal men and women. Though still only a

Scout, he was a proud Son of Dorn all the same, an Imperial Fist. He would strike with the Emperor's own righteous fury. That was his duty. That was his honour.

THE FIVE IMPERIAL Fists thundered east across the desert, maintaining their vanguard formation with rigid discipline. The greenskins were closing fast, coming right up behind.

In contrast with the regimented formation of the Fists, the morning sun glinting on the golden yellow and jet-black of their armour and bikes, the greenskins were a ragtag assortment of monsters, their vehicles belching exhaust and rumbling like unending death-rattles. But they were no slower, for all of that, thundering after the Fists like a fast approaching storm front.

Glancing back, Scout Zatori steeled his nerves as he saw an ork warbike roaring up behind, tantalisingly close to his own back tyre. Bike and rider were both covered in red, the colour of new-spilt arterial blood, with a banner fluttering madly from a rear-mounted stanchion, marking the rider as the warband's leader.

The ork leader waved an axe overhead, his wide-mouthed howls lost to the wind. Then he fired a prolonged burst from the twin-linked guns forward mounted before him. Zatori might have fallen there and then if not for the fact that the warbike bucked and spun wildly out of control as soon as the poorly balanced guns were fired, sending the shots wide of the mark. As it was, the explosive shells passed so near Zatori's left shoulder as they flew by that the Scout fancied he could feel the heat of their passage.

Zatori glanced to the right, and caught a glimpse of a pair of warbuggies approaching du Queste and Kelso's flank. On the back of each of the two-man attack vehicles stood gunners on weapons platforms, and in the brief instant that Zatori's gaze took in the scene, he saw one of the gunners fire off a pair of rockets. As the rockets dug into the ground only metres from Kelso's back tyre, sending up a gout of dust and rock, Zatori turned his attention back to the ground before his own wheels.

Like the rest of the Scouts, Zatori was waiting for Veteran Sergeant Hilts to give the signal. Their orders called for them to maintain close formation after first enemy contact, right up until the sergeant gave the word, and then the next stage of their mission plan would be put into motion.

Zatori just hoped he survived long enough to follow the order.

'Squad,' Veteran Sergeant Hilts voxed at last, 'evasive pattern alpha.'

'Confirmed,' Zatori chorused back with the others, and then as one they broke formation, the left flank jinking right and the right flank jinking left, their paths twisting like DNA helixes as they gunned forward, leaving the disorderly orks in pursuit to compensate.

Now the Scouts would have to remain mobile long enough to see how the greenskins would respond.

DUST GRITTED IN Rotgrim's eyes, the carcasses of countless insects entombed between his teeth. He whirled his axe overhead, urging the rest of the warband to greater speeds.

A dozen metres to his right, a skorcha let loose a gout of flame at the nearest of the humans, the huge vats of promethium mounted on the rear of the buggy fuelling the heavy-duty flamethrowers operated by a pair of Evil Sunz. The flame was all but spent by the time the last flickering tongues of the stream lapped the back of one of the human riders, doing little more than scorching his armour, but it was a start, at least.

Rotgrim fired off another round from the twin-linked dakkaguns on the front of his ride, the irregular percussive sound music in his ears. The shots went wide of the human he was tailing, and Rotgrim found little satisfaction in the puffs of dust and rock kicked up where the explosive shells finally struck the ground, far ahead.

A warbiker off to Rotgrim's left kept firing off shots from his rifle, laying down cover to keep the humans off balance while Rotgrim and the others narrowed the distance. Another warbuggy fired off a few shots with a mega-blaster, and another loosed a pair of rockets from its launcher. None of the shots, large or small, did much more than kick up dust, like Rotgrim's had done, but the humans were forced to jag back and forth to avoid the orks' fire, which served to slow them down.

And then, seemingly all at once, the distance had shrunk to nothing. Instead of just pursuing the humans, Rotgrim's crew was right in with them. Close enough for melee action, for close combat weapons rather than unreliable ranged fire.

This was where the fun really started. Not in lobbing shots at distant targets, hoping against hope that something hit home. But instead in taking the fight right to the enemy, dive-bombing them head on like a bomber coming in for the kill, speed against speed, motion against motion.

An evil grin curled Rotgrim's rubbery lips, exposing vicious, yellowed teeth, dotted with insect carcasses like sunspots on a jaundiced star. This *was* going to be fun.

Scout Zatori couldn't help but be reminded of the words of Rhetoricus, who long centuries before had codified the Rites of Battle by which the Imperial Fists guided their actions. In the estimation of the Chapter, Rhetoricus was surpassed only by the Primarch Rogal Dorn himself. Rhetoricus had penned any number of tracts, codices, and lexicons, but principal among them was *The Book of Five Spheres*, the catechism of the sword. In it, Rhetoricus had stressed the importance of knowing the advantages and shortcomings of each weapon in a warrior's arsenal. He had spoken of the importance of ranged weapons in the open field, of flame weapons and meltas in entrenched defence, of heavy ordnance for bombardment and of blast weapons for barrage. But more than any other, he had sung the praises of the sword in close combat.

It was seldom, if ever, that a battle-brother of the Imperial Fists Chapter went into the field of battle without a sword in his fist or at his hip, and not uncommon for Fists to enter the fray with no weapon save his trusted blade. Some, like Captain Eshara of the Third Company, even went into battle with a sword in each hand, testing his skill with the blade against all enemies of the Golden Throne. Even the Master of the First Company – to say nothing of being First Captain, Overseer of the Armoury, and Watch Commander of the *Phalanx* – the legendary Captain Lysander had wielded nothing but a sword in the undertaking on Malodrax, scouring the Iron Warriors from the planet and reclaiming his master-crafted thunder hammer, the Fist of Dorn, which had been first given to him by the martyred Captain Kleitus more than a millennium before Zatori was born.

In *The Book of Five Spheres*, Rhetoricus wrote, 'The sword is at its most advantageous in confined places, or in the melee, or in close quarters – any situation in which you can close with an opponent.' And later, 'The soul of the Imperial Fist can be found in his sword.' Also, 'When the odds are innumerable against you, and there is little hope for victory, still a holy warrior with a sword in his hand can prevail, if his intent is righteous and pure.'

So as the greenskin warbiker with the massive axe barrelled towards him, Zatori tightened his grip on his sword, his other hand gripping his bike's handlebars, and silently repeated the *Litany of the Blade*. As the ork swung his axe overhand at Zatori's bare head, just as their two bikes were about to careen into one another, the Scout muttered a prayer to Dorn and the Emperor that his parry would be sufficient to the task.

* * *

ROTGRIM BROUGHT HIS axe down in a one-handed swing, right at the human's naked head. But before the blade bit into skin and skull, the human managed to turn the axe away with his sword, sending up a shower of sparks. Just as their blades struck, their two bikes collided off one another with a bone-crunching jar. As the two riders fought to maintain their balance, offsetting the force of the impact, they veered away from one another once more, each readying for another blow.

Teeth bared, Rotgrim hurled abuse at the human, who suddenly let go of his handlebars. It would have been funny, seeing a human riding a little bike hands free, if that hand hadn't come back up another moment later with a big gun in it.

Rotgrim yanked his forks to the right just in time to miss the torrent of heat that poured out of the gun, hot enough to fuse the sand on the ground into glass.

With a grim snarl, Rotgrim couldn't help but chuckle. The human wasn't the only one with a holdout.

Steadying his bike's forks with his knees, he let go of the handle and then yanked his dakkagun out of its holster.

THE MELTA GUN was a temporary deterrent at best, Zatori knew. It was only useful anyway over the shortest of distances, the promethium it excited into a sub-molecular state impossible to aim more than a few metres; but it was difficult to use any ranged weapons at high speed, anyway, so the trade-off between range and firepower for the Bike Scouts was deemed well worth it. As it was, between the melta guns for ranged firing and their swords for close combat, Veteran Sergeant Hilts had told the Scouts not to expect much opportunity to use their twin-linked bolters. After all, the bolters were designed to be fired at a target the bike was heading *towards*, and this mission would require them to head *away* from the enemy until the race was over. There would be enemies aplenty when – and if – they reached their goal, but even then the bike's bolters would be of little use, if all went to plan.

When he'd parried the greenskin's first blow, Zatori had known he'd need to reposition before he took another, or he'd be off his seat and sprawled in the dust. Though he'd trained to use the blade in either hand, still he was far less proficient with his left, and with the ork approaching from the left rear, he didn't have the option of switching the sword to his right. His defensive options would be limited, perhaps fatally so, if he had to cross his body to parry and block, and offensive options would be reduced to virtually nil, and so the sword in his left hand was the only option. But while his left arm was no less strong than his right, the level of skill was simply not the same in both, as he'd learned to his shame in duels on board the *Phalanx*.

After deflecting the ork's first blow, their bikes collided and then spun slightly apart, with the greenskin a short distance behind Zatori's bike. The next attack, Zatori knew, would be coming from that angle. Poorly braced as he was, there was simply too great a chance that the greenskin would unseat him, and then Zatori's race would be at an end, far too soon.

It was necessary, then, to change the parameters of the engagement. Or, as Rhetoricus put it in *The Book of Five Spheres*, 'When facing defeat or deadlock, seize the advantage by ascertaining the opponent's state and changing your approach.'

So as the greenskin readied for his next attack, Zatori risked letting go of his handlebars, pulled out his melta gun, and sent a blast of superheated gas shooting over. Then, when the ork responded as Zatori anticipated he would, by drawing his own firearm and returning fire, Zatori slammed the melta gun back into his holster, and yanked hard left on his handlebars, sending his bike careering towards the greenskin's. Damning the imprecise but no less deadly fire of the ork, Zatori's path took him barrelling right past the greenskin's, the Scout's forward tyre just missing the ork's rear wheel as they zoomed past, Zatori's sword swinging across his body as they drew near.

When Zatori felt the sword tug in his hand as he whizzed past the ork's rear, he hoped for a moment that he might have scored a hit against the greenskin, who'd been unable to raise his axe in time to parry. Glancing back Zatori now saw that the ork was unharmed, but that the stanchion that had held the banner aloft had been cut clean through, the grimacing red ork emblazoned on it now fluttering down to the churned earth.

In that instant Zatori's gaze locked with the greenskin's, and he saw murder in the ork's flashing eyes.

FUN WAS ONE thing. Rotgrim couldn't blame a human for taking a few potshots in battle, or for trying to stick Rotgrim with his pointy blade. It was only fair, after all. Rotgrim'd kill him, sooner or later, but the little guy had a right to fight back. Wouldn't be any fun, otherwise.

But knocking the Evil Sunz standard down into the dirt? Now *that,* that just wasn't right.

Rotgrim jammed his dakkagun back into its holster. He wasn't going to use bullets or shells for this one. He was going to take care of this one with his *hands*.

ZATORI WAS STEERING back around so that his front forks were aiming towards the mountains when he heard a voice buzzing over the vox.

'Zatori, on your right!'

The next instant, Scout Kelso rammed by at top speed, crossing Zatori's path from right to left, barely avoiding a collision.

'Want to trade?' Kelso voxed as he slewed around, dust flying in a wide arc. He jerked a thumb back the way he'd come, at the flame-belching warbuggy following a short distance behind him.

Zatori glanced over his own shoulder at the ork warbiker following in his wake, a murderous scowl on his green face.

Before he could answer, though, Kelso gunned his engine and went racing right at the warbiker. 'My thanks, Zatori. I was getting bored.'

In the next moment, the warbuggy that previously had been pursuing Kelso roared behind Zatori, between him and the warbiker, the flamethrowers' attention now turned to their new target. In the dance of death between the Scouts and the orks, Zatori and Kelso appeared to have traded partners.

Zatori still found Kelso's manner difficult to understand. All Imperial Fists found some measure of satisfaction in carrying out their holy duty, but Kelso seemed to find some strangely manic *joy* in battle, and often conducted himself in a way that the more choleric Zatori found all but impossible to understand. It was perhaps not as noxious to him as the laconic attitude of du Queste, nor the seemingly emotionless reserve of s'Tonan, but still and above all Zatori found Kelso's joyous abandon in battle difficult to reconcile with the sombre duties of an Astartes.

Blistering tongues of flame lapped at the ceramite of Zatori's armour as the warbuggy veered in pursuit, and the Scout poured on speed to keep from getting roasted alive.

ROTGRIM ROARED IN annoyance as the skorcha trundled between him and his prey, but when the other human biker came racing towards him, sword swinging overhead and a joyous smile on his face, the Nob figured this new human would serve as an adequate appetiser. If he could not take vengeance on the one that had dishonoured the Evil Sunz standard just yet, he could first colour his axe with the blood of this one.

The human was riding straight at Rotgrim, and the ork wasn't sure if it was playing dare, to see which of them would veer away first, or else wanted to joust like horseback warriors on some feral world. The strange thing was that the human almost looked like he was *laughing*.

Well, if it was the speed that was tickling him, Rotgrim could almost understand it.

Of course, in another second or two, it would be Rotgrim's axe that would be tickling the inside of the human's brainpan, and he wouldn't be laughing so much after that.

THE GROUND BENEATH Zatori's tyres was getting rougher the farther east they raced. Where there had been only scattered rocks and small promontories breaking the level horizon of the salt flats to the west, as they moved eastward there were increasing numbers of larger rocks rising like the tips of icebergs above the salty ground, some almost as large as Zatori's bike. With these obstacles in his path, he was no longer able simply to open up the throttle and thunder ahead, but was forced to zigzag to keep from colliding with stones large enough to arrest his forward motion in a bone-smashing crash.

The warbuggy pursuing him, unfortunately, was raised on four fat tyres, its supercharged engine powerful enough to push it up and over the smaller rocks with scarcely any loss of forward momentum. So while Zatori was forced to bleed off speed as he zigged and zagged back and forth, the warbuggy ploughed on ahead at full tilt, closing the gap between them.

The promethium-fuelled torches at the back of the warbuggy bathed Zatori in a cascade of flame, and he grit his teeth against the searing pain. He could feel the skin at the back of his neck blistering and cracking, the close-cropped hair on his scalp singing off, and while he knew his blood would already be flooding with Larraman cells from the implant in his chest, creating instant scar tissue and staunching the flow of blood to the affected area, that knowledge did little to lessen the agony itself.

Fortunately, Zatori had spent his time in the Pain Glove, as Initiate, Neophyte, and Scout, and had cleaved to the sacred words of Rhetoricus: 'Pain is the wine of communion with heroes.' If he could learn to endure prolonged periods with that tunic of electrofibres, suspended for what seemed an eternity within the steel gibbet deep within the *Phalanx*, meditating on the image of Rogal Dorn and learning to focus past the pain, remaining fully conscious throughout – if Zatori could do that, then he could endure the mere *discomfort* of having his flesh cooked off the bone by burning promethium.

He knew that, if the greenskins were in close enough proximity for their flamethrowers to paint him, then they were also close enough for Zatori's own melta gun to return the compliment.

With a silent prayer for forgiveness to the spirit of his blade, Zatori slammed his sword into the sheath on his back in one smooth motion, and then whipped his melta gun out of its holster on the side of his bike. Without wasting a moment, he twisted at the waist as far as he was able, swung the melta gun around and sent a blast of superheated gas back at the pursuing warbuggy.

ROTGRIM AND HIS human prey were less than an eye blink apart now, each with their blades on high. At the last possible instant, the human jinked to the left, swinging his sword at Rotgrim's broad chest. But Rotgrim had seen the swing coming, and just as the human pulled to the left, the ork slammed on the brakes for the briefest instant, arresting his speed just long enough for the swing to whistle by harmlessly, while at the same time whirling his axe in a wide arc aimed at the soft meat of the human neck rising above the neck of his armour.

Rotgrim punched his bike to speed almost immediately after braking, and so could scarcely feel the tug of resistance as his axe sliced through the human's neck. But glancing back he saw the human's bike careening off, veering wildly left and right, as the headless rider flopped back on the seat, sword still held in his lifeless hand, the head bouncing and skipping along on the ground behind.

Rotgrim noted the incarnadined edge of his axe with satisfaction. It was a nice shade of red now. But it needed to get redder.

Zatori's melta blast struck the greenskin driver head on, all but vaporising him instantly from the abdomen up, leaving only a pair of dismembered hands dangling lifeless from the steering wheel and an oozing puddle of viscera pooling atop the burnt remains of his hips and legs.

The flamethrower operators on the rear platform tried to direct another stream of incendiary his way, but their attempt was stymied by the warbuggy careering wildly out of control, driverless, into one of the larger rocks. With a squeal of metal on stone, the warbuggy came to an abrupt halt, and the pair of greenskins were sent hurtling through the air, tumbling end over end. The vat of promethium, jarred by the impact, spilled over, and as the liquid sloshed into the open flames of the throwers it caught fire, the resultant blast engulfing the warbuggy in a crumping black cloud of smoke and heat.

It was only as he turned his attention back to the ground ahead that he saw the headless body of Scout Kelso crashing into the dust a hundred or so metres off. Kelso's head, bouncing along the dead seabed far behind his body, wasn't smiling anymore.

Rotgrim saw the skorcha explode, a mushroom of black smoke rising into the air as the thunderclap of the explosion rumbled through the dry air, just audible above the throaty roar of his warbike's engine. The humans were down a rider, with only four left in the saddle, and even with the loss of the skorcha the Evil Sunz still had nearly a dozen vehicles on the move.

Scanning the horizon, Rotgrim could just glimpse the human who'd defiled the Evil Sunz standard, zipping off to the east. There were too many obstacles in between for Rotgrim to catch up quickly, and there were easier targets closer anyway, that deserved the attention of his axe first.

It was getting high time to bring this particular race to a close, though.

Drawing his dakkagun, he fired a few quick bursts into the air in a set pattern, two long, four short, one long. The noise of the shots would carry over the growl of even supercharged engines, and every biker boy of the warband would recognize the sequence, and what it meant.

Rotgrim's orders were clear – it was time to stop racing for the sake of racing, and to start driving their quarry into the endgame.

'Hilts to Zatori,' came the voice of the Veteran Sergeant over the vox. 'What's your status?'

'Kelso is down, sir,' Zatori voxed back in clipped tones. 'I'm still up and running towards the east' – he glanced back, and saw the attack bike now coursing after him – 'and am pursued by a greenskin biker. I had a clash with their leader, but I've lost sight of him.'

'Acknowledged.' Then, after a pause, 'I think I've picked up the leader. Big monster in red gear on a red bike. But I don't see the clan standard...'

Zatori could not suppress a small grin as he made a tight swerve around a waist-high rock in his path. 'That would be my fault, sergeant. I cut it down and left it in the dust.'

The Scout could hear Veteran Sergeant Hilts's short, dry chuckle buzzing through the comm-bead he wore in his ear. 'No wonder he looks so displeased.'

'I didn't intend to win his pleasure.'

A small-arms round pinged off the gold and jet ceramite of Zatori's armour, the shot thudding into his left shoulder as the pursuing attack bike attempted to pick him off with a firearm. A second shot followed, also on his left but further down, nearer his waist. Each time, he reflexively leaned to the right, pulling away from the shot.

'Their tactics have changed,' Veteran Sergeant Hilts voxed, after a moment's silence. 'They're stopped going for kill shots, and are using nuisance tactics, instead.'

Zatori glanced to his right, and could see the sergeant angling towards him, their trajectories meeting somewhere ahead of them, and behind the sergeant the red-clad leader of the warband.

When Hilts remained silent, Zatori realized that the veteran sergeant was giving him the opportunity to divine the significance of his words. Hilts had trained Scouts of the Imperial Fists for longer than Zatori had been alive, and was always looking for a teachable moment, whether in the sparring ring or in the battlefield, an opportunity for the novices under his command to learn an essential combat lesson.

'They are herding us,' Zatori said at last, as confidently as he was able.

'Yes,' Hilts allowed. 'Exactly as we'd hoped.'

'Your orders, sir?'

'Allow yourself to be herded,' Hilts replied. 'And try not to get killed doing it.'

ROTGRIM WATCHED AS the power fist-wearing human biker he was pursuing pulled alongside another, and a single glance was enough to tell him that this second human was the one who had cut down the banner stanchion and disgraced the Evil Sunz. Trailing the human was another biker boy, a pistol in his fist, planting careful shots on the human's back, steering his quarry just as Rotgrim's signal had ordered.

The plan was to allow all of the humans still upright to stay moving until they got to the wall, where they'd stop and have a final bit of fun. But seeing the bare head of the human bastard who'd knocked the standard in the dirt convinced Rotgrim that maybe one or two of them could still fall along the way. The few who reached the wall would have to be enough fun for the others.

Rotgrim whirled his axe overhead, signalling the other biker boy. A quick jab of his finger, first at the pair of humans, then at his own massive chest, was a simple enough message to carry even over the dust-filled air: These humans were *his*.

Zatori caught a glimpse of Scouts du Queste and s'Tonan veering in from the right, pursued by a trio of warbuggies. It was clear he'd been right, and that the greenskins were herding them, steering their advance towards the west. He just hoped the orks were driving them where Hilts *thought* they were heading.

He and Hilts were riding side by side now, jinking back and forth to dodge the ever-growing number of rocky protuberances and outcroppings, ever larger as they continued eastward, the largest of them now taller than Zatori when astride his bike.

There had been two greenskin bikes in their wake, but when Zatori chanced a glance back to see how close they had come, one of the orks was peeling off to cover their left flank. Only the warband's leader, the red of Kelso's blood still staining his axe blade the same shade as his leathers and ride, was still in pursuit, and closing fast.

'Zatori to Hilts,' he voxed. 'The leader is gaining.'

Hilts spared an instant to look back over his shoulder, then turned back to face forward. 'Tighten up, Zatori. This may get bumpy.'

The mountains on the eastern edge of the salt flats now towered before them. The sun was nearing its zenith, and the shadows had shrunk almost to nothing, making it more difficult to spot some of the smaller rocks in their path.

As they headed into the maze-like network of rocks and ridges that stretched out from the base of the mountains, Rotgrim gauged it impossible to pull up between the two humans, as he'd intended, laying about him on both sides with his axe. And since the human who'd disgraced the standard was now riding slightly ahead of the other one with the power fist, it meant that Rotgrim would have to get through him first before taking out his vengeance on the human bastard.

An evil grin tugged up the corners of Rotgrim's wide mouth as an idea struck. He hung his axe on his belt, then reached behind him and snapped off the broken spar which was all that remained of the stanchion that had once held the Evil Sunz banner aloft.

As the two humans pulled into a relatively open stretch of ground, Rotgrim punched his warbike into a sudden burst of speed, pulling up alongside them on the right. As the human on the right turned to grab at Rotgrim with his power fist, the ork leaned over as far over to the left as he could go without tipping his bike over, and drove the broken spar like a lance between the spokes of the human's front wheel.

The power fist closed on empty air as the front wheel pegged, and with a squeal of metal on metal the human's bike flipped end over end.

Before Rotgrim even had a chance to savour the destruction, though, a blast of superheated air shot right across his path, and he was forced to veer off hard to the right to avoid the next shot from the twice-damned human's heat gun.

'Squad! Cover needed!' Zatori voxed urgently, as he watched Veteran Sergeant Hilts tumbling through the air. A melta blast had been enough to drive the ork leader away, if only for a moment, but it wouldn't keep him off Zatori's back for long. And if their mission had any hope for success, Zatori couldn't let Hilts lie wherever he fell.

In response to Zatori's call, the other two scouts, du Queste and s'Tonan, came roaring over at speed, swords swinging and bolts flashing from their twin-linked bolters. They threw themselves at the ork leader, slewing in between him and Zatori, giving the latter a few moments grace to act.

While the ork leader was occupied with du Queste and s'Tonan, Zatori ground to a halt where Hilts had come to rest. The sergeant was pinned between the massive rock that had arrested his forward motion and the heavy bike that had arrived a split second after. The bike itself was a mangled mess, bent out of its true shape, the forward forks snapped off and the tyre still trundling away in the dust. Hilts was in little better shape. At the speeds they'd been travelling, the force of the impact with the massive rock outcropping had been enough to dent his ceramite armour in several places, and he was bleeding generously from wounds that his Larraman cells had not yet been able to staunch. One leg was bent forwards at an obscene angle, and his left arm appeared to be pulled completely from its socket. The impact of the bike had only worsened the damage.

'Take... take it...' Zatori heard Hilts say, not over the vox – the sergeant's ability to transmit no doubt compromised by the crash – but the words instead rasping out through Hilts's damaged visor.

The sergeant raised his power fist, and Zatori could see the small device affixed to the gauntlet's cuff.

'Sorry, sir,' Zatori said, leaping off his bike and rushing to Hilts's side. With a grunt of effort, he heaved the mangled bike off of the sergeant. 'We're already a rider down, and I can't conscience leaving another behind.'

Slipping both hands beneath the sergeant's battered form, Zatori straightened and lifted Hilts into the air.

Hurrying to his bike, Zatori draped the sergeant over the back like saddlebags, and after securing him in place jumped back into the seat.

'Scout…' Hilts said, as Zatori gunned the engine, his voice scarcely audible. Zatori knew that, in the face of such massive injuries, Hilts would be going into a fugue state as his body attempted to repair itself. 'Press on… No matter what… Press…'

The sergeant slipped into unconsciousness, his body's full attention on its injuries.

'Squad!' Zatori voxed, as he kicked his bike into motion, driving towards the mountains which now loomed before them. 'The sergeant's with me. Now let's end this race!'

THEY THUNDERED TO the east, the Scouts pulling just ahead of the Evil Sunz, and as they neared the foothills of the mountains, the rocky protuberances and outcroppings grew larger and more numerous, rising like ghost ships above the dead seabed. The way forward was difficult, and Scouts and orks alike were forced to jink constantly back and forth to avoid running aground.

And with each passing instant the mountains grew ever closer, ever larger, swelling to fill the horizon as far as the eye could see.

ROTGRIM RUMBLED IN grim satisfaction as he saw the three human bikers approach the end of the race.

There was nowhere for them to run. Just as Rotgrim had ordered, the warband had herded the humans across the salt flats, through the maze of stones, to a defile that ran a hundred or so metres deep into the living rock of a mountain before ending at a solid rock face. And it was to this wall of stone that the humans had run their bikes.

Rotgrim ground his bike to a halt, and the rest of the warband skidded in behind him. He snarled, hefting his axe.

The three humans were on their feet now, swords and guns in hand, ringed protectively around the fallen human draped over one of the bikes.

It was almost funny, Rotgrim thought. The humans acted like they even had a *chance*. And who knows, against Rotgrim and his crew of biker boyz, maybe they might have.

But what the humans didn't know was that it *wasn't* just Rotgrim and his crew they had to worry about.

Now the fun would start, Rotgrim thought, climbing off his warbike. He hit the transmitter on his belt, signalling that they had arrived.

The humans turned at the sound of the hidden hatch opening in the rock face behind them. Even before the hatch was clear a dozen orks were spilling through, axes, guns, and pistols armed and ready.

THERE WERE DOZENS at first, then hundreds, pouring out of the hatch that led to the passages and caverns hidden beneath the mountain.

Zatori kept close to his bike, with Veteran Sergeant Hilts still draped over the back like saddlebags, his massive power fist dangling just centimetres above the hard packed dirt.

The Scout could hear the hideous laughter of the green-skinned monsters, and knew that they must find some humour in the fact that the squad had failed to outrun them.

But what the orks did not know was that Zatori and the others never *meant* to outrun them, but merely outpace them. And now they had reached the end of the run.

Zatori smiled as he reached down and detached the small device attached to the power fist's cuff. He held it aloft, and as he thumbed the switch the miniature teleport homer began to hum faintly.

There was a flash of light and a sudden, deafening boom, and before Zatori stood a towering Space Marine, his ceramite armour finished golden yellow and jet black, a storm shield on one arm and a massive thunder hammer in his other hand. A cloak fluttered behind him in the dry, hot wind, and above the Space Marine's shoulders rose a stanchion surmounted by a wreathed death's-head, bearing a scroll-shaped crossbar on which was emblazoned his name: LYSANDER.

'Primarch!' Captain Lysander shouted, swinging his thunder hammer the Fist of Dorn overhead. 'To your glory and the glory of Him on Terra!'

With a snarl on his lips, Captain Lysander charged towards the orks massed before the open hatch, without hesitation, without pause. Just as the captain cleared the patch of dirt upon which he had appeared, another Space Marine flashed into existence, and then another, and another, all with thundering war cries on their lips, all with their swords drawn and ready for blood. An entire squad of Veterans of the Imperial Fists, each of them in Terminator armour, each of them rushing to close with the ork invaders.

The Veterans of the First Company tore into the massed greenskins, swords biting. Already Captain Lysander was plunging into the hidden underground complex beyond the open hatch, laying waste to all he found.

ROTGRIM STOOD DUMBLY for a moment, watching the armoured humans smashing into his brother orks. And all he could think was that this was all the fault of the humans he'd been chasing, and of that twice-damned human in particular. He could picture the standard of the Evil Sunz laying somewhere out there in the salty dust.

He tightened his grip on his axe, rubbery lips curling in a snarl.

This race wasn't over yet, he realised.

Not until he'd got his vengeance.

* * *

ZATORI AND THE other two Scouts gathered around the supine form of Veteran Sergeant Hilts at the extraction point, waiting for the gunship that was thundering in to extract them. From where they stood, some distance from the base of the mountain, they could hear the sound of battle as the Veteran squad clashed with the orks, the greenskins ill-prepared for such an assault.

'I would have liked to stay and watch the Terminator squad in action,' s'Tonan said, eyeing the horizon.

The bike squad's run across the desert had been a subterfuge all along, to get the homer deep enough into the enemy ranks for the Terminators to take them out from within, in one fell swoop.

'And I would like to get clear of the greenskins' stench,' answered du Queste, picking bugs from his teeth.

Zatori didn't have a chance to say just what he would like, as they were interrupted by a bellowing roar coming from the direction of the mountains.

It was the red-clad leader of the warband, rushing towards them at full tilt, his enormous axe held high overhead. He was driving straight at Zatori with murder in his eyes, an animalistic howl reverberating from between his cracked and massive teeth.

Zatori didn't waste an instant by dropping into a defensive posture, or by reciting the abbreviated *Litany of the Blade*, or by raising his sword into the en garde position. Instead, he simply drew his melta gun, squeezed the trigger, and melted the oncoming ork into a puddle of ooze and charred bone with a single prolonged blast.

'And what would Rhetoricus say about *that* manoeuvre?' du Queste asked, eyes narrowed and a slight smile tugging the corners of his lips.

'Simple,' Zatori answered. 'I ascertained the opponent's state,' he hefted his melta gun, 'and seized the advantage by changing my approach.'

RENEGADES

Gav Thorpe

THE GROWLING OF engines and the roar of battle cannons reverberated around the massive hall, the echoes overlapping into a constant thunder of destruction. Intricately designed mosaics upon the wall shattered into thousands of multi-coloured shards under the impact of shells and las-fire. The marble tiles of the flooring cracked and heaved under iron treads as battle tanks lumbered forwards. Soldiers garbed in long black overcoats hurried from cover to cover; sheltering behind the immense pillars supporting the ceiling, scurrying to and fro behind mounds of rubble and leaping into craters gouged into the once-gleaming floor.

The tumult of war drowned out the shouted commands of the rebels' leaders, who waved forward their men from atop the blasted remains of armoured transports and the plinths of ravaged statues of former Imperial commanders. Their men chanted new slogans in defiance of their ousted commanders; battle cries filled with hate and calls for justice.

All along the mile-long hall the forces of the insurrectionists surged forwards under the cover of their tanks' guns.

Ahead of them the Astartes of the Avenging Sons Chapter stood defiant, their blue armour covered in dust and grime. They had come to quell a rebellion, only to find a world gripped by civil war. They had arrived to execute the rebel leaders and restore the rule of the Imperial commander, now they defended the same man against a whole world risen up against the tyranny of their ruler. The fighting had taken a bloody toll. There were thirty of them left; thirty Space Marines of the one hundred and three who had first come to Helmabad.

From behind makeshift barricades of twisted metal, heaps of lumpen rockcrete and barriers of piled bodies the Astartes poured fire into their attackers. The air was alight with the flickering rocket trails of bolter rounds, while blinding lascannon blasts blazed out to sear through armoured hulls and flesh alike. The crunch of heavy bolter fire and the crackling roar of plasma howled the Space Marines' fury.

Behind the wall of armoured giants cowered the relatively few men that still remained loyal to Commander Mu'shan, snapping off shots from their lasguns in scattered moments of bravery. Once they had been the elite, the lauded Sepulchre Guard of Helmabad. Now the ire of those they had once sworn to protect had humbled them. Their death's head masks seemed comical rather than grim. Their gold brocade and epaulettes were tattered and their black carapace armour pitted, scarred and filthy.

Amidst the fire and devastation strode Brother-Captain Gessart of the Avenging Sons. Like his battle-brothers he wore armour marked from much fighting. Its blue paint was burnt and cracked ceramite showed through his livery in dozens of places. His left shoulder pad was a plain, dull white; a hasty replacement for the one he had lost two days ago. His golden helmet was slicked with a layer of dust, and blood stained the silver eagle upon his chest; the blood of enemies a better badge of honour than the symbol it obscured.

Gessart barked commands as he led the defenders, each order punctuated by a salvo of shots from the storm bolter in his hands.

'Dispersive fire on the left,' he growled, loosing off three rounds that tore through a junior officer half-hidden behind the tangled remains of an iron bench. The men the dead officer had been attempting to rally melted away into the dust clouds and smoke.

Just behind the captain stood Librarian Zacherys, a nimbus of energy glowing from the Librarian's psychic hood, the force sword in his right fist blazing with power. Helmetless, Zacherys's face was a mask of strain as he projected an invisible wall of force around the Space Marines. With sparks of warp energy, las-bolts and auto-gun rounds crackled into oblivion around the psyker.

'Show them no mercy!' bellowed Herdain, the Company Chaplain, as he stepped up onto a pile of rubble and loosed a succession of plasma bolts from his pistol. The conversion field hidden within the Chaplain's rosarius intermittently blazed into blinding life as enemy fire converged on the grim custodian.

'How can so many be so misguided?' said Rykhel, his bolter raised to his shoulder, his shots controlled and precise. 'They are blind to their doom.'

'Pick your targets,' said Gessart. 'Make every shot count.'

'It's hard to miss,' laughed Lehenhart, his bolter spewing rounds that chewed through a rebel squad dashing across the open area directly in front of the Space Marines. 'We haven't had such easy targets since those orks charged us on Caraphis.'

'You'll lead us to victory, captain,' said Willusch. 'The primarch favours you.'

'Just stay focused,' said Gessart as he loosed off another burst of fire.

The firefight continued for several more minutes, the Space Marines manoeuvring and concentrating their fire wherever the rebels looked to be gathering in numbers.

'Recon walkers on the right flank; three, possibly four,' warned Willusch. He swung his heavy bolter in a slow arc, his volley hammering through plasteel and rockcrete at the rebels cowering behind. 'I can't draw on them from here.'

'Lehenhart, Herdain, Nicz and Rykhel with me,' Gessart snapped. 'Ready grenades for counterattack.'

The five Space Marines pounded to the right along the barricade line. A long gallery ran alongside this side of the hall, the wall between cracked and holed in places, through which the captain saw the gawky forms of the Sentinel walkers advancing. If they were allowed to continue they would reach the end of the line and would be able to pour fire from behind the defence works.

'Breach on my signal,' Gessart called out.

They were less than a dozen paces from the wall when Gessart unleashed a long burst from his storm bolter, the rounds punching into the rockcrete and gouging great holes with their detonations. The others did the same, ripping up the wall with their fire.

'Breach!' shouted Gessart, lowering his left shoulder and charging full speed at the damaged rockcrete. The blasted wall shattered under the impact of the massive Space Marine and the captain smashed through into the gallery beyond amidst a cloud of stone splinters and crumbling plaster. To his left and right the others made similarly dramatic entrances.

The Avenging Sons had breached just behind four Sentinel walkers. The rearmost turned awkwardly, its double-jointed legs buckling as it struggled over a mound of rubble. The pilot's eyes widened with horror inside the open cockpit as Rykhel's frag grenade landed in his lap. He reached up to slap the release buckle on his restraining belt. A moment later the grenade detonated, spraying the inside of the walker with lethal shrapnel. The pilot was shredded, his bloodied, ragged form disembowelled. Its controls destroyed, the walker swayed to the left and then nose-dived to the right, the impact buckling its chin-mounted multilaser.

The three others were beginning to turn, but not quickly enough to bring their weapons to bear. Nicz had a krak grenade in his hand. He leapt forwards and slammed the magnetic explosive onto the lower joint of the closest Sentinel's left leg before jumping back. The grenade detonated, shearing away the walker's steel limb. The Sentinel toppled backwards and Nicz punched his gauntleted fist through its exposed underside, tearing free a handful of wires and hydraulics. Red fluid spurted from the severed lines, spraying like arterial blood from the critically wounded Sentinel.

Gessart jumped up towards the next Sentinel, his free hand grabbing hold of the edge of the cockpit. The pilot pulled out a laspistol and fired it point blank into Gessart's chest as the captain heaved himself up, the shots flickering harmless from the solid plastron of his armour. Gessart swung his storm bolter around and fired two shots; the first round ripped apart the pilot's chest, the second disintegrated his head in a shower of gore; blood and brain matter spattered across Gessart's golden helm. The Sentinel jerked spasmodically as the dead man's muscles contracted at the controls, throwing Gessart to the ground in its mechanical death throes.

The last pilot fired his multilaser, the shots falling well wide, as he tried to steer his walker to face his attackers. Lehenhart reached up and grabbed the swivelling weapon with his right hand. The creak of hydraulics competed with the whine of servos as the Sentinel's systems battled against the artificial muscles of Lehenhart's bionic arm and power armour. With a screech and a shower of sparks the Sentinel's actuators lost the fight and Lehenhart ripped the multilaser from its housing. Herdain's plasma pistol tore a glowing hole through the walker's engine block which exploded in a ball of blue flame, sending Lehenhart and the Chaplain crunching into the rubble littering the gallery floor.

The pilot of the walker crippled by Nicz pulled himself free of the cockpit and dragged himself a few paces across the grit of the floor, his leg shattered by the same blow that had destroyed his machine. Lehenhart picked himself up and grabbed the back of the man's flak jacket. Casually lifting the soldier into the air, the Space Marine turned to Gessart.

'Anyone want a new pet?' Lehenhart asked.

'Perhaps we can interrogate him for intelligence,' said Nicz.

Gessart glanced at the wounded man. Tears made tracks through the filth on his smoke-grimed face beneath the peak of his skewed leather helmet. The man's distress meant nothing to the captain. He was the enemy, that was all that mattered.

'There's nothing he can tell us that we don't know already,' said the captain with a dismissive shake of the head.

Lehenhart shrugged, the actuators beneath his shoulder pads whining in protest as they tried to replicate the expressive gesture. With a swing of his arm, the Space Marine smashed the pilot against the wreckage of his walker, dashing in his skull and snapping his spine with one blow. Lehenhart let the limp corpse drop from his fingers.

Gessart checked down the gallery to see if any other rebels had been following the walkers. He could see nothing and guessed they had been waiting until the sentinels secured a forward position. Still, he could not defend the gallery and the hallway at the same time; not if the rebels made a determined push along both. He was thankful that the rebel commanders, whoever they now were after overthrowing the Imperial commander's regime, seemed to place a tactically-limiting value on their follower's lives. An enemy with a more detached attitude would have overrun the hall on the first attack.

'Back to the line,' Gessart ordered.

For another six hours the battle for the audience hall raged. There had been little let-up in the fighting and even Gessart was beginning to feel the strain of the constant vigilance required; not just on the line here but from more than forty days of continuous war since they had arrived on Helmabad.

Smoke billowing from four wrecked tanks hung heavily in the still air, obscuring growing numbers of shadowy figures beyond. The rebels were clearly massing for another attack, as they had done three times before in the last twenty hours.

'Ammunition check,' said Gessart, ejecting his own empty magazine and slamming another drum into place on the side of the storm bolter.

'Last belt, captain,' Brother Willusch reported on the comm.

'Seven rounds left, captain,' warned Brother Rykhel.

'Power pack at thirty-five per cent,' said Brother Heynke.

As the rest gave their reports it was quickly apparent that every Space Marine was running low. Gessart looked out at the hundreds of soldiers now creeping closer and closer to their line. Some were less than fifty metres away, firing blind from their hiding places to cover the advance of their comrades. Gessart knew that they would be moving up heavier weaponry and the Space Marines would feel the full wrath of the rebels' attack soon.

Another Leman Russ tank rumbled into view. It foolishly shouldered aside the wreckage of a transport and crawled forwards, its cannon swinging towards Gessart's position. Obviously the men inside had not learnt from the mistakes of their fellow tank crews. The captain fearlessly stared down the bore of the gun for a moment.

'Heynke!' Gessart called out, but his warning was unnecessary; even as the name left his lips Heynke's lascannon spat out a blast of energy that slammed into the turret of the tank. The shot ignited the shells stored inside and the whole of the turret erupted into a blossom of fire and smoke, hurling a burning body out onto the blood-soaked marble.

'Power pack at thirty per cent,' warned Heynke. 'No more than half a dozen shots left, brother-captain. What are your orders, captain?'

'We are outgunned,' said Rykhel. 'We need to defend a more enclosed area.'

'It is our duty to press forward and drive these scum from the palace, captain,' snapped Herdain. 'Remember the teachings of Guilliman!'

Las- and heavy weapons fire intensified around the knot of Space Marines as more and more rebels got into position. Las-bolts, shrapnel and splinters of rockcrete pattered from their armour. Gessart could see only two options: retreat to the next position or counterattack and drive back the soldiers with hand to hand combat. He chose the former.

'Colonel, fall back to the access way,' Gessart directed his order to Colonel Akhaim, the leader of the Sepulchre Guard.

The Guardsmen needed no further encouragement and were soon scrambling and scrabbling over the wreckage towards the corridor behind them. A few minutes later Gessart signalled his own squads to withdraw. The Avenging Sons pulled back from the line, facing their foes all the while. No shots were fired to cover their retreat; the Space Marines were contemptuous of the rebels' weapons, and they needed to save every last shred of ammunition if they were to continue the war.

As they passed into the corridor the Space Marines retreated past a ring of melta-bombs secured to the walls and ceiling. When they were clear of the area Gessart sent the detonation signal. The ground underfoot shuddered as the captain watched the gateway into the audience hall disappear under tons of rockcrete and twisted steel. Now there was only one way in to and out of the central sepulchre where the Imperial commander was hidden.

'Reminds me of Archimedon,' said Nicz from behind the captain.

Gessart turned to look at the Space Marine, unable to see Nicz's expression hidden inside his helmet.

'Keep that thought to yourself,' snarled Gessart.

THE SEPULCHRE WAS the inner reaches of the Imperial commander's palace; a maze of corridors and chambers dug into the heartrock that were the foundations of the citadel. Before the uprising they had been home to functionaries and courtiers, now they were a makeshift hospital, communications station and headquarters. The brick tunnels were now choked with storage crates and wounded men on bloodstained bedding. The ghostly echoes of the dying resounded along the long, low tunnels.

Having left some of his warriors to defend the last gateway to the surface, Gessart led the remnants of his company through the winding subterranean passages. He ignored the moans of the wounded and the scared chatter of the Sepulchre Guard. Here and there a radio squawked out tinny propaganda transmitted by the rebels – a crude but effective jamming of the loyalists' communications.

Passing an archway the captain heard laughter and swearing from the chamber beyond. He stooped under the low arch into the room. Inside were a handful of Guardsmen clustered around a battered vox-caster.

'You'll be getting the same as your dog-faced friends,' their sergeant was saying into the pick-up. 'Just try to come through the east gate and the Avenging Sons will send you crying to your mothers.'

Gessart's massive armoured boot crushed the vox-caster, which died with a piercing screech.

'No communication with the enemy!' bellowed the captain.

The Guardsmen cowered before Gessart's anger as he loomed over them.

'This endless chatter gives the enemy vital information,' the captain told them. It was not the first time that he had been forced to explain his edict for radio silence. 'Fools such as you tell them where we keep our supplies, where our defences are strongest, where we intend to strike. If you wish to help the rebels at least have the courage to do it with your guns.'

Suitably cowed the Guardsmen muttered their apologies, avoiding the disconcerting gaze of the captain's blank eye lenses.

'Hopeless,' muttered Gessart as he turned back into the corridor.

The captain soon led the others into the central chamber; an octagonal meeting place of the main thoroughfares that radiated outwards to the far reaches of the sepulchre. Rykhel was already waiting; his helmet removed to reveal a lean face and agitated grey eyes.

'We have less than two hundred bolter rounds left,' the Space Marine explained with a grim expression. 'Less than fifty heavy shells for Willusch. Power packs are still plentiful.'

'One engagement,' said Heynke.

'A short one, perhaps,' said Lehenhart, his mood unusually subdued. 'It'll be short for the wrong reasons.'

'It's only through good fire discipline we've made our supplies last this long,' said Rykhel. 'We weren't equipped for an elongated campaign. We're already seventy days over our predicted combat threshold.'

'Tell me something I don't already know,' said Gessart. 'Other weapons?'

Rykhel strode across the chamber and picked up one of the many Guard-issue lasguns stacked against the walls. Its barrel crumpled in the augmented grip of his hand.

'Useless for our purposes,' said Rykhel, tossing the remnants of the lasgun aside. 'Simply not durable enough. We would be better using our fists.'

'If that is what we must do, that is what we shall do,' said Herdain. His skull helm turned slowly as the Chaplain looked at the assembled Space Marines. 'We fight to the last breath.'

Gessart did not reply, for his own thoughts were very different. Instead he looked towards Zacherys. The Librarian had pulled off his helmet, his black hair plastered with waxy sweat across his face. He leaned against the wall, the bricks behind him cracking under the strain as if in sympathy for the laboured psyker.

'Have you detected any sign of relief or reinforcement?' Gessart asked. 'Any vision or message?'

The Librarian shook his head silently.

'Nothing at all?' Gessart continued. 'No warp-chatter? No ship wakes?'

'Nothing,' said Zacherys in a cracked whisper. 'There is a veil upon Helmabad that I cannot pierce. I cannot see beyond the curtain of blood.'

'Rest,' said Gessart, crossing the chamber to lay a hand upon the Librarian's head. 'Regather your strength.'

Zacherys nodded and pushed himself upright.

'I do not wish to bring woe, but this does not augur well,' croaked the Librarian. The others watched as he straightened and walked from the vault with as much dignity as he could muster.

'His reticence worries me,' said Herdain once Zacherys was out of earshot.

'I trust no one more than Zacherys,' said Gessart. 'He guided us here. I trust he will lead us on the right path.'

'As he did on Archimedon?' asked Nicz. 'You followed his prophecy then and what did we get? A penitence patrol that has brought us to this Emperor-forsaken war.'

'I said not to speak of that place,' said Gessart, squaring off to Nicz. 'Your indiscipline borders on insubordination.'

'If I have my doubts it is not wise to keep them hidden,' said Nicz, looking at Herdain. 'Is it not true that the doubt that is buried festers into heresy, Brother-Chaplain?'

'There is a time and a place for voicing concerns,' Herdain replied evenly. 'This is neither. Respect your superiors or there will be consequences.'

'All I am saying is that we were never prepared for this fight,' said Nicz. 'You brought us here to put down a... What was it? A "small uprising", wasn't it? This world has been wracked in civil war for eight years. We should not have stayed.'

'The Chapter will respond,' said Herdain. 'More will come, either to aid us, or to avenge us.'

'Zacherys did not seem so certain,' said Heynke. 'All he talks about is the "curtain of blood" that surrounds this place. His messages have gone nowhere.'

'Then here we will make our last stand,' said Herdain. 'We live for battle and we shall die for battle.'

'We lay down our lives for victory,' said Gessart. 'I am not convinced there is any victory to be won here.'

GESSART WAS ALONE in one of the many chambers of the sepulchre, performing the rituals of maintenance on his storm bolter. The captain sat with his back to a crumbling vault wall, the storm bolter cradled delicately in his hands. He had removed his helm to see better and his craggy features were illuminated by the flicker of candles in small alcoves around the chamber. By the dim light he worked a cloth over the exposed innards of the weapon, inspecting each piece carefully before replacing it.

Now and then a detonation would set the whole network of corridors trembling, showering mortar dust from the walls and ceiling. The rebels' bombardment had been continuous, trying to force a breach through the gateways since the Space Marines had withdrawn from the upper levels. Though the defences were strong, the men who defended the catacombs were weary and disillusioned. Once the gates collapsed – perhaps two days, perhaps three or four – there would be nothing left but a last stand against an unstoppable army.

'Captain?' said Willusch from the doorway. He had stripped his armour of backpack, helm and shoulder pads. It made Willusch look strangely thin and weak, something Gessart knew to be utterly wrong. 'May I speak with you?'

Gessart looked up and waved in the Space Marine, placing his storm bolter to one side. Willusch did not sit.

'I have concerns, captain,' said Willusch.

'Our Brother-Chaplain is always ready to listen,' said Gessart.

'It is with Herdain that I have an issue,' Willusch said, his hands clasped at his waist.

'How so?' asked Gessart.

'I know that you forbade us from speaking of Archimedon, but I must,' said Willusch.

'Say what you must, brother,' said Gessart with a sigh.

'Thank you, captain,' Willusch said. He remained absolutely still as he spoke, his scarred face a picture of intense sincerity. 'We were right to do what we did on Archimedon. It is not in the teachings of the primarch to throw our lives away in needless sacrifice. We could not defend the space port any longer against the enemy. It had to be destroyed.'

'I do not need to justify my actions,' Gessart said angrily. 'As I told you all at the time, thousands would die, but not in vain. If the renegades had captured the port they would have been able to wreak unknown terror and destruction.'

'Yet the masters of the Chapter felt that you were in error,' said Willusch. 'They have punished us for that decision; a punishment that has led us to this place.'

'A chance of fate, perhaps,' said Gessart with a shake of the head. 'There is no divine justice in our coming here, merely the happenstance of location and the vagaries of astrotelepathy.'

'I concur, captain,' said Willusch. 'Yet Herdain lectured us when you departed. He told us that we were about to lay our lives upon the altar of battle for the glory of the Chapter.'

'And perhaps we will,' said Gessart. 'I see no way for us to break out of our predicament. The enemy number in their billions. Billions, Willusch! In all likelihood it is well that Herdain resigns us to our doom.'

'He not only expects it, he craves it,' said Willusch, now growing more animated. 'He would have us throw away our lives as a gesture of penance for Archimedon. He was not there yet he attributes us with a great shame for the judgement of the Chapter upon us. He does not seek victory, he seeks to absolve us with our deaths!'

Before Gessart replied a wailing shout echoed along the stone labyrinth; the cry of Zacherys. The captain pushed himself to his feet and strode out of the chamber, Willusch close on his heels. The pair marched quickly through the winding corridors, following the source of the shouts that continued to cry out. When they arrived at Zacherys's quarters Gessart saw that many of his warriors were already there.

The chamber was dark, lit by a single guttering lantern overhead. In the centre of the circle of Space Marines, Nicz was on one knee, the Librarian's head cradled in his armoured lap. Motes of energy danced around the psyker's lips as he shouted wordlessly, but the Librarian was otherwise utterly inert. Gessart noticed thick blood oozing from Zacherys's gums as he wailed.

'What is happening?' demanded Herdain as he entered from the opposite doorway.

'I just found–' began Nicz.

Zacherys's eyes snapped open and a blast of power exploded from him, hurling the Space Marines to the ground. Nicz was flung against the wall and flopped to the ground, dazed. The others groped their way back to their feet as the Librarian stood. His eyes were a liquid crimson and his teeth stained with blood.

'The curtain of blood is parting,' Zacherys whispered. 'The realm beyond breaks through. The legion across the divide awaits. The clarions of Chaos call loud.'

'What do you see?' demanded Gessart, striding across the small chamber. He reached out to touch the Librarian but held back his hand at the last moment.

'Death is coming!' hissed Zacherys. He turned his otherworldly eyes on Gessart. 'Yet, you are not destined to die here.'

With a shuddering gasp, the psyker fell to his knees and slumped forwards onto all fours. When he raised his head again, his eyes were once more the pale blue they had always been. Gessart crouched beside his friend and laid a comforting hand on his left shoulder pad.

'What did you see?' he asked again, his voice now gentle, barely audible.

'The warp opens,' said Zacherys.

There was a moment of murmuring discontent from the other Space Marines and Gessart shot them a fierce glance to quell it.

'Traitors?' asked Herdain.

'Worse,' said Zacherys, getting to his feet with the aid of Gessart. 'Chaos Incarnate. The Evil Given Life. A Nightmare Host.'

'Daemons,' muttered Rykhel.

'The rebels,' the Librarian continued. 'They know not what they do, but their fear and their loathing beckons the apparitions. They idly whisper the names of ancient powers lost in antiquity and draw the gaze of them to this world.'

'How long do we have to get ready for the festivities?' asked Lehenhart.

'Less than a day,' the Librarian replied. 'Hours, more likely. I can feel the rift opening, out in the stars above the city. They will come here first. Everything will die.'

'Not us,' said Herdain. 'We shall fight on gloriously. You said yourself that we will not die here.'

'He said that I would not die here,' said Gessart. 'I didn't hear him mention your name.'

'Yet how would you survive while we perish?' said Nicz, who had recovered and was pushing himself to his feet, using the wall to keep his balance.

'None need to die here,' said Gessart. He turned his dark gaze upon his Space Marines. 'This world is lost; to the rebels or the daemons. It matters not which darkness devours Helmabad; only that we survive to warn of its fall.'

'So we cut and run again?' said Nicz.

'That would not be my choice of phrase,' said Gessart.

'There is no honour in empty sacrifice,' said Willusch, taking a step to stand beside his captain.

'Sacrifice is the honour,' snapped Herdain. 'The Astartes were created to lay down their lives in battle. This cowardice will not be tolerated.'

'It's not cowardice, it's survival,' said Lehenhart. 'Humanity will not be guarded by our corpses.'

'I will not let you repeat the sins of Archimedon,' said Herdain, rounding on Gessart. 'You failed in your leadership then and you are failing now. You are no longer fit to lead this company.'

'Company?' laughed Nicz. 'There is no company here. No Chapter. We are all that remain. I will not die here in a vain gesture.'

'Heresy!' roared Herdain, snatching his plasma pistol from its holster and pointing it at Nicz. 'Pay no heed to this treachery, brothers.'

Rykhel held up his hands and stepped forwards.

'I swore an oath to the Chapter,' he said. 'I am Astartes, of the Avenging Sons. My life was forfeit the day I took that oath, as were all of yours. It is not our place to pick and choose our fates, but to fight until we can fight no more.'

There was a chorus of assent from several of the Space Marines, most of them newer recruits to the company, brought in to replace the losses of Archimedon. Gessart looked at the assembly and saw a mixture of hope and doubt in their eyes. Willusch gave him a reassuring nod.

'We cannot stand divided,' said Gessart. 'I am your captain, your commander. I alone lead this company, what remains of it.'

'I still follow where you lead,' said Willusch.

'And I,' said Zacherys. 'There is no defeating this foe.'

'I was taught to fight, not commit suicide,' said Lehenhart. 'Staying here would be suicide, by my reckoning.'

Herdain's face was a mask of hatred as he stared at Gessart and his companions. He turned his fell look upon Heynke.

'You, brother, what do you say?' the Chaplain demanded.

Heynke stood transfixed for a moment, his eyes shifting between Gessart and Herdain before straying around the room to look at his battle-brothers. He opened his mouth to speak and then closed it again.

'Is this the bravery of the Avenging Sons?' shouted Herdain, grabbing the rim of the breastplate at Heynke's throat and pulling him forward. 'Make your loyalties known! Show your purity!'

'I will fight!' declared Ruphen, drawing up his bolter to his shoulder and aiming at the group clustered around Gessart.

'This is insanity,' muttered Tylo, the company's Apothecary. His white armour stood out amongst the deep blue of his battle-brothers as he pushed his way forward. 'We cannot fail here and allow our gene-seed to fall into the clutches of traitors. We must seek to preserve the future.'

'What future is there without honour?' said Herdain, lowering his pistol, his eyes imploring.

The crack of a bolt-round rang out around the chamber and the Chaplain's head exploded in a blossom of blood and fragments of bone. Gessart stood with Zacherys's smoking pistol in his fist; the captain had not brought his own weapon with him.

'More future than death holds,' Gessart declared.

Ruphen opened fire with his bolter and anarchy filled the chamber. Gessart lunged to his left, pushing Zacherys clear of the Space Marine's fire. Nicz and Lehenhart opened up with their bolters. Within a second, the two camps were locked in bitter combat, blazing away with bolters and pounding each other with fists and chainswords, their harsh shouts accompanying the roar of weapons.

In a matter of moments four Space Marines lay dead on the rocky floor and six more were sorely wounded. Nicz loomed over brother Karlrech, one of those who had sided with Herdain. His bolter was inches from the bleeding Space Marine's face. Lehenhart was holding down Rykhel with the aid of two more battle-brothers. Heynke and a few others looked on with expressions of horror.

Gessart handed back the pistol to Zacherys and walked towards the subdued followers of the Chaplain.

'If you wish to die on Helmabad, I will grant that for you,' he said calmly, looking not only at those who had spoken against him but those who had remained silent. 'I hold no ill will against you, for we must each make a choice now. It will be quick for those who wish to preserve their honour. For those who swear anew to follow me, there will be no judgement on what has just passed.'

'I will follow the will of my brothers,' said Heynke. 'If it is their choice that we leave, then I shall be with them.'

'Death before dishonour!' spat Karlrech.

Gessart gave Nicz a nod, who pulled the trigger and ended Karlrech's protests with the angry retort of his bolter.

'Anybody else?' Nicz asked, straightening, his face a crimson mask of the dead Space Marine's blood.

Brother Hechsen stepped forwards and grabbed the muzzle of Nicz's bolter and placed it under his chin. He stared defiantly at Gessart.

'This is treachery,' said Hechsen. 'I name you all renegades, and I will not be numbered amongst you in the annals of shame. I am an Avenging Son and proud to die as such. You are less than cowards, for you are traitors.'

Gessart noticed a few of his warriors wince as Nicz fired again, but he kept his own eyes firmly fixed on those of Hechsen. He felt nothing. Inside he was empty, as he had been for several years; ever since Archimedon. He had not wished events to turn in this way, but he was accepting of whatever fate had dealt him.

No more Space Marines stepped forwards at Nicz's next inquiry and Gessart nodded approvingly. Lehenhart pulled Rykhel to his feet and patted him on the head. Tylo moved to the dead warriors and began the bloody process of removing their gene-seed as Gessart turned to Zacherys.

'We shall not die on Helmabad,' the captain said.

'Aye, captain,' said the Librarian with a weak smile.

'I hope you have a plan for how you're going to make that happen,' said Lehenhart. 'There's still millions of rebels camped outside, and we need to get off this world.'

'Captain!' Nicz called out and pointed towards one of the chamber doors.

Clustered outside was a handful of the Sepulchre Guard, who looked upon the awful scene with wide eyes and trembling lips.

'Nicz, Lehenhart, Heynke, Willusch,' Gessart snapped. 'Deal with them.'

As the Space Marines turned towards the doorway the Guardsmen bolted.

'Fists and knives,' Gessart added. 'Save what ammunition you can.'

THE CENTRAL CHAMBER of the sepulchre was deathly quiet, disturbed only by moans and whispers of dying Sepulchre Guards echoing from the corridors surrounding it. It was a large space, its wide floor decorated with tiles carved with the Imperial aquila, thirty pillars inscribed with the names of faithful Imperial servants supported the vaulted ceiling. At one end Imperial Commander Mu'shan sat upon a high-backed chair of dark red wood, his wizened face hidden by the cowl of his golden robe. Nicz stood to his left, bolter in hand, while Hurstreich loomed on the governor's right. Gessart leant against one of the pillars not far from the throne, talking to Lehenhart and Zacherys. Some of the other Space Marines stood guard at the entrance hall, others stood sentry behind the sealed east gate, whilst five had been despatched on a mission beyond the sepulchre by their captain.

'The breach is coming closer,' warned the Librarian, his voice low. 'I can feel the curtain of blood thinning. I hear the voices of the beasts that dwell on the other side. They are hungry, I can feel it. They sense the terror of this world and they thirst for it.'

'We could probably fight our way back to the Thunderhawk,' said Lehenhart. 'It's less than a mile from the north-west gate.'

'As a last resort, yes,' Gessart replied. 'I would rather not use up the remaining supplies fighting the rebels only to be unarmed when the daemons arrive. There is another way; one that carries less risk.'

'What do you have in mind?' asked Lehenhart.

'That is not your concern,' snapped Gessart. 'Be ready to move out on my word.'

'Of course,' said Lehenhart. 'You know, a little trust goes a long way.'

Gessart darted the Space Marine a scowl in reply and Lehenhart swiftly retreated, joining his comrades at the main door.

'What is your intent, renegade?' Mu'shan's high-pitched voice floated across the hall.

Gessart strode to the Imperial commander and stood in front of him, swathing the aging ruler with his shadow. He looked down at the shrivelled dignitary and wondered how such a decrepit specimen could ever have been trusted with the sovereign rule of Helmabad.

'It was not I that surrendered his world to the rebels,' said Gessart. 'The blame for all that has befallen you lies at your own feet. Your laxness in prosecuting the Emperor's will has been your undoing.'

'And so in hindsight you would hold me guilty of this, when it is you who are supposed to be our saviours?' Mu'shan spoke quietly but with defiance. 'What hope is there for mankind if our greatest defenders forget their oaths and put their survival ahead of their duty?'

'You speak to me of duties?' said Gessart with a sneer. 'How is it that three-quarters of your citizens rose up in revolt against your command? Explain to me why the Astartes should shed their blood to save the rulership of a man who did not defend it himself?'

'If I am weak, then it is beholden to you and your kind to remain strong,' said Mu'shan, pulling back his hood to reveal a thin, wrinkled face with alabaster-white skin. His eyes were dark blue and intent as he stared at Gessart. 'If I failed, it is because of my human weakness. You were created to be better than human; stronger, more devoted, dependable and unflinching. Has so much been lost these ten thousand years that the war-angels of the Astartes consider the protection of mankind beneath their dignity?'

'Has Man fallen so low that it must always look to the Astartes to cure every ill it suffers?' countered Gessart. 'We wage war for the protection of humankind, of the race, not in the defence of individuals. Did the Emperor grant you such a greater lot in your life, that it is worth our lives to defend you for a few hours more when we could live and save a billion others?'

Mu'shan stood slowly, awkwardly, lips pursed, his head barely reaching the chest of Gessart. His back was bent and as he reached forward a hand to lay it upon the eagle of Gessart's armour his skeletal limbs were plain to see.

'If you judge the worth of your battles by numbers alone, then you have already lost,' said Mu'shan. 'Beneath this breast of muscle and fused bone beats the heart of a man. Does it not tell you that what you do is wrong?'

Gessart gently brushed aside the commander's hand, fearful that so frail was Mu'shan that even this light touch might break his weak bones.

'I have read the *Tactica Imperialis* too,' said Gessart. 'It also says, "The mere slaughter of your foe is no substitute for true victory." A man's heart may beat in my chest, but beside it beats the secondary heart of the Space Marine. We are not alike. We share no common bond. You ask that I be human and sacrifice myself for you. The nature of the galaxy demands that I be more than human and live to fight further battles. To accept defeat, for our deaths will not prevent it here, is no courage at all. To accept death, no matter the circumstance, is the counsel of despair. I will listen to it no longer.'

Gessart turned away and heard Mu'shan wheeze as he sat down again. His ears also detected the tramp of heavy boots outside and a moment later the guards at the door parted to allow Willusch, Heynke and three other Space Marines to enter. Between them they carried the limp forms of four men, their greatcoats torn, insignias cut out. Rebels.

'Tylo!' Gessart called as the prisoners were dropped unceremoniously in the middle of the chamber.

The Apothecary walked over to the captives and, after giving them a brief inspection, nodded to confirm that they were still alive.

'Wake them up,' said Gessart.

Willusch strode across the chamber to the pile of crates and barrels in one corner, returning quickly with a glass demijohn of water. He tipped its contents over the faces of the men, who rose to wakefulness with splutters and coughs. They gazed at the Space Marines towering over them, their eyes full of fear, and their mouths aghast.

'Listen, do not speak,' snapped Gessart. 'Do as I say and you will live. Any defiance and you will be slain.'

The men nodded dumbly in understanding.

'That is well,' said Gessart, crouching down beside the prisoners, the joints of his armour creaking as he did so. He turned his gaze to Heynke. 'Fetch a vox-caster.'

Heynke headed back into the recesses of the hall without question and returned promptly carrying a comms unit under one arm. He placed it on the floor next to Gessart and knelt on one knee beside it.

'Who are we contacting?' Heynke said.

Gessart looked at the prisoners with a vicious smile.

'The enemy,' he said.

GESSART'S CAPTIVES WERE more than willing to give up the command frequencies of their superiors, and after several messages, the Space Marines worked their way up the chain to speak to those in charge.

'Whom am I addressing?' asked Gessart, the vox-caster's pick-up dwarfed by his huge fist.

'Serain Am'hep, Third Apostle of the Awakening,' a tinny voice crackled back.

'Third what?' snorted Lehenhart. 'Unbelievable!'

Gessart waved him into silence and pressed the transmit stud.

'Do you have the authority to discuss terms?' the captain asked.

'I am a member of the Revolutionary Council,' Serain Am'hep replied. 'I have with me the fourth and eighth Apostles and we speak for all members.'

'Finally!' said Gessart. He began to pace around the prisoners as he spoke. 'It is my desire to end this conflict.'

'You wish to discuss surrender?' Am'hep's incredulity was clear in the tone of his voice.

'Of course not,' said Gessart.

'There's no way we could possibly take you all prisoner!' Lehenhart called from behind his leader.

Gessart turned with a frown and wordlessly pointed towards the guards at the door. Lehenhart gave a sullen nod and departed to join them.

'Let me be direct with you,' said Gessart. 'I wish to arrange our safe departure in return for the delivery of Imperial Commander Mu'shan.'

'What?' came Mu'shan's choked cry from the end of the hall.

Surprise was written across the faces of many of the Space Marines. Nicz simply nodded with a grim smile.

'You will turn over the faithless Mu'shan to our justice?' asked Am'hep.

'Once we have departed, you will be free to enter the sepulchre without resistance and claim him for yourselves,' said Gessart.

'Why would we allow you to walk free?' said Am'hep. 'We have the manpower to storm the sepulchre any time that we wish.'

'You are welcome to expend the lives of thousands of your followers in the attempt,' said Gessart. 'I'm sure their deaths will not discourage the rest.'

There was a long pause as Am'hep undoubtedly conferred with his companions. Gessart glanced towards the throne, where Mu'shan was sat trembling, his eyes boring holes of hatred into the Space Marine captain. Gessart ignored him and looked away.

'What guarantee can we be given that you have not spirited Mu'shan away by some means?' said Am'hep.

'None,' replied Gessart. 'However, should you try to double-cross me, my strike cruiser in orbit has locked onto your comms-signal and is even now aiming its cannons at your position. If I fail to report to them once we leave the sepulchre they will reduce your camp to ashes, and you along with it.'

'Really?' whispered Willusch with a smile. 'I never knew we could do that.'

'He's lying, you idiot,' snapped Nicz. 'Even if we were actually in contact with the *Vengeful* they can't track a solitary carrier wave signal from orbit. We would have blasted their commanders to oblivion by now if we could.'

Gessart shook his head despairingly and clicked the transmit stud once more.

'I expect your reply within five minutes,' he told the rebel leaders. 'If I have not had confirmation by then, I will assume you wish the war to continue.'

He tossed the pick-up to the floor and walked away.

'What if they refuse?' asked Tylo. 'They could bombard us for days and reduce the sepulchre to rubble and trap us in here.'

'No,' Mu'shan called out. 'They're revolutionaries. They need to show their pawns that I have been truly overthrown. It is, however, a grave mistake to trust them. To defeat the Astartes will be a powerful symbol for them also.'

Gessart stalked along the hallway, his eyes fixed upon the Imperial commander.

'You try to goad me by speaking of defeat?' Gessart said as he walked. 'Your crude manipulations may have been sufficient to fool and subdue your council, but they do not work on me. You forget that we are trained to believe in the right of our cause. We do not flinch from the harsh truths that ordinary men would shy away from. Once committed to a cause we are indefatigable; swayed not by propaganda or deception.'

'You believe your actions here are justified?' croaked Mu'shan. 'You have made your decision and will no longer listen to reason?'

'The reason of men is filled with doubt and fear,' said Gessart as he stopped in front of the governor. 'Their logic is tainted by affection, compassion and mercy. They believe that life should be fair, rather than just.'

'I did not realise that the argument of semantics was part of your training,' said Mu'shan with a dismissive shake of the head. 'It has bred arrogance.'

'The insecure see self-assurance and call it hubris,' said Gessart. 'You call it semantics. In training it was called the shield of righteousness and the armour of contempt. We indeed learn of the trickery of words, so that we might spot the falsehoods presented as facts by our foes. Our minds are as hardened to doubt as our bodies are to injury. Your self-interest is plain, and so easily ignored.'

'My self-interest?' laughed Mu'shan bitterly. 'You flee this battle to save yourself!'

'It does not matter which course of action I have chosen,' said Gessart. 'Label it as you will. The fact remains that I am decided on it, and your so-called arguments are nothing more than a petty, irritating distraction. If you continue, I shall be forced to silence you.'

Mu'shan looked into Gessart's eyes and saw nothing but harsh sincerity. He shook his head once more and lifted up his cowl to hide his leathery face.

Gessart was halfway back to the vox-caster when it crackled into life.

'We have contacted our fellow Apostles and we have reached a decision,' said Am'hep. 'In two hours from now you shall assemble at the east gate and open it. You will be allowed to depart and will be given clear passage to your transport. You will not be hindered. When you have left we shall enter the sepulchre and arrest the treacherous Mu'shan. Are you agreed with this plan?'

Gessart took the proffered pick-up from Willusch and squeezed the transmit stud.

'The east gate, in two hours,' Gessart repeated. 'It is agreed.'

Dropping the handset to the floor he turned to his warriors.

'Scout the sepulchre for power packs, ammunition and all other supplies of use to us,' said Gessart. 'Armour up and be ready for action in ninety minutes. Tylo, prepare your gene-seed extractions for transit. Brothers, we are leaving Helmabad.'

GESSART'S SPACE MARINES were a peculiar sight as they gathered just inside the massive bastion of the east gateway. Helmeted once more, they assumed the appearance of faceless angels of death, but now tempered with the baggage of their war on Helmabad. Their armour was rent and pitted with damage from the long fighting, patched here and there with battlefield repairs. They carried kitbags from the slain Guardsmen stuffed with power packs and water canteens. Nicz had an ornate power sword looted from the body of Colonel Akhaim; it looked small in his armoured fist, but was still a valuable prize.

Some of them had promethium containers hung from their belts, and the small fragmentation grenades used by the Imperial commander's forces. Lehenhart had supplemented his bolter with an autocannon taken from its tripod, which he now carried over his shoulder, belts of shells hooked over one of the exhaust vents of his backpack.

They had been busy this last hour and a half, that was for sure.

'Ready?' asked Gessart. He received nods and affirmatives in response. He gave the signal to Heynke to start the gate-opening sequence.

He was stood at a rune panel set atop a lectern facing the huge armoured doors. Heynke's gauntleted hands moved quickly over the glowing screen. Gears hidden in the floor far below the sepulchre started to turn slowly, their rumbling causing the floor to shudder. A warning klaxon sounded and red lights flashed on and off in the mass of machinery above the Space Marines.

The inner gate creaked and squealed as it opened outwards, driven by massive pistons. Amber lights flickered into life in the high, narrow hallway beyond.

'Move out,' snapped Gessart.

With the four captured rebels in front of them, the Space Marines strode into the antechamber. Gessart gave Heynke the nod, who activated the outer door locks and then followed his leader into the gatehouse.

There was more grinding of huge engines beneath them and then a sliver of bright light appeared in the plasteel door ahead. The sliver became a crack and then widened into a shaft of blinding sunlight. It was sunset and Helmabad's star was low on the horizon, almost directly opposite the east gate. Gessart's visor darkened immediately as the auto-senses filtered out the sudden brightness.

Through the tint, Gessart could see a massive ruined hallway, with tall windows all along its length through which the light was streaming. A long colonnade, its columns broken in places, ran down the centre, lined with troops and vehicles. Hundreds of weapons from lasguns to battle cannons were directed towards the Space Marines as they emerged. Most of the roof had collapsed and the dusk sky provided a ruddy ceiling.

A shimmering aurora hung to the north, making the sky look like a curtain of blood. At the realisation, Gessart hurriedly glanced at Zacherys. The Librarian nodded meaningfully.

Ahead, and to the left, stood a knot of serious-looking men in grey robes. There were eight of them, each with his head shaven, his face and scalp painted black. Their white eyes stood out like pearls floating upon ink. Gessart looked at the Apostles of the Awakening but they all cast their gaze upon the rubble-strewn floor; out of disdain, fear or shame, Gessart could not tell.

The shattered plascrete crunched underfoot in the quiet, joined only by the throbbing of combustion engines. Gessart turned his eyes directly ahead and walked without fear down the steps of the eastern gatehouse and into the hall.

'Go,' he said to the captured rebels, waving them away. They gave grateful smiles and grins as they scurried across the debris to rejoin their insurrectionist comrades.

The Space Marines' advance along the hall was not hurried, but nor was it slow. Gessart was keen not to show any fear, but he was very aware that it was more than a mile to the Thunderhawk's landing pad up on the roof of the palace, and time was a resource that was rapidly running out.

The tramp of booted feet signalled an escort falling into place behind the Space Marines. Gessart glanced back and saw the fear etched into the faces of those that followed. If the Astartes chose to fight, the men closest to the Space Marines knew they would be the first to die.

Further on, tank engines belched into fuming life and the crunch and clatter of treads announced the armoured element of their guard was now getting underway. Gessart was not worried. At this close range, the presence of the tanks was for show rather than any real protection. With another glance towards the darkening red sky, he began to slowly increase his pace.

As the small group reached the end of the hall, Gessart turned back towards the sepulchre. Already squads of troops were streaming up the steps to search for the Imperial commander. Mu'shan wouldn't be hard to find;

Gessart had manacled him to his chair of office and transmitted the location of the inner chamber just before he'd left for the gatehouse.

Assured that there would be no treachery, Gessart lead his Space Marines onwards.

THE AVENGING SONS' last remaining Thunderhawk gunship sat atop one of the landing platforms of the palace's east wing, surrounded by a cordon of guards. The Avenging Sons had lost their other craft one by one during the course of many missions against the rebels, and Gessart had wisely decided to keep one of the gunships intact. Fearing the vessel to be booby-trapped the rebels had not interfered with the Thunderhawk or tried to gain entry; early in the campaign the traitors had tried to capture a damaged Rhino personnel carrier and the transport's machine-spirit had detonated its engines, slaying several dozen looters.

The Helmabadians guarding the craft withdrew into the palace as Gessart and his warriors approached, giving the Space Marines unimpeded access. Nicz moved to the assault ramp at the front of the slab-sided craft and opened the access controls while Gessart and the others scanned the surrounding gantries and rooftops for signs of heavy weapons ready to bring them down once they were airborne. Gessart could see nothing with enough firepower to down the Thunderhawk and gave Nicz the signal to open the ramp.

The ring of Space Marines collapsed back towards the gunship as the ramp growled down from the hull of the Thunderhawk. They were as alert now as they had been throughout the march from the sepulchre, expecting treachery but careful not to provoke a response from the rebels that had shadowed them. Gessart was the last to board, and gave a look towards the heavens where the night sky was dominated by the rippling waves of the red aurora. He slammed a hand onto the button that would close the ramp as he strode into the Thunderhawk's interior.

Nicz was already in the cockpit at the pilot's controls, Vanghort beside him in the navigator's position. Gessart stepped backwards into one of the flight alcoves along the flanks of the hull. Mechanics hissed as servo arms came down from the ceiling and detached the Space Marine's backpack and plugged it into the Thunderhawk's system to recharge. Even the compensating muscle-like fibre bundles of his power armour felt lighter without the backpack's reactor weighing him down. A quick check of the suit's systems in his visor display confirmed that his armour had internal power for several hours; more than enough for them to reach the strike cruiser in orbit. Thus freed of the bulky backpack, Gessart was able to work his way between the rows of benches into the control chamber and climb up into the command chair behind Nicz. He activated the comm-link and punched in the frequency of the strike cruiser's bridge.

'*Vengeful*, this is Gessart,' he said, the Thunderhawk's own communications system picking up his helmet's signal and amplifying it into orbit. 'Confirm extraction by Thunderhawk imminent. Stand in to low orbit above our position and beat to quarters. Be ready to leave at flank speed upon our arrival.'

'Captain!' came the surprised voice of Kholich Beyne, Gessart's chief functionary aboard the *Vengeful*. 'We thought you might be dead.'

'I still might be if you don't get ready to leave right now,' Gessart snarled. 'You can leave the celebrations until we're out-system.'

'Understood, captain,' said Beyne, his tone controlled once more. 'Will rendezvous over your position in one-eight standard minutes. Confirm.'

'Confirmed,' said Gessart before he closed the contact. He reached up and pulled down the restraint harness above his head, fixing its locking bolts into position on his shoulder pads. 'Everybody get secure for rapid departure!'

When the other Space Marines confirmed that they were in their positions Gessart reached out and patted Nicz on the back of the head. Without a word, Nicz gunned the engines into life, which kicked in with a throaty roar that set the whole gunship to juddering.

'Goodbye Helmabad,' said Lehenhart over the comm-net. As Nicz opened up the launch thrusters the Thunderhawk surged into the air upon columns of plasma fire. Gessart felt the gravitational forces pushing at him even through the pressurised balance of his armour and he gritted his teeth against the sickening sensation in his stomach.

Nicz rolled the Thunderhawk to the right as they pulled up into a steep climb, taking them over the ruins of the palace.

'Come take a look at this, captain,' said Heynke from his position at the starboard lascannon array.

Gessart glanced at the launch chronometer and saw that they were still over a hundred seconds from orbital thrust. Plenty of time to investigate. He punched the harness release and levered it back over his head. The Thunderhawk shaking under the tread of his magno-grip boots, Gessart made his way down the steeply inclined hull towards Heynke. The Space Marine pointed to the monitor displaying the image from the external gun camera. He had the magnification set at thirty times normal Space Marine vision and it showed the steps of the sepulchre eastern gate. Gessart could see thousands of rebels were crowded into the outer hall and tens of thousands more could be seen outside the palace and crushing into the galleries and on balconies. Through the remnants of the hall's roof the scene playing out upon the steps was clear to see.

The eight Apostles of the Awakening stood in a circle around a golden-robed figure: unmistakeably Mu'shan.

The dwindling light of the dusk glittered on blades as they struck him down and the surrounding rebels threw up their arms and cast their hats and helmets into the air in celebration. Lasrifle shots flashed into the sky as they fired victory volleys.

Heynke looked over his shoulder but said nothing. Gessart nodded in understanding and patted Heynke hard on the shoulder pad.

'It would have happened even if we had stayed,' said Gessart. 'He was slain swiftly. Perhaps it is better that he died at the hands of those who despised him than he survived to be taken by the daemons.'

Gessart clambered his way back to the control cabin and locked himself in once more. By now the Thunderhawk was shaking violently as its thrusters accelerated the gunship to hypersonic speeds. The external pick-ups of his helm relayed the creaks and groans of straining metal and ceramite as the Thunderhawk fought against gravity and friction. Looking out of the armoured canopy, Gessart could see the stubby nose of the craft beginning to glow with heat, and beyond that the great wound in reality like a pulsing red sheet of energy.

'Check seals for depressurisation,' Nicz said over the link. 'Orbital velocity in thirty seconds.'

Gessart hoped fervently that they reached the safety of the strike cruiser before the rift opened and the hellish legions that waited beyond were unleashed. He didn't need Zacherys's psychic insight to know that it would be close. Very close.

EVEN AS NICZ switched power to the landing thrusters and the Thunderhawk screamed into the docking bay of the *Vengeful* Gessart was already out of his seat. He tapped into the internal ship link to the bridge.

'Kholich, full power to engines, maximum acceleration!' he snapped.

'Understood, captain,' came Beyne's reply.

The roar of plasma was joined by the screech of metal as the Thunderhawk touched down onto the docking platform. Gessart leapt down into the main compartment and activated the assault ramp.

'Zacherys, with me,' he ordered as he thundered onto the lowering ramp. 'The rest of you get to battle stations and prepare the gun crews.'

Gessart was off the Thunderhawk before the ramp had finished lowering, leaping the last few metres to the decking, Zacherys a few strides behind him. The *Vengeful* was awash with tremors as her powerful engines burned into life. Stunned serfs looked up from their consoles and cranes as the Space Marines dashed past. Gessart exited the hangar into the main dorsal corridor at a run. Turning left he headed towards the nearest conveyor and punched in the code for the bridge.

'Report on the warp breach,' Gessart demanded as he waited for the conveyor to arrive.

'Activity increasing, captain,' said Beyne.

'It's opening,' whispered Zacherys. 'It's almost time.'

The conveyor arrived with a hiss of brakes and a clang. The doors squealed open at a touch of the runepad. Gessart stepped inside and almost dragged Zacherys with him. Closing the door, Gessart set the transporter into motion and forced himself to calm down. In the three minutes it took for the conveyor to arrive at the main bridge station he was back in control, his rising sense of urgency brutally quashed.

The armoured doors to the bridge grumbled open at his approach to reveal a scene of frenzied activity. The warp breach was front and centre of the main display, algorithms and symbols scrolling past as its energies were detected and measured.

Gessart was no more than a pace inside the bridge when Zacherys gave a cry of pain. Turning, Gessart saw the Librarian fall to one knee, his hands clasped to his head.

'The curtain of blood falls away!' he shouted. 'The rift opens!'

Gessart looked back at the screen and saw that the waving red energy seemed to part, unveiling a swirling maelstrom of colours. Though he had no psychic power at all even he could hear the screams and shouts of the daemonic host, like distant cries within his skull.

'Immediate warp jump,' snapped Gessart, focusing his attention back on the bridge.

Beyne stood to one side of the command chair; a young, bright-eyed retainer with long hair. He was dressed in blue service robes like the other serfs, though his rank was signified by the silver rope at his waist. He held a dataslab in one hand, forgotten now, his gaze distant as he listened to the inner voices now assailing everybody aboard.

'Activate warp shields,' shouted Gessart. 'Prepare for immediate jump.'

There was no reaction from the crew.

'Beyne!' Gessart yelled, grabbing the man by his arm, careful not to squeeze too tightly and shatter the bone. The pain brought Beyne out of his trance and he looked at Gessart with panicked eyes.

'Warp jump?' he stuttered. 'If we open a gate here the gravitational forces will pull us apart.'

'There's already a gate open, you imbecile!' said Gessart, thrusting a finger towards the pulsing daemonic rift.

'Enter that?' replied Beyne, the fear written across his youthful face.

'Heading zero-zero-eight by zero-seventeen by thirteen degrees,' Gessart bellowed, turning his attention to the helmsmen to his left. They nodded and their fingers danced across their control panels as they laid in the course that would take the *Vengeful* directly into the warp breach.

Satisfied that they were at least headed in the correct direction, Gessart turn to Zacherys, who was back on his feet, staring intently at the main screen.

'I need you to navigate, Zacherys,' Gessart said, stepping towards the Librarian. 'Can you do that?'

The Librarian nodded.

'Where are we heading?' he asked.

'Anywhere away from here,' said Gessart.

Zacherys turned on his heel and made his way back into the main corridor, heading towards the navigational pilaster above the bridge. The doors closed behind him with a resounding crash.

Gessart fixed his attention back to the main screen and the warp rift displayed upon it. It looked like a writhing miasma, interchanging between strangely-coloured flames, bright spirals of light and a seething ring of boiling reality. Faces appeared briefly and then faded from view. Swirls and counter-swirls of different hues rippled across its surface.

The sound of an alarm pinging from a console broke Gessart's fixation.

'Saviour pod launched from the third battery, captain,' announced one of the bridge attendants.

'What?' said Gessart. 'Who launched it?'

He strode across the bridge and shoved the serf out of his way. A schematic of the foremost starboard battery was on the screen, the saviour pod channel flashing green. A circular sensor display showed the evacuation craft on a trajectory towards the planet below. Gessart activated his ship-wide address.

'All Astartes, report in!' he barked.

As his warriors called in their locations, it became clear that Rykhel was missing. Gessart recalled that he had only been a reluctant convert to the departure from Helmabad.

'Get me a hail frequency for that pod,' Gessart demanded, rounding on the attendant who was nursing his arm from where Gessart had shoved him.

'Linking in to your helm comms, captain,' a serf at the communications bench told him.

'Rykhel?' Gessart said.

There was a hiss of static for a moment before the Space Marine replied.

'This is wrong, Gessart,' said Rykhel. 'I cannot be a part of this.'

'Coward,' snarled Gessart. 'At least the others faced me and took their fate as warriors.'

'The Chapter must hear of this treachery,' said Rykhel. 'You murdered Herdain and fled your duty. You cannot be allowed to go unpunished for this. You talked your way out of the recriminations for Archimedon; I cannot let you do that again. You have taken the first steps on a dark path and you have damned yourself and those that follow you.'

Gessart heard the snick of the connection cutting before he could reply. Thankfully Rykhel's accusations had been made on his command line, heard only by Gessart. He looked around the bridge and saw the serfs going about their work, ignorant of the exchange.

'Continue on course,' Gessart said, focusing on the screen once more.

He wasn't afraid of the consequences. Rykhel would die; at the hands of the rebels or the daemons. It was not important, for Gessart had resigned himself to his fate the moment he shot Herdain. The others had not yet realised that they were truly renegades now.

The warp breach was expanding even as the *Vengeful* hurtled towards it. It swelled in size until the main screen could not contain it even without magnification.

'I'm in position,' Zacherys reported in Gessart's ear.

A few minutes later Gessart felt the lurch in his body and mind that signified a jump into warp space. Dislocation throbbed through his being as the *Vengeful* burst into the immaterium. His nerves buzzed with energy and shadows played across his vision. The constant murmuring of the daemons became louder and for a moment Gessart was sure that insubstantial hands were clawing at him. He knew the sensations to be false; the psychic shields of the strike cruiser were operating normally. Controlling the unnatural dread that seeped into the corners of his mind, Gessart switched off the screen and turned away.

There was now no sensation of movement. All was calm as the *Vengeful* drifted upon the psychic tides, the raging tempest of energy held at bay by her warp screens.

'Can you plot a course?' Gessart asked as he hailed Zacherys.

The Librarian's reply was halting and suffused with strain.

'No fix on Astronomican,' he said. 'Heading for eye of storm. Need to concentrate.'

'Stand down from general quarters,' Gessart announced. 'Follow warp security rituals.'

Unseen and out of mind, the world of Helmabad descended into nightmare.

ONCE THE VENGEFUL was well clear of the Helmabad system and the roiling warp storm unleashed by the daemons, Gessart called his surviving Space Marines together. They gathered in the strike cruiser's chapel; a carefully considered choice by Gessart in relation to what he had to say.

The others entered to find Gessart already awaiting them, stripped of his armour, which was stowed on a frame to one side of the Chapter shrine. The small altar was bare of the ornaments and relics usually displayed. They had been the artifices of Herdain and Gessart had already disposed of them. In a similar vein, the company banner, which had remained on the ship for its safety, had been taken down and stowed away. Now the only reminder of the Space Marines' allegiance was the Chapter symbol engraved into the metal of the bulkhead. Gessart had already arranged for some of the serfs to etch it out with acid once he was finished here.

He stood with his arms folded across his broad chest as his battle-brothers attended him. Some looked at the bare wall and empty altar with confusion. Others were impassive, perhaps having already guessed the nature of Gessart's announcement. Nicz stood apart from the rest, his eyes narrowed as he hawkishly watched Gessart.

The last to enter was Zacherys. The Librarian still wore his armour, though within the confines of the ship's warp shield he had removed his psychic hood to allow him to better see the currents of the immaterium and guide the ship. He did not look at Gessart, but instead stayed at the door, perhaps having already seen what was unfolding.

Gessart said nothing. Instead he crossed the chapel to where his armour stood. Leaning down, he picked up a container of paint used by the serfs. Wordlessly, he dipped a thick brush into the black liquid within and drew the brush across the symbol upon his armour's shoulder pad. A few of the Space Marines gasped at this obvious affront to the armour's spirit and the obliteration of his rank insignia.

'I am no longer a captain,' Gessart intoned. He painted out the chest eagle. 'The Third Company is no more.'

Gessart continued to daub the pitch black onto his armour, his rough strokes eradicating the heraldry, campaign badges and honours displayed upon it.

'We cannot return to the Chapter,' Gessart said, putting down the paint and turning to face his men. 'They will not understand what it is that we have done. We have killed our battle-brothers, and to our former masters there is no greater heresy. Rykhel deserted us for fear of their vengeance and he was right to do so. Think with your hearts and remember the hatred you felt for the traitors we have faced before. We are now those traitors. We willingly stepped over a boundary that kept us in check. If ever the Chapter learns that we have survived, they will hunt us down without pity or remorse.'

Gessart picked up the paint once more and walked forwards. He proffered the container to Lehenhart who stood at one end of the group.

'You are an Avenging Son no longer,' Gessart said.

Lehenhart looked grim, in stark contrast to his usual ready laugh and lively eyes. He nodded, turning his gaze towards the deck. With a brushstroke Gessart covered up Lehenhart's Chapter symbol. Next in line was Gundar. He took the brush from Gessart and painted out the symbol himself.

Some of the Space Marines were eager to break the last of their ties, hoping that perhaps the guilt they felt would be destroyed along with the cross-crosslet of the Avenging Sons. Others hesitated, seeking some remorse in Gessart's eyes. They saw nothing but his iron-hard will to survive and realised that they were not being presented with a choice; they had made their decision back in the inner sepulchre of Helmabad. One by one the Space Marines destroyed that which had been most precious to them. A few had tears in their eyes, the first emotion they had felt since being brought to the Chapter as youths many war-torn years ago.

Nicz was the last, his eyes boring holes into Gessart as he took the brush from his former captain and splashed the dark paint across his shoulder.

'If you are captain no more, why do you still remain in command?' Nicz asked, handing the brush back to Gessart. 'By what authority do you give us orders?'

Gessart did not say anything immediately but instead met Nicz's cold stare with his own. Neither was willing to look away and they stood like that for several minutes.

'If you think you can kill me, take your shot,' Gessart eventually hissed, his eyes unwavering. 'When you do, make it count. I won't give you a second chance.'

Confident that his message was clear, Gessart stepped back, still eying Nicz, and then eventually broke contact to look at the others.

'What do we do now?' asked Willusch.

Gessart grinned. 'Whatever we want,' he replied.

'Where should we go?' said Tyrol.

'Where all the renegades go,' Gessart told them. 'The Eye of Terror.'

HONOUR AMONG FIENDS

Dylan Owen

'CONTACT ZERO-THIRTY!'

'You sure, Scaevolla? I see nothing.'

'Trust me, Larsus!'

Scaevolla stroked the trigger of his bolter. A dozen rounds barked into the obscuring green fog, and screams wailed from the soupy atmosphere ahead. He and his men pounded towards the cries, eight hulking warriors in black power armour trimmed with gold. A blazing eye was superimposed on the eight-pronged star of Chaos emblazoned on their right shoulder pads: the heraldry of the Black Legion.

The warriors whooped feral cries of joy. It had been a long journey through the void to this barren, mist-swathed planet, but now they could let off steam against the minions of the False Emperor ahead. Scaevolla almost felt sorry for the enemy. He needed one alive, to learn where fate had directed him, and to discover the name of the man he had sought since the visions made him leave the Eye of Terror a year ago.

It was always a nightmare that would inspire Scaevolla to lead his men on another hunt. A year ago he had woken screaming from such a dream: silver, unblinking eyes penetrating his sleep. Instinct had led him to navigate his battle frigate, *Talon of the Ezzelite,* out of the shifting spheres of the Eye of Terror into the reality of Imperial space. A series of portents had led him to this world of lethal mists. Dozens of battleships emblazoned with symbols of the Ruinous Powers blockaded the planet, the wreckage of Imperial vessels drifting amongst them. The *Talon* had evaded these and landed undetected among low, mist-shrouded hills on a continent wracked by war. A kilometre away was a sprawling city under siege, towards which Scaevolla's esoteric senses tugged. Whenever he closed his eyes, the image of a crowned skull seared his mind's vision, and he knew that the man he had to kill commanded the defenders here.

Las-rounds whined past or pattered harmlessly off the warriors' armour. Scaevolla felt one brush his temple, but felt no pain. He pumped off another dozen rounds into the fog, each shot followed by a scream, closer this time. At his left, Opus, the bull of the squad, howled a tuneless battle-dirge accompanied by the roar of his autocannon.

Lines of men in grey battle uniform emerged wraith-like from the mist, their masked helmets lending them an alien appearance – wide black eyes and metal snouts. The troopers' helmets depicted a silver double-headed eagle, the insignia of the Imperial Guard. The front rank of the platoon knelt and the second rank stood upright, lasguns at the ready while the fallen curled on the floor. Ethereal green tentacles probed the living and caressed the dead. A sergeant bellowed and another volley was unleashed, but the shrill hail washed over the attackers' power armour with no effect. Scaevolla calmly loosed a bolt and watched as the sergeant's head exploded into meat and bone. He had not expected to encounter any of the planet's defenders so soon after leaving the *Talon*.

Perhaps this platoon of troopers was as lost in the mists as his squad was.

Scaevolla and his men smashed into the enemy lines. When a man enters combat, his experience of time slows. For Scaevolla, the first second of the skirmish froze completely. He observed the tableau of impending destruction. Opus was mouthing a song, no doubt accompanying the infernal choir that sang ceaselessly inside his skull, his eyes rolled up into the sockets of his bald head, the death spitting from his autocannon hanging in mid-air. To Opus's left was Sharn, his helmet featureless, devoid even of eye-slits, his flamer bathing the troopers with liquid fire. Further away was Ferox, head flipped back at an unnatural angle as a smooth shaft of glistening muscle with a muzzle of snapping teeth began to emerge from his mouth. Ahead was Icaris, his face contorted with anguish, tears of blood frozen on his cheeks, the air patterned crimson where his chainaxe lopped his opponents' limbs. Icaris wept for his victims, who would never know the joys of serving the true gods.

Scaevolla glanced right. Lieutenant Larsus had bisected a Guardsman with his chainsword, and was caught in mid-laughter savouring the gore splashing his face. Beyond him was Surgit, towering over his foes, power sword scabbarded, pistol holstered, his horned helm scanning the platoon for a worthy foe. Finally came Manex, emptying a stream of ammunition from his two bolt pistols into the enemy line, mouth frothing and eyes bulging from the poisons that fed into his brain from the tubes within his armour. Pride swelled in Scaevolla's chest as he regarded his squad. Countless warzones had honed their battle skills, and none had ever failed him.

The frozen scene melted, the motionless fighters slamming back to life. Bodies piled around the feet of Icaris and Larsus, both a blur of whirring chainblades, and Ferox's monstrous tongue lashed among the troopers, flensing flesh, his hands erupting into vicious, slashing claws. Manex ripped torsos apart with the ferocity of his gunfire, and Opus howled aloud an incomprehensible opera, chorused by the deadly riff of his autocannon, while Sharn burned a hole in the enemy lines. Although outnumbered, the warriors of the Black Legion were carving bloody chunks in the ranks of the Imperial Guard, whose bayonets stabbed feebly at their power armour. The troopers' attempts at swamping their attackers through sheer weight of numbers were like the ocean lashing in vain at a tidal wall.

A commissar in a leering skull mask rushed into the fray, power sword raised, haranguing the troopers to fight to the bitter end, cutting down those who dared take a step backwards. Surgit, ignoring the las-fire zipping around him, cackled in triumph, drew his power sword and ploughed through the troopers to meet the officer blow for blow.

A bayonet stabbed at Scaevolla, who opened a hole in its owner's skull with a shot from his boltgun. More bayonets bit into his armour. Scaevolla stepped back, firing indiscriminately, and the bayonets fell away into the fog. A single trooper stood his ground, clutching his ruined arm. Scaevolla reached out with his left hand and gently traced the leather of the man's mask with a claw of his armoured glove. He spoke softly. 'What year is this? What planet? Who leads your foes?'

The words choked weakly from behind the gas mask.

'Pl... planet? Zincali VI. We fight the Traitor-Lord H'raxor. The year? W... why...?'

'Who commands your defences?'

'Captain Demetros... of the Imperial Fists... he will cleanse your filth. The Emperor protects...'

With a flick of Scaevolla's clawed fingers, the material of the gas mask fell away, revealing a pale face, eyes dazed. The soldier took a deep breath and winced. He clamped his uninjured hand to his neck, his mouth gaping wide, throat gurgling, and as Scaevolla watched, dark green, fleshy shoots pushed their way out of the soldier's mouth, bulging his neck. The man sank to his knees, tiny vines growing from his nostrils. With a strangled groan, he toppled to his side, eyes glazed, and within seconds his corpse was wrapped in a vegetal embrace, roots snaking into the black earth, pinning the body to the ground.

Scaevolla breathed deeply, the spore-rich air bitter to the taste. He smiled at the frailty of lesser men.

The sounds of battle trailed away. The few Imperial Guard who had survived the onslaught had vanished like ghosts into the green mist. Where once had stood an ordered line of determined soldiers there now lay piles of broken corpses, green shoots sprouting from bloody wounds where the minute spores in the mist had seeded in flesh. The ground flared where Sharn's flamer incinerated the bodies of the half-dead, and in the fire's glow, Icaris mumbled the *Litany of Execration* over the corpses. Manex struggled in Opus's iron grip, pinned down until his frenzy subsided. Ferox was metamorphosing back, his hands already human, his eel-like appendage vomiting gobbets of half-digested meat as it shrank back into his distended mouth. For his outstanding valour, Ferox had been blessed by the gods with these mutations, which burst forth from his flesh under duress. While his comrades regarded Ferox with awe, Scaevolla did not share their admiration. He remembered the old Ferox that these gifts had consumed, who had bolstered the squad's morale with his easy manner and ready wit, now long disappeared.

There was no sign of Surgit. Scaevolla called out his name.

'Here!' The horns of the warrior's helmet lent him a daemonic appearance as he emerged from the clinging fog carrying the commissar's head. He sniffed. 'A disappointing match. His hatred made him clumsy. My blade feels sullied.'

'A fine fight you've led us to, captain.' Larsus approached, grinning through a mask of drying blood at Scaevolla. 'You never disappoint. Is our quarry here?'

'His name is Demetros. The visions were true. He commands the Corpse-Emperor's forces.' Scaevolla's voice became heavy. 'Lieutenant, do you ever tire of the chase?'

Larsus rapped the image of the Eye of Horus on Scaevolla's right shoulder pad. 'Never. So long as we fight, the legacy of the Warmaster lives on.'

It had been during the false Emperor's Great Crusade that Scaevolla and his men had learned their battlecraft, and bonded in blood and violence. In those days they had been Lunar Wolves, their armour white; innocents blind to the Emperor's weakness. Then Horus, beloved Warmaster, had cast the scales from their eyes, and they had fought as his devoted Sons to free themselves from the false Emperor's coils. At the edge of victory, the Warmaster fell, and his Legion had fled to the protective shadows of the warp, where it became known as the Black Legion. To mark the Legion's sorrow and disgrace, its warriors' power armour was lacquered black, although the edges of the armour gleamed with gold, for even the darkest night is banished by the gleam of a new dawn. Scaevolla's men believed that every minion of the Corpse-Emperor they slew brought closer a new golden age for their Legion.

Scaevolla's memory of those days was scarred by rage and betrayal. The past haunted him with the face of a murdered comrade. The pain had not dulled in... how many years? A hundred, a thousand... *ten thousand*? Time was exiled from the Eye of Terror, Scaevolla's life one long dream-like existence until he was spat out into reality to honour his oath.

Larsus broke Scaevolla's reverie. 'Captain, why the grim face? Is our small victory not sweet enough?'

'It's nothing,' Scaevolla shook his head to clear his mind. 'Gather the hounds, lieutenant. Let's see where the scent has led us to.'

* * *

Scaevolla hugged the brow of the hill. Piercing the sea of green fog that roiled in the valley below were uncountable battle standards, laden with gory trophies. The valley seemed to rumble under the advance of the obscured army. The bronze turrets of assault tanks and upper hulls of troop transports, crested with spikes, resembled an innumerable fleet of sea craft ploughing through ethereal waves. A score of monstrous war machines waded among them, each clanking on six steel legs like nightmarish metal spiders. The horde swept towards the horizon where a termites' nest of cyclopean buildings rose from the mist like an island. The city's ziggurats glittered with a million dots of light, their heights vanishing into red nimbus, and a thousand chimneys belched smoke into the sky. Circling the factory-city was a wall that dwarfed even the clanking war machines. Titanic bastions guarded the circuit, their cannons spitting plasma onto the advancing horde. Among the serried grey ranks of troopers manning the defences were phalanxes of power-armoured warriors, distinct in brilliant yellow, proud standards depicting a black-clenched fist on a white field; Space Marines of the Imperial Fists Chapter defended in force.

Larsus, crouched next to Scaevolla, gave a low whistle. 'A city of ten billion souls. H'raxor wants to build a mountain of skulls.'

'No,' whispered Scaevolla. 'If he only desired trophies, he would have attacked a less well-defended target.'

Blasts smacked the valley, yellow blossoms briefly parting the mists to reveal a circle of torn corpses, and a tank was hurled into the air ablaze, to land with a ripping explosion.

Scaevolla licked the air. 'These mists are rich in protein. Perhaps this planet's manufactorums process the atmosphere into food. The destruction of this world may mean famine for those Imperial outposts it feeds. This is the opening gambit of a major invasion. H'raxor has great ambition. We'll let him enjoy his petty conquest, as long as he doesn't interfere with our mission. Our quarry is in the city. I feel it. We must reach him quickly, before the defenders are overrun.'

'There.' Larsus pointed at a bronze-plated Land Raider battle tank, festooned with hooks and barbs, advancing at the foot of their hill in support of the army's reserve. 'We steal a ride.'

Scaevolla nodded. 'Get to work, lieutenant.'

While Larsus signalled orders to the squad waiting behind him, Scaevolla removed a small silver discus from his grenade belt and fingered a switch on its ornate shell. Raising the discus to his lips, he kissed it once then spun it at the vehicle below. There was a flash and the tank came to a halt with a squeal of engines, blue sparks rippling across its hull. Scaevolla and his squad pelted down the hill, penetrating the mist. The mutant soldiers hugging the vehicle for cover milled around in confusion, muffled curses escaping the crude respirators clamped around their mouths.

'Out of the way, scum!' roared Larsus, felling soldiers who failed to yield. The mutants gibbered as they pushed each other to escape.

Ferox and Icaris vaulted to the top of the vehicle, while the rest of the squad surrounded it. A crewman emerged from a hatch on the tank's upper hull, blue sparks playing across his brassy power armour. Icaris yanked him out and silenced him with a bolt. Ferox slid through the opening. There followed a muffled roar, then the portal closest to Manex slid open and another crewman toppled out, his bronze armour rent with gashes. Manex peppered him with bolts.

'Good work, brothers.' Larsus peered through the open portal. Inside the gore-splattered interior of the tank, Ferox straddled a third crewman, his head snapped back and the fleshy eel extended from his mouth, sucking at the innards of his victim.

'Inside,' urged Scaevolla. He followed his squad into the vehicle and pointed at the feeding Ferox. 'Calm him.' Larsus eased Ferox from his kill with gentle movements and a soft voice. Already, the eel was shrinking back into Ferox's throat, its recent meal sloshing onto the floor.

Icaris positioned himself at the controls, the blue sparks that danced across the console sputtering like dying flames. He caressed the array of switches as they flashed back to life. 'Power returning. Yes, here she comes. I think she likes us; she finds our antics... amusing.'

The portal and hatch clanged shut, the cabin shuddered as the engines roared, and the Land Raider lurched forward. Inside, its inner walls purred and blinked with myriad eyes at the new crew.

THE LAND RAIDER careened across the battlefield, crushing mutant soldiers beneath its treads. Fog clouded the viewports, but the intelligence fettered within the vehicle's shell guided it towards its destination, a heavily defended gate in the city wall. Halfway across, a missile rocketed into the Land Raider's hull, and the daemon-spirit keened in agony, but the damage was superficial. Soon the gateway loomed out of the mist, its portcullis buckled and scorched. A semi-circle of twisted mutant corpses defined the killing ground around the base of the gate, into which H'raxor's soldiers marched, chanting defiantly as they soaked up the defenders' precious ammunition.

As the Land Raider came into range of the gate's barbican it suffered sustained fire. Opus emerged head and shoulders from the vehicle's hatch to rake defenders off the battlements with the pintle-mounted gun, indifferent to the las-fire whining inches from his face and the explosions impacting off the hull. The Land Raider's lascannon strobed at the weakened gate, but the portal absorbed the laser fire intact.

'Ram the gates!' ordered Scaevolla desperately. Everyone in the troop compartment tensed. Manex inhaled deeply from his tox-tubes and Ferox began coughing strings of drool. Scaevolla knew they had to evacuate before the blood lust and the Dark Gods' gift took hold.

'Ram them now!'

The Land Raider rattled from a violent explosion and Opus dropped from the firing hatch, a face of burnt flesh, power armour embedded with shrapnel, his ruined lips mouthing demented lyrics.

Icaris screamed from the controls, 'The gates are not going to give!'

'Continue, Brother Icaris,' yelled Scaevolla. He braced himself. There was a crashing rip of torn metal, and every bone in his body seemed to jar from the impact. The keening of the daemon-spirit raked his eardrums. With a sharp crack, Ferox's head snapped back, his mutation probing from his throat.

'We're through!' shouted Icaris. 'Seventy per cent damage to auxiliary reactor, firing systems all down–'

'Open the hatches!'

'Impossible... locking rune overridden... she doesn't like us anymore!'

The eel snaked from Ferox's gullet. Then, with a feral roar, Manex gripped the rear hatch with both hands and wrenched it open. Green fronds of mist wisped into the cabin. With a single cry, Scaevolla and his squad bounded out of the vehicle.

Scaevolla felt the flow of time cease once again. Manex was down, a shield for his companions, his armour punctured a dozen times. Larsus and Surgit were behind him, their bolters loosing a ribbon of shots as they charged the phalanx of Imperial Fists that opposed them. Sharn was licking the enemy with flesh-melting heat, while Ferox, fully deformed, stretched towards the enemy, yellow gore spurting from a hit to his pulsing eel-muscle.

Scaevolla's sword was already in his hand, its blade long and slender, a single rune engraved at its tip. Scaevolla had been rewarded with the runeblade *Fornax* when he had laid the first skull before the floating Altar of the Four Gods on the daemon-world Sebaket. How long ago had that been? Now a pyramid of five hundred skulls marked his success in the hunt. He wondered what divine favour victory would win him this time?

There was only one reward which Scaevolla desired: an end to this eternal chase. The gods drove him without rest to fulfil his vow. While his men fought for the sheer joy of killing, Scaevolla could no longer share their enthusiasm. The deaths blurred into one, dulling the emotion of the kill. His swordplay failed to thrill him, no longer a display of skill but mechanistic rote. He felt hollow. He had prayed to his masters for clemency, for release from his oath, which he had fulfilled five hundred times, but they would never grant him manumission. The only way out was escape.

A bolt-round rebounded off Scaevolla's chest guard with a bang. The world slipped back into motion, and the wild charge of Scaevolla's warriors met the stoic wall of yellow power armour. Surgit rejoiced. 'At last! A foe worthy of my wrath!'

With a juddering retort, the heavy bolter atop the crippled Land Raider came to life as Icaris, who had manoeuvred himself to the gun-turret, pinned down reinforcements trying to enter the fight.

'Dreadnought!' Icaris's heavy bolter shells pattered uselessly against the walker striding powerfully towards the combat, its crushing claws poised to strike.

Scaevolla stepped in front of the war-hulk, sword pointed in challenge. For how long had the withered corpse inside this walking coffin been compelled to cheat death?

'By the four gods,' shouted Scaevolla, 'I will end your misery.'

The Dreadnought, liveried in the heraldry of the Imperial Fists, overshadowed Scaevolla, but the prayer scrolls and relic bones decorating the walker's hulk would be no ward against his runesword, which could penetrate any earthly metal.

A stray mortar exploded between them.

White light consumed Scaevolla's vision, then darkness. He was flying. He felt no pain. He panicked. It was not yet time to die! Scaevolla had chosen the manner of his death, and it was not this way.

Scaevolla landed with a crash and fought for breath. His vision cleared to reveal the Dreadnought, unscratched by the explosion, looming over him, fists crackling with energy. The fingers of Scaevolla's outstretched left hand brushed the hilt of his runesword.

With a bestial snarl, a giant lurched from the wreckage of the Land Raider. Opus, his head in tatters, pounded the Dreadnought's hull with tactical artillery from his autocannon.

Scaevolla's grip folded around the handle of his sword and he lunged at the reeling Dreadnought, its armour scorching where the glowing runesword penetrated. Scaevolla slid the blade out and leapt back. The Dreadnought's oculus flashed green then faded to black, and the metal behemoth crashed forward.

Scaevolla raised his blade in salute. Something ancient had just perished. Scaevolla swallowed his envy.

The warriors of the Black Legion had decimated the line of Imperial Fists, though a few persevered despite severed limbs and mortal wounds. One Space Marine lay prone, his legs a crimson ruin, loosing shots from his bolt pistol until silenced by Icaris's stamping boot. Another, his helmet cloven, his eyes dashed from his face, fought blind, almost decapitating Larsus with his blade until finished by the lieutenant's chainsword.

Surgit ran up to the wrecked Dreadnought, shaking his fist in Scaevolla's face. 'Whoreson! That should have been mine!'

Larsus pushed Surgit aside. 'Scaevolla, we have to go. Lord H'raxor's army has broken through.'

The gateway was choked with masked mutants fighting each other to be first through the breach. The defenders in the bastions concentrated their fire on the horde, but for every abomination they felled, two more stepped over the corpse. Behind the seething, dying mass, scarlet-armoured berserk warriors wearing rictus helms chopped through the scum with chainswords, chanting paeans to their bloody god.

Scaevolla's squad stood in a wide bailey that stretched between the defensive wall and the soaring buildings of the city. From the right clanked a wall of battle tanks to plug the breach. From the left marched lines of gas-masked troopers. Ahead, across the bailey, barely discernable through the fog, yawned the entrance to a manufactorum, the heights of the complex disappearing into red clouds. There was only one way forward before the jaws of flesh and metal closed.

'Follow me, men!' Scaevolla sprinted through the obscuring mist for the huge doors.

THE MANUFACTORUM WAS a cathedral of industry. Furnaces burned – altars of hungry flames – and huge vats steamed stinking vapours like sacred censers. Machinery hissed, impatient to be reanimated, and ducts and gantries spiralled up into echoing blackness. Holed by a single melta charge, the doors had proved no obstacle, and neither had the desultory force of factory guards; the innards of forty men decorated the floor.

Surgit spat at the corpses. 'We ran from an army to face mere factotums.'

'We did not run, brother,' retorted Larsus. 'We are on the hunt, remember. The chaff outside is not worth our while.'

'Calm,' snapped Scaevolla, and Surgit and Larsus backed away from each other. 'How is Manex?'

'Fit to shatter more skulls.' Manex had been dragged to safety by Opus. His armour was pitted with holes and half his face was fleshy pulp. 'I've suffered worse.'

'Ferox?'

Larsus shrugged. 'He'll find us when he's had his fill.'

'Sharn, Icaris, ready for battle?'

Sharn bowed, then returned to caressing the white flames of a nearby kiln. Icaris had sunk to his knees, cradling the severed head of a factory-drudge.

'Why do they fight us? We show them our might, yet they refuse to follow our path. We evangelise with sword and fire, but to what end? They perish in their millions for their faith in a dead God-Emperor. We offer the secret knowledge of the stars, yet they prefer to die ignorant. Why, my captain?' Icaris's cheeks were streaked with bloody tears.

Scaevolla softly cupped his battle-brother's chin with his armoured glove. The scars on the young face were testament to his many victories.

'The gods demand sacrifice, boy. We are the reapers who sate their eternal hunger. These men are mere animals, fit only for the holy pyre; don't weep for the fate of the weak.'

'But I must, captain. I will weep until the entire universe bends its knee to the gods.'

Scaevolla admired Icaris's devotion, but said nothing more. Let him enjoy the lie. Once Scaevolla too had believed it was his vocation to shatter the shackles of order that chained the galaxy, but he knew from bitter experience that the gods demanded war only for the sake of petty entertainment. Lord H'raxor fought in vain to win glory, for when the gods tired of him, he would be cast down and forgotten. Perhaps Horus's rebellion, too, had been nothing more than a brief diversion for the gods. Perhaps, at the brink of victory, it had delighted them to see their servant fall and watch his armies collapse into animosity. It was for their amusement that

Scaevolla scoured the galaxy on an unending blood-hunt.

As he contemplated the will of his divine masters, unwelcome memories invaded his mind…

…Scaevolla cradled the dying Space Marine, whose yellow power armour was spattered with the filth of battle. Scaevolla's pale armour was similarly grimed. The surrounding storm of war felt ten thousand years away. Scaevolla looked down at his battle-brother's face: a patrician's nose, a powerful chin, the well-defined skull of a noble warrior, defiant even at the approach of death. Silver eyes dimmed as the life drained away, their glassy stare haunting Scaevolla.

'Aleph, my friend, you could have saved yourself!' Scaevolla choked on the words. 'Why did you follow the lies of the False Emperor? Your liege-lord is Horus. You know it, brother. Say it!'

Life beat weakly within the Space Marine, but Aleph's lips did not move. The silence stoked Scaevolla's anger.

'Damn you, Aleph! We swore to conquer galaxies together, unstoppable, our crusade unending. Remember how we cleansed the Haruspex of Crore? How we defended the monastery of Satrapos alone against the ork hordes of the Star-biter?'

During the Great Crusades, when Scaevolla's Legion had been called the Lunar Wolves, the Imperial Fists had fought alongside them in many battles. It was common lore that Horus, primarch of the Lunar Wolves, had, as a mark of respect, joked that a war between his Legion and the Imperial Fists would last for eternity.

At the battle of Thrael Falls on Cestus II, Scaevolla had rescued Captain Aleph of the Imperial Fists from the anak, the planet's monstrous aboriginals. The two Space Marines bonded in friendship and fought together in many battles when the paths of their Legions crossed. But when Horus declared his true colours, Scaevolla failed to convince his friend that the road to glory lay with the Warmaster. The rebellion parted them and they would not meet again until the siege of the Emperor's palace on Terra, when the Sons of Horus assaulted the Eternity Gate, guarded by the Imperial Fists. Across the carnage of the battlefield, Scaevolla had sought out his former battle-brother. They had fought, and Aleph had fallen, pierced by Scaevolla's sword.

Scaevolla remembered his final words to the dying Space Marine. 'All the glory we fought for, my brother, gone to dust.'

It was only then that Aleph's lips moved. 'It was not our glory, brother,' he spat out the word with a phlegm of blood. 'The glory was the Emperor's.'

Scaevolla sneered. 'Your Emperor fights to defend dishonourable men, weaklings, slaves, who cower while we, men of virtue, spill our sacred blood on their behalf. Your Emperor could have been a god, and we his angels, but instead he chose servitude to protect his bleating flock.' Urgency touched Scaevolla's words. 'Look into your heart. You know I am right.'

Aleph shook his head.

Hot tears coursed Scaevolla's cheeks. 'I offer you freedom, brother, and you choose death.'

A hundred wounds Scaevolla had suffered, but none had bitten as deep as this. Aleph had rebuked the Warmaster, and had forced Scaevolla's hand to fratricide. Aleph had betrayed his battle-brother.

'Fool!' snarled Scaevolla. 'I rescued you. You owe me your life. Listen to me. I can save you again: disown the false Emperor and join me.'

Aleph chuckled hoarsely. 'Had the Emperor granted me foresight, I would have preferred to have been torn alive by the anak than rescued by the whelp of an insane blackguard.'

Rage conquered Scaevolla. His bitter agony turned to anger, sweet to taste.

'You dare mock the Warmaster! I swear, with the four gods as my witness, I shall avenge your insults a thousandfold.'

Laughter echoed madly in Scaevolla's head.

'I shall hunt down and kill your progeny, to the end of time. Your sons will suffer by my blade for your devotion to your weakling Emperor.'

Scaevolla tore Aleph's armour from his chest and dug deep into the flesh. With a sickening squelch, he removed a gland from the mess, his armoured gloves wet and red. As the light in Aleph's eyes vanished, Scaevolla taunted him with the bloody trophy. 'I shall replay this moment of victory over you again and again.'

With reverence, he nestled the organ in Aleph's dead hands. The progenoid gland contained the gene-seed necessary to cultivate Aleph's successor. Apothecaries scoured the battlefield under fire, collecting the precious material. When they recovered Aleph's progenoid gland, his essence would live on in a new recruit implanted with his gene-seed. Scaevolla would pursue each of Aleph's genetic heirs and make them suffer the same fate as their progenitor. In invoking the four gods, he had bound himself to this oath.

Scaevolla stood and addressed the corpse. 'I shall build a monument to the gods you spurned with the skulls of your descendants. Yours shall be the foundation stone.'

With a swift swipe of his blade he decapitated his former battle-brother. As he stooped to pick up the fallen head, Larsus appeared, stumbling on the wreckage of the battlefield, panic on his bloodied face. Scaevolla paled as he heard his words.

'Captain, all hope is lost. The Warmaster is dead! We must go!'

'What did you say?'

Larsus repeated himself, louder…

…The past faded. Scaevolla gathered his wits back to the present. Larsus was shaking his shoulder.

'Captain, we must go. H'raxor's army has broken the outer defences.'

Outside, the triumphant battle cries of the invading horde were drowning out the defenders' screams. Scaevolla paused, inhaling deeply. His quarry was close. His senses were drawn to the factory's heights.

'We go up.'

* * *

Scaevolla watched the trooper pirouette towards a gaping vat far below and vanish with a splash into the volcanic brew, the last of those who had engaged his squad as they clambered up ladders and along gantries to the higher levels of the factory, led by their leader's instinct.

The squad stood before a set of sturdy doors. Scaevolla could almost taste his quarry's presence beyond them. Quietly, he took Larsus to one side. 'Lieutenant, whatever happens, do not intervene to save me. If I should fall, it is the will of the gods. Bear my head to Sebaket and top the altar with my skull as a mark of my failure.'

Larsus looked stunned. 'What do you mean, captain? There is no soul in this galaxy who could best you.'

Scaevolla turned away from his lieutenant. He pointed at the doors. 'Opus?'

The bull ran at the doors and shouldered them open. Daylight spilled from the breach. Scaevolla followed, the rest of his men close behind.

Outside was a wide plaza, open to the gusting wind, with a view across the mist-wreathed killing fields far below. Low clouds, an angry red, obscured the sky. A platoon of Imperial Fists ranged across the plaza. The tallest was cloaked in sweeping blue, crowned with the golden laurels of an officer. An ornate sword hissed with energy in his hands.

Scaevolla thrilled. Aleph's features were etched on Captain Demetros's noble face. He barked his orders. 'The captain is mine. Destroy the others.'

The screech of bolters greeted the warriors' charge, their black armour soaking up the deadly hail. Scaevolla watched his squad advance.

'Farewell,' he whispered sadly, then muttered a pledge to the gods. 'Now it's time to end your sport. I will lay no more skulls before your altar.'

Scaevolla walked forward, singling out the captain with his runesword. Five hundred times he had re-enacted this scene. Five hundred times he had vanquished his silver-eyed opponent, heir of Aleph, and removed his head as a trophy. His rage had been satisfied long ago. He'd had to endure the pain of murdering his comrade over and over again, but he could endure it no longer.

Scaevolla circled, a black wolf stalking its prey. His rival adopted a duelling posture, power sword balanced to parry or bite. As he closed, Scaevolla saw Demetros's silver eyes narrow with faint recognition. That silver stare pinned Scaevolla's gaze, transporting him to another time, another place...

...The sounds of battle roared, explosions and gunfire and the screams of the dying. The ground shuddered to the tread of a Titan's foot, scattering squads of Imperial Fists before it. The magnificent Eternity Gate, glowering over the battlefield, shook to the fiery kiss of a hundred missiles. A gunship screeched overhead, spitting death, and a dozen advancing pale-armoured Sons of Horus fell in a shower of flame. Mud from the explosions spattered Scaevolla's pale armour, but he did not flinch. The cacophony of battle was a mere murmur to him as he circled his opponent, the surrounding blur of violence an illusion.

'Brother Scaevolla.' Scaevolla's silver-eyed adversary broke the silence. 'I have missed you.'

'And I you, Brother Aleph.' Scaevolla smiled ruefully. 'Surrender your sword. You've laid low many of the Warmaster's servants but I will vouch for you before him. He will forgive.'

'Why should I give my heart to a traitor?' spat Aleph. His eyes steeled. 'His madness has destroyed everything the Emperor has fought for. Your Warmaster has stolen your reason, Scaevolla. You may live your lie for ten millennia, but your heart will weary of your lusts, and you'll be left an empty husk.' Aleph breathed deeply, his features pulled with sorrow. 'Let me end it here, my friend. On the point of my blade. I cannot save you from your past, but I can save you from the future.'

Their eyes continued to lock.

Aleph nodded slowly. 'So be it. We fight…'

…Scaevolla was jolted back into the present as Demetros's blade sprang from nowhere. He blocked with a rapid parry, his runesword sparking as it slid down his rival's power weapon. With a flick of his blade, Demetros tried to disarm him, but Scaevolla was too nimble and returned with a counter-blow. Demetros inclined his head slightly, and the runesword's sweep skimmed his cheek.

A hideous ululation broke the duellist's concentration. Fury burst from the plaza doors, clad in baroque armour slick with gore. Odes to the Blood God howled from rictus battle-helms as the berserkers fell on the Imperial Fists, chainaxes chopping. One of the crazed attackers sliced apart a Space Marine, but was in turn disembowelled by Surgit, whose kill he had stolen. Soon the plaza was a confused melee: black, yellow and crimson power armour battling each other.

Five berserkers converged on Captain Demetros.

'No!' screamed Scaevolla, decapitating one with a swing of his blade.

The headless corpse tottered forward, flailing past the startled Space Marine. Scaevolla turned to engage two of the surviving berserkers. Demetros was forced to defend against the other pair. Together they stood almost side by side, blocking every frenzied attack. Though their assailants' blows were everywhere, their defences blurred in reply. A chainaxe buzzed past Demetros's head, who ducked and rammed his blade deep into its wielder's chest. Another berserker lunged enthusiastically at Scaevolla, who cut his legs from under him, the severed stumps smoking where the runesword had bitten.

With a crunch, a chainaxe penetrated Demetros's shoulder guard. He shrugged off the wound, but tottered back, unbalanced. Howling, the devotee of the Blood God raised his weapon to deal the death blow, but the axe stopped centimetres from Demetros's skull, met by Scaevolla's sword. Scaevolla raked his blade down the weapon's shaft, slicing through its guard and ruining the fingers clutching the hilt, before decapitating its wielder with a whirling blow. Demetros rolled to a kneeling position to gut the final attacker. Scaevolla spun to face the Imperial Fist, who rose to his feet, the berserker's corpse slipping from his blade.

Scaevolla gave a slight bow. 'Just like old times.'

Demetros frowned. 'I have seen you fight before.'

'We have never met,' Scaevolla smiled slyly. 'But I have spilled your blood many, many times.'

Demetros shook his head slowly. 'You are insane.'

Around the duellists, Scaevolla's warriors had formed a defensive ring. Berserkers and Space Marines lay in a crimson circle at their feet.

'Shield the captain!' yelled Larsus as a howling tide of berserkers and mutants flowed into the plaza.

'Fresh meat!' cried Surgit with satisfaction, swinging his power sword above his head.

The fighting was chaotic, Imperial Fists and berserkers hacking at each other, and mutants caught in the melee, chopped into a crimson spray. Amidst this tumult, Scaevolla's warriors cut down any that attempted to breach their circle. As they fought, Opus sang, Icaris wept, Manex roared and Sharn slew silently.

Scaevolla and Demetros stood undisturbed in their arena.

Demetros frowned. 'You defend me against your own kind. You are jealous for my death. Why?'

'For the sins of your father,' replied Scaevolla. 'He did my liege lord a great disservice once. But fortune smiles on you, Demetros. You are the one who will win back your father's honour. Let us finish this. My men are strong, but they cannot hold out against two armies.'

Scaevolla tipped his runesword to his forehead in salute. Demetros stood motionless. Blades blurred, then the two were statues. Neither betrayed exertion. A feint from the Space Marine, a retort from Scaevolla, swift attack and counterattack blocked and blocked again. Scaevolla twisted his blade and his opponent's sword flew from his grasp, to land with a clatter between them. Scaevolla's runesword glowed, as though excited by the impending kill, but Scaevolla dipped his blade and flipped the fallen power sword back at Demetros, who deftly caught it.

'A hero should never be defenceless,' said Scaevolla.

Demetros replied with a lightning thrust, but Scaevolla parried. Then Demetros executed a brilliant side step, and his sword was beyond Scaevolla's guard.

The world stilled around Scaevolla, the blade hovering a second away from his heart. At this, the final moment, he felt alive; fear and elation mingled in one delicious cocktail. His vow was broken; at last he would sleep.

But if Scaevolla shifted his torso a fraction to the right, the blade would slide parallel to his armour, cutting a flesh wound, deep but not mortal.

Scaevolla remained still.

Reality surged back with a sucking roar, and the blade plunged through black power armour. Scaevolla smiled. The power sword had punctured his heart and split the back of his armour. When the blade slid free, Scaevolla was still standing.

'A fine blow, my friend. A blow worthy of my death.'

Scaevolla wondered how a dead man could speak. There was no pain. The tumult of the surrounding battle did not ebb away.

Demetros backed off, enraged. 'How can this be? Daemon!'

Scaevolla looked down at the gash in his chest. Where there should have been spilling gore, there was instead a hole. As though torn through the fabric of space, a thousand stars swirled like gloating eyes within the wound. Laughter echoed madly in Scaevolla's head: four terrible voices. He opened his mouth, but it was their voice which spoke.

'You think a scratch can fell a champion of the Dark Gods? It will take more than a cur of the Dog-Emperor to cut this puppet's strings!'

Scaevolla struggled to control his tongue. 'You cannot kill me. Run, brother. Save yourself!'

Demetros scoffed. 'Run? I am a Space Marine of the Imperial Fists. I do not run.'

Scaevolla's runesword glowed hungrily. He cried out to the sky. 'I will not slay him! There is no honour in this fight!'

As Demetros closed in for the kill again, Scaevolla tried to bare his neck to the oncoming blade, but his runesword wrestled his will, and it blocked the strike with a clash. Scaevolla swiped again, his limbs not his own, and Demetros shuffled backwards, a thread of scorched flesh lining his throat. The Space Marine fell to his knees, expressionless, his power sword clattering to the ground.

Over the noise of the Imperial Fists' battle hymns, the wild canticles of the berserkers and screams of dying mutants, Larsus cried out to his captain. 'It is finished. We must leave – now!'

Scaevolla gazed at the corpse of Demetros. He would order Sharn to incinerate the body, destroying the progenoid glands, ending the hunt here.

Suddenly, onto the plaza tore a mass of pulsing muscle straining within a black carapace fused to flesh. A voracious eel-like member gnashed and swallowed. Ferox had been rewarded with the warp's ultimate boon: the gift of spawnhood. He would slaughter mindlessly for the pleasure of the gods.

Scaevolla's order died on his lips. Watching what once had been Ferox whine and gibber as it slew, Scaevolla realised what fate awaited him should he attempt to renege on his oath. He chilled. The gods would never allow the chase to end. Sullenly, he bowed to his dead foe. It was better to embrace enslavement than have the remnants of his humanity eaten away. 'Until next we meet, my friend.' The words left a bitter taste.

With his sword, he sheared off Demetros's head and picked up the trophy by the hair: one more skull for the floating altar.

Larsus yelled an order. 'Squad, converge! We return to the *Talon*.'

The defensive circle tightened to a knot around Scaevolla, who flicked a device on his belt, and the squad shimmered and disappeared, the maelstrom of battle flooding into the space they left.

THE APOTHECARY DARTED among the corpses of his fallen battle-brothers, ignoring the violence swirling around him as he harvested their precious gene-seed. He knelt over the body of Captain Demetros.

'Emperor's tears,' he exclaimed. 'They've taken his head!' With a heavy heart, he muttered the orison of passing and extracted the vital fluid from the progenoid gland in the corpse's chest with his reductor. 'Your line will live on to avenge this atrocity, my captain.'

SOMEWHERE IN THE ether, laughter rippled. The game would continue.

FIRES OF WAR

Nick Kyme

'Give me some good news, Helliman,' growled Colonel Tonnhauser. The old soldier spoke out the side of his mouth, a cigar smouldering between his lips.

He ducked instinctively as another explosion rocked the walls of the workshop, sending violent tremors through the floor and chips of rockcrete spitting from the ceiling onto the map-strewn bench below.

'That was closer...' Tonnhauser muttered, blowing smoke as he brushed away the dislodged dust and debris for the umpteenth time.

It's a hard thing for a man to lose his own city to an enemy. When that enemy comes from within, it's even more repugnant. But that was the stark reality facing Abel Tonnhauser of the 13th Stratosan Aircorps. He'd given too much ground already to the endless hordes of insurgent cultists, and still they pushed for more. Soon there'd be nothing left. The defence of the three primary cities of Stratos was on the brink of failure. The cloud and bolt badge he wore, though tarnished by weeks of fighting, was pinned proudly to a double-breasted tan leather jacket. It was only made of brass, but felt about as heavy as an anvil.

The workshop structure in which he'd made his command post was full of disused aeronautical equipment and machinery, more or less a refit and repair yard for dirigibles and other flying craft that were a necessary part of life on Stratos. Air tanks, pressure dials and coils of ribbed hosing were strewn throughout the building. The one in which Tonnhauser conferred with Sergeant Helliman, while Corpsman Aiker monitored the vox-traffic, was broad and long with vast angular arches and tall support columns, all chrome and polished plasteel.

Typical of the Stratosan architectural style, it had been beautiful once but was now riddled with bullet holes and crumbling from shell damage. A demo-charge rigged by insurgents to a ballast tractor had taken out most of the south-facing wall, the bulk of the colonel's command staff with it. With no time to effect repairs, a sheet of plastek had been piston-drilled to cover the hole.

This largely pointless measure did little to keep out the stutter of sporadic gunfire and incessant explosions from tripped booby traps and purloined grenade launchers. Sergeant Helliman had to raise his voice to be heard.

'Three loft-cities remain under the control of the insurgents, sir: Cumulon, here in Nimbaros, and Cirrion. They have also collapsed all except the three major sky-bridges into these areas.'

'What of our ground forces, any progress there?' asked Tonnhauser, lifting his peaked cap to run a hand across his receding hairline and wishing dearly that the expulsion of the insurgents was someone else's job.

Helliman looked resigned, the young officer grown thinner over the passing weeks, and pale as a wraith.

'Heavy resistance is dogging our efforts to make any inroads into the cities. The insurgents are dug in and well organised.'

Helliman paused to clear his dry throat.

'There must be at least ninety thousand of the cities' total populations corrupted by cult activity. They hold all of the materiel factorums and are equipping themselves with our stockpiles. Armour too.'

Tonnhauser surveyed the city maps on the bench, looking for potential avenues of assault he might have missed. He saw only bottlenecks and kill-zones in which the Aircorps would be snared.

Helliman waited anxiously for Tonnhauser's response, and the void in conversation was filled by the frantic chatter coming from the command vox. Corpsman Aiker, crouched by the boxy unit in one corner of the workshop, tried his best to get a clear signal but static ran riot over all channels in the wake of the destruction of the antenna towers. Tonnhauser didn't need to hear the substance of the vox-reports to know it was bad.

'What *do* we hold then?' he asked at last, looking up into the sergeant's tired eyes.

'Our safe zones are–'

A shuddering explosion slapped against the workshop, cutting Helliman off. Fire spilled through the plastek towards the sergeant in a tide. It funnelled outwards, the plastek becoming fluid in the intense heat wave, and melted around the hapless Helliman.

Tonnhauser swore loudly as he was dumped on his arse, but had enough presence of mind to pull out his service pistol and shoot the screaming sergeant through the head to spare him further agony.

Ears still ringing from the blast, Tonnhauser saw a figure scuttle through the fire-limned gouge in the plastek. It was a man, or at least a dishevelled interpretation of one, clad in rags and flak armour. His hair was sheared roughly all the way down to the skull. Hate-filled eyes caught sight of Tonnhauser as the wretch cast about the room. But it was the mouth of the thing that gave the loyal Stratosan pause. It was sewn shut with thick black wire, the lips and cheeks shot through with purple-blue veins.

At first, Tonnhauser thought the insurgent was unarmed. Then he saw the grenade clutched in his left hand...

'Holy Emperor...'

Tonnhauser shot him through the forehead. As the cultist fell back there was an almighty thunderclap as the grenade went off, blasting the bodily remains of the insurgent to steaming chunks of meat.

The metal workbench spared Tonnhauser from the explosion, but he had little time to offer up his thanks to the Throne. Through the smoke and falling debris three more insurgents emerged, mouths sewn shut just like the first. Two carried autoguns; one had a crude-looking heavy stubber.

Squeezing off a desultory burst of fire, Tonnhauser went to ground behind the solid bench just as metal rain ripped into the workshop. It chewed up the room with an angry roar, tearing up the walls and disused machinery, perforating Corpsman Aiker where he crouched.

Crawling on his hands and knees, Tonnhauser pressed himself tighter into cover, discharging the spent clip from his pistol before reaching for another with trembling fingers.

No way could he kill them all...

Through the incessant barrage of gunfire, Tonnhauser first heard the *plink-plink* of a small metal object nearby, then saw the tossed grenade land and roll to within a metre of his foot. Survival instinct taking over, he lurched towards the grenade and kicked. It went off seconds later, heat, noise and pressure crashing over Tonnhauser in a violent wave, close enough for a shard of shrapnel to embed itself in his outstretched leg.

The colonel bit down so he wouldn't cry out.

Won't give this scum the satisfaction, he thought.

A sudden rash of las-fire spat overhead and abruptly the shooting ceased.

'Colonel,' an urgent voice called out from across the workbench a few moments later.

'Behind here,' Tonnhauser growled, wincing in pain as he saw the jagged metal sticking out of his leg.

Five Stratosan Aircorpsmen ran around the side of the bench, lasguns hot.

Tonnhauser read the first man's rank pins.

'Impeccable timing Sergeant Rucka, but aren't you supposed to be with Colonel Yonn and the 18th at the Cirrion border?'

A second corpsman carried a portable vox. Reports were drumming out on all frequencies, accompanied by a throbbing chorus of explosions and muted gunfire from across the length and breadth of Nimbaros.

'Colonel Yonn is dead, sir. And the 18th are pulling out of Cirrion. The city is totally lost, all safe zones are compromised,' Rucka told him. 'We've got to get you out.'

Tonnhauser grimaced as two of the other corpsmen helped him to his feet.

'What about Cumulon? Has that fallen too?' he asked, passing the dead bodies of the three cultists, and staggering out of the back entrance to the workshop.

The sergeant's tone was hollow but pragmatic.

'We've lost them all, sir. We're in full retreat, back beyond the city limits and across the sky-bridge to Pileon.'

Once out into the city streets the noise of the encroaching gun battle grew exponentially louder. Tonnhauser looked up to the dome roof of the city and saw a stormy sky through the reinforced plastek above him. Scudding smoke clouded his view as the upper atmosphere of the loft-city was lost from sight. As he fell back with Sergeant Rucka and his squad, Tonnhauser risked a glance over his shoulder. A mass retreat was in effect. Distant insurgents closed on their position en masse, clutching various guns and improvised weapons. Their battle cries were muted by the wire lacing their lips together – the effect was unnerving. Tonnhauser didn't need to hear them to tell the enemy was pressing a large-scale attack.

A gas-propelled rocket roared close by overhead, forcing Tonnhauser and the others to duck. It struck the side of a mag-tram depot and exploded outwards, engulfing an entrenched Aircorps gunnery position. The three-man team died screaming amidst brick and fire.

Rucka altered course abruptly, taking Tonnhauser and his men away from the destruction of the depot and down a side alley.

'Throne, how did this happen?' Tonnhauser asked when Rucka had them stop in the alley to wait for the all clear to proceed. 'We were pressing them back, weren't we?'

'Took us by surprise,' said Rucka, ducking back into the alley as a bomb blast lit up the road beyond. 'Set off a chain of booby traps that decimated our troops then launched a mass ground offensive. They're using advanced military tactics. No way can we retake the cities like this. We'll have to regroup. Maybe then we can get Nimbaros and Cumulon back, but Cirrion...' The sergeant's words trailed away, telling Tonnhauser everything he needed to know about the capital's fate.

'What about Governor Varkoff?'

'He's alive, bunkered down in Pileon. It's the nearest of the minor sky-cities that's still under our control. That's where we are headed now. He's enacted official distress protocols on all Imperial astropathic and comm-range frequencies, requesting immediate aid.'

'Do something for me will you, corpsman,' said Tonnhauser. The colonel had moved to the end of the alley and watched as another explosion took out a statue of the first Stratosan governor. It was a symbol of Imperial rule and order. It shattered as it struck the ground wrapped in fire.

'What's that, sir?'

'Get on your knees and pray,' Tonnhauser said, 'pray for a bloody miracle...'

* * *

For the last forty years, the dream hadn't changed.

At first there was only a vague sensation of heat, and then Dak'ir was back in the hot dark of the caves of Ignea on Nocturne. In his dream he was only a boy, the rock wall of that hostile place coarse and sharp against his pre-adolescent skin as he touched it. Mineral seams glinted in the glow of lava pools fed by the river of fire that was the lifeblood of the mountain above him. Ignea then faded, and the light from the river of fire died with it, resolving into a new vista...

The Cindara Plateau stretched before Dak'ir's sandaled feet, its edge delineated by rock-totems, its surface the colour of rust and umber. Ash scudded in drifts across the Pyre Desert below, obscuring scaled saurochs as they hunted for sustenance amongst the crags. Above there came the sound of thunder, as if Mount Deathfire was about to erupt flame and smoke to blot out the heavens. But the great mountain of Nocturne slumbered still. Instead, Dak'ir looked up and saw a fiery blaze of a different kind, the engines of a vast ship slowly coming to land.

A ramp opened in the side of the vessel as it came to rest at last, and a warrior stepped out, tall and powerful, clad in armour of green plate and emblazoned with the symbol of the salamander, the noble creatures that lived in the heart of the earth. Others joined the warrior, Dak'ir knew some of them; he had worked beside them rebuilding and rock-harvesting after the Time of Trial. His heart quailed at the sight of these giants, though. For he knew they had come for him...

The image changed again, and this time Dak'ir had changed too. He now wore the mantle of warrior, carried the tools of war. His body was armoured in carapace, a holy bolt pistol gripped in his Astartes fist, his onyx flesh a stark reminder of his superhuman apotheosis. Monoliths of stone and marble loomed above Dak'ir like grey sentinels, ossuary roads paved the streets and the acrid stench of grave dust filled the air. This was not Nocturne; this was Moribar, and here the skies were wreathed in death.

Somewhere on the horizon of that grey and terrible world, Dak'ir heard screaming and the vision in his mind's eye bled away to be filled by a face on fire. He had seen it so many times, 'the burning face', agonised and accusing, never letting him truly rest. It burned and burned, and soon Dak'ir was burning too, and the screams that filled his ears became his own...

'We were only meant to bring them back...'

DAK'IR'S EYES SNAPPED open as he came out of battle-meditation. Acutely aware of his accelerated breathing and high blood pressure, he went through the mental calming routines as taught to him when he had first joined the superhuman ranks of the Space Marines.

With serenity came realisation. Dak'ir was standing in the half-darkness of his isolation chamber, a solitorium, one of many aboard the strike cruiser *Vulkan's Wrath*. It was little more than a dungeon: sparse, austere and surrounded on all sides by cold, black walls.

More detailed recollection came swiftly.

An urgent communication had been picked up weeks ago via astropathic messenger and interpreted by the Company Librarian, Pyriel. The Salamanders were heading to the Imperial world of Stratos.

A prolific mining colony, one of many along the Hadron Belt in the Reductus Sector of Segmentum Tempestus, Stratos had great value to the Imperium for its oceanic minerals as well as its regular tithe of inductees to the Imperial Guard. Rescue of Stratos, liberation for its inhabitants from the internecine enemies that plagued it, was of paramount importance.

Hours from breaking orbit, Captain Ko'tan Kadai had already assigned six squads, including his own *Inferno Guard*, to be the task force that would make planetfall on Stratos and free the world from anarchy. As Promethean belief dictated, all Salamanders about to embark on battle must first be cleansed by fire and endure a period of extended meditation to focus their minds on self-reliance and inner fortitude.

All, but Dak'ir, had been untroubled in their preparations.

Such a fact would not go unnoticed.

'My lord?' a deep and sonorous voice asked.

Dak'ir looked in its direction and saw the hooded form of Tsek. His brander-priest was dressed in emerald green robes with the Chapter icon, a snarling salamander head inside a ring of fire, stitched in amber-coloured wire across his breast. Half-concealed augmetics were just visible beneath the serf's attire in the flickering torchlight.

The chamber was small, but had enough room for an Astartes' attendants.

'Are you ready for the honour-scarring, my lord?' asked Tsek.

Dak'ir nodded, still a little disoriented from his dream. He watched as Tsek brought forth a glowing rod, white-hot from the embers of the brazier-cauldron that Dak'ir was standing in barefooted. The Astartes barely registered the pain from the fire-wrapped coals beneath him. There was not so much as a globule of sweat across his bald head or onyx-black body, naked but for a tribal sash clothing his loins.

The ritual was part of the teachings of the Promethean Cult, to which all warriors of the Salamanders stoically adhered.

As Tsek applied the branding rod to Dak'ir's exposed skin he embraced the pain it brought. His fiery eyes, like red-hot coals themselves, watched approvingly. First, Tsek burned three bars and then a swirl bisecting them. It conjoined the many marks he and other brander-priests had made upon Dak'ir's body where they'd healed and scarred into a living history of the Salamander's many conflicts. Each was a battle won, a foe vanquished. No Salamander went into battle without first being marked to honour it and then again at battle's end to commemorate it.

Dak'ir's own marks wreathed his legs, arm and some of his torso and back. They were intricate, becoming more detailed as each new honour scar was added. Only a veteran of many campaigns, a Salamander of centuries' service, ever bore such markings on his face.

Tsek bowed his head and stepped back into shadow. A votive-servitor shambled forward in his wake on reverse-jointed metal limbs, bent-backed beneath the weight of a vast brazier fused to its spine. Dak'ir reached out and plunged both hands into the iron caldera of the brazier, scooping up the fragments of ash from the burned matter collected at its edges.

Dak'ir smeared the white ash over his face and chest, inscribing the Promethean symbols of the hammer and the anvil. They were potent icons in Promethean lore, believed to garner endurance and strength.

'Vulkan's fire beats in my breast...' he intoned, making a long sweep with his palm to draw the hammer's haft.

'...With it I shall smite the foes of the Emperor,' another voice concluded, letting Dak'ir cross the top of the haft with his palm to form the hammer's head before revealing himself.

Brother Fugis stepped into the brazier's light, clanking loudly as he moved. He was already clad in his green power armour, but went unhooded. His blood-red eyes blazed vibrantly in the half-dark. As befitted a Space Marine of his position, Fugis bore the ash-white of the Apothecaries on his right shoulder pad, though the left still carried the insignia of his Chapter on a jet-black field, the snarling salamander head there a blazing orange to match the pauldrons of his Third Company battle-brothers.

Thin-faced and intimidating, some in the company had suggested Fugis might be better served in a more spiritual profession than the art of healing. Such 'suggestions' were never voiced out loud, however, or given in front of the Apothecary, for fear of reprisal.

Dak'ir's response to the Apothecary's sudden presence was less than genial.

'What are you doing here, brother?'

Fugis did not answer straight away. Instead, he scanned a bio-reader over Dak'ir's body.

'Captain Kadai asked me to visit. Examinations are best conducted before you're armoured.'

Fugis paused as he waited for the results of the bio-scan, his blade-thin face taut like wire.

'Your arm, Astartes,' he added without looking up, but gesturing for Dak'ir's limb.

Dak'ir held his arm out for the Apothecary, who took it by the wrist and syringed off a portion of blood into a vial. A chamber in his gauntlet then performed a bio-chemical analysis after the vial was inserted into its miniature centrifuge.

'Are all of my brothers undergoing such rigorous conditioning?' asked Dak'ir, keeping the annoyance from his voice.

Fugis was evidently satisfied with the serology results, but his tone was still matter of fact.

'No, just you.'

'If my brother-captain doubts my will, he should have Chaplain Elysius appraise me.'

The Apothecary seized Dak'ir's jaw suddenly in a gauntleted fist and carefully examined his face. 'Elysius is not aboard the *Vulkan's Wrath*, as you well know, so you will have to endure my *appraisal* instead.'

With the index finger of his other hand Fugis pulled down the black skin beneath Dak'ir's left eye, diffusing its blood-red glow across his cheek.

'You are still experiencing somnambulant visions during battle-meditation?' he asked. Then, apparently satisfied, he let Dak'ir go.

The brother-sergeant rubbed his jaw where the Apothecary had pinched it.

'If you mean, am I dreaming, then yes. It happens sometimes.'

The Apothecary looked at the instrument panel on his glove, his expression inscrutable.

'What do you dream about?'

'I am a boy again, back on Nocturne in the caves of Ignea. I see the day I passed the trials on the Cindara Plateau and became an Astartes, my first mission as a neophyte…' The Salamander's voice trailed away, as his expression darkened in remembrance.

The burning face…

'You are the only one of us, the only Fire-born, ever to be chosen from Ignea,' Fugis told him, eyes penetrating as he looked at Dak'ir.

'What does that matter?'

Fugis ignored him and went back to his analysis.

'You said, "We were only meant to bring them back". Who did you mean?' he asked after a moment.

'You were there on Moribar,' Dak'ir uttered and stepped off the brazier-cauldron, hot skin steaming as it touched the cold metal floor of his isolation cell. 'You know.'

Fugis looked up from his instruments and his data. His eyes softened fleetingly with regret. They quickly narrowed, however, sheathed behind cold indifference.

He laughed mirthlessly, his lip curling in more of a sneer than a smile.

'You are fit for combat, brother-sergeant,' he said. 'Planetfall on Stratos is in less than two hours. I'll see you on assembly deck six before then.'

Fugis then saluted, more by rote than meaning, and turned his back on his fellow Salamander.

Dak'ir felt relief as the Apothecary departed.

'And Brother Dak'ir... Not all of us *want* to be brought back. Not all of us *can* be brought back,' said Fugis, swallowed by the dark.

THE SURFACE OF Stratos writhed with perpetual storms. Lightning streaked the boiling tumult and thunderheads collided in violent flashes, only to break apart moments later. Through these ephemeral gaps in the clouds tiny nubs of chlorine-bleached rock and bare earth were revealed, surrounded by a swirling maelstrom sea.

The Thunderhawk gunships *Fire-wyvern* and *Spear of Prometheus* tore above the storm's fury, turbofans screaming. They were headed for the conglomeration of floating cities in Stratos's upper atmosphere. Named 'loft-cities' by the Stratosan natives, these great domed metropolises of chrome and plascrete were home to some four point three million souls and linked together by a series of massive sky-bridges. Due to the concentrated chlorine emissions from their oceans the Stratosans had been forced to elevate their cities with massive plasma-fuelled gravitic engines; so high, in fact, that each required its own atmosphere in order for the inhabitants to breathe.

The words of Fugis were still on Dak'ir's mind and he willed the furore inside the Chamber Sanctuarine of the *Fire-wyvern* to smother his thoughts. The gunship's troop hold was almost at capacity – twenty-five Astartes secured in standing grav-harness as the Thunderhawk made its final descent.

Brother-Captain Kadai was closest to the exit ramp, his gaze burning with courage and conviction. He was clad in saurian-styled artificer armour and, like his charges, had yet to don his helmet. Instead, he had it clasped to his armour belt, a simulacrum of a snarling fire drake fashioned in metal. His close-cropped hair was white and shaven into a strip that bisected his head down the middle. Alongside him was his command squad, the Inferno Guard: N'keln, Kadai's second in command, a steady if uncharismatic officer; Company Champion Vek'shen, who had bested countless foes in the Chapter's name, and gripped his fire-glaive; Honoured Brother Malicant who bore the company's banner into battle, and Honoured Brother Shen'kar clasping a flamer to his chest. Fugis was the last of them. The Apothecary nodded discreetly in Dak'ir's direction when he saw him.

It was dark in the chamber. Tiny ovals of light came from the Salamanders, their red eyes aglow. As Dak'ir's gaze left Fugis it settled on another's, one that burned coldly.

Brother-Sergeant Tsu'gan glared from across the hold.

Dak'ir felt his fists clench.

Tsu'gan was the epitome of Promethean ideal. Strong, tenacious, self-sacrificing – he was everything a Salamander should aspire to be. But there was a vein of arrogance and superiority hidden deep within him. He was born in Hesiod, one of the seven Sanctuary Cities of Nocturne, and the principal recruiting grounds for the Chapter. Unlike most on the volcanic death world, Tsu'gan was raised into relative affluence. His family were nobles, tribal kings at the tenuous apex of Nocturnean wealth and influence.

Dak'ir, as an itinerant cave-dwelling Ignean, was at its nadir. The fact that he became Astartes at all was unprecedented. So few from the nomadic tribes ever reached the sacred places where initiates underwent the trials, let alone competed and succeeded in them. Dak'ir was, in many ways, unique. To Tsu'gan, he was an aberration. Both should have left their human pasts behind when they were elevated to Astartes, but centuries of ingrained prejudice were impossible to suppress.

The Thunderhawk banked sharply as it made for the landing zone adjacent to the loft-city of Nimbaros, breaking the tension between the two sergeants. The exterior armour plate shrieked in protest with the sudden exertion, the sound transmitting internally as a dull metal moan.

'A portent of the storm to come?' offered Ba'ken in a bellow.

The bald-headed Astartes was Dak'ir's heavy weapons trooper, his broad shoulders and thick neck making him ideally equipped for the task. Ba'ken, like many of his Chapter, was also a gifted artisan and craftsman. The heavy flamer he had slung on his back was unique amongst Tactical squads, and he had manufactured the weapon himself in the blazing forges of Nocturne.

'According to the Stratosan's reports, the traitors are dug in and have numbers. It will not be–'

'*We* are the storm, brother,' Tsu'gan interjected, shouting loudly above the engine din before Dak'ir could finish. 'We'll cleanse this place with fire and flame,' he snarled zealously, 'and purge the impure.'

Ba'ken nodded solemnly to the other sergeant, but Dak'ir felt his skin flush with anger at such blatant disrespect for his command.

An amber warning light winked into existence above them and Brother-Captain Kadai's voice rang out, preventing any reprisal.

'Helmets on, brothers!'

There was a collective *clank* of metal on metal as the Astartes donned battle-helms.

Dak'ir and Tsu'gan fitted theirs last of all, unwilling to break eye contact for even a moment. In the end Tsu'gan relented, smiling darkly as he mouthed a phrase.

'Purge the impure.'

'CUMULON IN THE east and Nimbaros in the south are still contested, but my troops are taking more ground by the hour and have managed to secure the sky-bridges that link the three cities,' explained a sweating Colonel Tonnhauser over the crackling pict-link of Kadai's Land Raider Redeemer, *Fire Anvil*. 'We're using them to siphon out civilian survivors. There are still thousands trapped behind enemy lines though, my men amongst them.'

'You have done the Emperor's work here, and have my oath as a Salamander of Vulkan that if those men can be saved, I will save them,' Kadai replied, standing inside the hold of his war machine as it shuddered over the sky-bridge to Cirrion. Four armoured Rhinos rumbled behind it in convoy, transporting the rest of the battle-group.

Once the Salamanders had made planetfall outside Nimbaros, Kadai had ordered Brother Argos, Master of the Forge, to make a structural assessment of the approach road to Cirrion. Using building schematics from the Stratosan cities inloaded to the *Vulkan's Wrath*'s cogitators and then exloaded back to a display screen on the *Fire-wyvern*, the Techmarine had determined the sky-bridges were unfeasible locations for the gunships to land and redeploy the Astartes.

Less than twenty minutes later, three Thunderhawk transporters had descended from orbit and deployed the Salamanders' dedicated transport vehicles.

Kadai had held his Salamanders at the landing zone in squad formation, ready for the arrival of the transports. There had been no time for a tactical appraisal with the Stratosan natives. That would have to be conducted en route to Cirrion.

'I pray to the Emperor that some yet live,' Tonnhauser continued over the pict-link, network-fed to all of the Astartes transports. 'But I fear Cirrion is lost to us, lord Astartes,' he added, lighting up a fresh cigar with shaking fingers. 'There's nothing left there but death and terror, now.' He seemed to be avoiding eye contact with the screen. Kadai had taken off his helmet during the ride over the sky-bridge and the human clearly found his appearance unsettling.

'Wars have been won on the strength of that alone,' he remembered the old Master of Recruits telling him almost three hundred years ago when he had first been given the black carapace.

'Tell me of the enemy,' Kadai said, face hardening at the thought of such suffering.

'They call themselves the Cult of Truth,' said Tonnhauser, the pict-link breaking up for a moment with the static interference. 'Until roughly three months ago, they were merely a small group of disaffected Imperial citizens adept at dodging the mauls of the city proctors. Now they are at least fifty thousand strong, and dug in all throughout Cirrion. They're heavily-armed. Most of the Stratosan war-smiths are based in the capital, as are our dirigible fleets, our airships. They carry a mark on their bodies, usually hidden, like a tattoo in the shape of a screaming mouth. And their mouths...' he said, taking a shuddering breath, 'their mouths are sewn shut with wire. We think they might remove their tongues, too.'

'What makes you say that?'

Tonnhauser met the captain's burning gaze in spite of his fear.

'Because no one has ever heard them speak.' Tonnhauser paled further. 'To fight an enemy that does not cry out, that does not shout orders. It's not natural.'

'Do they have a leader, this *cult*?' said Kadai, showing his distaste at such depravity.

Tonnhauser took a long drag on his cigar, before crushing it in an ash tray and lighting another.

'Our gathered intelligence is limited,' he admitted. 'But we believe there is a hierophant of sorts. Again, this is unconfirmed, but we think he's in the temple district. What we do know is that they call him the *Speaker*.'

'An ironic appellation,' Kadai muttered. 'How many troops do you have left, colonel?'

Tonnhauser licked his lips.

'Enough to hold the two satellite cities. The rest of my men in Cirrion are being pulled out as we speak. Civilians too. I've lost so many...' Tonnhauser's face fell. He looked like a man with nothing more to give.

'Hold those cities, colonel,' Kadai told him. 'The Salamanders will deal with Cirrion, now. You've done your duty as a servant of the Imperium and will be honoured for it.'

'Thank you, my lord.'

The pict-link crackled into static as Kadai severed the connection.

The captain turned from the blank display screen to find Apothecary Fugis at his shoulder.

'Their courage hangs by a thread,' he muttered. 'I have never seen such despair.'

'Our intervention is timely then.' Kadai glanced over Fugis's shoulder and saw the rest of his command squad. N'keln was readying them for battle, leading them in the rites of the Promethean Cult.

'Upon the anvil are we tempered, into warriors forged...' he intoned, the others solemnly following his lead. They surrounded a small brazier set into the floor of the troop hold. Offerings to Vulkan and the Emperor burned within the crucible, scraps of banners or powdered bone, and one by one the Inferno Guard took a fistful of the ash and marked their armour with it.

'Guerrilla warfare is one thing, but to defeat an entire Imperial Guard regiment... Do you think we face more than a cult uprising here?' asked Fugis, averting his gaze from the ritual and resolving to make his own observances later.

Kadai brought his gaze inward as he considered the Apothecary's question.

'I don't know yet. But something plagues this place. This so-called Cult of Truth certainly has many followers.'

'Its spread is endemic, suggesting its root is psychological, rather than ideological,' said the Apothecary.

Kadai left the implication unspoken.

'I can't base a strategy on supposition, brother. Once we breach the city, then we'll find out what we're facing.' The captain paused a moment before asking, 'What of Dak'ir?'

Fugis lowered his voice, so the others could not hear him.

'Physically, our brother is fine. But he is still troubled. Remembrances of his human childhood on Nocturne and his first mission...'

Kadai scowled, 'Moribar... Over four decades of battles, yet still this one clings to us like a dark shroud.'

'His memory retention is... *unusual*. And I think he feels guilt for what happened to Nihilan,' offered Fugis.

Kadai's expression darkened further.

'He is not alone in that,' he muttered.

'Ushorak, too.'

'Vai'tan Ushorak was a traitor. He deserved his fate,' Kadai answered flatly, before changing the subject, 'Dak'ir's spirit will be cleansed in the crucible of battle; that is the Salamander way. Failing that I will submit him to the Reclusiam and Chaplain Elysius for conditioning.'

Kadai re-activated the open vox-channel, indicating that the conversation was over.

It was time to address the troops.

'BROTHERS...' DAK'IR HEARD the voice of his captain over the vox. 'Our task here is simple. Liberate the city, protect its citizens and destroy the heretics. Three assault groups will enter Cirrion on a sector by sector cleanse and burn – *Hammer*, *Anvil* and *Flame*. Sergeants Tsu'gan and Dak'ir will lead *Anvil* and *Flame*, into the east and west sectors of the city respectively. Devastator heavy support is Sergeant Ul'shan's Hellfire Squad for *Anvil* and Sergeant Lok's Incinerators for *Flame*. I lead *Hammer* to the north with Sergeant Omkar. Flamers with all units. Let nothing stay your wrath. This is the kind of fight we were born for. In the name of Vulkan. Kadai out.'

Static reigned once more. Dak'ir cut the link completely as the convoy rumbled on slowly past sandbagged outposts crested with razor wire. Weary troops with hollow eyes manned those stations, too tired or inured by weeks of fighting to react to the sight of the Astartes.

'This is a broken force,' muttered Ba'ken, breaking the silence as he peered out of one of the Rhino's vision slits.

Dak'ir followed his trooper's gaze. 'They are not like the natives of Nocturne, Ba'ken. They are unused to hardship like this.'

A lone file of Stratosan Aircorps passed the convoy, marching in the opposite direction. They trudged like automatons, nursing wounds, hobbling on sticks, lasguns slung loose over their shoulders. Every man wore a respirator, and a tan storm-coat to ward off the chill of the open atmosphere. Only the cities were domed, the sky-bridges lay open to the elements, though they had high walls and were suspended from rugged-looking towers by thick cables.

The gate of Cirrion loomed at the end of the blasted road. The way into the capital city was huge, all bare black metal, and hermetically sealed to maintain its atmospheric integrity.

'I heard a group of corpsmen talking before we mustered out,' offered Ba'ken as they approached the gate. 'He said that Cirrion was how he imagined hell.'

Dak'ir was checking the power load of his plasma pistol before slamming it back into its holster. 'We were born in hell, Ba'ken... What do we have to fear from a little fire?'

Ba'ken's booming laughter thundered in the Rhino all the way up to the gate.

DEEP WITHIN THE bowels of Cirrion the shadows were alive with monsters.

Sergeant Rucka fled through shattered streets, his pursuers at his heels. His heart was pounding. Cirrion's principal power grid had collapsed, leaving failing backup generators to provide intermittent illumination for the city via its lume-lamps. With every sporadic blackout, the shadows seemed to fill with new threats and fresh enemies. It didn't help matters.

Rucka had been at the front of the second push in the capital city. The attack had failed utterly. Something else was stalking the darkened corridors of Cirrion, and it had fallen upon his battalion with furious wrath. It was totally unexpected. In strategising his battalion's assault Rucka had deliberately taken an oblique route, circumventing the main battle zones, to come through the northern sector of the city.

All Stratosan gathered intelligence had suggested that insurgent resistance would be light. It wasn't insurgents that had wiped out five hundred men.

Rucka was the last of them, having somehow escaped the carnage, but now the cultists had found him. They were gaining too. His once proud city was in ruins. He didn't know this dystopian version of it. Where there should have been avenues there were rubble blockades. Where there should be plazas of chrome there were charred pits falling away into stygian darkness. Hell had come here. There was no other word to describe it.

Rounding another corner, Rucka came to abrupt halt. He was standing at the mouth to a mag-tram station; on one side a stack of industrial warehouses, on the other a high wall and an overpass. The trams themselves littered the way ahead, just burnt out wrecks, daubed in crude slogans. But it was the tunnel itself that caught the sergeant's attention. Something skittered there in the abject darkness.

Behind him, Rucka heard the pack. They'd slowed. He realised then he'd been steered to this place.

Slowly the skittering from the tunnel became louder and the pack from behind him closer. The cultists scuttled into view. Rucka counted at least fifty men and women, their mouths sewn shut, blue veins threading from their puckered lips. They carried picks and shards of metal and glass.

It wasn't the end that Rucka had envisaged for himself.

The sergeant had picked out his first opponent and was about to take aim with his lasgun when a piece of rockcrete clattered down onto the street. Rucka traced its trajectory back to the overpass and saw the silhouettes of three armoured giants in the ambient light.

The brief spark of salvation given life in Rucka's mind was quickly crushed when he realised that these creatures were not here to save him.

Thunder roared and muzzle flares tore away the darkness a second later.

Rucka read what was about to happen and went to ground just before the onslaught. The deadly salvo lasted heartbeats, but it was enough. The cultists were utterly annihilated – their broken, blasted bodies littered the street like visceral trash.

Rucka was on his back, still dazed from the sudden attack. When he couldn't feel his legs, he realised he'd been hit. Heat blazed down his side like an angry knife ripping at his skin. His fatigues were wet, probably with his own blood. A sudden earth tremor shook the rockcrete where Rucka lay prone, sending fresh daggers of pain through his body, as something large and dense smashed into the ground. More impacts followed, landing swift and heavy like mortar strikes.

Vision fogging, the sergeant managed to turn his head... His blood-rimed eyes widened. Crouched in gory armour, two bloody horns curling from its snarling dragon helm, was a terrible giant. It rose to its feet, like some primordial beast uncurling from the abyss, to reveal an immense plastron swathed in red scales. Heat haze seemed to emanate from its armoured form as if it had been fresh-forged from the mantle of a volcano.

'The vault, where is it?' the dragon giant asked, fiery embers rasping through its fanged mouth-grille as if it breathed ash and cinder.

'Close...' said another. Its voice was like cracked parchment but carried the resonance of power.

Though he couldn't see them in his eye-line, Rucka realised the secondary impacts had been the giant warrior's companions.

'We are not alone,' said a third, deep and throaty like crackling magma.

'Salamanders,' said the dragon giant, his vitriol obvious.

'Then we had best be swift,' returned the second voice. 'I do not want to miss them.'

Rucka heard heavy footfalls approaching and felt the ominous gaze of one of the armoured giants upon him.

'This one still lives,' it barked.

Rucka's vision was fading, but the sergeant could still smell copper coming off its armour, mangled with the acrid stench of gun smoke.

'No survivors,' said the second voice. 'Kill it quickly. We have no time for *amusement*, Ramlek.'

'A pity...'

Rucka tried to speak.

'The Empe–'

Then his world ended in fire.

THE BLACK IRON gates of Cirrion parted with slow inevitability.

The armoured Astartes convoy rumbled through into the waiting darkness. After a few moments the gates shut behind them. Halogen strip lights flickered into life on the flanking walls revealing a large metal chamber, wide enough for the transports to travel abreast.

Abandoned Stratosan vehicles lay abutting the walls, dragged aside by clearance crews. Caches of discarded equipment were strewn nearby the forlorn AFVs. Webbing, luminator rigs and other ancillary kit had been left behind, but no weapons – all the guns were needed by the human defenders.

Hermetically sealed from the outside to preserve atmospheric integrity, the holding area had another gate on the opposite side. This second gate opened when the Salamanders were halfway across the vast corridor with a hiss of pressure, and led into Cirrion itself.

The outskirts of the benighted city beckoned.

Deserted avenues bled away into blackness and buildings lay in ruins like open wounds. Fire seared the walls and blood washed the streets. Despair hung thick in the air like a tangible fug. Death had come to Cirrion, and held it tightly in its bony grasp.

Akin to a hive, Cirrion was stacked with honeycomb levels in the most densely packed areas. Grav-lifts linked these plateau-conurbations of chrome and blue. Sub-levels plunged in other places, allowing access to inverted maintenance spires or vast subterranean freight yards. Above, a dense pall of smoke layered the ceiling in a roiling mass. Breaks in the grey-black smog revealed thick squalls of cloud and the flash of lightning arcs from the atmospheric storm outside and beyond the dome.

Tactically, the city was a nightmarish labyrinth of hidden pitfalls, artificial bottlenecks and kill-zones. Tank traps riddled the roads. Spools of razor wire wreathed every alleyway. Piled rubble and wreckage created makeshift walls and impassable blockades.

The Salamanders reached as far as Aereon Square, one of Cirrion's communal plazas, when the wreckage-clogged, wire-choked streets prevented the transports from going any further.

It was to be the first of many setbacks.

'Salamanders, disembark,' Kadai voiced sternly over the vox. 'Three groups, quadrant by quadrant search. Vehicles stay here. We approach on foot.'

'NOTHING,' BA'KEN'S VOICE was tinny through his battle-helm as he stood facing the doorway to one of Cirrion's municipal temples. It yawned like a hungry maw, the shadows within filled with menace.

From behind him, Dak'ir's order was emphatic.

'Burn it.'

Ba'ken hefted his heavy flamer and doused the room beyond with liquid promethium. The sudden burst of incendiary lit up a broad hallway like a flare, hinting at a larger space in the distance, before dying back down to flickering embers.

'Clear,' he shouted, stepping aside heavily with the immense weapon, allowing the sergeant and his battle-brothers through.

Sergeant Lok and his Devastators were assigned to the rearguard and took up positions to secure the entrance as Ba'ken followed the Tactical squad inside.

Dak'ir entered quickly, his squad fanning out from his lead to cover potential avenues of attack.

They'd been travelling through the city for almost an hour, through three residential districts filled with debris, and still no contact with friend or foe. Regular reports networked through the Astartes' comm-feeds in their helmets revealed the same from the other two assault groups.

Cirrion was dead.

Yet, there were signs of recent abandonment: lume-globes flickering in the blasted windows of tenements, sonophones playing grainy melodies in communal refectories, the slow-running engines of dormant grav-cars and the interior lamps of mag-trams come to an all-stop on the rails. Life here had ended abruptly and violently.

Numerous roads and more conventional routes were blocked by pitfalls or rubble. According to Brother Argos, the municipal temple was the most expedient way to penetrate deeper into the east sector. It was also postulated that it was a likely location for survivors to congregate. The Techmarine was back in Nimbaros with Colonel Tonnhauser, guiding the three assault groups via a hololithic schematic, adjusting the image as he was fed reports of blockades, street collapses or structural levelling by Salamanders in the field.

'Brother Argos, this is *Flame*. We've reached the municipal temple and need a route through,' said Dak'ir. Even through his power armour, he was aware of the dulcet hum of the plasma engines keeping the massive city aloft and reminded of the precariousness of their battlefield.

Putting the thoughts out of his mind, he swept the luminator attached to his battle-helm around the vast hall. Within its glare a lozenge-shaped chamber with racks of desks on both flanking walls was revealed. Overhead, exterior light from the city's lume-lamps spilled through a glass-domed ceiling in grainy shafts illuminating patches on the ground. Lightning flashes from Stratos's high atmosphere outside augmented it.

Parchments and scraps of vellum set ablaze by Ba'ken's flamer skittered soundlessly across a polished floor, or twisted like fireflies on an unseen breeze. More of the papers were fixed to pillars that supported the vaulted roof above, fluttering fitfully – some stuck with votive wax, others hammered fast with nails and stakes. The messages were doubtless pinned up by grieving families long since given in to despair

'These are death notices, prayers for the missing,' intoned Brother Emek, using the muzzle of his bolter to hold one still so he could read it.

'More here,' added Brother Zo'tan. He panned the light from his luminator up a chrome-plated staircase at the back of the room to reveal the suited bodies of clerks and administrators entangled in the balustrade. Torn scrolls were pinned to the banister, and gathered over the corpses on the steps like a paper shroud.

'There must be thousands…' uttered Sergeant Lok, who had entered the lobby. The hard-faced veteran looked grimmer than ever as he surveyed the records of the dead with his bionic eye.

'Advance to the north end of the hall,' the Techmarine's voice returned, cracked with interference as it called the Salamanders back. 'A stairway leads to a second level. Proceed north through the next chamber then east across a gallery until you find a gate. That's your exit.'

Dak'ir killed the comm-feed. In the sudden silence he became aware of the atmospheric processors droning loudly in the barrier wall around the city, purifying, recycling, regulating. He was about to give the order to move out when the sound changed abruptly. The pitch became higher, as if the processing engine were switched to a faster setting.

Dak'ir re-opened the comm-feed in his battle-helm.

'Tsu'gan, are you detecting any variance in the atmospheric processors in your sector?'

Crackling static returned for a full thirty seconds before the sergeant replied.

'It's nothing. Maintain your vigilance, Ignean. I have no desire to haul your squad out of trouble when you let your guard slip.'

Tsu'gan cut the feed.

Dak'ir swore under his breath.

'Move out,' he told his squad. He hoped they'd find the enemy soon.

'He should never have been chosen to lead,' muttered Tsu'gan to his second, Iagon.

'Our brother-captain must have his reasons,' he replied, his tone ever sinuous but carefully neutral.

Iagon was never far from his sergeant's side, and was ever ready with his counsel. His body was slight compared to most of his brethren, but he made up for sheer bulk with guile and cunning. Iagon gravitated towards power, and right now that was Tsu'gan, Captain Kadai's star ascendant. He also carried the squad's auspex, maintaining a watch for unusual spikes of activity that might prelude an ambush, walking just two paces behind his sergeant as they stalked through the shadows of a hydroponics farm.

Tiny reservoirs of nutrient solution encased in chrome tanks extended across an expansive domed chamber. The chemical repositories were set in serried ranks and replete with various edible plant life and other flora. The foliage inside the vast gazebo of chrome and glass was overgrown, resembling more an artificial jungle than an Imperial facility for the sector-wide provision of nutrition.

'Then that is his folly,' Tsu'gan replied, and signalled a sudden halt.

He crouched, peering into the arboreal gloom ahead. His squad, well-drilled by their sergeant, adopted overwatch positions.

'Flamer,' he growled into the comm-feed.

Brother Honorious moved forwards, the igniter of his weapon burning quietly. The Salamander noticed the blue flame flicker for just a moment as if reacting to something in the air. Slapping the barrel, Honorious muttered a litany to the machine-spirits and the igniter returned to normal.

'On your order, sergeant.'

Tsu'gan held up his hand.

'Hold a moment.'

Iagon low-slung his bolter to consult the auspex.

'No life form readings.'

Tsu'gan's face was fixed in a grimace.

'Cleanse and burn.'

'We would be destroying the food supply for an entire city sector,' said Iagon.

'Believe me Iagon, the Stratosans are long past caring. I'll take no chances. Now,' he said, turning back to Honorious, 'cleanse and burn.'

The roar of the flamer filled the hydroponics dome as the sustenance of Cirrion was burned to ash.

* * *

'THEY ARE DRAWING us in,' said Veteran Sergeant N'keln over the comm-feed. He was in the lead, tracking his bolter left and right for any sign of the enemy.

'I know,' Kadai agreed, trusting his and N'keln's warrior instincts. The captain held his inferno pistol by his side, thunder hammer crackling quietly in his other hand. 'Remain vigilant,' he hissed through his battle-helm, his squad treading warily with bolters ready.

The city loomed tall and imposing as the Salamanders advanced slowly down a narrow road choked with wreckage and Stratosan corpses – 'remnants' of the battalions Tonnhauser had mentioned. The hapless human troopers had erected sandbagged emplacements and makeshift barricades. Habs had been turned into bunkers, and bodies hung forlornly from their windows like rags. The defences had not availed them. The Stratosan infantry had been crushed.

Fugis was crouched over the blasted remains of a lieutenant, scowling.

'Massive physical trauma,' muttered the Apothecary as Captain Kadai approached him.

'Colonel Tonnhauser said the cultists were heavily armed,' offered N'keln alongside him.

Fugis regarded the corpse further. 'Rib cage is completely eviscerated, chest organs all but liquefied.' Looking up at his fellow Salamanders, his red eyes flared behind his helmet lenses. 'This is a bolter wound.'

Kadai was about to respond when Brother Shen'kar called from up ahead.

'I have movement!'

'KEEP IT TIGHT,' warned Dak'ir as he advanced up the lobby stairs towards a large chrome archway leading to the second level of the municipal temple.

The igniter on Ba'ken's heavy flamer spat and flickered furiously until he reduced the fuel supply down the hose.

'Problem?'

'It's nothing sergeant,' he replied.

Dak'ir continued up the stairway, battle-brothers on either side of him, the Devastators still in the lobby below, ready to move up if needed. When he reached the summit he saw another long hallway beyond, just as Brother Argos had described. The room was filled with disused cogitators and other extant machinery. Sweeping his gaze across the junk, Dak'ir stopped abruptly.

In the centre of the hall, surrounded by more dead Administratum workers, was a boy. An infant, no more than eight years old, he was barefoot and clad in rags. Dirt and dried blood encrusted his body like a second skin. The boy was staring right at Dak'ir.

'Don't move,' he whispered to his battle-brothers through the comm-feed. 'We have a survivor.'

'Mercy of Vulkan...' breathed Ba'ken, alongside him.

'Stay back,' warned Dak'ir, taking a step.

The boy flinched, but didn't run. Tears were streaming down his face, cutting through the grime and leaving pale channels in their wake.

Dak'ir scanned the hall furtively for any potential threats, before deeming the way was clear. Holstering his plasma pistol and sheathing his chainsword, he then showed his armoured palms to the boy.

'You have nothing to fear...' he began, and slowly removed his battle-helm. Dak'ir realised his mistake too late.

This infant was no native of Nocturne. One look at the Salamander's onyx-black skin and burning eyes and the child yelped and fled for his life back across the hall.

'Damn it!' Dak'ir hissed, ramming his battle-helm back on and re-arming himself. 'Sergeant Lok, you and your squad secure the room and await our return,' he ordered through the comm-feed. 'Brothers, the rest of you with me – there may be survivors, and the boy will lead us to them.'

The Salamanders gave chase, whilst the Devastators moved up the stairs behind them. Dak'ir was halfway across the hall with his squad when he felt the tiny pressure of a wire snapping against his greave. He turned, about to shout a warning, when the entire room exploded.

'Dead end,' stated Brother Honorious, standing before the towering barricade of heaped grav-cars and mag-trams.

Tsu'gan and *Anvil* left the hydroponics farm a smouldering ruin and had advanced into the city. Directed by Brother Argos, they'd passed through myriad avenues in the urban labyrinth until reaching a narrow defile created by tall tenement blocks and overhanging tower-levels. A hundred metres in and they'd rounded a corner only to find it blocked.

'We'll burn through it,' said Tsu'gan, about to order Sergeant Ul'shan's Devastators forward. The multi-meltas would soon–

'Wait...' said Tsu'gan, surveying the tall buildings reaching over them. 'Double back, we'll find another way.'

At the opposite end of the alleyway a huge trans-loader rolled into view, cutting off their exit. Slowly at first, but with growing momentum it rumbled towards the Salamanders.

'Multi-meltas now! Destroy it!'

Sergeant Ul'shan swung his squad around to face the charging vehicle just as the cultist heavy weapon crews emerged from their hiding places in the tenements above and filled the alleyway with gunfire.

'Eyes open,' hissed Captain Kadai.

The Inferno Guard, together with Omkar's Devastators, were crouched in ready positions spread across the street. The dangers were manifold – every window, every alcove or shadowed corner could contain an enemy.

Kadai's gaze flicked back to Fugis, as the Apothecary hurried, head low, towards a distant gun emplacement. A Stratosan lay slumped next to its sandbagged wall, alive but barely moving. Kadai watched the trooper's hand flick up for the third time as he signalled for aid.

Something didn't feel right.

The trooper's movements were limp, but somehow forced.

Sudden unease creeping into the pit of his stomach, Kadai realised it was a trap.

'Fugis, stop!' he yelled into the comm-feed.

'I'm almost there, captain...'

'Apothecary, obey my ord–'

The roar of a huge fireball billowing out from the emplacement cut Kadai off. Fugis was lifted off his feet by the blast wave, the slain Stratosans buoyed up with him like broken dolls. Chained detonations ripped up the road, rupturing rockcrete, as an entire section of it broke apart and fell away creating a huge chasm.

Flattened by the immense explosion, Captain Kadai was still struggling to his feet, shaking off the blast disorientation, when he saw Fugis lying on his chest, armour blackened by fire, gripping the edge of the artificial crater made during the explosion. Kadai cried out as the Apothecary lost his hold and slipped down into the gaping black abyss of Cirrion's underbelly, vanishing from sight.

From the hidden darkness of the city, the depraved cultists swarmed into the night and the shooting began...

Shrugging off the effects of the explosion, Dak'ir saw figures moving through the settling dust and smoke.

One loomed over him. Its mouth was stitched with black wire; blue veins infected its cheeks. Eyes filled with fervour, the cultist drove a pickaxe against the Space Marine's armour. The puny weapon broke apart on impact.

'Salamanders,' roared Dak'ir, rallying his squad as he pulverised the cultist's face with an armoured fist. He took up his chainsword, which had spilled from his grip in the blast, eviscerating three more insurgents as they came at him with cudgels and blades.

Reaching for his plasma pistol, he stopped short. The atmospheric readings in his battle-helm were showing a massive concentration of hydrogen; the air inside the dome was saturated with it.

To Dak'ir's left flank, Ba'ken was levelling his heavy flamer as a massive surge of cultists spilled into the hall...

'Wai–'

'Cleanse and burn!'

As soon as the incendiary hit the air, the weapon exploded. Ba'ken was engulfed in white fire then smashed sideways, through the rockcrete wall and into an adjoining chamber where he lay unmoving.

'Brother down!' bellowed Dak'ir, Emek offering suppressing fire with his bolter as he came forward, chewing up cultists like meat sacks.

More were piling through in a steady stream, seemingly unaffected by the bolt storm. Picks and blades gave way to heavy stubbers and autocannons, and Dak'ir saw the first wave for what it was: a flesh shield.

Another Salamander came up on the sergeant's other flank, Brother Ak'sor. He was readying his flamer when Dak'ir shouted into the comm-feed.

'Stow all flamers and meltas... the air thick with a gaseous hydrogen amalgam. Bolters and secondary weapons only.'

The Salamanders obeyed at once.

The press of cultists came on thickly now, small-arms fire whickering from their ranks as the heavy weapons were prepared to shoot. Dak'ir severed the head from one insurgent and punched through the sternum of another.

'Hold them,' he snapped, withdrawing a bloody fist.

Ak'sor had pulled out a bolt pistol. Bullets pattered against his armour as he let rip, chewing up a bunch of cultists with autoguns. The dull *thump-thud* of the heavier cannons starting up filled the room and Ak'sor staggered as multiple rounds struck him. From somewhere in the melee, a gas-propelled grenade whined and Ak'sor disappeared behind exploding shrapnel. When the smoke had cleared, the Salamander was down.

'Retreat to the lobby, all Salamanders,' shouted Dak'ir, solid shot rebounding off his armour as he hacked down another cultist that came within his death arc.

The Astartes fell back as one, two battle-brothers coming forward to drag Ba'ken and Ak'sor from the battle. As Dak'ir's squad reached the stairs and started to climb down, Sergeant Lok rushed in. Due to the presence of the explosive hydrogen gas the Incinerators were down to a single heavy bolter, strafing the doorway and ripping up cultists with a punishing salvo.

There was scant respite as the enemy pressed its advantage, wired-mouthed maniacs hurling themselves into the furious bolter fire in their droves. Brother Ionnes was chewing through the belt feed of his heavy bolter with abandon, his fellow Salamanders adding their own weapons to the barrage, but the cultists came on still. Like automatons, they refused to yield to panic, the fates of their shattered brethren failing to stall, let alone rout them.

'They're unbreakable!' bellowed Lok, smashing an insurgent to pulp with his power fist, whilst firing his bolter one-handed. A chainsaw struck his outstretched arm seemingly from nowhere and he grimaced, his weapon falling from nerveless fingers. Red-eyed eviscerator priests were moving through the throng, wielding immense double-handed chainblades. Dak'ir crushed the zealot's skull with a punch, but realised they were slowly being enveloped.

'Back to the entrance,' he cried, taking up Lok's fallen bolter and spraying an arc of fire across his left flank. The ones he killed didn't even scream. Step by agonising step, the Salamanders withdrew. There was a veritable bullet hail coming from the enemy now, whose numbers seemed limitless and came from every direction at once.

Inside the comm-feed it was chaos. Fragmented reports came in, plagued by static interference, from both *Anvil* and *Hammer*.

'Heavy casualties… enemy armour moving in… thousands everywhere… brother down!'

'Captain Kadai…' Dak'ir yelled into the vox. 'Brother-captain, this is *Flame*. Please respond.'

After a long minute, Kadai's broken reply came back.

'Kadai… here… Fall… back… regroup… Aereon Square…'

'Captain, I have two battle-brothers badly injured and in need of medical attention.'

Another thirty seconds passed, before another stuttering response.

'Apothecary… lost… Repeat… Fugis is gone…'

Gone. Not wounded or down, just gone. Dak'ir felt a ball of hot pain develop in his chest. Stoic resolve outweighed his anger – he gave the order for a fighting withdrawal to Aereon Square, and then raised Tsu'gan on the comm-feed.

'VULKAN'S BLOOD! I will not retreat in the face of this rabble,' Tsu'gan snarled at Iagon. 'Tell the Ignean, I have received no such order.'

Anvil had, under Tsu'gan's steely leadership, broken free of the ambush without casualties, though Brother Honorious was limping badly and Sergeant Ul'shan had lost an eye when the trans-loader hit and the drums of incendiary heaped onboard had exploded.

Without use of their multi-meltas, Tsu'gan had torn through the vehicle wreckage himself, scything cultists down on the other side with his combi-bolter. They were falling back to defended positions in the wider street beyond when Dak'ir's message came through.

At some point during the fighting, Tsu'gan had damaged his battle-helm and he'd torn it off. Since then he'd been relying on Iagon for communication with the other assault groups.

'We are Salamanders, born in fire,' he raged zealously, 'the anvil upon which our enemies are broken. We do not yield. *Ever!*'

Iagon dutifully relayed the message, indicating his sergeant's refusal to comply.

Further up the street, something loud and heavy was rumbling towards them. It broke Tsu'gan's stride for just a moment as a tank, festooned with armour plates and daubed with the gaping maw symbol of the Cult of Truth, came into view. Swinging around its fat metal turret, the tank's battle cannon fired, jetting smoke and rocking the vehicle back on its tracks.

Tsu'gan had his warriors in a defensive battle line, strafing the oncoming cultist hordes with controlled bursts of bolter fire. The tank shell hit with all the force of a thunderbolt, and tore the ragged line apart.

Salamanders were tossed into the air with chunks of rockcrete chewed out of the road, and fell like debris.

'Close ranks. Hold positions,' Tsu'gan snarled, crouching down next to a partially destroyed barricade once occupied by Stratosan Aircorps.

Iagon shoved one of the bodies out of the way, so he could rest his bolter in a makeshift firing lip.

'Still nothing from the captain,' he said between bursts.

Tsu'gan's reaction to the news was guarded, his face fixed in a perpetual scowl.

'Ul'shan,' he barked to the sergeant of the Devastators, 'all fire on that tank. In the name of Vulkan, destroy it.'

Bolter fire *pranged* against the implacable vehicle, grinding forward as it readied for another shot with its battle cannon. In the turret, a crazed cultist took up the heavy stubber and started hosing the Salamanders with solid shot.

'You others,' bellowed Tsu'gan, standing up and unhitching something from his belt, 'grenades on my lead.' He launched a krak grenade overarm. It soared through the air at speed, impelled by Tsu'gan's strength, and rolled into the tank's path. Several more followed, *thunking* to earth like metal hail.

At the same time, Iagon's bolter fire shredded the cultist in the stubber nest, whilst Sergeant Ul'shan's heavy bolters hammered the tank's front armour and tracks. An explosive round from the salvo clipped one of the krak grenades just as the armoured vehicle was driving over it. A chained detonation tore through the tank as the incendiaries exploded, ripping it wide open.

'Glory to Prometheus!' roared Tsu'gan, punching the air as his warriors chorused after him.

His fervour was dampened when he saw shadows moving through the smoke and falling shrapnel. Three more tanks trundled into view.

Tsu'gan shook his head in disbelief.

'*Mercy of Vulkan...*' he breathed, just as the comm-link with Captain Kadai was restored. The sergeant glared at Iagon with iron-hard eyes.

They were falling back to Aereon Square.

Dak'ir had been right. Tsu'gan felt his jaw tighten.

'Hold the line!' Kadai bellowed into the comm-feed. 'We make our stand here.'

The Salamanders held position stoically, strung out across the chewed-up defences, controlled bursts thundering from their bolters. Behind them were the armoured transports. Storm bolters shuddered from turret mounts on the Rhinos and *Fire Anvil*'s twin-linked assault cannon whirred in a frenzy of heavy fire, though the Land Raider's flamestorm side sponsons were powered down.

The Salamanders had converged quickly on Aereon Square, the fighting withdrawal of the three assault groups less cautious than their original attack.

The slab floor of the square was cratered by bomb blasts and fire-blackened. Fallen pillars from adjacent buildings intruded on its perimeter. The centre of the broad plaza was dominated by a felled statue of one of Stratos's Imperial leaders, encircled by a damaged perimeter wall. It was here that Kadai and his warriors made their stand.

The cultists came on in the face of heavy fire, swarming from every avenue, every alcove, like hell-born ants. Hundreds were slain in minutes. But despite the horrendous casualties, they were undeterred and made slow progress across the killing ground. The corpses piled up like sandbags at the edge of the square.

'None shall pass, Fire-born!' raged Kadai, the furious zeal of Vulkan, his progenitor, filling him with righteous purpose. *Endure* – it was one of the central tenets of the Promethean Cult, *endure and conquer*.

The bullet storms crossed each other over a shortening distance as the cultist thousands poured intense fire into the Salamanders' defensive positions. Chunks of perimeter wall, and massive sections of the fallen statue, were chipped apart in the maelstrom.

Brother Zo'tan took a round in the left pauldron, then another in the neck, grunted and fell to his knees. Dak'ir moved to cover him, armour shuddering as he let rip with a borrowed bolter. Insurgent bodies were destroyed in the furious barrage, torn apart by explosive rounds, sundered by salvos from heavy bolters, shredded by the withering hail from assault cannons whining red-hot.

Still the cultists came.

Dak'ir gritted his teeth and roared.

'No retreat!'

Slowly, inevitably, the hordes began to thin. Kadai ordered a halt to the sustained barrage. Like smoke, dispersing from a doused pyre, the insurgents were drifting away, backing off silently into the gloom until they were at last gone from sight.

The tenacity of the Salamanders had kept the foe at bay this time. Aereon Square was held.

'Are they giving up?' asked Dak'ir, breathing hard underneath his power armour as he tried to slow his body down from its ultra-heightened battle-state.

'They crawl back to their nests,' Kadai growled. His jaw clenched with impotent anger. 'The city is theirs... for now.'

Stalking from the defence line, Kadai quickly set up sentries to watch the approaches to the square, whilst at the same time contacting Techmarine Argos to send reinforcements from *Vulkan's Wrath*, and a Thunderhawk to extract the dead and wounded. The toll was much heavier than he had expected. Fourteen wounded and six dead. Most keenly felt of all, though, was the loss of Fugis.

The Salamanders were a small Chapter, their near-annihilation during one of the worst atrocities of the Heresy, when they were betrayed by their erstwhile brothers, still felt some ten thousand years later. They had been Legion then, but now they were merely some eight hundred Astartes. Induction of new recruits was slow and only compounded their low fighting strength.

Without their Apothecary and his prodigious medical skills, the most severe injuries suffered by Kadai's Third Company would remain untended and further debilitate their combat effectiveness. Worse still, the gene-seeds of those killed in action would be unharvested, for only Fugis possessed the knowledge and ability to remove these progenoids safely. And it was through these precious organs that future Space Marines were engineered, allowing even the slain to serve their Chapter in death.

The losses suffered by Third Company then became permanent with the loss of their Apothecary, a solemn fact that put Kadai in a black mood.

'We will re-assault the city proper as soon as we're reinforced,' he raged.

'We should level the full weight of the company against them. Then these heretics will break,' asserted Tsu'gan, clenching a fist to emphasise his vehemence.

Both he and Dak'ir accompanied Kadai as he walked from the battle line, leaving Veteran Sergeant N'keln to organise the troops. The captain unclasped his battle-helm to remove it. His white crest of hair was damp with sweat. His eyes glowed hotly, emanating anger.

'Yes, they will learn that the Salamanders do not yield easily.'

Tsu'gan grinned ferally at that.

Dak'ir thought only of the brothers they had already lost, and the others that would fall in another hard-headed assault. The traitors were dug-in and had numbers – without flamers to flush out ambushers and other traps, breaking Cirrion would be tough.

Then something happened that forestalled the captain's belligerent plan for vengeance. Far across Aereon Square, figures were emerging through the smoke and dust. They crept from their hiding places and shambled towards the Salamanders, shoulders slumped in despair.

Dak'ir's eyes widened when he saw how many there were, 'Survivors... the civilians of Cirrion.'

'Open it,' rasped the dragon giant. His scaled armour coursed with eldritch energy, throwing sharp flashes of light into the gloom. He and his warriors had reached a subterranean metal chamber that ended in an immense portal of heavy plasteel.

Another giant wearing the red-scaled plate came forward. Tendrils of smoke emanated from the grille in his horned helmet. The silence of the outer vault was broken by the hissing, crackling intake of breath before the horned one unleashed a furious plume of flame. It surged hungrily through the grille-plate in a roar, smashing against the vault door and devouring it.

Reinforced plasteel bars blackened and corroded in seconds, layers of ablative ceramite melted away, before the adamantium plate of the door itself glowed white-hot and sloughed into molten slag.

The warriors had travelled swiftly through the mag-tram tunnel, forging deep into the lesser known corridors of Cirrion. None had seen them approach. Their leader had made certain that the earlier massacre left no witnesses. After almost an hour, they had reached their destination. Here, in the catacombs of the city, the hydrogen gas clouds could not penetrate. They were far from the fighting; the battles going on in the distant districts of Cirrion were dull and faraway through many layers of rockcrete and metal.

'Is it here?' asked a third warrior as the ragged portal into the vault cooled, his voice like crackling magma. Inside were hundreds of tiny strongboxes, held here for the aristocracy of Stratos so they could secure that which they held most precious. No one could have known of the artefact that dwelled innocuously in one of those boxes. Even upon seeing it, few would have realised its significance, the terrible destructive forces it could unleash.

'Oh yes...' replied the eldritch warrior, closing crimson-lidded eyes as he drew of his power. 'It is exactly where he said it would be.'

DESPERATE AND DISHEVELLED, the Stratosan masses tramped into Aereon Square.

Most wore little more than rags, the scraps of whatever clothed them when the cultists had taken over the city. Some clutched the tattered remnants of scorched belongings, the last vestiges of whatever life they once had in Cirrion now little more than ashen remains. Many had strips of dirty cloth or ragged scarves tied around their noses and mouths to keep out the worst of the suffocating hydrogen gas. A few wore battered respirators, and shared them with others; small groups taking turns with the rebreather cups. The hydrogen had no such ill-effects on the Salamanders, their Astartes multi-lung and oolitic kidney acting in concert to portion off and siphon out any toxins, thus enabling them to breathe normally.

'An entire city paralysed by terror...' said Ba'ken as another piece of shrapnel was removed from his face.

The burly Salamander was sat up against the perimeter wall, and being tended to by Brother Emek who had some rudimentary knowledge of field surgery. Ba'ken's battle-helm had all but shattered in the explosion that destroyed his beloved heavy flamer and, after being propelled through the wall, fragments of it were still embedded in his flesh.

'This is but the first of them, brother,' replied Dak'ir, regarding the weary passage of the survivors with pity as they passed the Salamander sentries.

Aereon Square was slowly filling. Dak'ir followed the trail of pitiful wretches being led away in huddled throngs by Stratosan Aircorps to the Cirrion gate. From there he knew an armoured battalion idled, ready to escort the survivors across the sky-bridge and into the relative safety of Nimbaros. Almost a hundred had already been moved and more still were massing in the square as the Aircorps struggled to cope with them all.

'Why show themselves now?' asked Ba'ken, with a nod to Emek who took his leave having finally excised all the jutting shrapnel. The wounds were already healing; the Larraman cells in Ba'ken's Astartes blood accelerating clotting and scarring, the ossmodula implanted in his brain encouraging rapid bone growth and regeneration.

Dak'ir shrugged. 'The enemy's withdrawal to consolidate whatever ground they hold, together with our arrival must have galvanised them, I suppose. Made them reach out for salvation.'

'It is a grim sight.'

'Yes...' Dak'ir agreed, suddenly lost in thought. The war on Stratos had suddenly adopted a different face entirely now: not one bound by wire or infected by taint, but one that pleaded for deliverance, that had given all there was to give, a face that was ordinary and innocent, and afraid. As he watched the human detritus tramp by, the sergeant took in the rest of the encampment.

The perimeter wall formed a kind of demarcation line, dividing the territory of the Salamanders and that held by the Cult of Truth. Kadai was adamant they would hold onto it. A pair of Thunderfire cannons patrolled the area on grinding tracks, servos whirring as their Techmarines cycled the cannons through various firing routines.

Brother Argos had arrived in Aereon Square within the hour, bringing the artillery and his fellow Techmarines with him.

There would be no further reinforcements.

Ferocious lightning storms were wreaking havoc in the upper atmosphere of Stratos, caused by a blanketing of thermal low pressure emanating off the chlorine-rich oceans. Any descent by Thunderhawks was impossible, and all off-planet communication was hindered massively. Kadai and the Salamanders who had made the initial planetfall were alone – a fact they bore stoically. It would have to be enough.

'How many of our fallen brothers will be for the long dark?' Ba'ken's voice called Dak'ir back. The burly Salamander was staring at the medi-caskets of the dead and severely wounded, aligned together on the far side of the perimeter wall. 'I hope I will never suffer that fate...' he confessed in a whisper. 'Entombed within a Dreadnought. An existence without sensation, as the world dims around me, enduring forever in a cold sarcophagus. I would rather the fires of battle claim me first.'

'It is an honour to serve the Chapter eternally, Ba'ken,' Dak'ir admonished, though his reproach was mild. 'In any case, we don't know what their fates will be,' he added, 'save for that of the dead...'

The fallen warriors of Third Company were awaiting transit to Nimbaros. Here, they would be kept secure aboard *Fire-wyvern* until the storms abated and the Thunderhawk could return them to the *Vulkan's Wrath* where they would be interred in the strike cruiser's *pyreum*.

All Salamanders, once their progenoids had been removed, were incinerated in the pyreum, still wearing their armour, their ashes offered in Promethean ritual to honour the heroic dead and empower the spirits of the living. Such practices were only ever conducted by a Chaplain, and since Elysius was not with the company at this time, the ashen remains would be stored in the strike cruiser's crematoria until he rejoined them or they returned to Nocturne.

Such morbid thoughts inevitably led to Fugis, and the Apothecary's untimely demise.

'I spoke to him before the mission, before he died,' said Dak'ir, his eyes far away.

'Who?'

'Fugis. In the isolation chamber aboard the *Vulkan's Wrath*.'

Ba'ken stood up and reached for his pauldron, easing the stiffness from his back and shoulders. The left one had been dislocated before Brother Emek had righted it, and Ba'ken's pauldron had been removed to do it.

'What did he say?' he asked, affixing the armour expertly.

Not all of us want *to be brought back. Not all of us* can *be brought back.*

'Something I will not forget...'

Dak'ir shook his head slowly, his gaze fixed on the darkness beyond Aereon Square. 'I do not think we are alone here, Ba'ken,' he said at length.

'Clearly not – we fight a horde of thousands.'

'No... There is something else, too.'

Ba'ken frowned. 'And what is that, brother?'

Dak'ir voice was hard as stone, 'Something worse.'

THE INTERIOR OF the *Fire Anvil*'s troop hold was aglow as Dak'ir entered the Land Raider. A revolving schematic in the middle of the hold threw off harsh blue light, bathing the metal chamber and the Astartes gathered within. The four Salamanders present had already removed battle-helms. Their eyes burned warmly in the semi-darkness, at odds with the cold light of the hololith depicting Cirrion.

Summoned at Kadai's request, Dak'ir had left Ba'ken at the perimeter wall to rearm himself, ready for the next assault on Cirrion.

'Without flamers and meltas we face a much sterner test here,' Kadai said, nodding to acknowledge Dak'ir's arrival, as did N'keln.

Tsu'gan offered no such geniality, and merely scowled.

'Tactically, we can hold Aereon Square almost indefinitely,' Kadai continued. 'Thunderfire cannons will bulwark our defensive line, even without reinforcement from the *Vulkan's Wrath* to compensate for our losses. Deeper penetration into the city, however, will not be easy.'

The denial of reinforcements was a bitter blow, and Kadai had been incensed at the news. But the granite-hard pragmatist in him, the Salamander spirit of self-reliance and self-sacrifice, proved the stronger and so he had put his mind to the task at hand using the forces he did possess. In response to the casualties, Kadai had combined the three groups of Devastators into two squads under Lok and Omkar, Ul'shan with his injury deferring to the other two sergeants. Without reinforcements, the Tactical squads would simply have to soak up their losses.

'With Fugis gone, I'm reluctant to risk more of our battle-brothers heading into the unknown,' Kadai said, the shadows in his face making him look haunted. 'The heretics are entrenched and well-armed. We are few. This would present little impediment should we have the use of our flamers, but we do not.'

'Is there a way to purify the atmosphere?' asked N'keln. He wheezed from a chest wound he'd sustained during the withdrawal to Aereon Square. N'keln was a solid, dependable warrior, but leadership did not come easily to him and he lacked the guile for higher command. Still, his bravery had been proven time and again, and was above reproach. It was an obvious but necessary question.

Brother Argos stepped forward into the reflected light of the schematic.

The Techmarine went unhooded. The left portion of his face was framed with a steel plate, the snarling image of a salamander seared into it as an honour marking. Burn scars from the brander-priests wreathed his skin in whorls and bands. A bionic eye gleamed coldly in contrast to the burning red of his own. Forked plugs bulged from a glabrous scalp like steel tumours, and wires snaked around the side of his neck and fed into his nose.

When he spoke, his voice was deep and metallic.

'The hydrogen emissions being controlled by Cirrion's atmospheric processors are a gaseous amalgam used to inflate the Stratosan dirigibles – a less volatile compound, and the reason why bolters are still functioning normally. Though I have managed to access some of the city's internal systems, the processors are beyond my knowledge to affect. It would require a local engineer, someone who maintained the system originally. Unfortunately, there is simply no way to find anyone with the proper skills, either alive amongst the survivors or amongst those still trapped in the city.' Argos paused. 'I am sorry, brothers, but any use of incendiary weapons in the city at this time would be catastrophic.'

'One thing is certain,' Kadai continued, 'the appearance of civilian survivors effectively prevents any massed assault. I won't jeopardise innocent lives needlessly.'

Tsu'gan shook his head.

'Brother-captain, with respect, if we do not act the collateral damage will be much worse. Our only recourse is to lead a single full-strength force into Cirrion, and sack it. The insurgents will not expect such a bold move.'

'We are not inviolable against their weapons,' Dak'ir countered. 'It is not only the Stratosans you risk with such a plan. What of my battle-brothers? Their duty ended in death. You would add more to that tally? Our resources are stretched thin enough as it is.'

Tsu'gan's face contorted with anger.

'Sons of Vulkan,' he cried, smacking the plastron of his power armour with his palms, 'Fire-born,' he added, clenching a fist, '*that* is what we are. Unto the Anvil of War, that is our creed. I do not fear battle and death, even if you do, Ignean.'

'I fear nothing,' snarled Dak'ir. 'But I won't cast my brothers into the furnace for no reason, either.'

'Enough!' The captain's voice demanded the attention of the bickering sergeants at once. Kadai glared at them both, eyes burning with fury at such disrespect for a fellow battle-brother. 'Dispense with this enmity,' he warned, exhaling his anger. 'It will not be tolerated. We have our enemy.'

The sergeants bowed apologetically, but stared daggers at each other before they stood down.

'There will be no massed assault,' Kadai reasserted. 'But that is not to say we will not act, either. These heretics are single-minded to the point of insanity, driven by some external force. No ideology, however fanatical, could impel such... madness,' he added, echoing Fugis's earlier theory. The corner of Kadai's mouth twinged in a brief moment of remembrance. 'The hierophant of the cult, this Speaker, is the key to victory on Stratos.'

'An assassination,' stated Tsu'gan, folding his arms in approval.

Kadai nodded.

'Brother Argos has discovered a structure at the heart of the temple district called Aura Hieron. Colonel Tonnhauser's intelligence has this demagogue there. We will make for it.' The captain's gaze encompassed the entire room. 'Two combat squads made up from the Devastators will be left behind with Brother Argos, who will be guiding us as before. This small force, together with the Thunderfire cannons will hold Aereon Square and protect the emerging survivors.'

Tsu'gan scowled at this.

'Aereon Square is like a refugee camp as it is. The Air-corps cannot move the survivors fast enough. All they are doing is getting in our way. Our mission is to crush this horde, and free this place from terror. How can we do that if we split our forces protecting the humans? We should take every battle-brother we have.'

Kadai leaned forward. His eyes were like fiery coals and seemed to chase away the cold light of the hololith.

'I will not abandon them, Tsu'gan. We are not the Marines Malevolent, nor the Flesh Tearers nor any of our other bloodletting brothers. Ours is a different creed, one of which we Salamanders are rightly proud. We will protect the innocent if–'

The *Fire Anvil* was rocked by a sudden tremor, and the dull *crump* of an explosion came through its armoured hull from the outside.

Brother Argos lowered the ramp at once and the Salamanders rushed outside to find out what had happened.

Fire and smoke lined a blackened crater in the centre of Aereon Square. The mangled corpses of several Stratosan civilians, together with a number of Aircorps were strewn within it, their bodies broken by a bomb blast. A woman screamed from the opposite side of the square. She'd fallen, having tried to flee from another of the survivors who was inexplicably clutching a frag grenade.

Tsu'gan's combi-bolter was in his hands almost immediately and he shot the man through the chest. The grenade fell from the insurgent's grasp and went off.

The fleeing woman and several others were engulfed by the explosion. The screaming intensified.

Kadai bellowed for order, even as his sergeants went to join their battle-brothers in quelling the sudden panic.

Several cultists had infiltrated the survivor groups, intent on causing anarchy and massed destruction. They had succeeded. Respirator masks were the perfect disguise for their 'afflictions', bypassing the Stratosan soldiery and even the Astartes.

Ko'tan Kadai knelt with the broken woman in his grasp, having gone to her when the smoke was still dissipating from the explosion. She looked frail and thin compared to his Astartes bulk, as if the rest of her unbroken bones would shatter at his slightest touch. Yet, they did not. He held her delicately, as a father might cradle a child. She lasted only moments, eyes fearful, spitting blood from massive internal trauma.

'Brother-captain?' ventured N'keln, appearing at his side.

Kadai laid the dead woman down gently and rose to his full height. A thin line of crimson dotted his ebon face, the horror there having ebbed away, replaced by anger.

'Two combat squads,' he asserted, his iron-hard gaze finding Tsu'gan, who was close enough to hear him, but wisely displayed no discontent. 'Everyone is screened... *Everyone.*'

'Now we know why the survivors came out of hiding. The cultists wanted them to, so they could do this...'

Ba'ken said softly to Dak'ir as the two Salamanders looked on.

Kadai touched the blood on his face then saw it on his fingers as if for the first time.

'We need only get a kill-team close enough to the Speaker to execute him and the cultists' resolve will fracture,' he promised. 'We move out now.'

FIVE KILOMETRES FILLED with razor wire, pit falls and partially-demolished streets. Cultist murder squads dredging the ruins for survivors to torture; human bombers hiding in alcoves, trembling fingers wrapped around grenade pins; eviscerator priests leading flocks with wire-sewn mouths. It was the most expedient route Techmarine Argos could find in order for his battle-brothers to reach Aura Hieron.

Only two kilometres down that hellish road, after fighting through ambushes and weathering continual booby traps, the Salamanders' assault had reached yet another impasse.

They stood before a long but narrow esplanade of churned plascrete. Labyrinthine track traps were dug in every three or four metres, crowned with spools of razor wire. The bulky black carapaces of partially submerged mines shone dully like the backs of tunnelling insects. Death pits were excavated throughout, well-hidden with guerrilla cunning.

A killing field; and they had to cross it in order to reach Aura Hieron. At the end of it was a thick grey line of rock-crete bunkers, fortified with armour plates. From slits in the sides constant tracer fire rattled, accompanied by the throbbing *thud-chank* of heavy cannon. The no-man's-land was blanketed by fire that lit up the darkness in gruesome monochrome.

The Salamanders were not the first to have come this way. The corpses of Stratosan soldiers littered the ground too, as ubiquitous and lifeless as sandbags.

'There is no way around.' Dak'ir's reconnaissance report was curt, having tried, but failed, to find a different angle of attack to exploit. In such a narrow cordon, barely wide enough for ten Space Marines to operate in, the Salamanders' combat effectiveness was severely hampered.

Captain Kadai stared grimly into the maelstrom. The Inferno Guard and Sergeant Omkar's Devastators were at his side, awaiting their rotation at the front.

No more than fifty metres ahead of them Tsu'gan and his squad were hunkered down behind a cluster of tank traps returning fire, Sergeant Lok and his Devastators providing support with heavy bolters. Each painful metre had been paid for with blood, and three of Tsu'gan's troopers were already wounded, but he was determined to gain more ground and get close enough to launch an offensive with krak grenades.

The battle line was stretched. They had gone as far as they could go, short of risking massive casualties by charging the cultists' guns head on. The insurgents were so well protected they were only visible as shadows until their twisted faces were lit by muzzle flashes.

Kadai was scouring the battle line, searching for weaknesses.

'What did you find, sergeant?' he asked.

'Only impassable blockades and un-crossable chasms, stretching for kilometres east and west,' Dak'ir replied. 'We could turn back, captain, get Argos to find another route?'

'I've seen fortifications erected by the Imperial Fists that put up less resistance,' Kadai muttered to himself, then turned to Dak'ir. 'No. We break them here or not at all.'

Dak'ir was about to respond when Tsu'gan's voice came through the comm-feed.

'Captain, we can make five more metres. Requesting the order to advance.'

'Denied. Get back here, sergeant, and tell Lok to hold the line. We need a new plan.'

A momentary pause in communication made Tsu'gan's discontent obvious, but his respect for Kadai was absolute.

'At once, my lord.'

'WE NEED TO get close enough to attack the wall with krak grenades and breach it,' said Tsu'gan, having returned to the Salamanders' second line to join up with Dak'ir and Kadai, leaving Lok to hold the front. 'A determined frontal assault is the only way to do it.'

'A charge across the killing ground is insane, Tsu'gan,' countered Dak'ir.

'We are wasting our ammunition pinned here,' Tsu'gan argued. 'What else would you suggest?'

'There must be another way,' Dak'ir insisted.

'Withdraw,' Tsu'gan answered simply, allowing a moment for it to sink in. 'Loath as I am to do it. If we cannot break through, then Cirrion is lost. Withdraw and summon the *Fire-wyvern*,' he said to Kadai. 'Use its missile payload to destroy the gravitic engines and send this hellish place to the ocean.'

The captain was reticent to agree.

'I would be condemning thousands of innocents to death.'

'And saving millions,' urged Tsu'gan. 'If a world is tainted beyond redemption or lost to invasion we annihilate it, excising its stain from the galaxy like a cancer. It should be no different for a city. Stratos *can* be saved. Cirrion cannot.'

'You speak of wholesale slaughter as if it is a casual thing, Tsu'gan,' Kadai replied.

'Ours is a warrior's lot, my lord. We were made to fight and to kill, to bring order in the Emperor's name.'

Kadai's voice grew hard.

'I know our purpose, sergeant. Do not presume to tell me of it.'

Tsu'gan bowed humbly.

'I meant no offence, my lord.'

Kadai was angry because he knew that Tsu'gan was right. Cirrion *was* lost. Sighing deeply, he opened the comm-feed, extending the link beyond the city.

'We will need Brother Argos to engage the Stratosan failsafe and blow the sky-bridges connecting Cirrion first, or it will take an entire chunk of the adjacent cities with it,' he said out loud to himself, before reverting to the comm-feed.

'Brother Hek'en.'

The pilot of the *Fire-wyvern* responded. The Thunderhawk was at rest on the landing platform just outside Nimbaros.

'My lord.'

'Prepare for imminent take off, and prime hellstrike missiles. We're abandoning the city. You'll have my orders within–'

The comm-feed crackling to life again in Kadai's battle-helm interrupted him. The crippling interference made it difficult to discern a voice at first, but when Kadai recognised it he felt his hot Salamander blood grow cold.

It was Fugis. The Apothecary was alive.

'I BLACKED OUT after the fall. When I awoke I was in the sub-levels of the city. They stretch down for about two kilometres, deep enough for the massive lifter-engines. It's like a damn labyrinth,' Fugis explained with his usual choler.

'Are you injured, brother?' asked Kadai.

Silence persisted, laced with static, and for a moment he thought they'd lost the Apothecary again.

'I took some damage, my battle-helm too. It's taken me this long to repair the comm-feed,' Fugis returned at last. In the short pauses it was possible to hear his breathing. It was irregular and ragged. The Apothecary was trying to mask his pain.

'What is your exact location, Fugis?'

Static interference marred the connection again.

'It's a tunnel complex below the surface. But it could be anywhere.'

Kadai turned to Dak'ir. 'Contact Brother Argos. Have him lock on to Fugis's signal and send us the coordinates.'

Dak'ir nodded and set about his task, all the while heavy cannon were chugging overhead.

'Listen,' said Fugis, the crackling static worsening, 'I am not alone. There are civilians. They fled down here when the attacks began, and stayed hidden until now.'

There was another short silence as the Apothecary considered his next statement.

'The city is still not ours.'

Kadai explained the situation with the hydrogen gas amalgam on the surface, how they could not use their flamers or meltas, and that it only compounded the fact that the cultists were well-prepared and dug in. 'It is almost as if they know our tactics,' he concluded.

'The gas has not penetrated this deep,' Fugis told him. 'But I may have a way to stop it.'

'How, brother?' asked Kadai, fresh hope filling his voice.

'A human engineer. Some of the refugees were fleeing from the gas as well as the insurgents. His name is Banen. If we get him out of the city and to the Techmarine, Cirrion can be purged.' A pregnant pause suggested an imminent sting. 'But there is a price,' Fugis explained through bursts of interference.

Kadai's jaw clenched beneath his battle-helm.

There always is...

The Apothecary went on.

'In order to cleanse Cirrion of the gas, the entire air supply must be vented. Its atmospheric integrity will be utterly compromised. With the air so thin, many will suffocate before it can be restored. Humans hiding in the outer reaches of the city, away from the hot core of the lifter-engines, will also likely freeze to death.'

Kadai's brief optimism was quickly crushed.

'To save Cirrion, I must doom its people.'

'Some may survive,' offered Fugis, though his words lacked conviction.

'A few at best,' Kadai concluded. 'It is no choice.'

Destroying the city's gravitic engines had been bad enough. This seemed worse. The Salamanders, a Chapter which prided itself on its humanitarianism, its pledge to protect the weak and the innocent, was merely exchanging one holocaust for another.

Kadai gripped the haft of his thunder hammer. It was black, and its head was thick and heavy like the ready tool of a forgesmith. He had fashioned it this way in the depths of Nocturne, the lava flows from the mountain casting his onyx flesh in an orange glow. Kadai longed to return there, to the anvil and the heat of the forge. The hammer was a symbol. It was like the weapon Vulkan had first taken up in defence of his adopted homeworld. In it Kadai found resolve and in turn the strength he needed to do what he must.

'We are coming for you, brother,' he said with steely determination. 'Protect the engineer. Have him ready to be extracted upon our arrival.'

'I will hold on as long as I can.'

White noise resumed.

Kadai felt the weight of resignation around his shoulders like a heavy mantle.

'Brother Argos has locked the signal and fed it to our auspex,' Dak'ir told him, wresting the Salamander captain from his dark reverie.

Kadai nodded grimly.

'Sergeants, break into combat squads. The rest stay here,' he said, summoning his second in command.

'N'keln,' Kadai addressed the veteran sergeant. 'You will lead the expedition to rescue Fugis.'

Tsu'gan interjected.

'My lord?'

'Once we make a move the insurgents will almost certainly redirect their forces away from here. We cannot hold them by merely standing our ground,' Kadai explained. 'We need their attention fixed where we want it. I intend to achieve that by charging the wall.'

'Captain, that is suicide,' Dak'ir told him plainly.

'Perhaps. But I cannot risk bringing the enemy to Fugis, to the human engineer. His survival is of the utmost importance. Self-sacrifice is the Promethean way, sergeant, you know that.'

'With respect, captain,' said N'keln. 'Brother Malicant and I wish to stay behind and fight with the others.'

Malicant, the company banner bearer, nodded solemnly behind the veteran sergeant.

Both Salamanders had been wounded in the ill-fated campaign to liberate Cirrion. Malicant leaned heavily on the company banner from a leg wound he had sustained during the bomb blast in Aereon Square, whereas N'keln grimaced with the pain of his crushed ribs.

Kadai was incensed.

'You disobey my orders, sergeant?'

N'keln stood his ground despite his captain's ire.

'Yes, my lord.'

Kadai glared at him, but his anger bled away as he realised the sense in the veteran sergeant's words and clasped N'keln by the shoulder.

'Hold off as long as you can. Advance only when you must, and strike swiftly. You may yet get past the guns unscathed,' Kadai told him. 'You honour the Chapter with your sacrifice.'

N'keln rapped his fist against his plastron in salute and then he and Malicant went to join the others already at the battle line.

'Make it an act of honour,' he said to the others as they watched the two Salamanders go. They were singular warriors. All his battle-brothers were. Kadai was intensely proud of each and every one. 'Fugis is waiting. Into the fires of battle, brothers...'

'Unto the anvil of war,' they declared solemnly as one.

The Salamanders turned away without looking back, leaving their brothers to their fate.

THE TUNNELS WERE deserted.

Ba'ken tracked his heavy bolter across the darkness, his battle-senses ultra-heightened with tension.

'Too quiet...'

'You would prefer a fight?' Dak'ir returned over the comm-feed.

'Yes,' Ba'ken answered honestly.

The sergeant was a few metres in front of him, the Salamanders having broken into two long files, either side of the tunnel. Each Space Marine maintained a distance of a few metres from the battle-brother ahead, watching his back and flanks in case of ambush. Helmet luminators strafed the darkened corridors, creating imagined hazards in the gathered shadows.

The Salamanders had followed the Apothecary's signal like a beacon. It had led them south at first, back the way they had come, to a hidden entrance into the Cirrion sub-levels. The tunnels were myriad and did not appear on any city schematic, so Argos had no knowledge of them. The private complex of passageways and bunkers was reserved for the Stratosan aristocracy. Portals set in the tunnel walls slid open with a ghosting of released pressure and fed off into opulent rooms, their furnishings undisturbed and layered with dust. Reinforced vaults lay unsecured and unguarded, their treasures still untouched within. Several chambers were jammed with machinery hooked up to cryogenic floatation tanks. Purple bacteria contaminated the stagnant gel-solutions within. Decomposed bodies, bloated with putrefaction, were slumped against the glass, their suspended existence ended when the power in Cirrion had failed.

Kadai raised his hand from up ahead and the Salamanders stopped.

Nearby, one step in the chain from Tsu'gan, Iagon consulted his auspex.

'Bio-readings fifty metres ahead,' he hissed through the comm-feed.

The *thud-chank* of bolters being primed filled the narrow space.

Kadai lowered his hand and the Salamanders slowly began to proceed, closing up as they went. They had yet to meet any cultist resistance, but that didn't mean it wasn't there.

Dak'ir heard something move up ahead, like metal scraping metal.

'*Hammer!*' a voice cried out of the dark, accompanied by the sound of a bolt round filling its weapon's breech.

'*Anvil!*' Kadai replied with the other half of the code, and lowered his pistol.

Twenty metres farther on, a wounded Salamander was slumped against a bulkhead, his outstretched bolt pistol falling slowly.

The relief in Kadai's voice was palpable.

'Stand down. It's Fugis. We've got him.'

BANEN STEPPED FROM the shadows with the small band of survivors. Short and unassuming, he wore a leather apron and dirty overallls that bulged with his portly figure. A pair of goggles framed his grease-smeared pate.

He didn't look like a man with the power to wipe out a city.

The gravitas of the decision facing Kadai was not lost on him as he regarded the human engineer.

'You can vent the atmosphere in Cirrion, cleanse the city of the gas?'

'Y-yes, milord.' The stammer only made the human seem more innocuous.

The Salamanders formed a protective cordon around the bulkhead where Fugis and the survivors were holed up, bolters trained outwards. The Apothecary's leg was broken, but he was at least still conscious, though in no condition to fight. With the discovery of the Apothecary an eerie silence had descended on the tunnel complex, like the air was holding its breath.

Salamanders encircling them, Kadai stared down at Banen.

I will be signing the death warrant of thousands...

'Escort them back to Aereon Square,' he said to Brother Ba'ken. 'Commence the cleansing of the city as soon as possible.'

Ba'ken saluted. The Salamanders were breaking up their defensive formation when the held breath rushed back.

A few metres farther down the tunnel, a lone insurgent dropped down from a ceiling hatch, a grenade clutched in her thin fingers.

Bolters roared, loud and throaty down the corridor, shredding the cultist. The grenade went up in the fusillade, the explosion sweeping out in a firestorm. The Salamanders met it without hesitation, shielding the terrified humans with their armoured bodies.

Hundreds of footsteps clattered down to them from the darkness up ahead.

'Battle positions!' shouted Kadai.

A ravening mob of insurgents rounded the corner. Further hatchways in the walls and ceilings suddenly broke open as cultists piled out like fat lice crawling from the cracks.

Kadai levelled his pistol.

'Salamanders! Unleash death!'

A team of cultists brought up an autocannon. Dak'ir raked them with bolter fire before they could set it.

'Iagon...' shouted Tsu'gan over the raucous battle din.

'Atmosphere normal, sir,' the other Salamander replied, knowing precisely what was on his sergeant's mind.

Tsu'gan bared his teeth in a feral smile.

'Cleanse and burn,' he growled, and the flamer attached to his combi-bolter roared.

Liquid promethium ignited on contact with the air as a superheated wave of fire spewed hungrily down the corridor.

Shen'kar intensified the conflagration with his own flamer. The cultists were obliterated in the blaze, their bodies becoming slowly collapsing shadows behind the shimmering heat haze.

It lasted merely seconds. Smoke and charred remains were all that was left when the flames finally died down. Dozens of insurgents had been destroyed; some were little more than ash and bone.

'THE FURY OF fire will win this war for the Salamanders,' said Fugis, as the Astartes were readying to split their forces once again. Ba'ken supported the Apothecary and was standing with the others that would be returning to Aereon Square.

Kadai was adamant that Fugis and the human survivors be given all the protection he could afford them. If that meant stretching his Salamanders thinly, then so be it. The captain would press on with only Tsu'gan, Dak'ir, Company Champion Vek'shen and Honoured Brother Shen'kar as retinue. The rest were going back.

'I am certain of it,' Kadai replied, facing him. 'But at the cost of thousands. I only hope the price is worth it, old friend.'

'Is any price ever worth it?' Fugis asked.

The Apothecary was no longer talking about Cirrion. A bitter remembrance flared in Kadai's mind and he crushed it.

'Send word when you've reached Aereon Square and the gas has been purged. We'll be waiting here until then.'

Fugis nodded, though it gave the Apothecary some pain to do so.

'In the name of Vulkan,' he said, saluting.

Kadai echoed him, rapping his plastron. The Apothecary gave him a final consolatory look before he had Ba'ken help him away. It gave Kadai little comfort as he thought of the thousands of innocents still in the city and their ignorance of what was soon to befall them, a fate made by his own hand.

'Emperor, forgive me...' he whispered softly, watching the Salamanders go.

AURA HIERON HUNG open like a carcass. It had been austerely beautiful once, much like the rest of Cirrion, stark silver alloyed with cold marble. Now it was an abattoir-temple. Blood slicked its walls, seeping down into the cracks of the intricate mosaic floor. Broken columns punctuated a high outer wall that ran around the temple's vast ambit. Statues set in shadowy alcoves had been beheaded or smeared in filth, their pale immortality defaced.

Crude sigils, exulting in the dark glory of the Cult of Truth, were daubed upon the stonework. A black altar, refashioned with jagged knives and stained with blood, dominated a cracked dais at the back of the chamber. Metal spars ripped from the structure of Cirrion's underbelly had been dragged bodily into the temple, tearing ragged grooves in the tarnished marble. Blackened corpses, the remains of loyal Stratosans, were hung upon them as offerings to the Chaos gods. A shrine to the Emperor of Mankind no longer, Aura Hieron was a haven for the corrupt now, where only the damned came to worship.

Nihilan revelled in the temple's debasement as he regarded the instrument of his malicious will from afar.

'We should not be here, sorcerer. We have what we came for,' rasped a voice from the shadows, redolent of smoke and ash.

'Our purpose here is two-fold, Ramlek,' Nihilan replied, his cadence grating. 'We have only achieved the first half.' The renegade Dragon Warrior overlooked the bloodied plaza of Aura Hieron from a blackened anteroom above its only altar. He was watching the Speaker keenly, beguiling and persuading the cultist masses basking in his unnatural aura with his dark-tongued rhetoric.

The brand Nihilan had seared into the hierophant's flesh over three months ago, when the Dragon Warriors had first come to Stratos, had spread well. It almost infected his entire face. The seed the sorcerer had embedded there would be reaching maturation.

'A life for a life, Ramlek; you know that. Is Ghor'gan prepared?'

'He is,' rasped the horned warrior.

Nihilan smiled thinly. The scar tissue on his face pulled tight with the rare muscular use. 'Our enemies will be arriving soon,' he hissed, psychic power crackling over his clenched fist, 'then we will have vengeance.'

EYES LIKE MIRRORED glass stared out from beneath a mausoleum archway, no longer seeing, unblinking in mortality. Tiny ice crystals flecked the dead man's lips and encumbered his eyelids so they drooped in mock lethargy. The poor wretch was arched awkwardly across a stone tomb, his head slack and lifeless as it hung backwards over the edge.

He was not alone. Throughout the temple district, citizens and insurgents alike lay dead, their breath and their life stolen away when the atmospheric processors had vented. Some held one another in a final desperate embrace, accepting of their fate; others fought, fingers clutched around their throats as they tried in vain to fill their lungs.

The ruins of the temple district were disturbingly silent. It was oddly appropriate: the quietude fell like a shroud over broken monoliths and solemn chapels; acres of cemeteries punctated with mausoleums and sepulchres; and hooded statues bent in sombre remembrance.

'So much death…' uttered Dak'ir, reminded of another place decades ago, and glanced to his captain. Kadai seemed to bear it all stoically, but Dak'ir could tell it was affecting him.

The Salamanders had passed through the city unchallenged, plying along the subterranean roads of the private tunnel complex. Though he had no map of the underground labyrinth, Techmarine Argos had extrapolated a route based on the position of the hidden entrance and his battle-brothers' visual reports, relayed to him as they progressed through its dingy confines. After an hour of trawling through the narrow dark, the Salamanders had emerged from a shadowy egress to be confronted with the solemnity of the temple district.

Kadai had told his retinue to expect resistance. Truthfully, he would have welcomed it. Anything to distract him from the terrible act he had been forced to commit against the citizens of Cirrion. But it was not to be – the Salamanders had passed through the white gates of the temple district without incident, yet the reminders of Kadai's act lurked in every alcove, in each darkened bolthole of the city.

Mercifully, Fugis and the others had arrived at Aereon Square without hindrance. Kadai was emotionally ambivalent when the Apothecary's communication had reached him over the comm-feed. It was a double-edged sword, salvation with a heavy tariff – annihilation for Cirrion's people.

'Aura Hieron lies half a kilometre to the north,' the metallic voice of Argos grated over the comm-feed, dispelling further introspection.

'I see it,' Kadai returned flatly.

He cut the link with the Techmarine, instead addressing his retinue.

'The people of Cirrion paid for a chance to end this war with their lives. Let us not leave them wanting. It ends this day, one way or the other. On my lead, brothers. In the name of Vulkan.'

Ahead, the temple of Aura Hieron loomed like a skeletal hand grasping at a pitch black sky.

DAK'IR CREPT THROUGH the darkened alcoves of the temple's west wall. Opposite him, across the tenebrous gulf of the temple's nave, Tsu'gan stalked along the other flanking wall.

Edging down the centre, obscured by shattered columns and the debris from Aura Hieron's collapsed roof, was Kadai and the rest of his retinue. They kept low and quiet, despite their power armour, and closed swiftly on their target.

Ahead of them cultists thronged in hundreds, respirators fixed over their sewn mouths, prostrate before their vile hierophant. The Speaker was perched on a marble dais and clad in dirty blue robes like his congregation of the depraved. Unlike the wire-mouthed acolytes abasing themselves before him, the Speaker was not mute. Far from it. A writhing purple tongue extruded from his distended maw, the teeth within just blackened nubs. The wretched appendage twisted and lashed as if sentient. Inscrutable dogma spewed from the Speaker's mouth, its form and language inflected by the daemonic tongue. Even the sound of his words gnawed at Dak'ir's senses and he shut them out, recognising the mutation for what it was – Chaos taint. It explained at once how this disaffected Stratosan native, who, up until a few months ago, had been little more than a petty firebrand, had managed to cajole such unswerving loyalty, and in such masses.

Surrounding the hierophant was the elite of those fanatical troops, a ring of eight eviscerator priests, kneeling with their chainblades laid out in front of them in ceremony.

It left a bitter tang in Tsu'gan's mouth to witness such corruption. Whatever foul rite these degenerate scum were planning, the Salamanders would end with flame and blade. He felt the zeal burn in his breast, and wished dearly that he was with his captain advancing down the very throat of the enemy and not here guarding shadows.

Let the Ignean skulk at the periphery, he thought. I am destined for more glorious deeds.

A garbled cry arrested Tsu'gan's arrogant brooding. Spewing an unintelligible diatribe, the Speaker gestured frantically towards Kadai and the other two Salamanders emerging from their cover to destroy him. His craven followers reacted with eerie synchronicity to their master's warning, and surged towards the trio of interlopers murderously.

Shen'kar opened up his flamer and burned down a swathe of maddened cultists with a war cry on his lips. Vek'shen charged into the wake of the blaze, the conflagration having barely ebbed, fire-glaive swinging. The master-crafted blade reaped a terrible harvest of sheared limbs and heads, spurts of incendiary immolating bodies with every flame-wreathed strike.

Kadai was like a relentless storm, and Tsu'gan's warrior heart sang to witness such prowess and fury. Channelling his fiery rage, the captain tore a ragged hole through one of the eviscerator priests with his inferno pistol, before crushing the skull of another with his thunder hammer.

As the wretched deacon went down, his head pulped, Kadai gave the signal and enfilading bolter fire barked from the alcoves as Tsu'gan and Dak'ir let rip.

As cultists fell, shot apart by his furious salvos, Tsu'gan could contain his battle lust no longer. He would not be left here like some sentry. He wanted to be at his captain's side, and look into his enemy's eyes as he slew them. Dak'ir could hold the perimeter well enough without his aid. In any case, the enemy was here amassed for slaughter.

Roaring an oath to Vulkan, Tsu'gan left his post and waded into the battle proper.

DAK'IR CAUGHT SIGHT of Tsu'gan's muzzle flare and cursed loudly when he realised he had abandoned his orders and left the wall deserted. Debating whether to press the attack himself, his attention was arrested when he noticed Kadai, having bludgeoned his way through the mob, standing scant feet from the Speaker and levelling his inferno pistol.

'In the name of Vulkan!' he bellowed, about to end the threat of the Cult of Truth forever, when a single shot thundered above the carnage and the Speaker fell, his head half-destroyed by an explosive round.

KADAI FELT THE meat and blood of the executed Speaker spatter his armour, and started to lower his pistol out of shock. A strange lull fell over the fighting, enemies poised in mid-attack, that didn't feel entirely natural as the Salamander captain traced the source of the shot.

Above him there was a parapet overlooking the temple's nave. Kadai's gaze was fixed upon it as a figure in blood-red power armour emerged from the gathered shadows, a smoking bolt pistol in his grasp.

Scales bedecked this warrior's battle-plate, like those of some primordial lizard from an archaic age. His gauntlets were fashioned like claws, with long vermillion talons, and eldritch lightning rippled across them in crackling ruby arcs. In one he clutched a staff, a roaring dragon's head at its tip rendered in silver; in the other his bolt pistol, which he returned to its holster. Broad pauldrons sat like hardened scale shells on the warrior's shoulders, a horn curving from each. He wore no battle-helm, and bore horrific facial scars openly. Fire had blighted this warrior's once noble countenance, twisting it, devouring it and remaking his visage into one of puckered tissue, angry wheals and exposed bone. It was the face of death, hideous and accusing.

A chill entered Kadai's spine as if he was suddenly drowning in ice. The spectre before him was a ghost, an apparition that died long ago in terrible agony. Yet, here it was in flesh and blood, called back from the grave like some vengeful revenant.

'Nihilan...'

'Captain,' the apparition replied, his voice cracked like dry earth baked beneath a remorseless sun, burning red eyes aglow.

Kadai's posture stiffened as the shock quickly passed, subjugated by righteous anger.

'Renegade,' he snarled.

WRACKING PAIN GRIPPED Dak'ir's chest as he beheld the warrior and was wrenched back into the otherworld of his dream...

The temple faded as the grey sky of Moribar engulfed all. Bone-monoliths surged into that endless steel firmament, ossuary paths stretched into endless tracts of cemeteries, mausoleum fields and sepulchral vales. Through legions of tombs, across phalanxes of crypts, along battalions of reliquaries sunk in earthen catacombs, Dak'ir followed the grave-road until he reached its terminus.

And there beneath the cold damp earth, boiling, burning, its lambent glow neither warm nor inviting, was the vast churning furnace of the crematoria.

Pain lanced Dak'ir's body as the vision changed. He gripped his chest, but no longer felt his black carapace. He was a scout once more, observing from the edge of the crematoria, the massive pit of fire large enough to swallow a Titan, burning, ever burning, down into the molten heart of Moribar.

Dak'ir saw two Astartes clambering at the edge of that portal to fiery death. Nihilan clung desperately to Captain Ushorak, his black power armour pitted and cracked with the intense heat emanating from below.

The terrible conflagration was in turmoil. It bubbled explosively, plumes of lava spearing the air in fiery cascades, when a huge pillar of flame tore from the crematoria. Dak'ir shielded his eyes as a massive fire wall obliterated the warriors from view.

Strong hands grasped Dak'ir's shoulder and wrenched him away from the blaze as the renegades they had come to bring to justice, not to kill, were immolated. Barely visible through the solid curtain of flame, Nihilan was screaming as his face burned…

Dak'ir lurched back to the present, a sickening vertigo threatening to overwhelm him, and he reached out to steady himself. He tasted blood in his mouth and black spots marred his vision. Tearing off his battle-helm, he struggled to breathe.

Somewhere in the temple, someone was speaking…

'YOU DIED,' KADAI accused, looking up at the warrior on the parapet. He fought the invisible pressure stopping him from striking the renegade down, but his arms were leaden.

'I survived,' returned Nihilan, the effort to maintain the psychic dampening that held the battle in stasis against the Salamander's will creasing his scarred face.

'You should have faced justice, not death,' Kadai told him, then smiled vindictively. 'Overloading the crematoria, stirring up the volatile core of Moribar, you provoked it in order to escape and kill me and my brothers into the bargain. Ushorak's destruction was your doing, yours *and* his.'

'Don't you speak of him!' cried Nihilan, red lightning coursing through his eyes and clenched fists, writhing around his force staff and spitting off in jagged arcs. Exhaling fury, the Dragon Warrior recovered his composure. '*You* are the murderer here, Kadai – a petty marshal who'd do anything to catch his quarry. But perhaps you're right... I did die, and was *reborn*.'

Kadai raised his inferno pistol a fraction. Nihilan's grip was loosening. He was readying for it to slip completely, and slay the traitor where he stood, when the Speaker's body started to convulse.

'It doesn't matter anymore,' the Dragon Warrior added, stepping back into the shadows of the parapet. 'Not for you...'

Kadai fired off his inferno pistol, melting away a chunk of parapet as Nihilan released his psychic hold. The Salamander was about to chase after him when a terrible aura enveloped the Speaker, lifting his prone corpse inexplicably so that it dangled just above the ground like meat on an invisible hook.

Slowly, agonisingly slowly, he raised his chin to reveal a ruined face destroyed by the bolt pistol's explosive round. Slick red flesh, wrapped partially around a bloody skull, shimmered in the ambient light. What remained of the Speaker's cranium was split open like an egg. Luminous cobalt skin was revealed beneath. Cracking bone gave way to a leering visage called forth from a dark unreality as something... *unnatural*... pulled itself forth into the material plane.

A lidless eye of fulgent black glared with otherworldly malevolence. The eight-pointed star, once burned into the Speaker's forehead, was now glowing upon this new horror. It was raw and vital, pulsing like a wretched heart as the warp-thing grew hideously. Bulbous protrusions tore from mortal flesh, spilling out with thickets of spines. Fingers splayed as if pulled taut by unseen threads, talons rupturing from them, long, sharp and black. The thing's distended maw, in mimicry of the Speaker's original mutation, stretched further and wider until it was a terrible lipless chasm, the lashing tongue within three-pronged and spiked with bloodied bone.

Cultists shrieked in fear and adoration as the Speaker's corpse was possessed. Eviscerator priests pledged their mute allegiance, turning their chainblades towards the Salamanders once again.

The creature was primal, wrenched from ethereal slumber and only partially sentient, a deep soul-hunger driving it. Roaring in fury and anguish, it surged forwards devouring a pair of eviscerator priests closing on Kadai. Like some terrible basilisk, it consumed them whole, bones crunching audibly as it dragged the prey down its bulging gullet.

'Abomination...' Kadai breathed, gripping the haft of his thunder hammer as he prepared to smite the daemon. Nihilan had given his soul over to the dark powers now, and this was but a taste of his malfeasance.

'Die, hell-beast!' cried Vek'shen, stepping between his captain and the unbound daemon. Whirling his fire-glaive in a blazing arc, the Company Champion crafted an overhand blow that would've felled an ork warlord. The daemon met it with its talons and the glaive was held fast. Its tongue slid like lightning from its abyssal mouth, oozing swiftly around Vek'shen's power-armoured form. The Salamander gaped in a silent scream, breath pressed violently from his body, as he was crushed to death.

Kadai roared, launching himself at the beast, even as his battle-brother's flaccid corpse, dented where the daemon's tongue had clutched him, crashed to the ground.

DAK'IR WAS RECOVERING his senses. Though he hadn't seen how, the Speaker was dead, shot in the back of the head, his body lying at Kadai's feet. It wasn't all that he'd missed while he was under the influence of his memory-dream. In the time it had taken for his Astartes constitution and training to override the lingering nausea the remembrance had caused, Nihilan was already retreating into the shadows. Leaving his flank position,

Dak'ir ran towards the nave determined to pursue, when a swathe of cultists impeded him.

'Tsu'gan!' he cried, gutting an insurgent with his chainsword and firing his bolter one-handed to explode the face of another, 'Stop the renegade!'

The other Salamander nodded in a rare moment of empathy and sped off after Nihilan.

Dak'ir was battling through the frenzied mob when he saw the Speaker's corpse rising and felt the touch of the warp prickle his skin...

TSU'GAN BOLTED ACROSS the nave, pummelling cultists with his fists, chewing up packed groups with explosive bursts of fire. Shen'kar was just visible in his peripheral vision, immolating swathes of the heretical vermin with bright streaks of flame.

Smashing through a wooden door at the back of the temple, Tsu'gan found a flight of stone steps leading up to the parapet. He took them three at a time with servo-assisted bounds of his power-armoured legs, until he emerged into a darkened anteroom.

Something was happening below. He heard Vek'shen bellow a call to arms and then nothing, as if all sound had fled in a sudden vacuum.

Burning red eyes regarded him coldly in the blackness.

'Tsu'gan...' said Nihilan, emerging from the dark.

'Traitorous scum!' the Salamander raged.

But Tsu'gan didn't raise his bolter to fire, didn't vanquish the renegade where he stood. He merely remained transfixed, muscles clenched as if held fast in amber.

'Wha–' he began, but found his tongue was leaden too.

'Sorcery,' Nihilan told him, the surface of his force staff alive with incandescent energy. It threw ephemeral flashes of light into the gloom, illuminating the sorcerer's dread visage as he closed on the stricken Astartes.

'I could kill you right now,' he said levelly. 'Snuff out the light in your eyes, and kill you, just like Kadai killed Ushorak.'

'You were offered redemption.' Tsu'gan struggled to fashion the retort, forcing his tongue into compliance through sheer willpower.

The sinister cast to Nihilan's face bled away and was replaced by indignation.

'Redemption was it? Spiritual castigation at the hands of Elysius, a few hours with his chirurgeon-interrogators, is that what was offered?' He laughed mirthlessly. 'That sadistic bastard would only have passed a guilty judgement.'

Stepping closer, Nihilan took on a sincere tone.

'Ushorak offered life. Power,' he breathed. 'Freedom from the shackles forcing us to serve the cattle of men, when we should be ruling them.'

The Dragon Warrior clenched his fist as he said it, so close now that Tsu'gan could smell his copper breath.

'You see, *brother*. We are not so dissimilar.'

'We are nothing alike, traitor,' snapped the Salamander, grimacing with the simple effort of speaking.

Nihilan stepped back, spreading his arms plaintively.

'A bolter shot to the head to end my heresy then?' His upturned lip showed his displeasure. 'Or stripped of rank, a penitent brand in place of my service studs?'

He shook his head.

'No... I think not. Perhaps I will brand you, though, *brother*.' Nihilan showed the Salamander his palm and spread his fingers wide. 'Would your resistance to corruption be stauncher than the human puppet, I wonder?'

Tsu'gan flinched before Nihilan's approach, expecting at any moment for all the turpitude of Chaos to spew forth from his hand.

'Cull your fear,' Nihilan rasped, making a fist as he sneered.

'I fear nothing,' barked Tsu'gan.

Nihilan sniffed contemptuously. 'You fear everything, Salamander.'

Tsu'gan felt his boots scraping against the floor as he was psychically impelled towards the edge of the parapet against his will.

'Enough talk,' he spat. 'Cast me down. Break my body, if you must. The Chapter will hunt you, renegade, and there will be no chance of redemption for you this time.'

Nihilan regarded him as an adult would a simple child.

'You still don't understand, do you?'

Slowly, Tsu'gan's body rotated so that he could see out onto the battle below.

Cultists fell in their droves, burned down by Shen'kar's flamer, or eviscerated by Dak'ir's chainsword. His brothers fought tooth and nail, fending off the horde whilst his beloved captain fought for his life.

Kadai's artificer armour was rent in over a dozen places, a daemon-thing that wore the flesh of the Speaker assailing him. Talons like long slashes of night came down in a rain of blows against the Salamander captain's defence, but he weathered it all, carving great arcs in riposte with his thunder hammer. Vulkan's name was on his lips as the lightning cracked from the head of his master-forged weapon, searing the daemon's borrowed flesh.

'I was devoted to Ushorak, just as you are to your captain…' Nihilan uttered in Tsu'gan's ear as he watched the battle with the hell-spawn unfold.

Kadai smashed the daemon's shoulder, shattering bone, and its arm fell limp.

'…Kadai killed him,' Nihilan continued. 'He forced us to seek solace in the Eye. There we fled and there we stayed for decades…'

Ichor hissed from the tears in the daemon's earthly form, its hold on reality slipping as Kadai punished it relentlessly with fist and hammer.

'...Time moves differently in that realm. For us it felt like centuries had passed before we found a way out.'

A chorus of screams ripped from the distended throat of the daemon-thing, as Kadai crushed its skull finally and banished it back into the warp, the souls it had consumed begging for succour.

'...It *changed* me. Opened my eyes. I see much now. A great destiny awaits you, Tsu'gan, but another overshadows it.' Nihilan gave the faintest inclination of his head towards Dak'ir.

The Ignean was fighting valiantly, cutting down the last of the cultists and heading for Kadai.

'Even now he rushes to your captain's side...' Nihilan said, insidiously, 'Hoping to gain his favour.'

Tsu'gan knew he could not trust the foul tongue of a traitor, but the words spoken echoed his own long-held suspicions.

And so, unbeknownst to the Salamander, Nihilan *did* plant a seed. Not one born of daemonic essence. No, this came about through petty jealousy and ambition, through the very thing Tsu'gan had no aegis against – himself.

'This cult,' the Dragon Warrior pressed. 'It is *nothing*. Stratos is nothing. Even this city is meaningless. It was always about *him*.'

Kadai was leaning heavily on his thunder hammer, weakened after vanquishing the daemon.

Nihilan smiled, scarred flesh creaking.

'A captain for a captain...'

Realisation slid like a cold blade into Tsu'gan's gut.

Too late he saw the armoured shadow closing in. The Dragon Warriors springing their trap at last. By leaving his post, he had let them infiltrate the Salamanders' guard. The cultists were only ever a distraction; the true enemy was only now revealing itself.

He had been a fool.

'No!'

Sheer force of will broke Nihilan's psychic hold. Roaring the captain's name, Tsu'gan leapt off the parapet.

Hoarse laughter followed him all the way down.

DAK'IR HAD ALMOST reached Kadai when he saw the renegade hefting the multi-melta. Shouting a warning, he raced to his captain's side. Kadai faced him, hearing the cry of Tsu'gan from above at the same time, and then followed Dak'ir's agonised gaze...

An incandescent beam tore out of the darkness.

Kadai was struck, and his body immolated in an actinic flare.

An intense rush of heat smashed Dak'ir off his feet, backwash from the terrible melta blast. He smelled scorched flesh. A hot spike of agony tortured his senses. His face was burning, just like in the dream...

Dak'ir realised he was blacking out, his body shutting down as his sus-an membrane registered the gross trauma he had suffered. Dimly, as if buried alive and listening through layered earth, he heard the voice of Sergeant N'keln and his battle-brothers. Dak'ir managed to turn his head. The last thing he saw before unconsciousness claimed him was Tsu'gan slumped to his knees in front of the charred remains of their captain.

WHEN DAK'IR AWOKE he was laid out in the Apothecarion of the *Vulkan's Wrath*. It was cold as a tomb inside the austere chamber, the gloom alleviated by the lit icons of the medical apparatus around him.

With waking came remembrance, and with remembrance, grief and despair.

Kadai was dead.

'Welcome back, brother,' a soft voice said. Fugis was thin-faced and gaunter than ever, as he loomed over Dak'ir.

Emotional agony was compounded by physical pain and Dak'ir reached for his face as it started to burn anew.

Fugis seized his wrist before he could touch it.

'I wouldn't do that,' he warned the sergeant. 'Your skin was badly burned. You're healing, but the flesh is still very tender.'

Dak'ir lowered his arm as Fugis released him. The Apothecary injected a solution of drugs through an intravenous drip-feed to ease the pain.

Dak'ir relaxed as the suppressants went to work, catalysing his body's natural regenerative processes.

'What happened?' His throat felt raw and abrasive, and he croaked the words. Fugis stepped away from Dak'ir's medi-slab to check on the instrumentation. He limped as he walked, a temporary augmetic frame fitted over his leg to shore up the break he had sustained in his fall. Stubborn to the point of bloody-mindedness, nothing would prevent the Apothecary from doing his work.

'Stratos is saved,' he said simply, his back to the other Salamander. 'With the Speaker dead and our flamers restored, the insurgents fell quickly. The storms lifted an hour after we returned to Aereon Square,' he explained. 'Librarian Pyriel arrived twenty minutes later with the rest of the company to reinforce N'keln, who had taken the wall and was already en route to Aura Hieron...'

'But too late to save Kadai,' Dak'ir finished for him.

Fugis stopped what he was doing and gripped the instrumentation panel he'd been consulting for support.

'Yes. Even his gene-seed was unsalvageable.'

A long grief-filled silence crept insidiously into the room before the Apothecary continued.

'A ship, Stormbird-class, left the planet but we were too late to give chase.'

The rancour in Dak'ir's voice could've scarred metal.

'Nihilan and the other renegades escaped.'

'To Vulkan knows where,' Fugis replied, facing the patient. 'Librarian Pyriel has command of Third Company, until Chapter Master Tu'Shan can appoint someone permanent.'

Dak'ir frowned.

'We're going home?'

'Our tour of the Hadron Belt is over. We are returning to Prometheus to reinforce and lick our wounds.'

'My face...' Dak'ir ventured after a long silence, 'I want to see it.'

'Of course,' said Fugis, and showed the Salamander a mirror.

Part of Dak'ir's facial tissue had been seared away. Almost half of his onyx-black skin had been bleached near-white by the voracious heat of the melta flare. Though raw and angry, it looked almost human.

'A reaction to the intense radiation,' Fugis explained. 'The damage has resulted in minor cellular regression, reverting to a form prior to the genetic ebonisation of your skin when you became an Astartes. I cannot say for certain yet, but it shows no sign of immediate regeneration.'

Dak'ir stared, lost in his own reflection and the semblance of humanness there. Fugis arrested the Salamander's reverie.

'I'll leave you in peace, such as it is,' he said, taking away the mirror. 'You are stable and there's nothing more I can do at this point. I'll return in a few hours. Your body needs time to heal, before you can fight again. Rest,' the Apothecary told him. 'I expect you to be here upon my return.'

The Apothecary left, hobbling off to some other part of the ship. But as the metal door slid shut with a susurrus of escaping pressure, Dak'ir knew he was not alone.

'Tsu'gan?'

He could feel his battle-brother's presence even before he saw him emerge from the shadows.

'Brother,' Dak'ir croaked warmly, recalling the moment of empathy between them as they'd fought together in the temple.

The warmth seeped away, as a cold wind steals heat from a fire, when Dak'ir saw Tsu'gan's dark expression.

'You are unfit to be an Astartes,' he said levelly. 'Kadai's death is on your hands, Ignean. Had you not sent me after the renegade, had you been swift enough to react to the danger in our midst, we would not have lost our captain.' Tsu'gan's burning gaze was as chill as ice. 'I shall not forget it.'

Stunned, Dak'ir was unable to reply before Tsu'gan turned his back on him and left the Apothecarion.

Anguish filled his heart and soul as Dak'ir wrestled with the terrible accusations of his brother, before exhaustion took him and he fell into a deep and fitful sleep.

For the first time in over forty years, the dream had changed...

SITTING IN THE troop compartment of the Stormbird, Nihilan turned the device stolen from the vault in the depths of Cirrion over and over in his gauntlet. His fellow Dragon Warriors surrounded him: the giant Ramlek, breathing tiny gouts of ash and cinder from his mouth grille as he tried to calm his perpetual anger; Ghor'gan, his scaled skin shedding after he'd removed his battle-helm, cradling his multi-melta like a favoured pet; Nor'hak, fastidiously stripping and reassembling his weapons methodically; and Erkine his pilot, the other renegade left behind to watch the Stormbird, forearm bone-blades carefully sheathed within the confines of his power armour as he steered the vessel to its final destination.

The Dragon Warriors had risked much to retrieve the device, even going as far as to establish the elaborate distraction of the uprising to cloak their movements. Kadai's death as part of that subterfuge had been a particularly satisfying, but unexpected, boon for Nihilan.

The Stormbird had been primed and ready before the trap in Aura Hieron was sprung. With eager swathes of suicidal cultists to ensure their escape, the renegades had fled swiftly, leaving the atmosphere of Stratos behind them as the engines of their extant craft roared.

'How little do they realise...' Nihilan rasped, examining every facet of the gilt object in his palm. Such an innocuous piece of arcana; within its twelve pentagonal faces, along the geodesic lines of esoteric script that wreathed its dodecahedral surface, there was the means to unlock secrets. It was the very purpose of the *decyphrex*, to reveal that which was hidden. For Nihilan that enigma existed in the scrolls of Kelock, ancient parchments he and Ushorak had taken over forty years ago from Kelock's tomb on Moribar. Kelock was a technocrat, and a misunderstood genius. He created something, a weapon, far beyond what was capable with the crippled science of the current decaying age. Nihilan meant to replicate his work.

Over a thousand years within the Eye of Terror, patiently plotting revenge and now he finally was closing on the means to destroy his enemies.

'Approaching the *Hell-stalker*,' the sepulchral voice of Ekrine returned over the vox.

Nihilan engaged the grav-harness. As it crept over his armoured shoulders, securing him for landing, he peered out of the Stormbird's vision slit. There across a becalmed and cobalt sea, a vessel of molten-red lay anchored. It was an old ship with old wounds, and older ghosts. The prow was a serrated blade, ripping a hole in the void. Cannons arrayed its flanks, gunmetal grey and powder-blackened. Dozens of towers and antennae reached up like crooked fingers.

Hell-stalker had entered the Eye a mere battle-barge and had come out something else entirely. It was Nihilan's ship and aboard it his warriors awaited him – renegades, mercenaries and defectors; pirates, raiders and reavers. There they gathered to heed of his victory and the slow realisation of their ambition – the total and utter destruction of Nocturne, and with it the death of the Salamanders.

THE LABYRINTH

Richard Ford

CHAINSWORD MOTORS ROARED, bellowing at each other before their steel teeth clashed in a violent kiss, spitting sparks and black oil. They locked together, whining in fury, each relentless in its desire to rend and tear.

Invictus glared at his opponent across the biting blades, determined he would be triumphant, utterly convinced that he would be the victor this time.

It was not to be.

Genareas wrenched his weapon aside, pulling the whirring teeth apart and showering the battle deck with a metallic spray. Before Invictus could counter, the full weight of Genareas's shoulder guard smashed him in the face, sending him reeling. He lost his footing, arms flailing wildly in an attempt to keep his balance, but it was no good. He fell, the harsh clang of ceramite on corrugated steel filling the battle deck, and it was all Invictus could do to keep a hold on his buzzing chainsword. Before he could bring it to bear, Genareas had clamped his arm to the ground with a huge armoured foot, his own chainsword brandished threateningly, closing in towards his opponent's face. Invictus watched as the swirling teeth drew closer to his exposed flesh, and grimaced at their inevitable onslaught.

With a triumphant laugh, Genareas powered down the chainsword's motor, offering his arm to Invictus. 'Well fought, brother. But as we can see, you are still no match for me in the confines of the battle deck.'

Invictus took the proffered arm and was helped to his feet, once again feeling the sting of defeat pierce him more painfully than any physical wound ever could.

'One day, Brother Genareas,' he said. 'One day.'

Genareas only laughed the louder. 'Indeed, brother. And I look forward to that day. Now come. We are already late.'

Together they walked from the battle deck, Invictus several paces behind Genareas, as he always was. Though they were closer than any of their other battle-brothers among the Sons of Malice, having served together as Scouts and then Initiates, it seemed that Invictus was always in Genareas's shadow, always that one step behind. It was a failing that had plagued him for decades, despite the victories he had won in the service of his Chapter.

But tonight would be different – tonight Invictus would prove his worth.

They strode through the dimly illuminated passages of the Retaliator-class cruiser, until they arrived at the docking bay. As soon as the bay doors opened, the shrill hum of a thousand different voices assailed their ears. Servitors buzzed and whirred, piloting their automatons, driving the rows of prisoners of both familiar and extrinsic species onto the docking craft. Snouts mewled peevishly, jaws barked curses in alien tongues, and amidst them the all too familiar cries of weeping innocents pealed out to fill the bay with a cacophonous racket. They had brought offerings captured in every system they had travelled through, xenos from almost a hundred different species. Malice would undoubtedly be pleased with the largesse; the sacrificial pyre would burn brighter than ever before.

Such an extensive gathering of vile beings sickened Invictus to his core, but he knew it was necessary if the hunger of Malice was to be sated and his desires appeased. This pitiful host could not be silenced soon enough, and Invictus could only hope the slaughter would be underway soon.

With Genareas at his side, Invictus made his way across the packed hangar to where his brothers of the Sons of Malice waited. They were already filing into the belly of a growling Thunderhawk gunship, and the two tardy Space Marines were quick to join their fellows. As they boarded, Invictus could hear some of his brothers offering benediction through the vox-relay of his helmet. For himself he made no prayer as he strapped on his harness and prepared for take off – his trust in the skills of the pilot was absolute.

The ship's engines fired into life and it left the artificial gravity of the Retaliator's hangar. Through the gunship's narrow viewport, Invictus could see the colossal outline of a long-dead Imperial ship drawing closer, expanding in his field of vision like a vast beast inflating itself to ward off a curious predator. Every dent and surface burn was visible, and it was a wonder the gargantuan relic survived at all after spending millennia exposed in the vastness of space, with no defence against the empyreal elements.

It hung like a gargantuan, rotted hand – vast steel appendages spiralling out from the centre, some displaying their bulwarks to the cold vacuum of space like an eviscerated corpse. Here and there the ship vented a gaseous blast into the void as though snorting its last toxic breath. Twisted detritus meandered by, caught in the behemoth's gravitational field and forced to perform a perpetual waltz around the vast edifice.

They called it the *Labyrinth*. It had taken them a month of trawling the warp to return here, as they did once each century to honour the blood rites of their Chapter. It was consecrated ground for the Sons of Malice, the only place they could rally to since their home world of Scelus had been so wickedly defiled by the Astartes. No matter their commitments elsewhere, no matter the blood that had to be shed on other worlds, the Sons of Malice would always come back here at the appointed time, ready to make their sacrifices. Their rites had to be strictly observed to the abandonment of all other things.

It was the way of the Sons, and always had been.

The Thunderhawk weaved through the spinning flotsam surrounding the vast ship, and finally reached the *Labyrinth*'s docking hangar. There was a deafening roar as reverse thrusters were engaged, and the Thunderhawk glided in to gently greet the surface of the landing pad.

Once the doors opened, Invictus was quick to disembark, barely registering the flashing relay of information as it pattered across the inside of his visor, shining a blinking green light onto his face. It had been a hundred years since last he trod this sacred ground, and it never failed to fill him with awe.

The resplendence of the ship's bowels was in stark contrast to the desolate appearance of its outer shell. Rockcrete pillars soared a thousand feet into the air, linked by flying buttresses. These towering structures flanked ogival arches that led down shadowed passageways in every direction. Gargoyles of every conceivable shape and size leered from the darkness; antiquated depictions of whatever deities were worshipped here in aeons passed.

Now, only one deity was offered reverence in this cold empty vessel: the exalted Malice, the Renegade God, the Outcast, Malice the Lost, Hierarch of Anarchy and Terror. And He would soon receive nourishment aplenty when the feeding began.

* * *

THEY HAD DISCARDED their armour and steam was rising from their bare flesh in the firelight. Every one of his brothers was covered in the ichor of their victims, each warrior now gore-strewn and glutted in the great hall.

Invictus had sated himself better than most. The blood was still fresh on his lips and chin where he had gorged on the stone-hard body of a trussed Astartes. To his credit, the servant of the Carrion Lord had not cried out as Invictus sank his teeth into him again and again, rending the flesh and muscle from his bones and feasting for the glory of Malice. Now, little was left of the dead Space Marine but a bloody stump, hanging like a carved joint of meat from a rusted chain.

The other sacrifices had not been as silent as that of Invictus, and the lofty heights of the massive hall still echoed with the ring of their unheeded screams for mercy. All around, the pyres burned, hot coals glowing bright with the charred remains of the night's hecatomb.

Faintly echoing from the distant, unexplored confines of the dead ship, Invictus was sure he could hear a noise, like something bellowing from the depths of its inhuman lungs. It repeated a phrase again and again, the strength of its voice carrying the words over what may have been miles, but try as he might Invictus could not hear them clearly. In the end he chose to ignore the sound, allowing it to blend in with the background hum of the creaking ship and the aftermath of the night's sacrifice.

He turned his attention to a raised mezzanine at one end of the great hall, where stood Lord Kathal, the greatest of them all, Chapter Master of the Sons of Malice, bedecked in his armour of office. Invictus could see his ancient face leering down, satisfied with the oblation his warriors had made. Every one of the Sons was now watching him, waiting for him to honour them with his words.

Kathal simply stared with those eyes of ice, seeming to savour the moment before he broke the silence.

'Brothers.' Kathal's voice was deep and resonant, filling the hall all the way to its high, dark ceiling. 'Malice is truly honoured this night. We have raised to Him a thousand souls in agony and terror. It is fitting that we offer Him such a bounteous sacrifice in preparation for our coming crusade.'

Invictus clenched his fists in anticipation. It was common knowledge that the Sons of Malice would soon march to war, embarking on a crusade the likes of which their Chapter had never seen before.

'For such a struggle we will need unparalleled warriors, men who have proven themselves in the Challenge of the Labyrinth. Only by succeeding at this trial can any of you prove your worth, and your suitability to stride amongst the ranks of the Doomed Ones.'

He felt a bite of quick excitement, and he knew his brethren felt it too. Each century, when the Sons of Malice returned to the carcass of the huge and ancient vessel, a select few would volunteer to face the Challenge of the Labyrinth. None were ever seen again, but it was said that those strong and cunning enough to overcome the trials of the Labyrinth were elevated to the Doomed Ones, Malice's sept of holy warriors. Every member of this elite coterie was granted Malice's divine gifts of untold power and sent off to walk the dark paths of the galaxy, slaying their enemies with cold efficiency. It was a position Invictus had long coveted, and this year he finally felt ready to pursue it.

'Which of you is strong enough, resourceful enough, and courageous enough to face the Labyrinth?' asked Kathal.

His head held high, his body still dripping with the gore of his recent sacrifice, Invictus strode forward to present himself before Kathal. He did not bow or show fealty, but thrust out his chin in defiance, keen to show his lack of trepidation and his worthiness for the ordeal ahead.

Lord Kathal smiled down in satisfaction, his wide leer cracking that ancient face almost in two. And after Invictus, others began to move forward, spurred on by his example and eager to show themselves equally as worthy. In the end, twenty warriors stood shoulder to shoulder with Invictus, presenting themselves to face the perils of the Labyrinth.

Glancing to his side, Invictus saw that his brother, Genareas, had also chosen this year to join the trial. It was inevitable that they would take this challenge together, but this time Invictus was determined to step out of his brother's shadow.

When he was sure that no more would take up the challenge, Lord Kathal beckoned his twenty warriors away from the great hall. The grim procession marched further into the dark heart of the rotting ship until finally they reached their goal. Before them stood a simple steel hatchway, which barred the way to the unseen terrors of the Labyrinth.

'Beyond this door lies your destiny,' said Kathal. 'You will all enter here unarmed and unarmoured. There is no rank beyond this entrance; you are all equal within the Labyrinth. Use what resources you can scavenge, and have faith in one another. At the far side of the ship awaits a portal to freedom. Any who can find it and step within its hallowed confines will receive the benediction of Malice. The rest will find only oblivion. To those of you I will not see again – die well, my brothers.'

With that, Kathal turned the great wheel that secured the hatch and it swung open on rusted hinges. Within was only darkness, but Invictus did not pause – stepping inside and leading the way for his brothers to follow.

Once they were all within, he heard the great door close behind him.

Flickering strobes filled the corridor with a dim red light, and the warriors were forced to wait for their keen eyes to adjust to the gloom before proceeding. While they lingered, Invictus was sure he could hear that bellowing voice once more, though its origin was still too distant for him to ascertain any meaning. The noise filled Invictus with a chill, but he would not allow it to stop him. They would never find victory skulking in the dark corridor of some dead ship and, steeling himself against the fear, he led his battle-brothers forward.

AT FIRST THE going was easy, with the wide corridor funnelling them along an obvious route. As they moved, the warriors of the Sons scavenged what they could – steel bars, the sharp edges of torn bulwarks – anything that could be used as a weapon. Here and there they would discover an object of greater value gripped in the skeletal fingers of a long dead aspirant – a discarded bolter or a salvageable flamer. Invictus found a bolt pistol, its clip half full, and said silent thanks to Malice for his beneficence.

After an hour of tramping through the dimly lit passageways without incident, the twenty warriors came to a wide chamber. Six doors were set in the far wall, each one yawning wide, beckoning them forward into the blackness beyond.

'Which way?' asked Genareas.

The other warriors looked to one another uncertainly.

'Perhaps we should split our numbers here,' Invictus replied. 'If only death awaits us beyond one of these doors, then at least some of us might make it to the Labyrinth's end.'

Genareas nodded, as did the others. If the Labyrinth was as huge and dangerous as they feared, then splitting into smaller groups would serve them better than staying as a single unit and falling foul of the same deadly ensnarement.

The warriors quickly split into two squads, with Genareas and Invictus on opposing sides. Before they headed off through different passageways, Genareas offered his brother a nod – what might be a final salute. Whether he was wishing him luck or merely offering a silent challenge, Invictus did not know, but he returned the gesture in kind, and followed his own group into the dark.

INVICTUS LED THE way, his battle-brothers close behind. As they moved they could hear a tapping within the walls that grew more intense the further they delved into the shell of the dead ship. It was as though the noise were following their route along the arterial passageways. Several times they stopped, sensing unseen forms watching them, waiting to pounce at any moment, but each time their caution proved unfounded.

Again, something shuffled in the dark nearby, and the warriors quickly halted, brandishing their arms threateningly. They looked to one another uncertainly, until bold Brother Cainin stepped forward. He had fashioned a crude axe from the detritus of the tunnels and he held it forward, as though challenging the shadows themselves. With a quick swipe left and right Cainin cut the blackness from where the sound had emanated, as though attacking the shadows themselves.

Nothing.

He turned, shrugging with a smile as though they were all foolish – spooked by innocent sounds like a bunch of untested neophytes, not the cold, hard veterans they were.

It roared from the dark, huge arms clamping around Cainin, slavering jaws biting deep into his neck. He had no time to scream as he was pulled into the shadows, blood spurting from his wounds as a savage, twisted beast tore clumps of his flesh away.

The remaining warriors opened fire with what weapons they had and Invictus pumped bolter shells at the place where seconds before his battle-brother had stood. Brother Vallius, crude autogun in hand, stepped forward to unleash an angry tirade of fire and was answered with a bloodcurdling cry of pain.

The echo of gunfire subsided and the corridor fell silent. None of the warriors moved, each one staring at the dark, waiting for something to come screaming forward, ready to grasp them with powerful arms and rend their flesh asunder.

Blood suddenly began to pool across the decking, and Invictus took a step forward. Before he could get any closer a thick, foetid arm flopped raggedly from the dark, its clawed hand twitching in the winking light. Brother Angustine reached up and diverted one of the dull spotlights that hung limply from its housing to shed some illumination on the creature. It was large, and like no xenos Invictus had ever seen. The body bore obvious marks of mutation, as though the creature had been exposed to the warp. Its fangs were bared from a lipless maw and its dead eyes stared blankly, bereft of pupils. The skin was hard like leather and its body was covered with open sores, exuding a weird, musky scent.

As his brothers checked the lifeless body of Cainin, Invictus knelt beside the creature, keen to get a closer look at the kind of beast they would be facing during the trial. Instantly his eyes were drawn to the mutant's upper arm. It bore some kind of mark, faded by the years and the mutation of its flesh, but it was still barely discernible in the guttering light – the black and white skull symbol of Malice.

He thought it strange that the creature should bear such a mark, but before he could speak of it Brother Mortigan beckoned them on down the corridor.

'We must keep moving,' he said. 'We do not know how many more of these creatures are stalking us in the dark. Our shots may attract more of them to our position.'

With that, they began to move on, leaving the dead creature and the body of battle-brother Cainin in the shadows behind them.

Invictus gave no further thought to the mark. He had more pressing matters to attend to – such as not falling foul of any more of these twisted beasts in the stygian tunnels.

Over the next few hours they made good progress through the rotting bulwarks and rusted corridors of the dead ship, but the tricks and traps of the Labyrinth began to take their toll.

Brother Kado, who single-handedly repelled an ork ambush at the Battle of Uderverengin, was beheaded by hidden las-wire as they traversed a narrow bridge. Brother Vallius, who took the head of Lord Bacchus at the Ansolom Gate, was crushed by a blast door that had at first seemed inoperable. Brother Mortigan, who stood beside Invictus as they watched the exterminatus of Corodon IV, was doused in corrosive waste as they navigated a scoriation duct.

With each death Invictus felt the pall of dread close in further, but he forced himself on. If anyone was to survive this trial and take their place among the Doomed Ones it would be him, and he would let nothing stand in his way.

Eventually, the six remaining warriors found themselves at the entrance to a wide chamber. Its floor was peppered with huge holes, as though something massive had punched through the solid decking with spiked fists of steel.

Invictus tentatively led the way, stepping over the threshold of the room as though the floor beyond might burn his bare feet. There did not appear to be any cunning traps awaiting them inside, and Invictus signalled his brothers to follow him as he skirted the edge of one of the great holes. Looking down, he could see that the huge punctured deck disappeared into the darkness below, and a sudden sense of foreboding began to fill him.

'Move quickly,' he ordered, stepping gingerly between the twisted metal. 'There is something not right here.'

It took Invictus scant seconds to realise what had put him on edge – the entire room stank of the same musk as the creature they had slain earlier – but by then it was too late.

Brother Angustine cried out in alarm, firing wildly with his autogun as a ferocious mutant beast rushed from the dark. The blaring report of automatic fire suddenly filled the room as more of the creatures began to pour in from all around. Invictus raised his bolt pistol, ready to add his own stream of fire to the deluge, when another of the creatures burst from the shadows ahead. He immediately altered his sightline, squeezing hard on the trigger three times. Each shot hit its target, bursting against the mutant's face, explosive rounds mashing flesh and pulping bone with each deafening impact. But even as one assailant fell, Invictus was attacked by a second that leapt at him from above. He swung his pistol around, letting off a sweeping volley of fire, but it was not enough to stop the mutant's wild lunge. It smashed into him, gripping him tightly with razor claws and snapping its fangs at his throat. Invictus fell back, his hands barely grasping at the beast's jaws in time to stop it tearing out his throat, but as he did so he lost his footing, falling back into the void as he and the mutant were pitched into one of the huge holes.

All he could hear as the shadows enveloped him was the desperate sound of his remaining battle-brothers fighting valiantly for their lives...

HIS EYES FLICKED open, suddenly assailed by the intermittent blinking of another defective spotlight. Lifting a hand to his head, Invictus could feel blood caking the side of his face. He had fallen Malice-knew how far, and struck his head on something solid. There was no telling how long he had been unconscious.

Panic suddenly gripped him as he realised he had lost his weapon. His mutant attacker could be anywhere, even now stalking him, readying itself to pounce. He leapt to his feet, eyes scanning desperately for something he could use as a weapon, and instantly he saw there was little need for alarm.

The room he had fallen into was packed with detritus – sharp edged machinery and torn bulwark panels lay scattered all around. It was only by the grace of Malice that he had not been cut to ribbons by the forest of junk. The mutant he had fallen with, however, had not been so lucky. Its body was impaled by a steel girder, poking up from the pile of scrap metal like a slanted flagpole. The end of the torn steel protruded from its mouth, and its black eyes stared vacantly. It looked almost pitiful.

There was silence above – Invictus's battle-brothers had either perished, or moved on, thinking him lost. From here he would have to proceed alone.

Making a quick search of the surrounding junk, Invictus managed to retrieve the bolt pistol, and then set about trying to locate an exit from the stifling chamber.

As he scrabbled around in the dark something reached out, grasping his wrist and holding the bolt pistol firmly. Invictus stretched out with his free hand, keen to halt the mutant's jaws before they could clamp themselves around his throat, but he suddenly stopped as he saw that it was not the baleful eyes of a mutant beast that regarded him from the shadows, but one of his battle-brothers. Though it was no one he recognised, the mark of Malice was plain to see on his upper arm. But that was not all – his skin was marred by sores, and his face had taken on a feral cast. It was plain he was in the early stages of mutation.

'Mercy, brother,' he said. 'I mean you no harm.'

With that he released Invictus's wrist, but remained in the dark confines of the shadows, seeming to find solace within them.

Invictus took a wary step backwards, readying himself to raise the bolt pistol at the slightest provocation. 'What has happened to you?' he asked.

'The Labyrinth, brother. Prolonged exposure condemns us to this.' He raised his arm, showing the weeping pustules and fledgling talons. 'I too volunteered for the Challenge a century ago, heeding the words of our Chapter Master. There were six of us that made it to the portal and what we thought was our victory. But it seems Kathal did not tell us all there is to know about his test. Once the first of us passed through the portal, it ceased to operate for the rest. We were trapped down here, forced to fight for our lives. I am the last of those survivors, but as you can see, survival means nothing. This place is warp-touched. It will not be long before I am one of them.' He gestured towards the mutant, impaled on the vast spike.

'Then there can be only one victor in this Challenge?' said Invictus.

'Indeed.'

'Then I must hurry. Is there a way out of this place?'

His tainted battle-brother beckoned towards the shadows. 'An exit lies that way. But beware – their hive nestles along that path. It will be impossible to pass.'

'I will find a way.' Invictus took a step towards the door.

'Before you leave,' the mutant's voice sounded almost desperate. 'Perhaps there is something you could do for me in return...'

Invictus raised the bolt pistol and fired a single round, exploding his twisted battle-brother's face. Without a second look, he walked from the metallic bone yard and further into the Labyrinth.

THE SOUND OF boltgun reports and the stench of promethium emanated from up ahead. Invictus quickened his step, eager to join in the fray, feeling the red mist of his battle haze descending. As he moved along the tunnel the sounds and smells of combat intensified and his heart began to pound with anticipation.

He could see the desperate skirmish now. Five of his battle-brothers were fighting in a tight corridor, with mutants assailing them from further ahead. Genareas was among them, unleashing a hellish conflagration from the tip of his salvaged flamer. Any beasts that were not instantly immolated were riddled with bolter and autogun fire.

As Invictus joined his battle-brothers, Genareas looked across and smiled. 'Where is your squad? Have you lost them so soon?'

Invictus smiled back. 'They did not fare as well as I,' he replied. 'But I see that you are not without troubles of your own.'

More ravenous faces appeared at the end of the corridor, rushing towards their doom, and Invictus added the sound of his own bolt pistol to the staccato melody of gunfire.

'There is some kind of lair up ahead,' Genareas bellowed above the din. 'It is packed with these creatures. We cannot make it through.'

'Then we will have to go around,' shouted Invictus, pointing to a sign written in ancient and crumbling script above their heads. Genareas looked up, nodding his agreement as he read the word 'Airlock' on the sign.

'Withdraw,' ordered Genareas, flooding the corridor with another torrent of liquid flame.

One by one, the remaining warriors moved back along the passage in short sprints before turning and supporting their battle-brothers' withdrawal with bursts of fire. Within seconds they were at the airlock, leaving a trail of corrupted bodies in their wake.

Once all his battle-brothers were inside, Invictus pulled the ancient lever, sealing the outer lock. At once, more of the mutant brood appeared, flinging themselves at the reinforced hatch in their voracious attempts to get at the escaping warriors.

Genareas was already at the airlock controls, reducing the pressure within the room so that they were not blown out into the immaterium once the outer door's seals were broken. Invictus and his brothers could only watch and wait as the creatures smashed their fists and heads against the toughened plasglass, unyielding in their desire to destroy the warriors inside.

'These beasts are insane,' said Brother Crassus, staring intently at the mad creatures. 'They would destroy themselves just to get to us.'

Invictus laughed. 'Take a good look. These creatures are what we are destined to become. All but one of us.'

'What do you mean?' asked Agon, as Invictus's words sparked a murmur of doubt from the rest.

'These things were once our brothers, the product of Challenges past. One of them spoke to me – it revealed that only the first of us to the transportation portal will be relayed to safety. The rest will be left behind, left to the vagaries of the warp.'

The warriors began to eye one another warily, unsure of how to take the news.

'We should discuss this later,' said Genareas. 'For now, I would suggest a deep breath and a tight grip.'

With that there came a sharp hiss, as the outer seal of the airlock began to lift, revealing the stark oblivion of the immaterium beyond.

Genareas was the first to brave the cold vacuum, shouldering his flamer and gripping the corrugated hull of the great ship for dear life. He was closely followed by Agon, then Crassus and Septimon. Invictus looked to Moloch, offering him the next place in line but his battle-brother shook his head, eyeing him suspiciously. With a shrug, Invictus made his way into the void, his fingers gripping hard to the strip of weathered metal that was his only lifeline. Just as Moloch joined him on the outer hull there came an almighty blast of air as the plasglass finally gave way under its vicious assault, depressurising the corridor within and blowing flailing mutants into the immaterium.

Invictus and his brothers quickly made their way across the hull, with the mutated bodies of what were once proud warriors floating away into the black behind them like so much flotsam.

Though their mucranoid glands would offer protection against the vacuum it would not last indefinitely, and Invictus felt relief wash over him as he saw Genareas opening another airlock up ahead.

Genareas and Agon made their way into the ship, and the other warriors quickened their pace along the handrail of the hull. Crassus was next into the airlock and Septimon was about to climb inside when Invictus felt the railing suddenly yield under his weight. The iron bolts securing the rail to the hull began to give way, and separate from the ship's corrugated surface. Invictus glanced back at Moloch, a wicked plan quickly formulating in his mind. One less rival would take him one step closer to victory, and besides, Moloch had always been his inferior.

Panic suddenly crossed Moloch's face as he saw Invictus's look of loathing.

Both Space Marines moved faster, desperate to reach the airlock before the railing came free altogether. Invictus managed to grip the inside of the door, feeling a strong hand grasp his wrist. With a last look back at Moloch, he pulled hard on the railing, wrenching the remaining rusted bolts from their housing and sending his battle-brother reeling into the immaterium. Moloch's mouth opened wide in a silent scream as he floated off, and Invictus was pulled inside to safety.

The warriors began to breath easily once more as the outer seal was brought down with a hiss. Invictus looked to his brothers and saw that more than one of them was regarding him accusatorially.

'What happened to Moloch?' said Agon, bringing his autogun to bear.

'Do you accuse me, brother?' Invictus replied, reaching for the bolt pistol in his belt.

Before anyone could move, both battle-brothers had aimed their weapons. There was a sudden flurry of movement, as Genareas raised his flamer to point at Agon, and in turn Septimon and Crassus pointed their own weapons at Invictus.

'We have enough enemies without turning on each another,' said Genareas. 'If we cull our own numbers there is less chance we will even reach the portal to freedom. Once we find it, then we should allow our strength of arms to decide which of us survives. Until then, we are still brothers, we are still the Sons of Malice.'

Invictus slowly lowered his bolt pistol, and Agon did the same.

'Well met,' said Genareas. 'Let's get moving. It may not take these creatures long to work out our strategy.' With that he led the way from the airlock and along yet another seemingly endless tunnel.

The rest of the warriors followed in his stead, but they all regarded each other with a warier eye than they had previously – especially Invictus.

THE TUNNEL DIPPED, drawing them ever downward as though into the abyss itself. Invictus knew that to be a ridiculous notion – they were on the foundering carcass of an ancient spaceship, and despite its artificial suspensors giving the illusion of gravity, there was no 'up' or 'down'.

Nevertheless, they seemed to be drawn deeper into the Labyrinth, and moisture began pooling at their feet. The further they penetrated, the deeper the waters got until they were soon wading waist deep through foetid green sludge.

Once again, that bellowing voice emanated from some hidden part of the ship, but this time it was much closer. Invictus strained to hear what was being said but he could still not discern the meaning. The phrase consisted of three words, each of a single syllable, howled over and over again. What foul litany, and whatever ancient alien tongue it was in, was impossible to tell, but one thing was for sure – the speaker was no ordinary mortal.

A sudden scream pierced the tunnel, rising louder than the distant roar, and every man turned as one. It was Crassus, who had been bringing up their rear. The warriors aimed their weapons as their brother was lifted into the air by some unseen hand, his body clearing the water that oozed all around them. Blood spurted from his mouth as he tried to scream once more, his body pierced from behind by a huge, spiked tentacle that burst through his chest and flailed around as though probing for another victim.

As the lifeless body of Crassus was discarded to sink below the surface of the mire, the squad opened fire, shredding the putrid thing that had impaled their brother. More appendages began to rise from the water all around, blindly searching for prey.

'Retreat,' yelled Agon. 'There are too many!'

Invictus began to wade through the morass as tentacles rose all around. Bolter fire streaked past him as he moved down the tunnel and up ahead he could see the passage rising out of the water to safety. Agon and Septimon fired over his head, pulverising the foul smelling feelers as they reached out towards him, and as Invictus moved past him, Genareas blasted a cloud of molten fire into the corridor.

The water level around them dropped as they climbed the passageway, but the probing tentacles still relentlessly pursued them. If they could make it through the open doorway ahead they would be free, but as they neared it, a blast hatch began to slowly descend, threatening to trap them in the corridor with the deadly spiked limbs.

Septimon was the first to the doorway, dropping his weapon and grasping the hatch as it lowered. Invictus could hear the grinding of gears as Septimon's great strength fought against the ancient mechanism that sought to entomb them.

Agon was the first through the gap braced open by his brother Septimon, and he was quickly followed by Genareas. As Invictus passed through he gave one last glance to Septimon, his face grimly set as he held open the heavy steel door. Then he was gone, the metal portal slamming down and sealing his brother in with the horde of disembodied tentacles.

Invictus sat in the dark corridor, panting for air. Genareas offered him his arm, and Invictus gratefully accepted it, rising to his feet, his every fibre seeming to ache.

'Where is Agon?' said Genareas, glancing down the corridor.

'He must think us near to our goal.'

'And he wishes to claim his place amongst the Doomed Ones and leave us to our fate in this place.'

'Then we must hurry,' Invictus replied, moving off down the passageway.

With their last reserves of energy, the two warriors pursued their errant brother, and this time it was Invictus who led the way, for once a step in front of Genareas.

The passageway gradually turned and widened into a dark hall, deep shadows cloistering it on either side. Great statues rose upwards from the dark, ancient sentinels that lined the hall, but Invictus paid them no heed, for up ahead was a much more majestic sight.

A great portal stood at the far end of the massive chamber, fulgurating blue disks dancing up and down its length, tempting Invictus – beckoning him ever closer. But between he and it was the sprinting form of Agon, way ahead, ready to claim the prize that was rightfully his.

'Agon!' Genareas cried.

As he neared the portal, Agon stopped, slowly turning with a smile.

'I am truly sorry, my brothers. But it seems I must leave you. I wish you–'

Something streaked from the dark, cutting Agon off mid sentence. A huge chitin claw, ancient and battered, gripped him around the waist, lifting him five metres into the air. Agon screamed, blood gurgling from his mouth as the claw squeezed tight. The two halves of his body fell to the ground, innards spilling onto the hard steel decking.

Then it walked from the shadows.

Four massive limbs carried its great bulk forward. It was a mass of flesh and steel, metal plates cauterised to a body of seething blubber. Two great claws reached out to the fore and clacked together menacingly. But it was the head that was the most hideous – a twisted, bloated replica of a face that might once have been human, but was now so savage and malign as to be almost unrecognisable.

As Invictus watched in horror, its great jaws opened and it bellowed forth its incessant call.

'LET. ME. OUT!' it screamed, filling the hall with its ear splitting roar.

It was now all too clear. This was no ancient war cry Invictus had been hearing – it was simply the maddened ranting of an insane mutant, caged for centuries and left to the mercy of the warp's corrupting influence.

And now it was the only thing standing in the way of victory.

Genareas was the first to move, stepping forward and unleashing a gout of flame that consumed the monster's head. When the inferno subsided, Invictus could see that the flames had not even left a mark on the beast's hardened carapace. He raised his bolt pistol, firing at the creature's eye, but the explosive rounds did nothing but cause it annoyance.

It roared once more, repeating its interminable request for release, before stomping forward on those thick and hideous limbs.

'I have only one shot left,' said Invictus. 'We must make this last round count.'

'I understand, brother,' Genareas replied, grasping his flamer by the stock.

The beast opened its maw, ready to bellow at them again, and Genareas took his chance, flinging the flamer into its gaping jaws.

Invictus raised the bolt pistol, waiting for his moment. He had only a split second window in which to fire, but he was a veteran of the Sons of Malice, a warrior unmatched on the field. A split second was more than he would ever need.

An explosive round pierced the promethium canister just as the flamer entered the behemoth's mouth, igniting the liquid flame within. It exploded, blowing the top of the mutant's head clean off, and silencing it forever. For a few seconds the body of the twisted juggernaut staggered on its four limbs, uncertain of whether or not it was dead. Then, like a tower suddenly robbed of its foundations, it collapsed to the ground.

Genareas smiled at his brother. 'And so it is just us two remaining,' he said. 'It is fitting that we should face one another this last time. We will fight, with nothing but our bare hands and our stone resolve, and the victor will claim the spoils.' He gestured towards the portal, which still flashed and quivered seductively. 'How I have waited for this day, Invictus. Ours is a kinship forged in a hundred battles, and tempered in the blood of a thousand vanquished enemies. This will be a battle to end all battles. I am only sorry that we cannot both march from here triumphant, but as you know, there can be only one champion.'

Invictus nodded his agreement. 'I too am sorry, brother,' he said, raising the bolt pistol. 'For when I said I had only a single round remaining; I lied.'

Genareas had little time to protest before Invictus squeezed the trigger, sending his brother's brains exploding from the back of his head.

Discarding the now empty pistol, Invictus strode towards the coruscating portal and stepped within the threshold of its glorious light.

HE STOOD AT the centre of a wide, carved circle. Ancient sigils intersected one another across its face, eliciting the notion of daemonic faces in his mind, but as soon as he tried to focus on them the faces were gone.

Surrounding him on all sides was the faint sparking light of a containment shield. Invictus found it hard to imagine what awaited him that would require such a safeguard; there was no way he would flinch in the face of his destiny. Nevertheless, he was not about to question the dictates of Lord Kathal.

Lining the periphery of the great hall were his brothers of the Sons of Malice, fully regaled in their armour, bearing the standards and livery of the Chapter. The sides of the hall rose in tiers, allowing each and every man to view the proceedings. Each would be able to watch as the ceremony took place, each would see as Invictus was elevated to the ranks of the Doomed Ones. This had never happened before, and Kathal must have deemed his victory in the Labyrinth a historic one to break with tradition in such a way.

From one end of the great hall, Invictus saw Lord Kathal approaching, flanked by his Librarians and their priestly attendants, bedecked in their cerulean robes. Servitors carried the Chapter's ancient tomes, and liturgies droned from the automated vox-units that hovered alongside the procession. But there was more; huge caskets pulled along by the grasping mechadendrites of the Chapter's Techmarines. What was in these caskets Invictus had no idea, but something about their unexpected appearance began to fill him with a sense of unease.

As the huge room filled with the scent of burning incense, a macabre silence seemed to descend upon the proceedings. It was an unnerving quiet, and Invictus's unease began to intensify into a stolid feeling of dread. This was not the exultant ritual he had been anticipating – it was more like a funeral march.

As the feeling intensified, Kathal approached him, his stone face grim in the hazy darkness.

'You have proven yourself the best among us, Invictus. You have proven you are without peer for your strength and cunning. You are the most potent, the latest to prove himself worthy to join the Doomed Ones.'

The Librarians had surrounded him now, a monotonous chant emanating from within their hooded robes. The ancient, dark language that was spewed forth by the vox-units grew louder with every passing second, and Invictus could feel something metallic on the air, as though a storm were brewing within the confines of the hall. The Techmarines had positioned the caskets, ten in all, in a circle around Invictus. They ceremoniously released the holy seals that bound their locks and revealed what was inside. Ten blank faces stared out at Invictus – ten silent warriors, their bodies still robust but their minds vacuous.

His unease suddenly turned to cold panic. He told himself this was all part of the ritual, that there was nothing to fear, but his base instincts were crying out for him to flee this place. With the containment field binding him in place though, flight was impossible.

'You are the eleventh hero, Invictus, the eleventh and final warrior. Look to your battle-brothers,' he gestured to the blank faces that glared with vacant expressions. 'Your predecessors, each one succeeding in the Challenge of the Labyrinth for the honour of joining the ranks of the Doomed Ones. For a thousand years have we searched for champions worthy of Him. And tonight, finally you are all assembled.

'Our crusade can now begin. Now we will be strong enough to take back that which was stolen from us –

Scelus, our home world. None will stand in our way – not the forces of the foul Ruinous Powers nor the servants of the Carrion Lord. Not with Him by our side.'

Terror gripped Invictus as he looked down at the circle beneath his feet. Eldritch light was beginning to emanate from the carved runes, dancing and gambolling, flashing green and blue and red.

'Now you will learn what it is to be among the Doomed Ones,' continued Lord Kathal, taking a step backwards. 'Now Malice will show you what your victory has wrought.'

Invictus tried to speak, to demand to know what was happening to him, but he found his jaw would not move. The words simply would not come. The whisper of the Librarians rose, as did the vox-units, and they soon reached a crescendo. The light at Invictus's feet grew brighter, lashing upwards to sting his legs and bathe him in its iniquitous light.

'You are truly worthy, Invictus of the Sons,' Kathal screamed, raising his arms to the shadows of the rooftop. 'Can you hear Him calling? He has come to accept your tribute. He has come for the Labyrinth's eleven. He has come to walk among us.'

Invictus followed Kathal's gaze, lifting his head to the ceiling. Through the shadows he could see the outline of something huge, something that stared down with baleful eyes. Something wicked in the dark.

He screamed. Screamed for the pain that engulfed his body. Screamed for the terror in the depths of his soul. But no amount of screaming could halt the ritual now.

It began to descend, pulling with it the dark and the pain. Invictus raised his voice in a last tumultuous cry as his flesh began to flay from his bones.

As his body was consumed, he realised that not even the kindly release of oblivion could save him now...

* * *

In the great hall all was silent.

The Sons had watched as the light consumed the body of their brother Invictus, along with the ten other heroes of the Labyrinth, their limbs immolated, their torsos eviscerated, their heads contorting and twisting, writhing within a pool of black light.

And now what stood before them was no longer their brothers. Invictus and the rest were gone – gone to join the ranks of the legendary Doomed Ones.

What stood before them was the revenant they had worshipped for millennia. The eidolon that would stand at their vanguard as they retook what was rightfully theirs.

He could only be summoned by sacrifice – only by giving unto Him their best and most praiseworthy warriors could He walk among them.

And here He stood, gazing with eyes of fire – the Renegade God, the Outcast, the Lost, Hierarch of Anarchy and Terror…

…Malice.

HEADHUNTED

Steve Parker

SOMETHING VAST, DARK and brutish moved across the pin-pricked curtain of space, blotting out the diamond lights of the constellations behind it as if swallowing them whole. It was the size of a city block, and its bulbous eyes, like those of a great blind fish, glowed with a green and baleful light.

It was a terrible thing to behold, this leviathan – a harbinger of doom – and its passage had brought agony and destruction to countless victims in the centuries it had swum among the stars. It travelled, now, through the Charybdis Sub-sector on trails of angry red plasma, cutting across the inky darkness with a purpose.

That purpose was close at hand, and a change began to take place on its bestial features. New lights flickered to life on its muzzle, shining far brighter and sharper than its eyes, illuminating myriad shapes, large and small, that danced and spun in high orbit above the glowing orange sphere of Arronax II. With a slow, deliberate motion, the leviathan unhinged its massive lower jaw, and opened its mouth to feed.

At first, the glimmering pieces of debris it swallowed were mere fragments, nothing much larger than a man. But soon, heavier, bulkier pieces drifted into that gaping maw, passing between its bladelike teeth and down into its black throat.

For hours, the monster gorged itself on space-borne scrap, devouring everything it could fit into its mouth. The pickings were good. There had been heavy fighting here in ages past. Scoured worlds and lifeless wrecks were all that remained now, locked in a slow elliptical dance around the local star. But the wrecks, at least, had a future. Once salvaged, they would be forged anew, recast in forms that would bring death and suffering down upon countless others. For, of course, this beast, this hungry monster of the void, was no beast at all.

It was an ork ship. And the massive glyphs daubed sloppily on its hull marked it as a vessel of the Deathskull clan.

RE-PRESSURISATION BEGAN THE moment the ship's vast metal jaws clanged shut. The process took around twenty minutes, pumps flooding the salvage bay with breathable, if foul-smelling, air. The orks crowding the corridor beyond the bay's airlock doors roared their impatience and hammered their fists against the thick metal bulkheads. They shoved and jostled for position. Then, just when it seemed murderous violence was sure to erupt, sirens sounded and the heavy doors split apart. The orks surged forward, pushing and scrambling, racing towards the mountains of scrap, each utterly focused on claiming the choicest pieces for himself.

Fights broke out between the biggest and darkest skinned. They roared and wrestled with each other, and snapped at each other with tusk-filled jaws. They lashed out with the tools and weapons that bristled on their augmented limbs. They might have killed each other but for the massive suits of cybernetic armour they wore. These were no mere greenskin foot soldiers. They were orks of a unique genus, the engineers of their race, each born with an inherent understanding of machines. It was hard-coded into their marrow in the same way as violence and torture.

As was true of every caste, however, some among them were cleverer than others. While the mightiest bellowed and beat their metal-plated chests, one ork, marginally shorter and leaner than the rest, slid around them and into the shadows, intent on getting first pickings.

This ork was called Gorgrot in the rough speech of his race, and, despite the sheer density of salvage the ship had swallowed, it didn't take him long to find something truly valuable. At the very back of the junk-filled bay, closes to the ship's great metal teeth, he found the ruined, severed prow of a mid-sized human craft. As he studied it, he noticed weapon barrels protruding from the front end. His alien heart quickened. Functional or not, he could do great things with salvaged weapon systems. He would make himself more dangerous, an ork to be reckoned with.

After a furtive look over his shoulder to make sure none of the bigger orks had noticed him, he moved straight across to the wrecked prow, reached out a gnarled hand and touched the hull. Its armour-plating was in bad shape, pocked and cratered by plasma fire and torpedo impacts. To the rear, the metal was twisted and black where it had sheared away from the rest of the craft. It looked like an explosion had torn the ship apart. To Gorgrot, however, the nature of the ship's destruction mattered not at all. What mattered was its potential. Already, visions of murderous creativity were flashing through his tiny mind in rapid succession, so many at once, in fact, that he forgot to breathe until his lungs sent him a painful reminder. These visions were a gift from

Gork and Mork, the bloodthirsty greenskin gods, and he had received their like many times before. All greenskin engineers received them, and nothing, save the rending of an enemy's flesh, felt so utterly right.

Even so, it was something small and insignificant that pulled him out of his rapture.

A light had begun to flash on the lower left side of the ruined prow, winking at him from beneath a tangle of beams and cables and dented armour plates, igniting his simple-minded curiosity, drawing him towards it. It was small and green, and it looked like it might be a button of some kind. Gorgrot began clearing debris from the area around it. Soon, he was grunting and growling with the effort, sweating despite the assistance of his armour's strength-boosting hydraulics.

Within minutes, he had removed all obstructions between himself and the blinking light, and discovered that it was indeed a kind of button.

Gorgrot was extending his finger out to press it when something suddenly wrenched him backwards with irresistible force. He was hurled to the ground and landed hard on his back with a snarl. Immediately, he tried to scramble up again, but a huge metal boot stamped down on him, denting his belly-armour and pushing him deep into the carpet of sharp scrap.

Gorgrot looked up into the blazing red eyes of the biggest, heaviest ork in the salvage bay.

This was Zazog, personal engineer to the mighty Warboss Balthazog Bludwrekk, and few orks on the ship were foolish enough to challenge any of his salvage claims. It was the reason he always arrived in the salvage bay last of all; his tardiness was the supreme symbol of his dominance among the scavengers.

Zazog staked his claim now, turning from Gorgrot and stomping over to the wrecked prow. There, he hunkered down to examine the winking button. He knew well enough what it meant. There had to be a working power source onboard, something far more valuable than most scrap. He flicked out a blowtorch attachment from the middle knuckle of his mechanised left claw and burned a rough likeness of his personal glyph into the side of the wrecked prow. Then he rose and bellowed a challenge to those around him.

Scores of gretchin, puniest members of the orkoid race, skittered away in panic, disappearing into the protection of the shadows. The other orks stepped back, growling at Zazog, snarling in anger. But none dared challenge him.

Zazog glared at each in turn, forcing them, one by one, to drop their gazes or die by his hand. Then, satisfied at their deference, he turned and pressed a thick finger to the winking green button.

For a brief moment, nothing happened. Zazog growled and pressed it again. Still nothing. He was about to begin pounding it with his mighty fist when he heard a noise.

It was the sound of atmospheric seals unlocking.

The door shuddered, and began sliding up into the hull.

Zazog's craggy, scar-covered face twisted into a hideous grin. Yes, there *was* a power source on board. The door's motion proved it. He, like Gorgrot, began to experience flashes of divine inspiration, visions of weaponry so grand and deadly that his limited brain could hardly cope. No matter; the gods would work through him once he got started. His hands would automatically fashion what his brain could barely comprehend. It was always the way.

The sliding door retracted fully now, revealing an entrance just large enough for Zazog's armoured bulk to squeeze through. He shifted forward with that very intention, but the moment never came.

From the shadows inside the doorway, there was a soft coughing sound.

Zazog's skull disintegrated in a haze of blood and bone chips. His headless corpse crashed backwards onto the carpet of junk.

The other orks gaped in slack-jawed wonder. They looked down at Zazog's body, trying to make sense of the dim warnings that rolled through their minds. Ignoring the obvious threat, the biggest orks quickly began roaring fresh claims and shoving the others aside, little realising that their own deaths were imminent.

But imminent they were.

A great black shadow appeared, bursting from the door Zazog had opened. It was humanoid, not quite as large as the orks surrounding it, but bulky nonetheless, though it moved with a speed and confidence no ork could ever have matched. Its long adamantium talons sparked and crackled with deadly energy as it slashed and stabbed in all directions, a whirlwind of lethal motion. Great fountains of thick red blood arced through the air as it killed again and again. Greenskins fell like sacks of meat.

More shadows emerged from the wreck now. Four of them. Like the first, all were dressed in heavy black ceramite armour. All bore an intricate skull and 'I' design on their massive left pauldrons. The icons on their right pauldrons, however, were each unique.

'Clear the room,' barked one over his comm-link as he gunned down a greenskin in front of him, spitting death from the barrel of his silenced bolter. 'Quick and quiet. Kill the rest before they raise the alarm.' Switching comm channels, he said, 'Sigma, this is Talon Alpha. Phase one complete. Kill-team is aboard. Securing entry point now.'

'Understood, Alpha,' replied the toneless voice at the other end of the link. 'Proceed on mission. Extract within the hour, as instructed. Captain Redthorne has orders to pull out if you miss your pick-up, so keep your team on a tight leash. This is *not* a purge operation. Is that clear?'

'I'm well aware of that, Sigma,' the kill-team leader replied brusquely.

'You had better be,' replied the voice. 'Sigma, out.'

* * *

It took Talon squad less than sixty seconds to clear the salvage bay. Brother Rauth of the Exorcists Chapter gunned down the last of the fleeing gretchin as it dashed for the exit. The creature stumbled as a single silenced bolt punched into its back. Half a second later, a flesh-muffled detonation ripped it apart.

It was the last of twenty-six bodies to fall among the litter of salvaged scrap.

'Target down, Karras,' reported Rauth. 'Area clear.'

'Confirmed,' replied Karras. He turned to face a Space Marine with a heavy flamer. 'Omni, you know what to do. The rest of you, cover the entrance.'

With the exception of Omni, the team immediately moved to positions covering the mouth of the corridor through which the orks had come. Omni, otherwise known as Maximmion Voss of the Imperial Fists, moved to the side walls, first the left, then the right, working quickly at a number of thick hydraulic pistons and power cables there.

'That was messy, Karras,' said Brother Solarion, 'letting them see us as we came out. I told you we should have used smoke. If one had escaped and raised the alarm...'

Karras ignored the comment. It was just Solarion being Solarion.

'Give it a rest, Prophet,' said Brother Zeed, opting to use Solarion's nickname. Zeed had coined it himself, and knew precisely how much it irritated the proud Ultramarine. 'The room is clear. No runners. No alarms. Scholar knows what he's doing.'

Scholar. That was what they called Karras, or at least Brothers Voss and Zeed did. Rauth and Solarion insisted on calling him by his second name. Sigma always called him Alpha. And his battle-brothers back on Occludus, homeworld of the Death Spectres Chapter, simply called him by his first name, Lyandro, or sometimes simply Codicier – his rank in the Librarius.

Karras didn't much care what anyone called him so long as they all did their jobs. The honour of serving in the Deathwatch had been offered to him, and he had taken it, knowing the great glory it would bring both himself and his Chapter. But he wouldn't be sorry when his obligation to the Emperor's Holy Inquisition was over. Astartes life seemed far less complicated among one's own Chapter-brothers.

When would he return to the fold? He didn't know. There was no fixed term for Deathwatch service. The Inquisition made high demands of all it called upon. Karras might not see the darkly beautiful crypt-cities of his home world again for decades... if he lived that long.

'Done, Scholar,' reported Voss as he rejoined the rest of the team.

Karras nodded and pointed towards a shattered pict screen and rune-board that protruded from the wall, close to the bay's only exit. 'Think you can get anything from that?' he asked.

'Nothing from the screen,' said Voss, 'but I could try wiring the data-feed directly into my visor.'

'Do it,' said Karras, 'but be quick.' To the others, he said, 'Proceed with phase two. Solarion, take point.'

The Ultramarine nodded curtly, rose from his position among the scrap and stalked forward into the shadowy corridor, bolter raised and ready. He moved with smooth, near-silent steps despite the massive weight of his armour. Torias Telion, famed Ultramarine Scout Master and Solarion's former mentor, would have been proud of his prize student.

One by one, with the exception of Voss, the rest of the kill-team followed in his wake.

THE FILTHY, RUSTING corridors of the ork ship were lit, but the electric lamps the greenskins had strung up along pipes and ducts were old and in poor repair. Barely half of them seemed to be working at all. Even these buzzed and flickered in a constant battle to throw out their weak illumination. Still, the little light they did give was enough to bother the kill-team leader. The inquisitor, known to the members of Talon only by his call-sign, Sigma, had estimated the ork population of the ship at somewhere over twenty thousand. Against odds like these, Karras knew only too well that darkness and stealth were among his best weapons.

'I want the lights taken out,' he growled. 'The longer we stay hidden, the better our chances of making it off this damned heap.'

'We could shoot them out as we go,' offered Solarion, 'but I'd rather not waste my ammunition on something that doesn't bleed.'

Just then, Karras heard Voss on the comm-link. 'I've finished with the terminal, Scholar. I managed to pull some old cargo manifests from the ship's memory core. Not much else, though. Apparently, this ship used to be a civilian heavy-transport, Magellan-class, built on Stygies. It was called *The Pegasus*.'

'No schematics?'

'Most of the memory core is heavily corrupted. It's thousands of years old. We were lucky to get that much.'

'Sigma, this is Alpha,' said Karras. 'The ork ship is built around an Imperial transport called *The Pegasus*. Requesting schematics, priority one.'

'I heard,' said Sigma. 'You'll have them as soon as I do.'

'Voss, where are you now?' Karras asked.

'Close to your position,' said the Imperial Fist.

'Do you have any idea which cable provides power to the lights?'

'Look up,' said Voss. 'See those cables running along the ceiling? The thick one, third from the left. I'd wager my knife on it.'

Karras didn't have to issue the order. The moment Zeed heard Voss's words, his right arm flashed upwards. There was a crackle of blue energy as the Raven Guard's claws sliced through the cable, and the corridor went utterly dark.

To the Space Marines, however, everything remained clear as day. Their MkVII helmets, like everything else in their arsenal, had been heavily modified by the Inquisition's finest artificers. They boasted a composite low-light/thermal vision mode that was superior to anything else Karras had ever used. In the three years he had been leading Talon, it had tipped the balance in his favour more times than he cared to count. He hoped it would do so many more times in the years to come, but that would all depend on their survival here, and he knew all too well that the odds were against them from the start. It wasn't just the numbers they were up against, or the tight deadline. There was something here the likes of which few Deathwatch kill-teams had ever faced before.

Karras could already feel its presence somewhere on the upper levels of the ship.

'Keep moving,' he told the others.

THREE MINUTES AFTER Zeed had killed the lights, Solarion hissed for them all to stop. 'Karras,' he rasped, 'I have multiple xenos up ahead. Suggest you move up and take a look.'

Karras ordered the others to hold and went forward, careful not to bang or scrape his broad pauldrons against the clutter of twisting pipes that lined both walls. Crouching beside Solarion, he realised he needn't have worried about a little noise. In front of him, over a hundred orks had crowded into a high-ceilinged, octagonal chamber. They were hooting and laughing and wrestling with each other to get nearer the centre of the room.

Neither Karras nor Solarion could see beyond the wall of broad green backs, but there was clearly something in the middle that was holding their attention.

'What are they doing?' whispered Solarion.

Karras decided there was only one way to find out. He centred his awareness down in the pit of his stomach, and began reciting the *Litany of the Sight Beyond Sight* that his former master, Chief Librarian Athio Cordatus, had taught him during his earliest years in the Librarius. Beneath his helmet, hidden from Solarion's view, Karras's eyes, normally deep red in colour, began to glow with an ethereal white flame. On his forehead, a wound appeared. A single drop of blood rolled over his brow and down to the bridge of his narrow, angular nose. Slowly, as he opened his soul fractionally more to the dangerous power within him, the wound widened, revealing the physical manifestation of his psychic inner eye.

Karras felt his awareness lift out of his body now. He willed it deeper into the chamber, rising above the backs of the orks, looking down on them from above.

He saw a great pit sunk into the centre of the metal floor. It was filled with hideous ovoid creatures of every possible colour, their tiny red eyes set above oversized mouths crammed with razor-edged teeth.

'It's a mess hall,' Karras told his team over the link. 'There's a squig pit in the centre.'

As his projected consciousness watched, the greenskins at the rim of the pit stabbed downwards with cruelly barbed poles, hooking their prey through soft flesh. Then they lifted the squigs, bleeding and screaming, into the air before reaching for them, tearing them from the hooks, and feasting on them.

'They're busy,' said Karras, 'but we'll need to find another way through.'

'Send me in, Scholar,' said Voss from the rear. 'I'll turn them all into cooked meat before they even realise they're under attack. Ghost can back me up.'

'On your order, Scholar,' said Zeed eagerly.

Ghost. That was Siefer Zeed. With his helmet off, it was easy to see how he'd come by the name. Like Karras, and like all brothers of their respective Chapters, Zeed was the victim of a failed melanochromic implant, a slight mutation in his ancient and otherwise worthy geneseed. The skin of both he and the kill-team leader was as white as porcelain. But, whereas Karras bore the blood-red eyes and chalk-white hair of the true albino, Zeed's eyes were black as coals, and his hair no less dark.

'Negative,' said Karras. 'We'll find another way through.'

He pushed his astral-self further into the chamber, desperate to find a means that didn't involve alerting the foe, but there seemed little choice. Only when he turned his awareness upwards did he see what he was looking for.

'There's a walkway near the ceiling,' he reported. 'It looks frail, rusting badly, but if we cross it one at a time, it should hold.'

A sharp, icy voice on the comm-link interrupted him. 'Talon Alpha, get ready to receive those schematics. Transmitting now.'

Karras willed his consciousness back into his body, and his glowing third eye sealed itself, leaving only the barest trace of a scar. Using conventional sight, he consulted his helmet's heads-up display and watched the last few percent of the schematics file being downloaded. When it was finished, he called it up with a thought, and the helmet projected it as a shimmering green image cast directly onto his left retina.

The others, he knew, were seeing the same thing.

'According to these plans,' he told them, 'there's an access ladder set into the wall near the second junction we passed. We'll backtrack to it. The corridor above this one will give us access to the walkway.'

'If it's still there,' said Solarion. 'The orks may have removed it.'

'And backtracking will cost us time,' grumbled Voss.

'Less time than a firefight would cost us,' countered Rauth. His hard, gravelly tones were made even harder by the slight distortion on the comm-link. 'There's a time and place for that kind of killing, but it isn't now.'

'Watcher's right,' said Zeed reluctantly. It was rare for he and Rauth to agree.

'I've told you before,' warned Rauth. 'Don't call me that.'

'Right or wrong,' said Karras, 'I'm not taking votes. I've made my call. Let's move.'

KARRAS WAS THE last to cross the gantry above the ork feeding pit. The shadows up here were dense and, so far, the orks had noticed nothing, though there had been a few moments when it looked as if the aging iron were about to collapse, particularly beneath the tremendous weight of Voss with his heavy flamer, high explosives, and back-mounted promethium supply.

Such was the weight of the Imperial Fist and his kit that Karras had decided to send him over first. Voss had made it across, but it was nothing short of a miracle that the orks below hadn't noticed the rain of red flakes showering down on them.

Lucky we didn't bring old Chyron after all, thought Karras.

The sixth member of Talon wouldn't have made it out of the salvage bay. The corridors on this ship were too narrow for such a mighty Space Marine. Instead, Sigma had ordered the redoubtable Dreadnought, formerly of the Lamenters Chapter but now permanently attached to Talon, to remain behind on Redthorne's ship, the *Saint Nevarre*. That had caused a few tense moments. Chyron had a vile temper.

Karras made his way, centimetre by centimetre, along the creaking metal grille, his silenced bolter fixed securely to the magnetic couplings on his right thigh plate, his force sword sheathed on his left hip. Over one massive shoulder was slung the cryo-case that Sigma had insisted he carry. Karras cursed it, but there was no way he could leave it behind. It added twenty kilogrammes to his already significant weight, but the case was absolutely critical to the mission. He had no choice.

Up ahead, he could see Rauth watching him, as ever, from the end of the gangway. What was the Exorcist thinking? Karras had no clue. He had never been able to read the mysterious Astartes. Rauth seemed to have no warp signature whatsoever. He simply didn't register at all. Even his armour, even his bolter for Throne's sake, resonated more than he did. And it was an anomaly that Rauth was singularly unwilling to discuss.

There was no love lost between them, Karras knew, and, for his part, he regretted that. He had made gestures, occasional overtures, but for whatever reason, they had been rebuffed every time. The Exorcist was unreachable, distant, remote, and it seemed he planned to stay that way.

As Karras took his next step, the cryo-case suddenly swung forward on its strap, shifting his centre of gravity and threatening to unbalance him. He compensated swiftly, but the effort caused the gangway to creak and a piece of rusted metal snapped off, spinning away under him.

He froze, praying that the orks wouldn't notice.

But one did.

It was at the edge of the pit, poking a fat squig with its barbed pole, when the metal fragment struck its head. The ork immediately stopped what it was doing and scanned the shadows above it, squinting suspiciously up towards the unlit recesses of the high ceiling.

Karras stared back, willing it to turn away. Reading minds and controlling minds, however, were two very different things. The latter was a power beyond his gifts. Ultimately, it wasn't Karras's will that turned the ork from its scrutiny. It was the nature of the greenskin species.

The other orks around it, impatient to feed, began grabbing at the barbed pole. One managed to snatch it, and the gazing ork suddenly found himself robbed of his chance to feed. He launched himself into a violent frenzy, lashing out at the pole-thief and those nearby. That was when the orks behind him surged forward, and pushed him into the squig pit.

Karras saw the squigs swarm on the hapless ork, sinking their long teeth into its flesh and tearing away great, bloody mouthfuls. The food chain had been turned on its head. The orks around the pit laughed and capered and struck at their dying fellow with their poles.

Karras didn't stop to watch. He moved on carefully, cursing the black case that was now pressed tight to his side with one arm. He rejoined his team in the mouth of a tunnel on the far side of the gantry, and they moved off, pressing deeper into the ship. Solarion moved up front with Zeed. Voss stayed in the middle. Rauth and Karras brought up the rear.

'They need to do some damned maintenance around here,' Karras told Rauth in a wry tone.

The Exorcist said nothing.

BY COMPARING SIGMA's schematics of *The Pegasus* with the features he saw as he moved through it, it soon became clear to Karras that the orks had done very little to alter the interior of the ship beyond covering its walls in badly rendered glyphs, defecating wherever they pleased, leaving dead bodies to rot where they fell, and generally making the place unfit for habitation by anything save their own wretched kind. Masses of quivering fungi had sprouted from broken water pipes. Frayed electrical cables sparked and hissed at anyone who walked by. And there were so many bones strewn about that some sections almost looked like mass graves.

The Deathwatch members made a number of kills, or rather Solarion did, as they proceeded deeper into the ship's belly. Most of these were gretchin sent out on some errand or other by their slavemasters. The Utramarine silently executed them wherever he found them and stuffed the small corpses under pipes or in dark alcoves. Only twice did the kill-team encounter parties of ork warriors, and both times, the greenskins announced themselves well in advance with their loud grunting and jabbering. Karras could tell that Voss and Zeed were both itching to engage, but stealth was still paramount. Instead, he, Rauth and Solarion eliminated the foe, loading powerful hellfire rounds into their silenced bolters to ensure quick, quiet one-shot kills.

'I've reached Waypoint Adrius,' Solarion soon reported from up ahead. 'No xenos contacts.'

'Okay, move in and secure,' Karras ordered. 'Check your corners and exits.'

The kill-team hurried forward, emerging from the blackness of the corridor into a towering square shaft. It was hundreds of metres high, its metal walls stained with age and rust and all kinds of spillage. Thick pipes ran across the walls at all angles, many of them venting steam or dripping icy coolant. There were broken staircases and rusting gantries at regular intervals, each of which led to gaping doorways. And, in the middle of the left-side wall, an open elevator shaft ran almost to the top.

It was here that Talon would be forced to split up. From this chamber, they could access any level in the ship. Voss and Zeed would go down via a metal stairway, the others would go up.

'Good luck using that,' said Voss, nodding towards the elevator cage. It was clearly of ork construction, a mishmash of metal bits bolted together. It had a blood-stained steel floor, a folding, lattice-work gate and a large lever which could be pushed forward for up, or pulled backwards for down.

There was no sign of what had happened to the original elevator.

Karras scowled under his helmet as he looked at it and cross-referenced what he saw against his schematics.

'We'll have to take it as high as it will go,' he told Rauth and Solarion. He pointed up towards the far ceiling. 'That landing at the top; that is where we are going. From there we can access the corridor to the bridge. Ghost, Omni, you have your own objectives.' He checked the mission chrono in the corner of his visor. 'Forty-three minutes,' he told them. 'Avoid confrontation if you can. And stay in contact.'

'Understood, Scholar,' said Voss.

Karras frowned. He could sense the Imperial Fist's hunger for battle. It had been there since the moment they'd set foot on this mechanical abomination. Like most Imperial Fists, once Voss was in a fight, he tended to stay there until the foe was dead. He could be stubborn to the point of idiocy, but there was no denying his versatility. Weapons, vehicles, demolitions... Voss could do it all.

'Ghost,' said Karras. 'Make sure he gets back here on schedule.'

'If I have to knock him out and drag him back myself,' said Zeed.

'You can try,' Voss snorted, grinning under his helmet. He and the Raven Guard had enjoyed a good rapport since the moment they had met. Karras occasionally envied them that.

'Go,' he told them, and they moved off, disappearing down a stairwell on the right, their footsteps vibrating the grille under Karras's feet.

'Then there were three,' said Solarion.

'With the Emperor's blessing,' said Karras, 'that's all we'll need.' He strode over to the elevator, pulled the lattice-work gate aside, and got in. As the others joined him, he added, 'If either of you know a Mechanicus prayer, now would be a good time. Rauth, take us up.'

The Exorcist pushed the control lever forward, and it gave a harsh, metallic screech. A winch high above them began turning. Slowly at first, then with increasing speed, the lower levels dropped away beneath them. Pipes and landings flashed by, then the counterweight whistled past. The floor of the cage creaked and groaned under their feet as it carried them higher and higher. Disconcerting sounds issued from the cable and the assembly at the top, but the ride was short, lasting barely a minute, for which Karras thanked the Emperor.

When they were almost at the top of the shaft, Rauth eased the control lever backwards and the elevator slowed, issuing the same high-pitched complaint with which it had started.

Karras heard Solarion cursing.

'Problem, brother?' he asked.

'We'll be lucky if the whole damned ship doesn't know we're here by now,' spat the Ultramarine. 'Accursed piece of ork junk.'

The elevator ground to a halt at the level of the topmost landing, and Solarion almost tore the lattice-work gate from its fixings as he wrenched it aside. Stepping out, he took point again automatically.

The rickety steel landing led off in two directions. To the left, it led to a trio of dimly lit corridor entrances. To the right, it led towards a steep metal staircase in a severe state of disrepair.

Karras consulted his schematics.

'Now for the bad news,' he said.

The others eyed the stair grimly.

'It won't hold us,' said Rauth. 'Not together.'

Some of the metal steps had rusted away completely leaving gaps of up to a metre. Others were bent and twisted, torn halfway free of their bolts as if something heavy had landed hard on them.

'So we spread out,' said Karras. 'Stay close to the wall. Put as little pressure on each step as we can. We don't have time to debate it.'

They moved off, Solarion in front, Karras in the middle, Rauth at the rear. Karras watched his point-man carefully, noting exactly where he placed each foot. The

Ultramarine moved with a certainty and fluidity that few could match. Had he registered more of a warp signature than he did, Karras might even have suspected some kind of extra-sensory perception, but, in fact, it was simply the superior training of the Master Scout, Telion.

Halfway up the stair, however, Solarion suddenly held up his hand and hissed, 'Hold!'

Rauth and Karras froze at once. The stairway creaked gently under them.

'Xenos, direct front. Twenty metres. Three big ones.'

Neither Karras nor Rauth could see them. The steep angle of the stair prevented it.

'Can you deal with them?' asked Karras.

'Not alone,' said Solarion. 'One is standing in a doorway. I don't have clear line of fire on him. It could go either way. If he charges, fine. But he may raise the alarm as soon as I drop the others. Better the three of us take them out at once, if you think you can move up quietly.'

The challenge in Solarion's words, not to mention his tone, could hardly be missed. Karras lifted a foot and placed it gently on the next step up. Slowly, he put his weight on it. There was a harsh grating sound.

'I said *quietly*,' hissed Solarion.

'I heard you, damn it,' Karras snapped back. Silently, he cursed the cryo-case strapped over his shoulder. Its extra weight and shifting centre of gravity was hampering him, as it had on the gantry above the squig pit, but what could he do?

'Rauth,' he said. 'Move past me. Don't touch this step. Place yourself on Solarion's left. Try to get an angle on the ork in the doorway. Solarion, open fire on Rauth's mark. You'll have to handle the other two yourself.'

'Confirmed,' rumbled Rauth. Slowly, carefully, the Exorcist moved out from behind Karras and continued climbing as quietly as he could. Flakes of rust fell from the underside of the stair like red snow.

Rauth was just ahead of Karras, barely a metre out in front, when, as he put the weight down on his right foot, the step under it gave way with a sharp snap. Rauth plunged into open space, nothing below him but two hundred metres of freefall and a lethally hard landing.

Karras moved on instinct with a speed that bordered on supernatural. His gauntleted fist shot out, catching Rauth just in time, closing around the Exorcist's left wrist with almost crushing force.

The orks turned their heads towards the sudden noise and stomped towards the top of the stairs, massive stubbers raised in front of them.

'By Guilliman's blood!' raged Solarion.

He opened fire.

The first of the orks collapsed with its brainpan blown out.

Karras was struggling to haul Rauth back onto the stairway, but the metal under his own feet, forced to support the weight of both Astartes, began to scrape clear of its fixings.

'Quickly, psyker,' gasped Rauth, 'or we'll both die.'

'Not a damned chance,' Karras growled. With a monumental effort of strength, he heaved Rauth high enough that the Exorcist could grab the staircase and scramble back onto it.

As Rauth got to his feet, he breathed, 'Thank you, Karras… but you may live to regret saving me.'

Karras was scowling furiously under his helmet. 'You may not think of me as your brother, but, at the very least, you are a member of my team. However, the next time you call me psyker with such disdain, you will be the one to regret it. Is that understood?'

Rauth glared at him for a second, then nodded once. 'Fair words.'

Karras moved past him, stepping over the broad gap then stopping at Solarion's side. On the landing ahead, he saw two ork bodies leaking copious amounts of fluid from severe head wounds.

As he looked at them, wailing alarms began to sound throughout the ship.

Solarion turned to face him. 'I told Sigma he should have put me in charge,' he hissed. 'Damn it, Karras.'

'Save it,' Karras barked. His eyes flicked to the count-down on his heads-up display. 'Thirty-three minutes left. They know we're here. The killing starts in earnest now, but we can't let them hold us up. Both of you follow me. Let's move!'

Without another word, the three Astartes pounded across the upper landing and into the mouth of the corridor down which the third ork had vanished, desperate to reach their primary objective before the whole damned horde descended on them.

'So MUCH FOR keeping a low profile, eh, brother?' said Zeed as he guarded Voss's back.

A deafening, ululating wail had filled the air. Red lights began to rotate in their wall fixtures.

Voss grunted by way of response. He was concentrating hard on the task at hand. He crouched by the coolant valves of the ship's massive plasma reactor, power source for the vessel's gigantic main thrusters.

The noise in the reactor room was deafening even without the ork alarms, and none of the busy gretchin work crews had noticed the two Deathwatch members until it was too late. Zeed had hacked them limb from limb before they'd had a chance to scatter. Now that the alarm had been sounded, though, orks would be arming themselves and filling the corridors outside, each filthy alien desperate to claim a kill.

'We're done here,' said Voss, rising from his crouch. He hefted his heavy flamer from the floor and turned. 'The rest is up to Scholar and the others.'

Voss couldn't check in with them. Not from here. Such close proximity to a reactor, particularly one with so much leakage, filled the kill-team's primary comm-channels with nothing but static.

Zeed moved to the thick steel door of the reactor room, opened it a crack, and peered outside.

'It's getting busy out there,' he reported. 'Lots of mean-looking bastards, but they can hardly see with all the lights knocked out. What do you say, brother? Are you ready to paint the walls with the blood of the foe?'

Under his helmet, Voss grinned. He thumbed his heavy-flamer's igniter switch and a hot blue flame burst to life just in front of the weapon's promethium nozzle. 'Always,' he said, coming abreast of the Raven Guard.

Together, the two comrades charged into the corridor, howling the names of their primarchs as battle cries.

'WE'RE PINNED,' HISSED Rauth as ork stubber and pistol fire smacked into the metal wall beside him. Pipes shattered. Iron flakes showered the ground. Karras, Rauth and Solarion had pushed as far and as fast as they could once the alarms had been tripped. But now they found themselves penned-in at a junction, a confluence of three broad corridors, and mobs of howling, jabbering orks were pouring towards them from all sides.

With his knife, Solarion had already severed the cable that powered the lights, along with a score of others that did Throne-knew-what. A number of the orks, however, were equipped with goggles, not to mention weapons and armour far above typical greenskin standards. Karras had fought such fiends before. They were the greenskin equivalent of commando squads, far more cunning and deadly than the usual muscle-minded oafs. Their red night-vision lenses glowed like daemons' eyes as they pressed closer and closer, keeping to cover as much as possible.

Karras and his Deathwatch Marines were outnumbered at least twenty to one, and that ratio would quickly change for the worse if they didn't break through soon.

'Orders, Karras,' growled Solarion as his right pauldron absorbed a direct hit. The ork shell left an ugly scrape on the blue and white Chapter insignia there. 'We're taking too much fire. The cover here is pitiful.'

Karras thought fast. A smokescreen would be useless. If the ork goggles were operating on thermal signatures, they would see right through it. Incendiaries or frags would kill a good score of them and dissuade the others from closing, but that wouldn't solve the problem of being pinned.

'Novas,' he told them. 'On my signal, one down each corridor. Short throws. Remember to cover your visors. The moment they detonate, we make a push. I'm taking point. Clear?'

'On your mark, Karras,' said Solarion with a nod.

'Give the word,' said Rauth.

Karras tugged a nova grenade from the webbing around his armoured waist. The others did the same. He pulled the pin, swung his arm back and called out, 'Now!'

Three small black cylinders flew through the darkness to clatter against the metal floor. Swept up in the excitement of the firefight, the orks didn't notice them.

'Eyes!' shouted Karras and threw an arm up over his visor.

Three deafening bangs sounded in quick succession, louder even than the bark of the orks' guns. Howls of agony immediately followed, filling the close, damp air of the corridors. Karras looked up to see the orks reeling around in the dark with their great, thick-fingered hands pressed to their faces. They were crashing into the walls, weapons forgotten, thrown to the floor in their agony and confusion.

Nova grenades were typically employed for room clearance, but they worked well in any dark, enclosed space. They were far from standard-issue Astartes hardware, but the Deathwatch were the elite, the best of the best, and they had access to the kind of resources that few others could boast. The intense, phosphor-bright flash that the grenades produced overloaded optical receptors, both mechanical and biological. The blindness was temporary in most cases, but Karras was betting that the orks' goggles would magnify the glare.

Their retinas would be permanently burned out.

'With me,' he barked, and charged out from his corner. He moved in a blur, fixing his silenced bolter to the mag-locks on his thigh plate and drawing his faithful force sword, Arquemann, from its scabbard as he raced towards the foe.

Rauth and Solarion came behind, but not so close as to gamble with their lives. The bite of Arquemann was certain death whenever it glowed with otherworldly energy, and it had begun to glow now, throwing out a chill, unnatural light.

Karras threw himself in among the greenskin commandos, turning great powerful arcs with his blade, despatching more xenos filth with every limb-severing stroke. Steaming corpses soon littered the floor. The orks in the corridors behind continued to flail blindly, attacking each other now, in their sightless desperation.

'The way is clear,' Karras gasped. 'We run.' He sheathed Arquemann and led the way, feet pounding on the metal deck. The cryo-case swung wildly behind him as he moved, but he paid it no mind. Beneath his helmet, his third eye was closing again. The dangerous energies that gave him his powers were retreating at his command, suppressed by the mantras that kept him strong, kept him safe.

The inquisitor's voice intruded on the comm-link. 'Alpha, this is Sigma. Respond.'

'I hear you, Sigma,' said Karras as he ran.

'Where are you now?'

'Closing on Waypoint Barrius. We're about one minute out.'

'You're falling behind, Alpha. Perhaps I should begin preparing death certificates to your respective Chapters.'

'Damn you, inquisitor. We'll make it. Now if that's all you wanted...'

'Solarion is to leave you at Barrius. I have another task for him.'

'No,' said Karras flatly. 'We're already facing heavy resistance here. I need him with me.'

'I don't make requests, Deathwatch. According to naval intelligence reports, there is a large fighter bay on the ship's starboard side. Significant fuel dumps. Give Solarion your explosives. I want him to knock out that fighter bay while you and Rauth proceed to the bridge. If all goes well, the diversion may help clear your escape route. If not, you had better start praying for a miracle.'

'Rauth will blow the fuel dumps,' said Karras, opting to test a hunch.

'No,' said Sigma. 'Solarion is better acquainted with operating alone.'

Karras wondered about Sigma's insistence that Solarion go. Rauth hardly ever let Karras out of his sight. It had been that way ever since they'd met. Little wonder, then, that Zeed had settled on the nickname '*Watcher*'. Was Sigma behind it all? Karras couldn't be sure. The inquisitor had a point about Solarion's solo skills, and he knew it.

'Fine, I'll give Solarion the new orders.'

'No,' said Sigma. 'I'll do it directly. You and Rauth must hurry to the command bridge. Expect to lose comms once you get closer to the target. I'm sure you've sensed the creature's incredible power already. I want that thing eliminated, Alpha. Do not fail me.'

'When have I ever?' Karras retorted, but Sigma had already cut the link. Judging by Solarion's body language as he ran, the inquisitor was already giving him his new orders.

At the next junction, Waypoint Barrius, the trio encountered another ork mob. But the speed at which Karras and his men were moving caught the orks by surprise. Karras didn't even have time to charge his blade with psychic energy before he was in among them, hacking and thrusting. Arquemann was lethally sharp even without the power of the immaterium running through it, and orks fell in a great tide of blood. Silenced bolters coughed on either side of him, Solarion and Rauth giving fire support, and soon the junction was heaped with twitching green meat.

Karras turned to Rauth. 'Give Solarion your frags and incendiaries,' he said, pulling his own from his webbing. 'But keep two breaching charges. We'll need them.'

Solarion accepted the grenades, quickly fixing them to his belt, then he said, 'Good hunting, brothers.'

Karras nodded. 'We'll rendezvous back at the elevator shaft. Whoever gets there first holds it until the others arrive. Keep the comm-link open. If it goes dead for more than ten minutes at our end, don't waste any time. Rendezvous with Voss and Zeed and get to the salvage bay.'

Solarion banged a fist on his breastplate in salute and turned.

Karras nodded to Rauth. 'Let's go,' he said, and together, they ran on towards the fore section of the ship while Solarion merged with the shadows in the other direction.

'DIE!' SPAT ZEED as another massive greenskin slid to the floor, its body opened from gullet to groin. Then he was moving again. Instincts every bit as sharp as his lightning claws told him to sidestep just in time to avoid the stroke of a giant chainaxe that would have cleaved him in two. The ork wielding the axe roared in frustration as its whirring blade bit into the metal floor, sending up a shower of orange sparks. It made a grab for Zeed with its empty hand, but Zeed parried, slipped inside at the same instant, and thrust his right set of claws straight up under the creature's jutting jaw. The tips of the long slender blades punched through the top of its skull, and it stood there quivering, literally dead on its feet.

Zeed stepped back, wrenching his claws from the creature's throat, and watched its body drop beside the others.

He looked around hungrily, eager for another opponent to step forward, but there were none to be had. Voss and he stood surrounded by dead xenos. The Imperial Fist had already lowered his heavy flamer. He stood admiring his handiwork, a small hill of smoking black corpses. The two comrades had fought their way back to Waypoint Adrius. The air in the towering chamber was now thick with the stink of spilled blood and burnt flesh.

Zeed looked up at the landings overhead and said, 'No sign of the others.'

Voss moved up beside him. 'There's much less static on the comm-link here. Scholar, this is Omni. If you can hear me, respond.'

At first there was no answer. Voss was about to try again when the Death Spectre Librarian finally acknowledged. 'I hear you, Omni. This isn't the best time.'

Karras sounded strained, as if fighting for his life.

'We are finished with the reactor,' Voss reported. 'Back at Waypoint Adrius, now. Do you need assistance?'

As he asked this, Voss automatically checked the mission countdown.

Not good.

Twenty-seven minutes left.

'Hold that position,' Karras grunted. 'We need to keep that area secure for our escape. Rauth and I are–'

His words were cut off in mid-sentence. For a brief instant, Voss and Zeed thought the kill-team leader had been hit, possibly even killed. But their fears were allayed when Karras heaved a sigh of relief and said, 'Damn, those bastards were strong. Ghost, you would have enjoyed that. Listen, brothers, Rauth and I are outside the ship's command bridge. Time is running out. If we don't make it back to Waypoint Adrius within the next twelve minutes, I want the rest of you to pull out. Do *not* miss the pick-up. Is that understood?'

Voss scowled. The words *pull out* made him want to smash something. As far as his Chapter was concerned, they were curse words. But he knew Karras was right. There was little to be gained by dying here. 'Emperor's speed, Scholar,' he said.

'For Terra and the Throne,' Karras replied then signed off.

Zeed was scraping his claws together restlessly, a bad habit that manifested itself when he had excess adrenaline and no further outlet for it. 'Damn,' he said. 'I'm not standing around here while the others are fighting for their lives.' He pointed to the metal landing high above him where Karras and the others had gotten off the elevator. 'There has to be a way to call that piece of junk back down to this level. We can ride it up there and–'

He was interrupted by the clatter of heavy, iron-shod boots closing from multiple directions. The sounds echoed into the chamber from a dozen corridor mouths.

'I think we're about to be too busy for that, brother,' said Voss darkly.

RAUTH STEPPED OVER the body of the massive ork guard he had just slain, flicked the beast's blood from the groove on his shortsword, and sheathed it at his side. There was a shallow crater in the ceramite of his right pauldron. Part of his Chapter icon was missing, cleaved off in the fight. The daemon-skull design now boasted only a single horn. The other pauldron, intricately detailed with the skull, bones and inquisitorial 'I' of the Deathwatch, was chipped and scraped, but had suffered no serious damage.

'That's the biggest I've slain in hand-to-hand,' the Exorcist muttered, mostly to himself.

The one Karras had just slain was no smaller, but the Death Spectre was focused on something else. He was standing with one hand pressed to a massive steel blast door covered in orkish glyphs. Tiny lambent arcs of unnatural energy flickered around him.

'There's a tremendous amount of psychic interference,' he said, 'but I sense at least thirty of them on this level. Our target is on the upper deck. And he knows we're here.'

Rauth nodded, but said nothing. *We?* No. Karras was wrong in that. Rauth knew well enough that the target couldn't have sensed him. Nothing psychic could. It was a side effect of the unspeakable horrors he had endured during his Chapter's selection and training programmes—programmes that had taught him to hate all psykers and the terrible daemons their powers sometimes loosed into the galaxy.

The frequency with which Lyandro Karras tapped the power of the immaterium disgusted Rauth. Did the Librarian not realise the great peril in which he placed his soul? Or was he simply a fool, spilling over with an arrogance that invited the ultimate calamity. Daemons of the warp rejoiced in the folly of such men.

Of course, that was why Rauth had been sequestered to Deathwatch in the first place. The inquisitor had never said so explicitly, but it simply had to be the case. As enigmatic as Sigma was, he was clearly no fool. Who better than an Exorcist to watch over one such as Karras? Even the mighty Grey Knights, from whose seed Rauth's Chapter had been born, could hardly have been more suited to the task.

'Smoke,' said Karras. 'The moment we breach, I want smoke grenades in there. Don't spare them for later. Use what we have. We go in with bolters blazing. Remove your suppressor. There's no need for it now. Let them hear the bark of our guns. The minute the lower floor is cleared, we each take a side stair to the command deck. You go left. I'll take the right. We'll find the target at the top.'

'Bodyguards?' asked Rauth. Like Karras, he began unscrewing the sound suppressor from the barrel of his bolter.

'I can't tell. If there are, the psychic resonance is blotting them out. It's... incredible.'

The two Astartes stored their suppressors in pouches on their webbing, then Rauth fixed a rectangular breaching charge to the seam between the double doors. The Exorcist was about to step back when Karras said, 'No, brother. We'll need two. These doors are stronger than you think.'

Rauth fixed another charge just below the first, then he and Karras moved to either side of the doorway and pressed their backs to the wall.

Simultaneously, they checked the magazines in their bolters. Rauth slid in a fresh clip. Karras tugged a smoke grenade from his webbing, and nodded.

'Now!'

Rauth pressed the tiny detonator in his hand, and the whole corridor shook with a deafening blast to rival the boom of any artillery piece. The heavy doors blew straight into the room causing immediate casualties among the orks closest to the explosion.

'Smoke!' ordered Karras as he threw his first grenade. Rauth discarded the detonator and did the same. Two, three, four small canisters bounced onto the ship's bridge, spread just enough to avoid redundancy. Within two seconds, the whole deck was covered in a dense grey cloud. The ork crew went into an uproar, barely able to see their hands in front of their faces. But to the Astartes, all was perfectly clear. They entered the room with bolters firing, each shot a vicious bark, and the greenskins fell where they stood.

Not a single bolt was wasted. Every last one found its target, every shot a headshot, an instant kill. In the time it took to draw three breaths, the lower floor of the bridge was cleared of threats.

'Move!' said Karras, making for the stair that jutted from the right-hand wall.

The smoke had begun to billow upwards now, thinning as it did.

Rauth stormed the left-side stair.

Neither Space Marine, however, was entirely prepared for what he found at the top.

SOLARION BURST FROM the mouth of the corridor and sprinted along the metal landing in the direction of the elevator cage. He was breathing hard, and rivulets of red blood ran from grape-sized holes in the armour of his torso and left upper arm. If he could only stop, the wounds would quickly seal themselves, but there was no time for that. His normally dormant second heart was pumping in tandem with the first, flushing lactic acid from his muscles, helping him to keep going. Following barely a second behind him, a great mob of armoured orks with heavy pistols and blades surged out of the same corridor in hot pursuit. The platform trembled under their tremendous weight.

Solarion didn't stop to look behind. Just ahead of him, the upper section of the landing ended. Beyond it was the rusted stairway that had almost claimed Rauth's life. There was no time now to navigate those stairs.

He put on an extra burst of speed and leapt straight out over them.

It was an impressive jump. For a moment, he almost seemed to fly. Then he passed the apex of his jump and the ship's artificial gravity started to pull him downwards. He landed on the lower section of the landing with a loud clang. Sharp spears of pain shot up the nerves in his legs, but he ignored them and turned, bolter held ready at his shoulder.

The orks were following his example, leaping from the upper platform, hoping to land right beside him and cut him to pieces. Their lack of agility, however, betrayed them. The first row crashed down onto the rickety stairs about two thirds of the way down. The old iron steps couldn't take that kind of punishment. They crumbled and snapped, dropping the luckless orks into lethal freefall. The air filled with howls, but the others didn't catch on until it was too late. They, too, leapt from the platform's edge in their eagerness to make a kill. Step after step gave way with each heavy body that crashed down on it, and soon the stairway was reduced almost to nothing.

A broad chasm, some thirty metres across, now separated the metal platforms that had been joined by the stairs. The surviving orks saw that they couldn't follow the Space Marine across. Instead, they paced the edge of the upper platform, bellowing at Solarion in outrage and frustration and taking wild potshots at him with their clunky pistols.

'It's raining greenskins,' said a gruff voice on the link. 'What in Dorn's name is going on up there?'

With one eye still on the pacing orks, Solarion moved to the edge of the platform. As he reached the twisted railing, he looked out over the edge and down towards the steel floor two-hundred metres below. Gouts of bright promethium flame illuminated a conflict there. Voss and Zeed were standing back to back, about five metres apart, fighting off an ork assault from all sides. The floor around them was heaped with dead aliens.

'This is Solarion,' the Ultramarine told them. 'Do you need aid, brothers?'

'Prophet?' said Zeed between lethal sweeps of his claws. 'Where are Scholar and Watcher?'

'You've had no word?' asked Solarion.

'They've been out of contact since they entered the command bridge. Sigma warned of that. But time is running out. Can you go to them?'

'Impossible,' replied Solarion. 'The stairs are gone. I can't get back up there now.'

'Then pray for them,' said Voss.

Solarion checked his mission chrono. He remembered Karras's orders. Four more minutes. After that, he would have to assume they were dead. He would take the elevator down and, with the others, strike out for the salvage bay and their only hope of escape.

A shell from an ork pistol ricocheted from the platform and smacked against his breastplate. The shot wasn't powerful enough to penetrate ceramite, not like the heavy-stubber shells he had taken at close range, but it got his attention. He was about to return fire, to start clearing the upper platform in anticipation of Karras and Rauth's return, when a great boom shook the air and sent deep vibrations through the metal under his feet.

'That's not one of mine,' said Voss.

'It's mine,' said Solarion. 'I rigged the fuel dump in their fighter bay. If we're lucky, most of the greenskins will be drawn there, thinking that's where the conflict is. It might buy our brothers a little time.'

The mission chrono now read eighteen minutes and forty seconds. He watched it drop. Thirty-nine seconds. Thirty-eight. Thirty-seven.

Come on, Karras, he thought. What in Terra's name are you doing?

KARRAS BARELY HAD time to register the sheer size of Balthazog Bludwrekk's twin bodyguards, before their blistering assault began. They were easily the largest orks he had ever seen, even larger than the door guards he and Rauth had slain, and they wielded their massive two-handed warhammers as if they weighed nothing at all. Under normal circumstances, orks of this size and strength would have become mighty warbosses, but these two were nothing of the kind. They were slaves to a far greater power than mere muscle or aggression. They were mindless puppets held in servitude by a much deadlier force, and the puppeteer himself sat some ten metres behind them, perched on a bizarre mechanical throne in the centre of the ship's command deck.

Bludwrekk!

Karras only needed an instant, a fraction of a second, to take in the details of the fiend's appearance.

Even for an ork, the psychic warboss was hideous. Portions of his head were vastly swollen, with great vein-marbled bumps extending out in all directions from his crown. His brow was ringed with large, blood-stained metal plugs sunk deep into the bone of his skull. The beast's leering, lopsided face was twisted, like something seen in a curved mirror, the features pathetically small on one side, grotesquely overlarge on the other, and saliva dripped from his slack jaw, great strands of it hanging from the spaces between his tusks.

He wore a patchwork robe of cured human skins stitched together with gut, and a trio of decaying heads hung between his knees, fixed to his belt by long, braided hair. Karras had the immediate impression that the heads had been taken from murdered women, perhaps the wives of some human lord or tribal leader that the beast had slain during a raid. Orks had a known fondness for such grisly trophies.

The beast's throne was just as strange; a mass of coils, cogs and moving pistons without any apparent purpose whatsoever. Thick bundles of wire linked it to an inexplicable clutter of vast, arcane machines that crackled and hummed with sickly green light. In the instant Karras took all this in, he felt his anger and hate break over him like a thunderstorm.

It was as if this creature, this blasted aberration, sat in sickening, blasphemous parody of the immortal Emperor Himself.

The two Space Marines opened fire at the same time, eager to drop the bodyguards and engage the real target quickly. Their bolters chattered, spitting their deadly hail, but somehow each round detonated harmlessly in the air.

'He's shielding them!' Karras called out. 'Draw your blade!'

He dropped the cryo-case from his shoulder, pulled Arquemann from its scabbard and let the power of the immaterium flow through him, focusing it into the ancient crystalline matrix that lay embedded in the blade.

'To me, xenos scum!' he roared at the hulking beast in front of him.

The bodyguard's massive hammer whistled up into the air, then changed direction with a speed that seemed impossible. Karras barely managed to step aside. Sparks flew as the weapon clipped his left pauldron, sending a painful shock along his arm. The thick steel floor fared worse. The hammer left a hole in it the size of a human head.

On his right, Karras heard Rauth loose a great battle cry as he clashed with his own opponent, barely ducking a lateral blow that would have taken his head clean off. The Exorcist's shortsword looked awfully small compared to his enemy's hammer.

Bludwrekk was laughing, revelling in the life and death struggle that was playing out before him, as if it were some kind of grand entertainment laid on just for him. The more he cackled, the more the green light seemed to shimmer and churn around him. Karras felt the resonance of that power disorienting him. The air was supercharged with it. He felt his own power surging up inside him, rising to meet it. Only so much could be channelled into his force sword. Already, the blade sang with deadly energy as it slashed through the air.

This surge is dangerous, he warned himself. *I mustn't let it get out of control.*

Automatically, he began reciting the mantras Master Cordatus had taught him, but the effort of wrestling to maintain his equilibrium cost him an opening in which he could have killed his foe with a stroke. The ork bodyguard, on the other hand, did not miss its chance. It caught Karras squarely on the right pauldron with the head of its hammer, shattering the Deathwatch insignia there, and knocking him sideways, straight off his feet.

The impact hurled Karras directly into Rauth's opponent, and the two tumbled to the metal floor. Karras's helmet was torn from his head, and rolled away. In the sudden tangle of thrashing Space Marine and ork bodies, Rauth saw an opening. He stepped straight in, plunging his shortsword up under the beast's sternum, shoving it deep, cleaving the ork's heart in two. Without hesitation, he then turned to face the remaining bodyguard while Karras kicked himself clear of the dead behemoth and got to his feet.

The last bodyguard was fast, and Rauth did well to stay clear of the whistling hammerhead, but the stabbing and slashing strokes of his shortsword were having little effect. It was only when Karras joined him, and the ork was faced with attacks from two directions at once, that the tables truly turned. Balthazog Bludwrekk had stopped laughing now. He gave a deafening roar of anger as Rauth and Karras thrust from opposite angles and, between them, pierced the greenskin's heart and lungs.

Blood bubbled from its wounds as it sank to the floor, dropping its mighty hammer with a crash.

Bludwrekk surged upwards from his throne. Arcs of green lightning lanced outwards from his fingers. Karras felt Waaagh! energy lick his armour, looking for chinks through which it might burn his flesh and corrode his soul. Together, blades raised, he and Rauth rounded on their foe.

The moment they stepped forward to engage, however, a great torrent of kinetic energy burst from the ork's outstretched hands and launched Rauth into the air. Karras ducked and rolled sideways, narrowly avoiding death, but he heard Rauth land with a heavy crash on the lower floor of the bridge.

'Rauth!' he shouted over the link. 'Answer!'

No answer was forthcoming. The comm-link was useless here. And perhaps Rauth was already dead.

Karras felt the ork's magnified power pressing in on him from all sides, and now he saw its source. Behind Bludwrekk's mechanical throne, beyond a filthy, blood-spattered window of thick glass, there were hundreds – no, thousands – of orks strapped to vertical slabs that looked like operating tables. The tops of their skulls had been removed, and cables and tubes ran from their exposed brains to the core of a vast power-siphoning system.

'By the Golden Throne,' gasped Karras. 'No wonder Sigma wants your ugly head.'

How much time remained before the ship's reactors detonated? Without his helmet, he couldn't tell. Long enough to kill this monstrosity? Maybe. But, one on one, was he even a match for the thing?

Not without exploiting more of the dangerous power at his disposal. He had to trust in his master's teachings. The mantras would keep him safe. They had to. He opened himself up to the warp a little more, channelling it, focusing it with his mind.

Bludwrekk stepped forward to meet him, and the two powers clashed with apocalyptic fury.

DARRION RAUTH WAS not dead. The searing impact of the ork warlord's psychic blast would have killed a lesser man on contact, ripping his soul from his body and leaving it a lifeless hunk of meat. But Rauth was no lesser man. The secret rites of his Chapter, and the suffering he had endured to earn his place in it, had proofed him against such a fate. Also, though a number of his bones were broken, his superhuman physiology was already about the business of re-knitting them, making them whole and strong again. The internal bleeding would stop soon, too.

But there wasn't time to heal completely. Not if he wanted to make a difference.

With a grunt of pain, he rolled, pushed himself to one knee, and looked for his shortsword. He couldn't see it. His bolter, however, was still attached to his thigh plate. He tugged it free, slammed in a fresh magazine, cocked it, and struggled to his feet. He coughed wetly, tasting blood in his mouth. Looking up towards the place from which he had been thrown, he saw unnatural light blazing and strobing. There was a great deal of noise, too, almost like thunder, but not quite the same. It made the air tremble around him.

Karras must still be alive, he thought. He's still fighting.

Pushing aside the agony in his limbs, he ran to the stairs on his right and, with an ancient litany of strength on his lips, charged up them to rejoin the battle.

KARRAS WAS FAILING. He could feel it. Balthazog Bludwrekk was drawing on an incredible reserve of power. The psychic Waaagh! energy he was tapping seemed boundless, pouring into the warlord from the brains of the tormented orks wired into his insane contraption.

Karras cursed as he struggled to turn aside another wave of roiling green fire. It buckled the deck plates all around him. Only those beneath his feet, those that fell inside the shimmering bubble he fought to maintain, remained undamaged.

His shield was holding, but only just, and the effort required to maintain it precluded him from launching attacks of his own. Worse yet, as the ork warlord pressed his advantage, Karras was forced to let the power of the warp flow through him more and more. A cacophony of voices had risen in his head, chittering and whispering in tongues he knew were blasphemous. This was the moment all Librarians feared, when the power they wielded threatened to consume them, when user became used, master became slave. The voices started to drown out his own. Much more of this and his soul would be lost for eternity, ripped from him and thrown into the maelstrom. Daemons would wrestle for command of his mortal flesh.

Was it right to slay this ork at the cost of his immortal soul? Should he not simply drop his shield and die so that something far worse than Bludwrekk would be denied entry into the material universe?

Karras could barely hear these questions in his head. So many other voices crowded them out.

Balthazog Bludwrekk seemed to sense the moment was his. He stepped nearer, still trailing thick cables from the metal plugs in his distorted skull.

Karras sank to one knee under the onslaught to both body and mind. His protective bubble was dissipating. Only seconds remained. One way or another, he realised, he was doomed.

Bludwrekk was almost on him now, still throwing green lightning from one hand, drawing a long, curved blade with the other. Glistening strands of drool shone in the fierce green light. His eyes were ablaze.

Karras sagged, barely able to hold himself upright, leaning heavily on the sword his mentor had given him.

I am Lyandro Karras, he tried to think. Librarian. Death Spectre. Space Marine. The Emperor will not let me fall.

But his inner voice was faint. Bludwrekk was barely two metres away. His psychic assault pierced Karras's shield. The Codicer felt the skin on his arms blazing and crisping. His nerves began to scream.

In his mind, one voice began to dominate the others. Was this the voice of the daemon that would claim him? It was so loud and clear that it seemed to issue from the very air around him. 'Get up, Karras!' it snarled. 'Fight!'

He realised it was speaking in High Gothic. He hadn't expected that.

His vision was darkening, despite the green fire that blazed all around, but, distantly, he caught a flicker of movement to his right. A hulking black figure appeared as if from nowhere, weapon raised before it. There was something familiar about it, an icon on the left shoulder; a skull with a single gleaming red eye.

Rauth!

The Exorcist's bolter spat a torrent of shells, forcing Balthazog Bludwrekk to spin and defend himself, concentrating all his psychic power on stopping the stream of deadly bolts.

Karras acted without pause for conscious thought. He moved on reflex, conditioned by decades of harsh daily training rituals. With Bludwrekk's merciless assault momentarily halted, he surged upwards, putting all his strength into a single horizontal swing of his force sword. The warp energy he had been trying to marshal crashed over him, flooding into the crystalline matrix of his blade as the razor-edged metal bit deep into the ork's thick green neck.

The monster didn't even have time to scream. Body and head fell in separate directions, the green light vanished, and the upper bridge was suddenly awash with steaming ork blood.

Karras fell to his knees, and screamed, dropping Arquemann at his side. His fight wasn't over. Not yet.

Now, he turned his attention to the battle for his soul.

RAUTH SAW ALL too clearly that his moment had come, as he had known it must, sooner or later, but he couldn't relish it. There was no joy to be had here. Psyker or not, Lyandro Karras was a Space Marine, a son of the Emperor just as he was himself, and he had saved Rauth's life.

But you must do it for him, Rauth told himself. You must do it to save his soul.

Out of respect, Rauth took off his helmet so that he might bear witness to the Death Spectre's final moments with his own naked eyes. Grimacing, he raised the barrel of his bolter to Karras's temple and began reciting the words of the *Mortis Morgatii Praetovo*. It was an ancient rite from long before the Great Crusade, forgotten by all save the Exorcists and the Grey Knights. If it worked, it would send Karras's spiritual essence beyond the reach of the warp's ravenous fiends, but it could not save his life.

It was not a long rite, and Rauth recited it perfectly.

As he came to the end of it, he prepared to squeeze the trigger.

War raged inside Lyandro Karras. Sickening entities filled with hate and hunger strove to overwhelm him. They were brutal and relentless, bombarding him with unholy visions that threatened to drown him in horror and disgust. He saw Imperial saints defiled and mutilated on altars of burning black rock. He saw the Golden Throne smashed and ruined, and the body of the Emperor trampled under the feet of vile capering beasts. He saw his Chapter house sundered, its walls covered in weeping sores as if the stones themselves had contracted a vile disease.

He cried out, railing against the visions, denying them. But still they came. He scrambled for something Cordatus had told him.

Cordatus!

The thought of that name alone gave him the strength to keep up the fight, if only for a moment. To avoid becoming lost in the empyrean, the old warrior had said, one must anchor oneself to the physical.

Karras reached for the physical now, for something real, a bastion against the visions.

He found it in a strange place, in a sensation he couldn't quite explain. Something hot and metallic was pressing hard against the skin of his temple.

The metal was scalding him, causing him physical pain. Other pains joined it, accumulating so that the song of agony his nerves were singing became louder and louder. He felt again the pain of his burned hands, even while his gene-boosted body worked fast to heal them. He clutched at the pain, letting the sensation pull his mind back to the moment, to the here and now. He grasped it like a rock in a storm-tossed sea.

The voices of the vile multitude began to weaken. He heard his own inner voice again, and immediately resumed his mantras. Soon enough, the energy of the immaterium slowed to a trickle, then ceased completely. He felt the physical manifestation of his third eye closing. He felt the skin knitting on his brow once again.

What was it, he wondered, this hot metal pressed to his head, this thing that had saved him?

He opened his eyes and saw the craggy, battle-scarred features of Darrion Rauth. The Exorcist was standing very close, helmet at his side, muttering something that sounded like a prayer.

His bolter was pressed to Karras's head, and he was about to blow his brains out.

'WHAT ARE YOU doing?' Karras asked quietly.

Rauth looked surprised to hear his voice.

'I'm saving your soul, Death Spectre. Be at peace. Your honour will be spared. The daemons of the warp will not have you.'

'That is good to know,' said Karras. 'Now lower your weapon. My soul is exactly where it should be, and there it stays until my service to the Emperor is done.'

For a moment, neither Rauth nor Karras moved. The Exorcist did not seem convinced.

'Darrion Rauth,' said Karras. 'Are you so eager to spill my blood? Is this why you have shadowed my every movement for the last three years? Perhaps Solarion would thank you for killing me, but I don't think Sigma would.'

'That would depend,' Rauth replied. Hesitantly, however, he lowered his gun. 'You will submit to proper testing when we return to the *Saint Nevarre*. Sigma will insist on it, and so shall I.'

'As is your right, brother, but be assured that you will find no taint. Of course it won't matter either way unless we get off this ship alive. Quickly now, grab the monster's head. I will open the cryo-case.'

Rauth did as ordered, though he kept a wary eye on the kill-team leader. Lifting Bludwrekk's lifeless head, he offered it to Karras, saying, 'The machinery that boosted Bludwrekk's power should be analysed. If other ork psykers begin to employ such things…'

Karras took the ork's head from him, placed it inside the black case, and pressed a four-digit code into the keypad on the side. The lid fused itself shut with a hiss. Karras rose, slung it over his right shoulder, sheathed Arquemann, located his helmet, and fixed it back on his head. Rauth donned his own helmet, too.

'If Sigma wanted the machine,' said Karras as he led his comrade off the command bridge, 'he would have said so.'

Glancing at the mission chrono, he saw that barely seventeen minutes remained until the exfiltration deadline. He doubted it would be enough to escape the ship, but he wasn't about to give up without trying. Not after all they had been through here.

'Can you run?' he asked Rauth.

'Time is up,' said Solarion grimly. He stood in front of the open elevator cage. 'They're not going to make it. I'm coming down.'

'No,' said Voss. 'Give them another minute, Prophet.'

Voss and Zeed had finished slaughtering their attackers on the lower floor. It was just as well, too. Voss had used up the last of his promethium fuel in the fight. With great regret, he had slung the fuel pack off his back and relinquished the powerful weapon. He drew his support weapon, a bolt pistol, from a holster on his webbing.

It felt pathetically small and light in his hand.

'Would you have us all die here, brother?' asked the Ultramarine. 'For no gain? Because that will be our lot if we don't get moving right now.'

'If only we had heard *something* on the link...' said Zeed. 'Omni, as much as I hate to say it, Prophet has a point.'

'Believe me,' said Solarion, 'I wish it were otherwise. As of this moment, however, it seems only prudent that I assume operational command. Sigma, if you are listening–'

A familiar voice cut him off.

'Wait until my boots have cooled before you step into them, Solarion!'

'Scholar!' exclaimed Zeed. 'And is Watcher with you?'

'How many times must I warn you, Raven Guard,' said the Exorcist. 'Don't call me that.'

'At least another hundred,' replied Zeed.

'Karras,' said Voss, 'where in Dorn's name are you?'

'Almost at the platform now,' said Karras. 'We've got company. Ork commandos closing the distance from the rear.'

'Keep your speed up,' said Solarion. 'The stairs are out. You'll have to jump. The gap is about thirty metres.'

'Understood,' said Karras. 'Coming out of the corridor now.'

Solarion could hear the thunder of heavy feet pounding the upper metal platform from which he had so recently leaped. He watched from beside the elevator, and saw two bulky black figures soar out into the air.

Karras landed first, coming down hard. The cryo-case came free of his shoulder and skidded across the metal floor towards the edge. Solarion saw it and moved automatically, stopping it with one booted foot before it slid over the side.

Rauth landed a second later, slamming onto the platform in a heap. He gave a grunt of pain, pushed himself up and limped past Solarion into the elevator cage.

'Are you wounded, brother?' asked the Ultramarine.

'It is nothing,' growled Rauth.

Karras and Solarion joined him in the cage. The kill-team leader pulled the lever, starting them on their downward journey.

The cage started slowly at first, but soon gathered speed. Halfway down, the heavy counterweight again whooshed past them.

'Ghost, Omni,' said Karras over the link. 'Start clearing the route towards the salvage bay. We'll catch up with you as soon as we're at the bottom.'

'Loud and clear, Scholar,' said Zeed. He and Voss disappeared off into the darkness of the corridor through which the kill-team had originally come.

Suddenly, Rauth pointed upwards. 'Trouble,' he said.

Karras and Solarion looked up.

Some of the ork commandos, those more resourceful than their kin, had used grapnels to cross the gap in the platforms. Now they were hacking at the elevator cables with their broad blades.

'Solarion,' said Karras.

He didn't need to say anything else. The Ultramarine raised his bolter, sighted along the barrel, and began firing up at the orks. Shots sparked from the metal around the greenskins' heads, but it was hard to fire accurately with the elevator shaking and shuddering throughout its descent.

Rauth stepped forward and ripped the lattice-work gate from its hinges. 'We should jump the last twenty metres,' he said.

Solarion stopped firing. 'Agreed.'

Karras looked down from the edge of the cage floor. 'Forty metres,' he said. 'Thirty-five. Thirty. Twenty-five. Go!'

Together, the three Astartes leapt clear of the elevator and landed on the metal floor below. Again, Rauth gave a pained grunt, but he was up just as fast as the others.

Behind them, the elevator cage slammed into the floor with a mighty clang. Karras turned just in time to see the heavy counterweight smash down on top of it. The orks had cut the cables after all. Had the three Space Marines stayed in the cage until it reached the bottom, they would have been crushed to a fleshy pulp.

'Ten minutes left,' said Karras, adjusting the cryo-case on his shoulder. 'In the Emperor's name, run!'

KARRAS, RAUTH AND Solarion soon caught up with Voss and Zeed. There wasn't time to move carefully now, but Karras dreaded getting caught up in another firefight. That would surely doom them. Perhaps the saints were smiling on him, though, because it seemed that most of the orks in the sections between the central shaft and the prow had responded to the earlier alarms and had already been slain by Zeed and Voss.

The corridors were comparatively empty, but the large mess room with its central squig pit was not.

The Space Marines charged straight in, this time on ground level, and opened fire with their bolters, cutting down the orks that were directly in their way. With his beloved blade, Karras hacked down all who stood before him, always maintaining his forward momentum, never stopping for a moment. In a matter of seconds, the kill-team crossed the mess hall and plunged into the shadowy corridor on the far side.

A great noise erupted behind them. Those orks that had not been killed or injured were taking up weapons and following close by. Their heavy, booted feet shook the grille-work floors of the corridor as they swarmed along it.

'Omni,' said Karras, feet hammering the metal floor, 'the moment we reach the bay, I want you to ready the shuttle. Do not stop to engage, is that clear?'

If Karras had been expecting some argument from the Imperial Fist, he was surprised. Voss acknowledged the order without dispute. The whole team had made it this far by the skin of their teeth, but he knew it would count for absolutely nothing if their shuttle didn't get clear of the ork ship in time.

Up ahead, just over Solarion's shoulder, Karras saw the light of the salvage bay. Then, in another few seconds, they were out of the corridor and charging through the mountains of scrap towards the large piece of starship wreckage in which they had stolen aboard.

There was a crew of gretchin around it, working feverishly with wrenches and hammers that looked far too big for their sinewy little bodies. Some even had blowtorches and were cutting through sections of the outer plate.

Damn them, cursed Karras. If they've damaged any of our critical systems...

Bolters spat, and the gretchin dropped in a red mist.

'Omni, get those systems running,' Karras ordered. 'We'll hold them off.'

Voss tossed Karras his bolt pistol as he ran past, then disappeared into the doorway in the side of the ruined prow.

Karras saw Rauth and Solarion open fire as the first of the pursuing orks charged in. At first, they came in twos and threes. Then they came in a great flood. Empty magazines fell to the scrap-covered floor, to be replaced by others that were quickly spent.

Karras drew his own bolt pistol from its holster and joined the firefight, wielding one in each hand. Orks fell before him with gaping exit wounds in their heads.

'I'm out!' yelled Solarion, drawing his shortsword.

'Dry,' called Rauth seconds later and did the same.

Frenzied orks continued to pour in, firing their guns and waving their oversized blades, despite the steadily growing number of their dead that they had to trample over.

'Blast it!' cursed Karras. 'Talk to me, Omni.'

'Forty seconds,' answered the Imperial Fist. 'Coils at sixty per cent.'

Karras's bolt pistols clicked empty within two rounds of each other. He holstered his own, fixed Voss's to a loop on his webbing, drew Arquemann and called to the others, 'Into the shuttle, now. We'll have to take our chances.'

And hope they don't cut through to our fuel lines, he thought sourly.

One member of the kill-team, however, didn't seem to like those odds much.

'They're mine!' Zeed roared, and he threw himself in among the orks, cutting and stabbing in a battle-fury, dropping the giant alien savages like flies. Karras felt a flash of anger, but he marvelled at the way the Raven Guard moved, as if every single flex of muscle and claw was part of a dance that sent xenos filth howling to their deaths.

Zeed's armour was soon drenched in blood, and still he fought, swiping this way and that, always moving in perpetual slaughter, as if he were a tireless engine of death.

'Plasma coils at eighty per cent,' Voss announced. 'What are we waiting on, Scholar?'

Solarion and Rauth had already broken from the orks they were fighting and had raced inside, but Karras hovered by the door.

Zeed was still fighting.

'Ghost,' shouted Karras. 'Fall back, damn you.'

Zeed didn't seem to hear him, and the seconds kept ticking away. Any moment now, Karras knew, the ork ship's reactor would explode. Voss had seen to that. Death would take all of them if they didn't leave right now.

'Raven Guard!' Karras roared.

That did it.

Zeed plunged his lightning claws deep into the belly of one last ork, gutted him, then turned and raced towards Karras.

When they were through the door, Karras thumped the locking mechanism with the heel of his fist. 'You're worse than Omni,' he growled at the Raven Guard. Then, over the comm-link, he said, 'Blow the piston charges and get us out of here fast.'

He heard the sound of ork blades and hammers battering the hull as the orks tried to hack their way inside. The shuttle door would hold but, if Voss didn't get them out of the salvage bay soon, they would go up with the rest of the ship.

'Detonating charges now,' said the Imperial Fist.

In the salvage bay, the packages he had fixed to the big pistons and cables on either side of the bay at the start of the mission exploded, shearing straight through the metal.

There was a great metallic screeching sound and the whole floor of the salvage bay began to shudder. Slowly, the ork ship's gigantic mouth fell open, and the cold void of space rushed in, stealing away the breathable atmosphere. Everything inside the salvage bay, both animate and inanimate, was blown out of the gigantic mouth, as if snatched up by a mighty hurricane. Anything that hit the great triangular teeth on the way out went into a wild spin. Karras's team was lucky. Their craft missed clipping the upper front teeth by less than a metre.

'Shedding the shell,' said Voss, 'in three... two... one...'

He hit a button on the pilot's console that fired a series of explosive bolts, and the wrecked prow façade fragmented and fell away, the pieces drifting off into space like metal blossoms on a breeze. The shuttle beneath was now revealed—a sleek, black wedge-shaped craft bearing the icons of both the Ordo Xenos and the Inquisition proper. All around it, metal debris and rapidly freezing ork bodies spun in zero gravity.

Inside the craft, Karras, Rauth, Solarion and Zeed fixed their weapons on storage racks, sat in their respective places, and locked themselves into impact frames.

'Hold on to something,' said Voss from the cockpit as he fired the ship's plasma thrusters.

The shuttle leapt forward, accelerating violently just as the stern of the massive ork ship exploded. There was a blinding flash of yellow light that outshone even the local star. Then a series of secondary explosions erupted, blowing each section of the vast metal monstrosity apart, from aft to fore, in a great chain of utter destruction. Twenty thousand ork lives were snuffed out in a matter of seconds, reduced to their component atoms in the plasma-charged blasts.

Aboard the shuttle, Zeed removed his helmet and shook out his long black hair. With a broad grin, he said, 'Damn, but I fought well today.'

Karras might have grinned at the Raven Guard's exagger-rated arrogance, but not this time. His mood was dark, despite their survival. Sigma had asked a lot this time. He looked down at the black surface of the cryo-case between his booted feet.

Zeed followed his gaze. 'We got what we came for, right, Scholar?' he asked.

Karras nodded.

'Going to let me see it?'

Zeed hated the ordo's need-to-know policies, hated not knowing exactly why Talon squad was put on the line, time after time. Karras could identify with that. Maybe they all could. But curiosity brought its own dangers.

In one sense, it didn't really matter *why* Sigma wanted Bludwrekk's head, or anything else, so long as each of the Space Marines honoured the obligations of their Chapters and lived to return to them.

One day, it would all be over.

One day, Karras would set foot on Occludus again, and return to the Librarius as a veteran of the Deathwatch.

He felt Rauth's eyes on him, watching as always, perhaps closer than ever now. There would be trouble later. Difficult questions. Tests. Karras didn't lie to himself. He knew how close he had come to losing his soul. He had never allowed so much of the power to flow through him before, and the results made him anxious never to do so again.

How readily would Rauth pull the trigger next time?

Focusing his attention back on Zeed, he shook his head and muttered, 'There's nothing to see, Ghost. Just an ugly green head with metal plugs in it.' He tapped the case. 'Besides, the moment I locked this thing, it fused itself shut. You could ask Sigma to let you see it, but we both know what he'll say.'

The mention of his name seemed to invoke the inquisitor. His voice sounded on the comm-link. 'That could have gone better, Alpha. I confess I'm disappointed.'

'Don't be,' Karras replied coldly. 'We have what you wanted. How fine we cut it is beside the point.'

Sigma said nothing for a moment, then, 'Fly the shuttle to the extraction coordinates and prepare for pick-up. Redthorne is on her way. And rest while you can. Something else has come up, and I want Talon on it.'

'What is it this time?' asked Karras.

'You'll know,' said the inquisitor, 'when you need to know. Sigma out.'

MAGOS ALTANDO, FORMER member of both biologis and technicus arms of the glorious Adeptus Mechanicus, stared through the wide plex window at his current project. Beyond the transparent barrier, a hundred captured orks lay strapped down to cold metal tables. Their skulls were trepanned, soft grey brains open to the air. Servo-arms dangling from the ceiling prodded each of them with short electrically-charged spikes, eliciting thunderous roars and howls of rage. The strange machine in the centre, wired directly to the greenskins' brains, siphoned off the psychic energy their collective anger and aggression was generating.

Altando's many eye-lenses watched his servitors scuttle among the tables, taking the measurements he had demanded.

I must comprehend the manner of its function, he told himself. Who could have projected that the orks were capable of fabricating such a thing?

Frustratingly, much of the data surrounding the recovery of the ork machine was classified above Altando's clearance level. He knew that a Deathwatch kill-team, designation *Scimitar*, had uncovered it during a purge of mining tunnels on Delta IV Genova. The inquisitor had brought it to him, knowing Altando followed a school of thought which other tech-magi considered disconcertingly radical.

Of course, the machine would tell Altando very little without the last missing part of the puzzle.

A door slid open behind him, and he turned from his observations to greet a cloaked and hooded figure accompanied by a large, shambling servitor which carried a black case.

'Progress?' said the figure.

'Limited,' said Altando, 'and so it will remain, inquisitor, without the resources we need. Ah, but it appears you have solved that problem. Correct?'

The inquisitor muttered something and the blank-eyed servitor trudged forward. It stopped just in front of Altando and wordlessly passed him the black metal case.

Altando accepted it without thanks, his own heavily augmented body having no trouble with the weight. 'Let us go next door, inquisitor,' he said, 'to the primary laboratory.'

The hooded figure followed the magos into a chamber on the left, leaving the servitor where it stood, staring lifelessly into empty space.

The laboratory was large, but so packed with devices of every conceivable scientific purpose that there was little room to move. Servo-skulls hovered in the air overhead, awaiting commands, their metallic components gleaming in the lamplight. Altando placed the black case on a table in the middle of the room, and unfurled a long mechanical arm from his back. It was tipped with a las-cutter.

'May I?' asked the magos.

'Proceed.'

The cutter sent bright red sparks out as it traced the circumference of the case. When it was done, the mechanical arm folded again behind the magos's back, and another unfurled over the opposite shoulder. This was tipped with a powerful metal manipulator, like an angular crab's claw but with three tapering digits instead of two. With it, the magos clutched the top of the case, lifted it, and set it aside. Then he dipped the manipulator into the box and lifted out the head of Balthazog Bludwrekk.

'Yes,' he grated through his vocaliser. 'This will be perfect.'

'It had better be,' said the inquisitor. 'These new orkoid machines represent a significant threat, and the Inquisition must have answers.'

The magos craned forward to examine the severed head. It was frozen solid, glittering with frost. The cut at its neck was incredibly clean, even at the highest magnification his eye-lenses would allow.

It must have been a fine weapon indeed that did this, Altando thought. No typical blade.

'Look at the distortion of the skull,' he said. 'Look at the features. Fascinating. A mutation, perhaps? Or a side effect of the channelling process? Give me time, inquisitor, and the august Ordo Xenos will have the answers it seeks.'

'Do not take *too* long, magos,' said the inquisitor as he turned to leave. 'And do not disappoint me. It took my best assets to acquire that abomination.'

The magos barely registered these words. Nor did he look up to watch the inquisitor and his servitor depart.

He was already far too engrossed in his study of the monstrous head.

Now, at long last, he could begin to unravel the secrets of the strange ork machine.

AND THEY SHALL KNOW NO FEAR...

Darren Cox

009.009.832.M41
04.52

'Three minutes until blackout.'

The vox crackle from the Land Raider's driver pulled Castellan Marius Reinhart from his silent liturgies. Bathed in the interior's red light, he released himself from his assault harness and stood. His armour's gyro-stabilisers steadied him against the buck of the transport's passage as he peered over the driver's shoulder.

Through the forward viewport he watched as flashes of lightning fractured the night and revealed a landscape of icy rock and jagged peaks. Above, strange auroras moved across a sea of churning storm clouds. Even over the rumble of the Land Raider's tracks he could hear the slow roll of thunder.

'How far are we from our target?'

The Land Raider's co-driver adjusted a series of brass dials on the forward console. 'At our current speed, auspex readings mark us thirty minutes out.'

'Do we have any readings from the keep, any residual power spikes?'

'Negative, Castellan, the storm is jamming the majority of our forward sensors. There is no way to say for certain.'

Reinhart growled a curse under his breath. They were going in blind. Atmosphereologists aboard the Black Templar flagship, the *Revenant*, had warned him and his Sword Brethren about the dangers of the electromagnetic storm raging over Stygia XII's upper polar region – and over their waiting target. The forge-world's storms could affect the machine-spirit of even the most basic device – a fact necessitating their insertion by Thunderhawk transports just beyond the storm's perimeter. Though a direct flight through the storm would have saved the most time, there was no way to tell if the Thunderhawk's systems could withstand the fury of the electromagnetic pulses. The risk was too great and their cargo too precious. The Land Raiders would have to get them as close as possible.

Reinhart keyed his vox, triggering the command channel connecting him to the rest of his battle-brothers in the convoy. 'Escalade Two, Escalade Three; we're approaching the storm's blackout perimeter. Be prepared for vox interference.'

Two of the twelve amber runes displayed on his visor flashed briefly. Chaplain Mathias, commanding the second Land Raider, and Brother-Sergeant Janus, commanding the third, had received and understood.

Through the viewport Reinhart could see the track ahead narrowing into a rocky defile.

'Understood, Escalade Three.' The driver turned in his seat, addressing Reinhart. 'We're moving into a single ingress line. Escalade Three will take point.'

Reinhart nodded and turned back to the Land Raider's hold, grasping an overhead stabiliser. In preparation, the interior of the hold had been stripped bare, leaving room only for its cargo and three occupants.

'Brother Cerebus, Brother Fernus, prepare the Ark's shield.'

On either side of the hold, two Techmarines, their helmets heavy with neural cables, turned towards him and nodded. They bowed over a great armoured casket – what they called the Ark. Its surface was incised with the baroque runes of the Adeptus Mechanicus, and grav-engines kept it suspended just above the floor.

Chanting the rites of activation, the Techmarines coupled their grafted servo-arms with the Ark's forward actuators. Moments later a heavy thrum vibrated through the hold. A pale shimmer began to enshroud the Ark. Reinhart could not help but watch in awe as the machine-spirit was drawn from its slumber by the warrior-priests.

He found himself joining them in a prayer of his own.

'Emperor, protect us in this hour of need, may you see the truth of our actions. Allow us to be the instruments of your will and steer our hands on this blessed duty.'

With the Techmarines' rite complete Reinhart could barely see the Ark through the coalescing motes of energy that surrounded it. Lexmechanics aboard the *Revenant* had built the shield to specifically retard the effects of Stygia XII's storms and protect the Ark's internal functions. If it failed, millions would pay the price.

'Castellan, we have contact. Escalade Three is taking fire.'

Reinhart whirled back to the viewport just as the heavy staccato thump of rounds stitched across the exterior of their own Land Raider. 'Where? Where is it coming from?' He braced himself as a violent shudder ripped through the hull of the transport. Alarms sounded in time with the strobing of combat lamps.

'They've taken out our starboard sponson!' The co-driver shouted over the hail of gunfire. 'It's an ambush, right and left, above us, from the cliffs–'

In front of them, Escalade Three blossomed into a searing ball of flame. Shrapnel from its shredded hide clanged against their forward armour. At once five runes disappeared from Reinhart's visor.

'Holy Throne!' The driver, panic evident in his eyes, glanced over his shoulder at Reinhart. 'They must have ruptured a fuel cell. Whoever they are, they have some heavy ordinance.'

Reinhart ignored him. Unwilling to admit their fate, he keyed his vox and tried to reach Escalade Three. Only static answered. Brother-Sergeant Janus plus Brothers Gorgon, Sangrill, Charsild and Eklain were five of the Templar's most experienced and bravest Sword Brethren, each of them champions and legends in their own right. Together, they had all survived countless battles on countless worlds, and now they were gone. The loss was staggering.

'Castellan, your orders? Do we search for survivors?'

Reinhart blinked. 'They're all dead. Drive – get us out of here.'

With the heavy growl of turbine engines, the driver punched the throttle forward. Reinhart looked back to Cerebus and Fernus, both of whom stood protectively to either side of the Ark. Their Mechanicus power axes were held ready, shoulder-mounted bolters on-line. 'Be ready! This is going to get rough!' he yelled over the cacophony.

Another violent lurch nearly sent him sprawling to the hold's decking. A second series of alarms began to wail.

'We can't take much more, Castellan! We have armour breaches in three locations! If we continue to sustain this–' A terrific blast of flame and smoke engulfed the cabin in front of Reinhart. Hot shrapnel flew in all directions, pinging off the ablative plates of his artificer-forged power armour. Beneath him, the Land Raider shuddered to a stop.

Oily smoke began to fill the hold. Cerebus inserted a diagnostic cable from his chest plate into the Land

Raider's secondary codifier. The machine's screenplate flickered as lines of scripture scrolled across its surface. The Techmarine's augmented voice came over Reinhart's vox reflecting nothing of the anarchy that boiled around them. 'The Land Raider is crippled, Castellan. Evacuation is the only option before the engine's plasma coils go critical.'

Reinhart nodded. 'Escalade Two, this is Escalade One; acknowledge.'

Amid the crackle of static, Mathias's vox keyed up. Reinhart heard the thunderous boom of bolter fire in the background. 'I acknowledge, Castellan. Your Land Raider is blocking the track. We can't get around. We are dismounting and moving to your position to secure the Ark.'

Good, Reinhart thought. The Ark comes first; all of them would willingly sacrifice their lives to protect it. He drew his filigreed bolt pistol, its balanced weight a perfect extension of his armoured gauntlet. Whispering his *Litany of Devotion*, he clasped the bolter's binding chain around his wrist, each link graven with the litany's sacred words.

'Brother Cerebus, Brother Fernus, exit forward.' He gestured towards the hatch beneath the smoking crew cabin where the remains of the driver and co-driver crisped in the dying flames. 'Chaplain Mathias and our battle-brothers in Escalade Two are moving to cover you. Get through to the target as quickly as possible. May the Emperor be with you.'

Without waiting for their response, Reinhart turned, flipped open an access panel, and punched the quick release of the port side hatch. Explosive bolts blew the armoured door outwards. With a roar, Reinhart leapt into the frozen night of Stygia XII.

Through swirling snow he was met by streaks of tracer fire lancing down from darkened figures in the crags. Las-pulses and solid shot tore up the ground around him in explosions of rock and ice.

Within moments the crunch of footfalls and the bellow of war chants alerted him to Brother Apollos's approach from the direction of Escalade Two. The giant Sword Brother marched through the gunfire as if striding through a heavy gale. Shells whined and spat off his ornate Terminator armour. He bore his giant thunder hammer chained to his wrist; in his other, a heavy bolt pistol tracked and fired. The newest of Castellan's squad – and the youngest – Apollos had been awarded his tabard just a year prior. In that time, Reinhart had met few who could match his fervour in battle.

Next to the hulking Terminator, a giant himself but dwarfed in Apollos's shadow, was Brother Ackolon. The prime helix of the Apothecarius was emblazoned on his shoulder pad, his narthecium strapped securely to his back. Together, the Space Marines laid down a withering fusillade of fire, their blazing muzzle flashes lending a daemonic cast to their already terrifying countenances.

Apollos reached the shadow of the burning Land Raider and crashed against its buckled armour, shielded against the fire from the opposite cliffside. He pulverised the rock face looming over them in a shower of bolter shells, sending shadowy foes diving for cover. Ackolon followed close behind and crouched next to Reinhart, slamming a fresh magazine into his bolter. 'Castellan, Chaplain Mathias with Brothers Dorner, Gerard, and Julius are moving up the right; your orders?'

'Keep moving,' Reinhart voxed over the hammer of his bolter, even as a smoking slug blew a chunk from his ceramite leg guard. 'They'll cut us to pieces if we remain exposed in this Throne-forsaken defile much longer!'

Ackolon nodded. 'The Emperor protects!' He motioned to Apollos and the two Space Marines burst from the cover of the crippled Land Raider, charging through the smoke and haze of gunfire. Reinhart fired a final volley, blowing two of the enemy from the cliff, then followed.

Ahead, he could see the towering forms of Cerebus and Fernus fighting their way through the defile – the Ark between them – its shield sparking each time a round found its surface. Paralleling him across the narrow track, Chaplain Mathias, his golden skull helm gleaming, led the three remaining Sword Brethren at a full run, their bolters streaking angry gouts of automatic fire.

Reaching the two Techmarines, Reinhart and his squad flowed seamlessly into a wide formation around the Ark. From their left, a rocket, spitting a fiery contrail, hissed through the air and detonated at Brother Julius's feet.

The blast vaporised his legs, blowing away his helmet and a good portion of his breastplate. The Templar fell, screaming hate around mouthfuls of bloody froth. Still, Julius's bolter roared. Ackolon dashed to him, and began dragging him along, firing from the hip. Brother Gerard moved to help. Before he could reach them, a stray round blew through the knee joint of his armour. Blood sprayed, steaming on the frozen ground.

Reinhart knew the situation was slipping from his grasp. Enemies they had yet to identify held the high ground, the rough terrain rendering them next to impossible to acquire. Worse yet, the storm of gunfire lacing the air around them only seemed to be intensifying.

With two battle-brothers down, the squad moved into a tight circle, doing their best to cover all angles of fire. A sudden, earth-shaking detonation washed the defile in blinding firelight – the crippled Land Raider had finally succumbed to its wounds. Then, as abruptly as it had started, the gunfire ceased.

From somewhere forward of their position, where the defile opened into a deep valley, came the echoing booms of multiple engines. Reinhart risked a glance upwards.

Dorner heard the booms as well, mistaking them for enemy fire. 'Incoming!' he yelled.

Reinhart held up a fist. 'Hold your fire; those are jump packs.' With the words barely uttered, the sound of thumping bolters filled the night once more. Tracer rounds streaked down from the sky into the enemy positions high in the rocks.

'Stay alert! Everyone hold their position.'

In the momentary respite, Reinhart removed his helmet, its vox and visor readings going dead from the interference of the storm. The others followed suit. None of them could risk being blind and unable to communicate if the fighting broke out again.

Reinhart moved to Brother Gerard. The injured Space Marine, blood colouring the lower leg of his power armour, stood over Ackolon and the stricken Brother Julius. The Castellan laid a hand on his shoulder. 'How is your knee, brother?'

Gerard continued to scan the defile, his bolter sweeping left and right. 'A minor wound. I can still fight,' he said.

Reinhart looked down at Ackolon. 'Brother Julius?'

Ackolon shook his head. 'Massive trauma. I've already removed his gene-seed.'

Reinhart scanned the rocks. He felt the stares of his men. He looked back at Ackolon. 'Then he will serve the Chapter in death,' he said loud enough for all of them to hear. 'So will we all, if that is what the Emperor's will demands of us.'

Overhead, the sound of bolter fire ceased, but Reinhart's heightened senses could pick out the faint echo of a more intense exchange from somewhere deeper in the valley. Subtle flashes flickered in the darkness. An ochre cast stained the sky, a great conflagration raging just out of sight. He knew it could only be coming from one place. What he did not know was what waited for them there.

Chaplain Mathias, the black cross of their Chapter tattooed on his forehead, moved to Reinhart's side. 'Castellan, our... *rescuers*... approach.'

Reinhart turned. He glanced at Mathias, the disgust of their situation evident on the Chaplain's grim face. From the direction of the valley a squad of women – armoured in crimson and sable – advanced. Catechisms of the Ecclesiarchy adorned their tabards, stitched in High Gothic around the blood red petals of a single rose. Each carried a finely worked, Godwyn Deaz-pattern bolter of gold and silver. It was the signature weapon of those female orphans raised in the schola progenium and inducted as Adepta Sororitas battle-sisters of the Orders Militant.

The lead sister broke from her flanking guard. Reinhart moved to meet her, Mathias a step behind.

Beneath short-cropped midnight-black hair, old scars lined what would have been an attractive face. Her marred beauty was accentuated by an augmetic targeting reticule that replaced her left eye; the jewelled lens glowed a baleful red. 'Brother Astartes,' she said, her voice as cold as the biting wind. 'I am Sister Superior Helena Britaine of the Third Celestian Squad of the Order of the Bloody Rose.'

'Castellan Marius Reinhart of the Sword Brethren of the Black Templars,' Reinhart gestured to Mathias. The Chaplain stepped forward, his skull helm held in the crook of his arm, his crozius arcanum – topped with a glittering Imperial eagle – cradled in the other. 'This is Chaplain Mathias Vlain.'

The Sister Superior nodded. 'Well met, brothers of the Emperor.' Her single blue eye drifted past the two Astartes to the others who still waited, bolters at the ready. 'My Seraphim have driven the enemy from the cliffs. It should be safe for the moment. I can offer medical assistance to any of your battle-brothers who require it.'

'We have our own Apothecary,' Reinhart said, then stepped closer, his voice low. 'What I do need are answers. How have you and your sisters come to be here?'

Sister Helena's eye narrowed. 'I would ask the same of you, Castellan. We were given no word of your coming.'

'We did not offer any word, Sister Superior, and if you are not willing to give me the answers I need, I suggest you take me to someone who will.'

Helena studied the towering Marine for a moment. 'Very well, Castellan,' she said finally. 'I will take you. But be warned: Chaos has assuredly tainted this place.'

INTERROGATOR EDWIN SAVAUL of the Ordo Hereticus took a ragged breath of the mountain air as he surveyed the siege's progress. He stood at a shattered casement high in an ancient tower, a tower his men dubbed 'the Spike.' With walls forged from the ironite stone indigenous to Stygia XII, the Spike was one of two towers guarding the entrance to the valley from the winding defile beyond. All that remained of the second was a finger of crumbling stone, a place avoided by the simple Guardsmen, who claimed the unquiet dead haunted its collapsed halls.

From his perch, Savaul could easily see the gothic fortress stretching into the night sky, commanding the far side of the valley like a dark cathedral cut from the stone of the mountain. From its decaying battlements glowing streaks of criss-crossing las-fire and tracer rounds webbed the valley floor. Explosions rocked the broken landscape just beneath the walls, an area that had also received a name: 'the cemetery.' Everywhere, flashing light illuminated the forms of struggling soldiers.

Savaul turned to face the chamber's dank interior. A ring of flickering lumoglobes circled the room, their snaking power cables stretching across the floor's cracked flagstones. The harsh light stung his eyes. 'Are we any closer?' he asked.

Veteran Captain Dremin Vlorn of the 4th Inquisitorial storm-trooper regiment emerged from where he waited in the chamber's entry portal. He limped into the room, his grizzled face streaked with soot and dried blood. A stylized 'I' – the mark of Inquisitorial conditioning – stood out on either ridge of his sunken cheeks. He placed his helmet on the only piece of furniture: a large, smoke-blackened quarter panel of a blasted Vindicator tank turned into a makeshift table. The captain's exhaustion was palpable. 'The gates hold, interrogator. Our troops still can't get close enough to plant the breaching charges.'

Savaul stepped from the ruined window, one hand in the pocket of his ankle-length storm coat, its high black collar framing a face devoid of pigment. 'Where is Sister Superior Helena? I expected her report along with yours.'

'She should be just behind me,' the captain replied, tugging his gloves free. 'She took her Celestian and Seraphim squads to investigate a disturbance in the defile about an hour ago. I saw them descending the switchbacks as I entered the Spike.'

'A disturbance?'

Vlorn shrugged. 'There were reports of gunfire.'

Savaul's disturbingly blue eyes searched the captain's face. He had become adept at detecting a man turned by the warp. It appeared Veteran Captain Vlorn's conditioning remained uncorrupted. Savaul engaged the safety of the laspistol in his pocket and placed the weapon on the table. Vlorn looked up in alarm.

'None of us are safe from the warp's taint, veteran captain. Especially here. I would expect you to deal with me in the same manner, were I no longer... pure.'

Vlorn inclined his head. 'Understood, interrogator.'

A sound brought both men around. Footsteps echoed from the shadows beyond the chamber's portal – slow and measured, like the tread of a Titan. As they grew nearer, dust began to sift from the ceiling stones. A moment later Sister Superior Helena entered the room, stepping aside to make way for the mammoth figure in her wake. Savaul sucked in a sharp breath at the sheer scale of the newcomer.

Astartes. He had seen one once from a distance, but nothing could match the awe or the terror of seeing one up close. They truly were monsters.

Helena stepped forward. 'Interrogator Savaul, I present Castellan Marius Reinhart of the Black Templars' Sword Brethren.'

Reinhart stared down at them, flint eyes sparkling, one half of his tanned face covered in tattooed lines of Gothic script. At close to three metres tall, encased in ornate black power armour, the Space Marine dominated the room. His tabard was the colour of aged parchment. Scorched and ripped, it bore the ebony cross of the Templars' heraldry. An ancient blade hung at his side.

Silent, the giant nodded in greeting and stepped around the table, his gaze drawn to the maps spread upon its scarred surface. Armoured fingers lifted the vellum schematics of the besieged fortress's walls and gridded layouts of troop dispersements. All of them watched, drawn into a hushed silence, entranced.

He let the maps fall back to the table. His gaze swept them all, and then his unwavering eyes locked with Savaul's. 'What troubles this place, interrogator?'

Savaul swallowed, feeling as though he had emerged from a dream. All the power and authority due an Inquisitorial agent flooded back in an instant. He straightened. 'Castellan, I welcome you,' he said, ignoring the Astartes' question. 'Your arrival is most propitious. I will require your forces to join the assault on the gates of the fortress. I'm sure you saw the situation on your descent from the defile.'

A strange, reverberating growl came from the Marine. It took a moment for Savaul to realize it was laughter.

'Interrogator,' he said, any hint of mirth now gone from his voice, 'If you think I have come here to relieve you, you are mistaken.'

'I... I'm afraid I don't understand. Surely you have come at our request for aid. My envoys left with the call three days ago.'

Reinhart glanced down, again studying the map of the fortress. 'Do you know, interrogator, what this place is that you lay siege to?'

Savaul looked from Helena to Vlorn, but neither noticed his glance. They simply stared at Reinhart, puzzlement evident on both of their faces. Savaul was beginning to feel as though he lacked some vital piece of information – a feeling he was not accustomed to. 'Planetary records on file with Stygia XII's Administratum centre in Capitalis Acheron report that this fortress was in existence upon the planet's settlement. Its builders are unknown, possibly xenos, a rumour causing it to be shunned by the local populace. They call it Stormhelm. Further records indicate–'

'Your records are lacking, interrogator,' Reinhart interrupted. Savaul, unused to such disrespect, stood open-mouthed. Reinhart moved to the room's gaping window, the glow of the siege-flames lighting his face. 'The bastion's true name is Montgisard; a chapter keep of my order founded by Marshal Gervhart during his execution of the Athelor Crusade. That was close to three thousand years prior to Stygia XII's official settlement date. After millennia of faithful service it was declared *Vox in Excelso* – dissolved – and thus abandoned. However, the memory of our Chapter is long, and none of our keeps are ever truly forgotten. We have returned at the behest of High Marshal Ludoldus to reclaim Montgisard.' Reinhart turned back to the table. 'So, I ask you again: who has defiled this place?'

Savaul said nothing for a moment, unable to comprehend how his ordo could have been ignorant of these facts. Still, it changed nothing. The needs of the Templars would have to come second, if at all. A world's fate hinged upon the Inquisition's success. Savaul chose his next words carefully.

'Castellan, I thank you for enlightening us on the history of this site. This fortress, whether you call it

Montgisard or Stormhelm, has become an infested hive of taint and corruption – and, as near as we can tell, is the Archenemy's base of operations on Stygia XII. We are here on orders from my master, Inquisitor Abraham Vinculus of the Ordo Hereticus, to cleanse this taint.' Savaul motioned to Helena.

The Battle Sister moved to the table and gestured to the map outlining troop placements. 'We arrived on-site a week ago,' she said. 'Shortly thereafter, the storm manifested, cutting our communication lines. Nothing in, nothing out.' She looked up at Reinhart. 'Our situation could not be more dire. The cult of the Archenemy has turned out to be much larger than anticipated. A sizeable portion of the Stygian Planetary Defence Force has turned traitor, enslaved by the warp's corruption.' She motioned to Vlorn. 'Veteran Captain Vlorn and his storm-troopers have executed the brunt of the assault, with my sisters acting as the tip of the spear.'

Vlorn's gruff voice cut in. 'The bastards have dug in and they have a taste for blood. Though we lay siege, it is actually we who are encircled. They've taken the high ground around us, and the gates of Stormhelm refuse to fall.' A touch of grudging admiration laced the veteran captain's words. 'You Astartes know how to build a door.'

'Why not simply pull out, fight your way back through the defile, and return with additional forces?'

Helena and Vlorn looked to Savaul, a sudden uneasiness to their features.

Savaul looked down, composed himself, and then raised his eyes to meet the full force of Reinhart's gaze. 'Retreat is not an option, Castellan. We–' Savaul hesitated.

The hulking Space Marine's voice cracked with impatience. 'Speak, man! My time is short!'

'As is ours, Castellan!' Savaul reached to the inner-pocket of his storm coat and withdrew a rolled parchment. 'Have you heard of a Necrolectifier?'

'No, interrogator, I have not.'

Savaul unrolled the scroll and placed it on the table. A coruscating mass of arcanographs and warp glyphs crawled across the blood-stained parchment. Reinhart snarled, stepping back from the table. 'What abomination is this?'

The interrogator laid a splayed hand across the parchment, never taking his eyes from Reinhart. 'This scroll holds the design of a warp gate, a physical portal between our universe and the realm of Chaos. It requires four artefacts, four Necrolectifiers, vile items capable of focusing enough daemonic energy to rip a hole through the fabric of our reality into the maelstrom of the warp. Castellan, they are planning to open this gate.'

'But you have captured this scroll,' Reinhart said. 'You have foiled their plan, correct?'

'No, Castellan, this scroll is not the key; it was drawn by a captured heretic during interrogation – a physical representation of the knowledge my excruciators drew from him. It tells us the cultists within Montgisard already hold the Necrolectifiers, the knowledge of their proper arrangement, and the rituals required to activate them. It tells us that on any given year, at the ninth hour of a ninth day of a ninth month, a portal may be opened, a portal through which the legions of the warp may pass.'

Savaul's voice lowered to a whisper. 'Castellan, this is the ninth day, of the ninth month of 832.M41 and very soon it will be the ninth hour. Unless this fortress is destroyed first, you can be assured this gate will open, then this world will burn – and the thousands of souls living here will burn with it.'

THE MEETING WITH the interrogator had taken longer than Reinhart expected. The time he had spent with Savaul made it plain to him the man's resolve was unbendable, and that the situation at Stormhelm posed a very real threat to the success of the Templars' mission. Now, more than ever, time was of the essence.

He found his battle-brothers waiting for him in one of the tower's undercrofts. Its western wall had collapsed, the rubble cleared to give easy access to the tower's exterior. Beyond the wall a marshalling yard had been levelled. A hive of activity swarmed across its packed surface. Ordinance officers bellowed while loading crews thronged around a handful of damaged Vindicator tanks awaiting the ministrations of overworked enginseers.

Dorner and Apollos stood watchful at the undercroft's crude exit, observing the tumult outside, their bolters at low guard. Gerard sat on a battered munitions crate, his leg elevated while Ackolon applied a battlefield dressing. Chaplain Mathias talked in hushed tones with the Techmarines, not far from the floating Ark. They all turned at Reinhart's approach.

Mathias stepped to the forefront. 'Castellan?'

Reinhart looked at each of them in turn. 'I will tell you simply, brothers: Chaos has gained a foothold here. The Archenemy occupies Montgisard. At minimum two regiments of traitor guard and PDF lie within. In three hours they will attempt to open a warp gate within the fortress's grand chapel, and this world will die in the apocalypse that follows.'

Mathias's face darkened. 'Then we dare not lose another moment. The power cells of the shield will last another two hours at most.'

'I am well aware of the cells' capacity, Chaplain,' he replied. He brushed past Mathias and strode to the Ark, running his hands across the shield's crackling surface. So much hope hinged on what lay within. 'The Inquisition's forces are desperate. They have been engaged here over a week and are no closer to breaking the fortress's gates.'

Mathias followed Reinhart to the Ark. 'Castellan, I am afraid I don't see how their situation has any bearing on our mission here.'

'It bears on our mission, Chaplain Mathias, because I have told them we would help–'

'By Terra,' Mathias snapped. 'You told them what? I must protest this!' he growled, the muscles in his jaw knotting. 'Were this any other circumstance I would agree.' He looked to the Marines around him. 'We all would, but aiding the Inquisition is not an option. We have an oath and only one directive here. The fate of this world, our lives if need be, are secondary.'

Reinhart felt Ackolon move up beside him. 'Castellan, you know we would follow you anywhere, but Chaplain Mathias is right. Stygia XII has not yet fallen. We can return once our task is done.'

Reinhart faced the Apothecary. 'Are the two of you done?'

Startled by the iron in the Castellan's tone, Ackolon stepped back. Dorner and Apollos exchanged concerned looks.

'I have pledged to help them, yes,' he repeated. 'But for the first time in my life I must betray my word. We must feign compliance with them because I suspect that our comrades in the Inquisition will not help us, and I fear that whatever lies in wait within those halls will be more than we can handle alone. You and Mathias are right, Ackolon. Our task is more important and I will see it done at any cost, even if we must turn our backs on them.'

Reinhart looked back to the Ark. 'And when that time comes, may the Emperor forgive us all.'

THE WIND HOWLED across the escarpment, snow and ice scouring the rock. It had taken the small battlegroup of Reinhart's men and the Sister Superior's Celestian squad just under an hour to climb the steep crags leading up to Montgisard's flank. It was an hour they could ill afford. The black ramparts of the fortress at last loomed above them.

Carved from the very rock and sheathed in armoured layers of rusting iron, the impregnable walls had bore witness to the week-long slaughter in the valley before them. Now, however, a haunting stillness cloaked the valley. Following the Castellan's orders, Veteran Captain Vlorn and his men had pulled back – every hand needed to prepare for the massed artillery barrage that was to come. In response, the enemy's guns had gone silent.

Reinhart squinted through the gale, double-checking the codifier readout in his vambrace. Lines of interference spiked across the display. With the storm raging he was surprised it worked at all. The glowing schematic of Montgisard – something all of the Templars had been given prior to making planetfall – showed the entrance to an auxiliary passage at this location. The hidden tunnel would give them access to the fortress's lower levels and hopefully allow them to approach their target with minimal contact. It had perturbed Interrogator Savaul, Vlorn and the Sister Superior that this piece of information was lacking from their own maps. To Reinhart, this boded well. If the Inquisition did not know about the passage, it was possible the enemy was equally ignorant.

To either side, the armoured forms of his battle-brothers, along with the twelve members of Sister Superior Helena's Celestian squad, hugged the steep walls of the mountain trail. Interrogator Savaul stood behind him, wrapped in the leather of his storm coat, breath frosting on the wind. Reinhart scowled. The man's albino skin was a beacon against the darkness. Luckily, the rocky outcroppings kept them shielded from the watchful eyes of the Archenemy's sentries patrolling the heights above.

Reinhart looked down at Cerebus where he knelt next to Fernus, the Techmarine's servo arms manipulating the tunnel door's locking mechanism hidden in the rock. 'How long?'

'Thirty seconds, Castellan.'

Reinhart nodded; he motioned for the battlegroup to prepare for entry. The silent gesture travelled down the line. Next to him, Savaul drew his silver-plated laspistol, its barrel stamped with the crimson sigil of the Inquisition.

The Castellan heard a loud hiss, a sound not unlike the sudden decompression of a Thunderhawk's airlock, and the rock face in front of the Techmarines split to reveal a shadowed portal. From the opposite side of the door Apollos side-armed a pair of glowing phosphorus rods into the tunnel beyond. The rods' fizzling light slowly grew steady. Motioning for the others to follow, Reinhart slid forward, his bolt pistol raised.

Silence greeted them, the low passage dark and empty. As they had hoped, the enemy had not discovered this part of the tunnel. After the last of them had filed through, Cerebus activated the door's inner mechanism and sealed the portal behind them. Reinhart moved to Gerard's side. 'Try your auspex,' he said.

Slinging his bolter, Gerard pulled his auspex from his belt and thumbed its activator switch. The scanner's display sputtered then blinked to life. Gerard looked over at Reinhart, relief evident on his face. 'The Emperor is watching over us.'

Reinhart nodded. They had expected the ironite walls of Montgisard to block the effects of the storm but couldn't know for certain until they had reached this point. None of them had relished the idea of descending into the fortress blind.

Keeping his voice low Reinhart addressed the rest of the group. 'Let's move. The generator room is straight ahead.'

They descended quickly through the tunnel and minutes later emptied into their first objective. The chamber they entered stretched away into the gloom: a long gallery of dormant generators lined its stone walls and disappeared into the upper shadows of the room.

Weapons braced, Helena and her battle-sisters fanned out. Cerebus and Fernus moved to an archaic panel of codifiers, and began working to restore the fortress's power. Chaplain Mathias entered last with the remaining Templars flanking the floating Ark. Reinhart noticed Savaul watching it, the hunger in his eyes warring with nervous anticipation.

Reinhart had told the interrogator the Ark was a high-yield reactor core capable of powering the fortress's system of defence turrets, part of the protocol required to reclaim the stronghold. However, it could be used in another capacity. Placed in the heart of Stormhelm, it could be rigged to detonate – the resultant explosion strong enough to destroy the fortress. For the interrogator it was an answer to his prayers: a weapon capable of foiling the Archenemy's plans in one fell strike. Reinhart only wished he could have told the man the truth.

They waited in the near darkness until, finally, a series of thumps travelled down the gallery as generators kicked on one by one, causing banks of suspended lumoglobes to flicker to life. Reinhart looked over to the Techmarines. 'Only quadrant sigma up to the grav lifts. We don't want the entire fortress to know we're here.'

'These grav lifts, they will take us to where we can plant the reactor?' Savaul asked, perspiration beading on his brow.

Reinhart hesitated; he could not look him in the eye. 'The grav lifts are as far as we go.' He turned and motioned Gerard to him. With a slight limp the Space Marine advanced to the Castellan's side. 'Take point with Apollos and keep me advised of any contact.'

Reinhart turned to address them all. 'I want noise discipline from this point forward. Sister Superior Helena, you and your squad have the rear. The Ark stays between your squad and mine.'

Helena nodded, her features lost beneath the 'sabbat' pattern of her helm.

From a great distance, the percussive boom of massed ordinance vibrated down through the halls. Captain Vlorn and his men had begun their bombardment as planned. With any luck, it would pull the enemy from the lower levels.

With drilled precision, the small force moved into the halls of ancient Montgisard.

For what seemed like miles, they stalked through the fortress's lower chambers. Thankfully, they were empty of enemy troops. Vlorn's bombardment appeared to have done its job in pulling them to the surface levels. Each step took the battlegroup deeper into the nightmare that had once been the Templar stronghold. Everywhere, the walls were awash in horrific glyphs and grotesque scenes depicted in rotting blood and viscera. Even to the Space Marines the stench was nearly unbearable.

'Contact, twenty metres.' Gerard knelt in the vaulted corridor, the green glow of his auspex tinting his face. Reinhart's raised fist halted the formation behind him. He moved to Gerard's shoulder.

'How many?'

'It looks like a patrol; I count fifteen, just around the next junction.'

Apollos looked over at Reinhart, a hard grin splitting his face. 'I guess they want to know who turned the lights on.'

Reinhart motioned to Dorner. 'Spread the word, contact in two minutes,' he said. 'We will take them. The sisters and Savaul will protect the Ark with Cerebus and Fernus.'

Dorner glanced over his shoulder at the waiting Sororitas. 'They might not like that.'

Reinhart drew his ancient battle blade, a massive bastard sword blessed and inscribed with the sacred oaths of his Chapter. 'Once this begins,' he said, 'there will be plenty for them to do.'

To Apollos and Mathias, he said: 'We will lead the strike. Gerard, Dorner and Ackolon, you will support us with bolter fire. No one gets through our line, understood?'

They all nodded. Reinhart stepped to the forefront, flanked by Apollos and Mathias as Dorner rushed off to warn the rest of the battlegroup. The sound of disruptive energy crackled through the air as Mathias triggered his crozius arcanum. Apollos activated his thunder hammer, waves of gleaming power rolling across its surface.

Moments later, Dorner returned. He nodded to Reinhart. 'We're ready.'

Gerard took a final reading from his auspex. 'Twenty metres and still approaching'

Reinhart glanced to the rear and saw the battle-sisters spreading out in a formation around the Ark.

Mathias's voice brought him around. 'Here they come.'

The patrol rounded the corner; a dozen lost souls of the PDF clad in armour streaked with gore and marked with foul symbols of Chaos. The cultists stumbled to a halt, shocked at what lay before them.

With a thunderous roar, Reinhart charged followed closely by Apollos and Mathias. Superheated bolter rounds screamed past them to shred the enemy's forward rank, exploding flesh, blood and bone. In seconds, the Astartes were among them. The deafening crack of Apollos's thunder hammer splintered the armour of a former guardsman. To Reinhart's left, Mathias waded into the fray, his crozius trailing bloody arcs through the air. Snarling, the Castellan ducked a thrusting rifle butt; with a savage two-handed downward cut, he opened the cultist from shoulder to hip. Blood washed the floor. Twirling the blade, he pivoted and swept the weapon in a tight arc, decapitating a charging foe.

It was over in a heartbeat, the floor littered with the enemy's crushed and eviscerated bodies. Reinhart whirled to check their rear. He could see Savaul, his white face paler still at the brutal effectiveness of the Sword Brethren.

Gerard activated his auspex again, his smoking bolter still ready in the opposite hand. 'I've got more, converging from the last junction to our rear.' He looked closer. 'And ahead. Throne! They're crawling all over the main plasma coil chamber.'

Reinhart knew they couldn't afford to get bogged down in a protracted fight. Pumping his arm, he yelled back to the others through the haze that filled the corridor. 'The game is up! Expect contact forward and to our rear! We've got to punch through to the grav lifts! Move! Move!'

They broke into a run, Cerebus and Fernus increasing the output of the Ark's propulsion engines to keep pace. The reverberating thump of the battle-sisters' bolters exploded from behind them. Reinhart heard a sucking *whoosh* followed by an eruption of gurgling screams. The air grew hot, the stench of promethium masking that of decay as a Sororitas flamer did its holy work.

The embattled force stormed down the last few metres of the corridor and plunged through a yawning doorway. Close on Apollos's heels, Reinhart burst into the seemingly infinite space of the plasma coil chamber. Floor after floor of open gantries ringed the room and stretched upwards into the cavernous void above. Rising from a deep pit, the plasma coil dominated the chamber's centre: a monstrous pillar of brass machinery that arced and crackled with pent-up energies. Stabilising beams sprouted from its skin like the disjointed spokes of an endless wheel, each strut hung with scarlet rags, banners scrawled with the blasphemous litanies of Chaos.

Former guardsman swarmed the gantries above, their Imperial uniforms now a mockery of filth and gore. Gunfire spewed down from the heretics' positions as Reinhart's force dashed across the room. Firing upwards, the Castellan waved his men past. One Sister stumbled as multiple rounds tore through her armour. Her body twisted under the impacts; unable to stop her momentum, she fell screaming over the edge of the coil's pit.

Apollos reached the exit at the far side of the chamber and turned; his bolter blazing, he provided covering fire for the rest of the squad who rushed through. Dorner hurried into position at his side. Together, they answered the cultists with a hellish barrage of their own. Bolters roared, and a gruesome rain of torn and mangled bodies fell from the upper floors.

Bringing up the rear, Savaul and Helena raced towards Reinhart. The Sister Superior's helmet was gone, a bloody gash down her face. Both fired blindly behind them.

'Move, Castellan! They're right behind us!' Helena yelled.

Reinhart fell in step behind them, back-pedalling and firing a furious volley into the horde of screaming cultists that burst from the corridor they had just vacated. He grunted in annoyance as a lucky shell punched through his shoulder joint, lodging near his collarbone. Already off-balance, a blast of auto fire stitched across his breastplate and sent him sprawling.

Seeing him fall, Helena and Savaul turned back. Helena slung her bolter and, together with Savaul, dragged the Astartes to his feet. As she did so, she tore a krak grenade from her belt, pulled the pin with her teeth, and pitched it into the oncoming mass. A horrific blast ripped through the horde, pulverising the thronged bodies into a cloud of blood vapour and shredded flesh.

Together, the three stumbled through the exit hatch between Apollos and Dorner. The Space Marines swung in behind them, letting loose a final round of fire before punching the hatch activator that sent the door booming closed behind them, the hollow thump of rounds continuing to bang against its armoured shell.

They stood now in another wide corridor, once again, thankfully devoid of the enemy.

Flexing his shoulder, Reinhart could feel the wound closing with the shell still lodged painfully against his collarbone. He had fought with worse injuries. He looked at Helena and Savaul. The Sister Superior was organising the eight remaining members of her squad. Savaul, attended by Ackolon, was bent against the wall catching his breath and holding his side where a grazing round had cut through. They made no mention of what they had done for him and neither did he.

Fernus, his red tabard in rags, moved past Dorner and Apollos to the hatch activator. He looked over his shoulder at Reinhart. 'This door has no locking mechanism; it won't hold them long.'

The sudden thunder of a bolter round startled them all. The hatch activator exploded in a shower of sparks. They all turned to see Mathias lowering his bolt pistol. 'It should hold them now,' he said. Holstering the weapon, Mathias stepped forward, raising his crozius arcanum. 'All of you steel yourselves. In this fateful hour, the Emperor's eyes are upon us. May we all go to Him knowing that we have done our duty and stayed true to His will.'

Reinhart could not help but think these last words were directed at him.

BY THE TIME they reached the grav lift chamber the Ark's shield had died and Reinhart's time had run out. He could no longer hide the true nature of his squad's mission. He could see this fact on all his men's faces as they set up a perimeter around the lifts. They and the sisters had bled together, a bond formed of shared hardship. Savaul and Helena had saved his life. Only Mathias seemed resolute in what they had to do. Reinhart knew he had to follow the Chaplain's example.

The Ark waited on the first of three grav lifts: circular pads set into the floor adorned with the Templar cross.

The battle-sisters had split. Two stood guard at each of the stairwells that emptied into the room's four corners. The Techmarines worked at a bank of codifiers that controlled the lifts.

'How far up do we have to plant the reactor?' Savaul asked, watching the Techmarines work. His face was sunken and splattered with dried blood; one hand still clutched his wounded side.

Reinhart looked behind him. Mathias stood at the foot of the Ark, his manner cold and aloof. Apollos and Ackolon locked eyes on the floor, unable to meet his gaze. Never had he felt the weight of duty as acutely as he did at that moment. He looked back to Savaul. Helena had come to stand beside the injured interrogator.

'We are not going up, interrogator.'

Savaul's head snapped around. 'What? I thought you said the reactor needed to be set near the ground floor.'

Reinhart hardened his voice. 'I mean we are not destroying the fortress, Savaul.' He motioned to the Ark. 'That is not a reactor and it cannot be rigged to detonate.'

Savaul turned to face him fully, his voice quivering with rage. 'What, by the Throne, are you talking about?'

'What I told you was a reactor core for Montgisard's defences is in fact a sarcophagus housing the body of one of our Chapter's most decorated Sword Brethren. His name is Ezekial Yesod, and he clings to life by a thread.'

Helena stepped forward, her face a mask of fury. 'Then what has all this been about, Castellan? Why have you brought us here, if not to exterminate this threat?'

'My battle-brothers and I have not come here to reclaim Montgisard, Sister Superior. We are here because this grav lift will take us down to the keep's lowest sepulchre, where one of our Chapter's most venerated Dreadnoughts sleeps. There, we will inter Brother Yesod so that he may continue to fight in the Emperor's name.'

Savaul pushed past Helena, to stand toe to toe with Reinhart. 'Is fighting in the Emperor's name not what we're already doing here? Throne, man! Don't you realise that by doing this you will condemn hundreds of thousands of His servants to death?'

Reinhart stared down at the trembling interrogator. 'This world is not yet lost.' He motioned to the waiting sarcophagus. 'But thousands of light years away, a battle is being fought. An entire system stands on the brink of destruction, and what lies in Brother Yesod's mind could mean the difference between victory and defeat. Interment within the Dreadnought is his only chance. The loss of Stygia XII would be a mere ripple in an ocean of lost souls if I were to let him die.'

He looked past Savaul to Helena. 'Come with us, all of you. Once our task is done we will return to our battle-barge and explain the conditions here. High Marshal Ludoldus will send aid, and we can return and save this planet before it is too late.'

Helena shook her head, a look of sorrow filling her eyes. 'It will be too late, Castellan. The Archenemy will already have opened the warp gate. We must do everything we can now to stop it.'

Gerard's voice cut the air. 'Castellan, contact again, approaching from the stairwells. Ten minutes, max.'

Reinhart stepped back, called to the Techmarines. 'Prepare the lift.' He looked again at Savaul and Helena. 'I will only offer this once more: come with us.'

Savaul's head sank, his shoulders wilting in defeat. 'Then we are on our own.'

'Unless you come with us, yes.'

Helena stepped forward. 'This man Ezekial, you claim that by saving him you will save millions of others?'

Reinhart nodded. 'That is correct, Sister Superior.'

Helena fixed him with a cold stare. 'You know you used us, you lied to us.'

'If there had been another way...' Reinhart let the words trail off.

Helena only smiled. She looked at Savaul. 'You have command, it's your choice.'

Savaul drew in a deep breath. 'I cannot let this atrocity go unanswered. We must try.' He looked at the empty lift next to him, then to Reinhart. 'Send us up and we will destroy the gate or die trying.'

Reinhart stared at him for a moment. He truly did wish there was another way. 'Send them up, Fernus,' he said finally.

Savaul turned without another word.

Helena looked up at Reinhart. 'Goodbye, Castellan. I ask you to remember one thing: Duty and honour do not always go hand in hand.'

Reinhart watched them gather on the lift, and then they were gone, shooting upwards into the heart of the keep and into the midst of the waiting enemy.

He turned. 'Everyone to the lift, prepare for descent.'

All of them moved, circling around the Ark. All of them except Apollos.

'Brother Apollos,' Reinhart said. 'I believe I gave an order.'

The young Terminator stared back at him. 'Castellan... I request permission to follow them, to lend the support of my bolter.'

Reinhart glanced to the others.

Gerard looked up from his auspex. 'Five minutes, Castellan.'

Apollos stepped to the lift. 'Castellan, Chaplain Mathias said the eyes of the Emperor are upon us. I believe he speaks the truth. I believe you can complete this task without me. Let me help them, Castellan.'

'Brother Apollos,' Mathias said, his voice edged with venom, 'Your Castellan has given you an order.'

Reinhart stepped from the lift. 'No, Mathias, Brother Apollos speaks true. The rest of you go and we will do what we can to help them. Take the Ark, inter Ezekial, and then get out. If we are unsuccessful in closing the gate advise the High Marshal of what you've seen here and return to save this world. It is our duty. This is my final order. May the Emperor go with you.'

THE CRYPT WAITED for them at the heart of Montgisard's deepest catacombs. Their approach from the grav lift had been a quiet one, Gerard's auspex showing no sign of the enemy, but they knew that wouldn't last for long. Following the schematics downloaded to their personal codifiers, the crypt's brass doors emerged from the darkness, glinting beneath the stark beams of their armour's search lamps. The formidable doors were an imposing sight, each at five metres tall and nearly as wide, their brass surface worked with the image of Dorn smiting the forces of Chaos at the gates of the Imperial Palace.

With Ackolon and Dorner flanking the portal, the Techmarines started to examine the doors but Mathias waved them back. He pulled an adamantium necklace from beneath his armour, an amulet of polished obsidian hanging from its beaded length.

'High Marshal Ludoldus bestowed this rosarius upon me before our departure,' he said in an awe-hushed voice. 'It belonged to Reclusiarch Gideon Amesaris. He served beneath High Marshal Gervhart.' The Chaplain knelt before the doors. 'It was he who designed these doors almost four thousand years ago.' With reverence Mathias fitted the sacred rosarius into an ornate depression within the door. He turned the amulet. A series of clicks answered and with a hiss the doors rumbled open.

Beyond, statues carved in the grim shapes of ancient Templars holding aloft iron lanterns circled the perimeter of the room. As the doors boomed open the lanterns guttered to life. Their amber glow filled the chamber; its sectioned walls covered in dusty, bas-relief carvings of forgotten battles.

In the chamber's centre stood the cyclopean hull of a venerable Dreadnought draped in cobwebs. Its chest plate was open, revealing a darkened cavity within.

Mathias stood. 'We must work quickly.'

Together, the Space Marines brought the Ark forward, resting it just above a low altar at the foot of the colossal war machine. The smell of holy oils and sacred unguents permeated the air. Stepping back, Gerard and Dorner took up posts at the crypt's threshold while Cerebus and Fernus flanked the Ark.

The Techmarines began to chant, manipulating a succession of rune-marked dials along the Ark's side. Piece by piece its armoured shell folded back to reveal a golden sarcophagus, its surface glinting in the amber light.

Gerard's voice once again brought the warning. 'They're coming,' he said. 'More than I can count.'

'Hold them back,' Mathias replied. 'At any cost. We only need minutes.'

Gerard and Dorner drew their chainswords and kicked them into life even as the sound of the screaming cultists began to echo through the darkness of the hall beyond. Ackolon put himself between the sarcophagus and the door's threshold, his bolter levelled. 'Hurry, Chaplain.'

REINHART AND APOLLOS found the battle-sisters and Savaul in a long gallery leading to Montgisard's chapel. They had formed a ragged line across the width of the hall. Step-by-step, they struggled through a seething mass of carnage, the space before them boiling with the streak of las-rounds, bolter shells and intermittent gouts of roaring flame. The stink of blood and promethium choked the air.

'Throne,' Apollos whispered.

Reinhart hefted his blade. 'Come, Apollos. For the sword of Dorn.'

The Terminator looked over at him. 'For the sword of Dorn, Castellan.'

Together, they charged into the centre of the battle-sisters line. Helena spotted them first. A grim smile crossed her features.

'The Templars are with us!' she shouted.

A cheer from the sisters rolled over the din.

With Reinhart and Apollos leading, they formed a wedge and drove into the screaming cultists. The writhing mass was frenzied to the point of suicide, hell-bent on keeping the Emperor's faithful from reaching the chapel. Within moments, the blood of the enemy dripped from Reinhart's armour, his blade a whirling blur of slaughter, his bolt pistol screaming its song of death. Through the carnage he could see Apollos. With every swing the Terminator's thunder hammer cleaved away huge swaths of cultists. Savaul fought in his shadow, a surgical grace to his movements, each shot of his laspistol toppling a crazed heretic.

Ahead of them lay their goal: the towering bronze doors of the chapel.

Reinhart ducked the swing of a whining chainaxe and blew the wielder's head away in a shower of gore. He vaulted the fallen heretic, watching as a Sister stumbled beneath the blow of a crackling power maul. Successive rounds tore her arm off and then her left leg below the knee. Her death grip discharged her flamer in a wide arc, the white flame incinerating all those standing before her. A cultist fell before Apollos, his ribcage crushed beneath the Terminator's armoured boot.

Reinhart breathed hard, his armour wrenched and scorched, the skin of his face blistered. Only four of Helena's sisters remained, but the doors were within reach. They had to keep moving.

'The doors, Apollos, the doors!'

Apollos nodded. With a thunderous bellow the Terminator dropped his shoulder and plunged through the heretics, striking the doors with the full force of his weight and shattering them in an explosion of fragmenting wood and twisted bronze.

Reinhart and the others followed close on his heels... into hell.

BROTHER DORNER DIED in the first moments of the cultists' charge. It was an errant shot, catching him in the throat and blowing out the back of his neck in a shower of blood. He fell to his knees, chainsword still raised in a blow that would never come, then pitched forward on his face. Gerard roared in fury and waded into the corridor. Hacking like a man possessed, the Sword Brother tore a bloody swathe through the maddened heretics. The floor became slick with blood and for a moment the foe recoiled from his savage onslaught.

At the threshold of the crypt, Ackolon pumped round after round into the melee; behind him, Mathias and the Techmarines continued their work. He risked a hurried glance.

The Chaplain stood before the altar and chanted the sacred rite of interment as the Techmarines' servo-arms lifted the sarcophagus up and into the yawning cavity of the Dreadnought. For a moment, through the fogged glass set into the sarcophagus's lid, the Apothecary caught a glimpse of an emaciated face. Brass tubes and wires inlaid with lexmechanical runes glistened from its eyes, ears, nose and mouth.

A scream of warning from Gerard brought him about just as a traitor PDF officer lunged at him with his sword. Ackolon caught the weapon in his gauntlet. Snarling he snapped the blade in half and put a bolter round through the officer's chest. With a startled look in his eyes, the heretic fell to the floor.

Ahead of him, Gerard continued to scream: not in warning but in pain. The Space Marine had dropped his bolt pistol and was pressing his hand against his temple as he fought. Blood ran from his eyes. Ackolon noticed the rime of frost that crackled its way up the crypt doors and then he spotted the robed psyker at the back of the corridor.

Gerard's agonised voice shrieked over the tumult. 'Get out, Ackolon! I can't hold it! Pull back! Close the do–' With a loud crack Gerard's head split.

Ackolon grunted as a las-round scorched across his check and burned away his ear. He dove for the door. Wrenching Mathias's rosarius from the lock, he rolled into the crypt firing on full auto to keep the heretics at bay.

The doors boomed shut and Ackolon swung to his feet. 'Chaplain Mathi–' He stared in horror at the scene before him. Cerebus and Fernus were sprawled across the altar, a single bolt shot through each of their heads. Mathias stood over them, his pistol drawn, his armour caked in psychic frost.

Mathias glared at him, blood haemorrhaging from his eyes and nose. The Chaplain staggered forward and fell to his knees. 'Ackolon... ki... kill me! The psyker, I... have expunged him, but I can't hold... at bay for... for long!' Even as he spoke, Mathias began to raise his pistol, his arm trembling. Behind them, the crypt doors started to buckle.

Ackolon placed his bolter to Mathias's head, closed his eyes, and fired. Then, dropping his weapon, he sank to his knees and waited for his own death.

The violent squeal of heavy pneumatics brought him around. Ackolon looked up in awe. Somehow, Cerebus and Fernus had completed the rite of interment before Mathias killed them.

Like a vengeful god of death, the Dreadnought rose above him. The hollow pitch of Ezekiel's voice trumpeted from the war machine's loudspeaker.

'Take me to the enemy, Apothecary.'

* * *

REINHART CHOKED ON the smell of corruption as he stormed through the shattered doors behind Apollos. The interior was a charnel house. Flayed bodies and blood-soaked banners hung from the flying buttresses ribbing the chapel's nave. Heaps of stone pews were piled like children's building blocks near the chapel doors to make room for an undulating mass of Chaos worshipers. Two massive fires, a nebulous green tint to their flames, burned at either side of the sacristy's altar. Within the flames, blackened human forms chained to iron stakes cried out in torment. At the Templars' appearance the heretics spun. Screaming their fury, they poured down the nave.

With Helena and Savaul beside him, the Castellan slammed against a toppled marble pew, his eyes burning in the acrid air. Apollos hunkered against the heap across from them while Helena's sisters turned and defended the splintered doors. They were surrounded.

Helena rose from the cover of the pew, her bolter kicking. 'By the Emperor, the altar!' she yelled, oblivious to the gunfire tearing up the marble around her.

Reinhart punched home a fresh magazine and stood to add his own firepower.

Where the sacristy's rear wall once stood a tenebrous ripple of sickening warp energies now spiralled, twisting the laws of reality between the four anchor points of the Necrolectifiers. At the altar's base nine robed warp priests chanted, their shaven skulls branded with ruinous curses.

'Is it open?' Apollos roared.

Helena shook her head. 'No, but almost. We only have minutes.'

'The priests! Aim for the priests!' Savaul screamed.

As one, they poured fire over the heads of the cultists only to see their shells detonate just short of their target.

Reinhart spat a curse. 'What is this heresy?'

'Psykers!' Savaul yelled.

Behind them one of the sisters fell, her body hacked apart as she was pulled through the doors.

'We're going to have to get close!' Apollos shouted.

Helena let loose another barrage and fell back behind cover. 'We'll never make it. We have no defence against the warp. Their energies will tear us apart even if that mob doesn't.'

Apollos raked down another wave of cultists. They were almost on them. 'We're running out of time!'

The warp gate began to darken.

Reinhart looked at his companions, each in turn. He knew there was only one option. The Emperor's eyes were upon him. 'Give me all of your grenades!' he yelled to Helena.

She looked at him, a question on her lips, even as understanding blazed in her eyes. Unclipping her last two, she handed them over.

Reinhart ripped away a portion of his tabard, binding up her grenades with two of his own. He kept one in his hand.

From across the streaking avenue of fire Apollos watched, realising Reinhart's intent. 'No!' he screamed. 'Let me go, I have the best chance!'

A sudden, deafening eruption blew apart what remained of the chapel doors. A shattered piece of lintel struck Apollos in the temple, knocking the young Terminator unconscious. Helena's remaining sisters simply ceased to exist, their bodies vaporised.

Reinhart shook himself from his dazed concussion, a heavy ringing in his ears. He felt warmth streaming down his chest. A bloody crater smoked just below his shoulder. Next to him, Helena coughed in the swirling dust, her face covered in blood from a deep gash across her forehead. Her left leg was gone. Savaul lay unconscious next to them. Through the roiling haze they could see a thronging horde of cultists climbing over the rubble of the devastated doorway.

'Can you hold them?' Reinhart asked.

Helena braced her bolter and nodded. She smiled at Reinhart. 'You do know what true honour is, Marius Reinhart.'

'The Emperor protects, Helena,' he said and briefly grasped her hand.

The Battle Sister smiled again. 'The Emperor protects, Castellan.'

Reinhart vaulted from cover. Hugging the grenades close to his body, he charged through the haze. It took a moment for the Chaos worshippers to realise what dashed between them. But, before they could react, the trembling discharge of an assault cannon shook the chapel's foundations and ripped them to bloody pulps. A grenade arced over the Castellan's head and detonated in a cloud of heavy smoke – masking his approach. Reinhart glanced over his shoulder as he covered the last few metres and saw the silhouette of an ancient Dreadnought in the shadow of the ruined threshold.

He whispered a word of thanks, then turned and emerged from the smoke in the midst of the unsuspecting psykers. Thumbing away the pin of his grenade, he barrelled onto the altar's landing. He felt the first stabs of pain within his mind but they were too late.

'The Emperor does protect,' he said, and the gate was shut amidst lightning and flame.

THEY FOUND HIM in the smoking rubble outside the chapel's entrance; his body and armour shattered, his features burnt. He awoke as a young Templar Neophyte knelt next to him. His crusted eyes cracked open, miraculously intact.

Ackolon blinked.

The shadowed forms of Templars picked their way past them, bolters aimed. He tried to focus on the man leaning over him.

'Brother,' the Neophyte said. 'Hold on. The Apothecaries will be here soon.'

Ackolon coughed, attempted to raise his head. He knew his wounds were mortal 'How... where?'

'The *Revenant*, brother, your flagship. High Marshal Ludoldus himself sent us after we received a call for aid from an Inquisitor named Vinculus. It appears we're working with the Ordo Hereticus now.' he said. 'A crusade has been called against the remainder of the cult you and Castellan Reinhart stopped here.'

'The others...'

'Brother Apollos and the interrogator live, sir, we are pulling them out now. Brother Yesod has already been extracted.'

Ackolon nodded. He began to go cold. What little feeling he had left was slowly fading. He struggled to rise again.

'What is your name, Neophyte?' he rasped.

'Helbrecht, sir.'

Ackolon fell back, his vision blurring. He thought he could hear Reinhart and the others calling his name. 'Tell them, Helbrecht,' he whispered, 'tell them we knew no fear...'

And then he too joined his battle-brothers.

NIGHTFALL

Peter Fehervari

'Terrible things wait amongst the stars and only a terror greater still may ward against them. So the Lords have taught us and thus have They shaped and shielded us through the hungry night. But strength demands sacrifice and Sarastus must pay its dues. Know then, that every thirteenth year, upon the dawn of the Black Star, our Lords shall descend and terrible will be their wrath should our tribute prove unworthy.'

'The Blind and the Bound'
The Revelations of True Night

SARASTUS WAS JUST another forgotten world left to rot in the backwaters of the Imperium. The life of a hive-world was measured by its productivity and when the seams of its industry ran dry, the planet had quietly slipped off the Imperial charts. Soon after that the darkness had come.

True Night had touched Sarastus three times, each visitation miring the planet deeper in damnation. Four of the great hive cities now lay silent, their will to live smothered beneath decades of fear. Carceri, once the greatest, was now merely the last. Blighting the plains like a vast scab, it was a black ziggurat of heaped tiers, its spires clutching hopelessly at the sky. The manufactorums were still, the hab-warrens shadow-haunted mausoleums. Of its massed millions perhaps some hundred thousand remained, huddling in the lowest tiers, far from the touch of the stars. The prophets of True Night ruled them with an iron hand, but they were as fearful as their thralls, for in the balance of Sarastus the only ones who truly mattered were the sacrifices.

To the prophets who chose them, they were the blessed; to the thralls who surrendered and mourned them, they were just the ghouls. All were ragged, skeletal shadows with gaunt faces and hungry eyes. Most would kill on a whim and many wouldn't hesitate to make a meal of the dead. Cast into the uppermost tier of the hive they scavenged and murdered beneath an open sky, striving to prove themselves worthy of the darkness. When True Night fell none were older than thirteen.

JUDGEMENT BEGAN WITH a song, a drone so deep it stirred the entire hive. Throughout the day it rose in pitch and complexity, blossoming as the sun waned, charging the air with potential. As night drew near, the planet itself seemed to hold its breath, as if playing dead for the stars. But while the thralls trembled and the priests mumbled prayers, the ghouls thrilled to it. This was *their* night!

Tantalising and threatening by turns, the call drew them to the walled plaza nestling at the peak of the hive. Long ago the square had hosted the elite of Carceri, but now only these feral youths remained to pass through the crumbling majesty of the gates. They came in a trickle and then a tide, none sparing a glance for the imperious faces glowering down from the lintels; they knew nothing of the past, and cared even less. They were here for the Needle, because tonight the Needle sang.

Gazing up at the gently vibrating monolith that dominated the centre of the plaza, Zeth felt the old awe welling up again. No matter how many times he saw it, the Needle was a shocking, impossible thing. About twenty feet across, it was a vast splinter woven from twisted iron spars, every inch encrusted with black barbs. One end was embedded deep in the rockcrete of the plaza, the other ascended in angular coils to disappear amongst the clouds. It was the brand of the star gods on Sarastus and it was Zeth's only friend.

Most of the ghouls feared the monolith, but Zeth had always been drawn to it. During the first terrifying days of his ordeal he'd hidden in its shadow, finding strength in its agonised contours. Soon afterwards the visions had begun. They were just teasing flashes – *a rich darkness glittering midnight blue – a black-feathered king dying from within and without – the howl of a hunter high above...* There were never enough pieces to complete the picture, but Zeth knew the Needle had given him an *edge*. He'd glimpsed enough of the future to get ahead of the game.

Losing himself in the Needlesong, Zeth remembered the words of the scarred prophet, 'Listen for the Needle. It's Their mark and your measure. Time will come when you'll hear it sing and then you'd best be ready, for the Lords will be close. Win their favour and you'll taste the stars, fail them and you'll be worse than dead...'

The weak would be culled and the strong would be taken. It was a simple promise that had become the vicious core of Zeth's soul. He was ready for the test. He was *hungry* for it. Impatiently he watched the sun bleed into the horizon.

AS WAS THEIR way, the masters of Sarastus returned on the eve of Nightfall. Their vessel was a jagged, jaundiced predator, slicing between the stars like a serrated knife. Its hull, a blue so deep it was almost black, bore no ornamentation or marks of allegiance. It was a creature of shadows, much like its crew.

From the shrouded recesses of his command throne, Vassaago observed the world he had enslaved. Flickering holo-reports veiled his bleakly handsome features in a web of light and shadow, but his eyes were changeless black orbs. Impassively he assessed the prospects for this harvest. Another hive had died and the last was teetering on the brink of extinction.

'Lord, I must prepare for the harrowing'. The words were spoken in a discordant electrical hiss and Vassaago frowned, turning to the thing hovering beside him.

The sorcerer had entered his service a mere century ago and he still considered it an outsider. It claimed an Astartes heritage, but its demeanour had more in common with the extremes of the Mechanicum. The tattered swathes of its robes completely hid its physique and Vassaago had never seen so much as a hand emerge from that formless mass. Stranger still was the absence of anything recognisable as a face. Perhaps the coarse iron sheet it wore was just a mask, but if so it made no concessions to anything remotely human. *Such as eyes…* It was an uncanny creature to be sure, but Vassaago had entertained stranger allies over the millennia.

'Do not dissemble with me, Yehzod. I know it is your precious Black Sun that draws you,' Vassaago challenged.

'Our interests are concordant. The anomaly will facilitate a prime yield.'

'Indeed? I believe this world has grown stale. Previously we took only six newbloods…'

'Six that proved exceptional,' Yehzod insisted, but Vassaago's attention had already returned to the holo-screens and after a moment the sorcerer took the opportunity to drift away. Watching the creature from the corner of his eye, Vassaago knew it was correct. The six *had* been exceptional. Perhaps there was still meat on this carcass after all...

STEALTHILY THE SHIP stalked the hive, following it into the planet's night side. As the sun was occluded the vessel's hull rippled with scintillating flashes of energy and its primal spirit stirred into troubled awareness. Neither wholly machine nor yet daemon, the ancient predator recognised this place and shuddered uneasily.

Crouched in the assault bay amongst his armoured brethren, Zhara'shan could sense the ship's disquiet, reading its mood in every nuance of the flight: the erratic pulse of the thrusters, the lethargy of the stabilisers, even the flicker of the lights... The old devil was skittish, as it always was when they hunted here. It was a wary beast and Zhara'shan sometimes grew tired of its reticence, but he had faith in it. Certainly he trusted it over his watchful, murderous brethren.

His eyes hidden beneath his helmet, he glanced warily at Haz'thur. Inevitably, the massive warrior had positioned himself just to Zhara'shan's right, not quite challenging his authority, but visibly staking a claim. The talonmaster regarded his unwelcome shadow with distaste. Haz'thur's armour was a fibrous mass of tumours and spines that pulsed with a life of its own, its monstrosity completed by the huge bone cleavers jutting from his wrists. Typically he disdained a helmet, revelling in the horror his serpentine features evoked in his prey. Although a youth beside Zhara'shan, the giant had embraced the ravages of the warp with zeal. Some amongst the talon even whispered of daemonic possession...

Zhara'shan grimaced. Like all his kind he had tasted the touch of the warp, but his own changes were refined, precise... *controlled*. The rampant perversions sported by Haz'thur could only end in madness and dissolution. If such abominations were the future then the Long War was already lost.

Abruptly the fierce jet streams of Sarastus caught them, buffeting and rattling the craft. They were entering the atmosphere and tradition demanded the vigil. Zhara'shan's bellow drew the eyes of the talon.

'Brothers, we ride the storm and the storm rides within our hearts!' He ignored the low, mocking chuckle from Haz'thur. 'We are masters of the tempest, never slaves. Seek the eye and chain the storm!' With a snarl Zhara'shan twisted his body into a stylised stance and became rigid. Swiftly the talon followed his lead, each warrior freezing into his own unique posture. Even Haz'thur obeyed, dropping into a bestial crouch.

Striving for perfect stillness they compensated for the turbulence with minute motions. Each knew that to slip or scuffle, even to make the slightest sound would invite the scorn of his brothers. Their discipline filled Zhara'shan with fierce pride. Balance was the lynchpin of their craft, enabling them to skim the warp without being consumed.

Like a menagerie of nightmare statues, the silent raptors waited for Nightfall.

NIGHTFALL. ZETH SHIVERED at the thought of it. Not just any night, but *True Night*. Soon all the pain and the horror was going to pay off...

'This is gonna be a bloodfest. We gotta evac this zone, chief.' Vivo's reedy voice broke Zeth's reverie and he scowled.

'You planning to run out on us, Vivo?' Zeth's tone dripped poison and the gangly youth blanched. He was the weakest link in Zeth's pack, but all of them were wired. He sighed theatrically. 'Listen up, it's Nightfall! Needle's where we gotta be. Just stick with the plan and I'll get you all to the stars.'

Shaking his head, Zeth scanned the plaza. Things *were* pretty wild. There were hundreds clustered around the Needle now: razers and flesheaters and darkscars all standing shoulder to shoulder, their gang rivalries on hold for Nightfall. But Zeth could already taste the violence in the air. High above, the sky rumbled.

A VIOLENT JUDDER shook the craft and Haz'thur felt himself slipping. Only an act of brutal concentration saved him and he snarled inwardly. Covertly he eyed Zhara'shan, certain that the ancient had caught his error. Doubtless the talonmaster would seek to humiliate him after the harvest, but the fool would never get the chance. The mood of the warband was changing and relics like Zhara'shan were losing favour. Already the talon was drawn to Haz'thur and when the time came none would defy him. Bristling beneath Zhara'shan's contempt, Haz'thur had long hungered to lash out, but the sorcerer had urged patience.

Thinking of the mystic, Haz'thur recalled the truths that had been revealed to him. He had seen the future! A future of slaughter unfettered by any justification save its own raw beauty, where his body would shape itself to the whims of the moment and the Long War would become the Eternal War! Seething with tension, Haz'thur endured the vigil.

LURKING AMONGST THE roiling clouds, the ship sensed the obscenity approaching. There was nothing its sensors could detect, nothing its tainted logic core could quantify, just an absolute certainty of *wrongness*. Bitterly it turned its attention to the stone-clad chamber that ached like a void in its guts.

Ensconced within his sanctum, levitating within a circle of arcane wards, Yehzod quietly decided the fate of the talonmaster and dismissed the ship's hatred. Like Zhara'shan, the ship was another vexing element of this warband that needed addressing, but for now the impending anomaly consumed his attention. The Black Sun was returning to Sarastus and every detail had to be recorded, every nuance evaluated. Despite decades dedicated to the enigma, he had made little progress in fathoming its nature, but its *promise* captivated him. Satisfied that his wards were intact, the sorcerer reached into the void to bear witness to impossibility.

IT ARRIVED WITH a silent scream, the insane potential sound of space being defiled by *otherness*. Reality itself recoiled, waves of causality twisted into chaos by the intruder's presence. Fighting back at some fundamental level, the materium coagulated around the rift, struggling to quarantine the infected space. Reality held and the invader was contained.

Contained, but not quite isolated. Trapped in a bubble of order it manifested as a vast black star radiating poisonous light.

True Night fell on Sarastus.

THE DARKNESS WAS sudden and complete, yet Zeth could see right across the plaza. Every pale face and glinting blade and grey charm, all raked the eyes with unnatural sharpness. It was all stark high-contrast detail, bleached of colour and every hint of warmth. *Ghost light...*

A voice whimpered, another answered, superstitious dread spreading through the crowd like wildfire. They wanted to flee, but the Needle's song held them. The monolith burned a bright white, like a negative image of its former self. It was alive with coruscating energy, arcs of black lightning crackling between its thorns. Suddenly its song flared into an awful, soul-scraping whine.

Something began to fracture inside the ghouls. With a lost wail someone raced forward, arms outstretched to embrace the metal siren. Immediately the boy was caught up in the crackling eddies swirling around the monolith and drawn up into the maelstrom. Spiralling up through the forest of thorns he was shredded and charred, rendered down into a ragged ruin before coming to rest impaled on the spines high above.

A second youth leapt into the whirlwind, then a third, a fourth. Soon dozens of supplicants had joined the lethal dance, gyrating about the Needle and screaming joyfully as it mangled them, body and soul.

On Zeth and his pack the tug was gentle, almost playful. He knew the Needle wanted him to win through, wanted him to make it to the stars. He didn't really know why, and his instincts told him there would be a price to pay, but Zeth figured he'd deal with that later. After all, he was already in hell, so what did he have to lose?

ABANDONING THE CAGE of his flesh, the sorcerer cast his spirit into the plaza and hovered invisibly above the chaos. Observing the shrieking monolith, Yehzod was filled with pride, remembering the tiny daemonseed he had planted there so long ago. Nurtured by the noxious light of the Black Sun and feeding on the decay of the hive, it had germinated into a titan! Unfortunately, while it was a useful tool for the harvest, it had revealed little about the sun. He had deduced that the anomaly violated space at a metaphysical level, literally corroding the soul of a planet, but the *mechanism* completely eluded him.

He turned his attention to the test animals and assessed the carnage. Once again the pitiful creatures displayed remarkable fortitude. For every one that succumbed to the lure, three more resisted. Many had fallen to their knees, hands clasped over their ears to block out the song. Others stood rigid, eyes screwed shut, their lips mouthing prayers or obscenities, focusing on anything but the call. They confirmed his hypothesis that brutality bred resistance to the anomaly. Even so, too many were dying and Lord Vassaago would expect a live yield from this harvest. It would be imprudent to disappoint him quite yet...

Reluctantly Yehzod commanded the monolith to desist. As always, it resisted and he lashed it with his will, brutally driving it into submission. Its strength had grown exponentially since the last harvest. It was more hostile, more enigmatic, *more a creature of the Black Sun...*

GRADUALLY THE CACOPHONY died down and the Needle subsided into a dull, lifeless grey. The ghouls gawked at the slumbering monster, their faces bright with ghost light. At some point during the slaughter it had begun to rain and now the first rumbles of thunder rolled across the plaza. Still the monolith remained silent. Slowly, uncertainly, a murmur washed through the crowd, beginning as relief and daring for jubilation.

Zeth almost pitied them. They thought the test was over when it had only just begun. Ignoring the whoops and cheers he watched the seething sky.

A SONOROUS BELL reverberated through the assault bay and the hatch swung open. Instantly the chamber was transformed into a riot of wind and rain. It would have scattered ordinary men, but for the raptors it was bliss. Exploding from the rigour of the vigil they scuttled towards the hatch. Hunched beneath their baroque jump packs, clawed feet skittering along the decking, they moved in ragged, avian bursts, hungry for freedom.

Thrusting aside an insolent brother Zhara'shan claimed the spearhead. As talonmaster the first jump was his by right! Instinctively he rounded on Haz'thur, the flensing claws springing free from his gauntlets, but the abomination was hanging back in the shadows. Surprised, Zhara'shan growled low in his throat. His instincts had been honed through the pitiless millennia and he knew something was wrong here...

Abruptly he realised his brothers were watching him expectantly. *Did they think he feared the jump?* The thought seared him with horror, swiftly followed by an overpowering need to kill. Already he could see the bay transformed into a blood-drenched charnel house. Savagely fighting down the fury, he swung around and plunged into the tempest.

Haz'thur stalked forward, noting with satisfaction that the others were giving him precedence. Already they understood the new shape the talon was taking. Contemptuously he appraised the stunted, almost uniform extent of their mutations. Yes, a new shape was undeniably called for. *Several in fact!* With a guttural chuckle he leapt after the talonmaster.

FREEFALLING THROUGH THE maelstrom, Zhara'shan urged the wind to flay him of doubt. He thrust his arms wide, recklessly obstructing his streamlined form and inviting the full wrath of the wind. It answered with a vengeance, raking the gnarled flesh of his armour and making him howl with release. At one with the storm, he tasted the only peace he recognised.

As he fell, Haz'thur fixed his eyes on the dark speck of the talonmaster far below and grinned savagely. He had received the command during the vigil, the sorcerer's words a silken whisper in his mind: *the talonmaster was not to return from the harrowing.*

Spying the tip of the monolith jabbing through the clouds, Zhara'shan reluctantly ignited his jetpack to veer away. The thing was a spawn of the Black Sun and not to be trusted. *Much like the faceless bastard who had led them on this trail...* With a clarity born of the storm, Zhara'shan suddenly knew he would kill the sorcerer. Lord Vassaago's schemes be damned, once this harvest was done he would tear out the cancer devouring his warband. With a satisfied snarl the talonmaster flipped into a knifing dive, streaking towards the distant spires.

CAUTIOUSLY ZETH APPROACHED the silent monolith. The pack kept their distance, but Zeth told himself he had nothing to fear. Tentatively he reached out towards a long, dagger-like thorn, hesitating at the thought of the remnants sizzling in the branches above.

'You want me for something...' *Something other than charred meat.* 'And I want...' *To break them all and unmake them all and bring them all down screaming and drowning in their own lies.* The words erupted unbidden from somewhere dark and hungry deep within Zeth's soul. They were shockingly alien, yet achingly familiar. *True words.*

Stunned, Zeth staggered back, the thorn snapping free in his grasp. He stared at it in confusion. When had he actually touched the thing? He'd reached out, but then he'd hesitated...

The thought was sliced apart by an ululating cry. Rippling down from the clouds, it was a bestial sound that froze the ghouls as surely as the Needle's lure. Zeth recognised it in a heartbeat.

A tall darkscar, his face a patchwork of ritual wounds, seized the moment, 'Hear the Midnight Fathers and open your hearts to True Night!' His voice was deep and rich, belying his youth. 'We have endured the Sacrament of Divine Shredding and now the Lords are come amongst us!'

Zeth could see he had them. In a crazy way he was even right. That cry from above had sealed the deal. All his visions had been real. The Lords were here!

'The things you've seen up here in the Spires, they're nothing! Up there...' The darkscar jabbed at the sky, 'Up there it's all pain and death! The only thing you've got to ask is this: am I a hunter... or am I just meat?'

And then something streaked out of the sky and the preacher was gone.

SOARING BACK INTO the clouds, his prey hooked delicately between the shoulder blades, Haz'thur whooped with delight. He lived for these moments of elegant slaughter, his perfect offerings to the chaos swirling at the heart of everything. But this time the true joy lay in cheating the talonmaster of the first kill!

Twisting into the wind he saw Zhara'shan watching him. They regarded each other from a hovering standstill as the others circled them. This affront had crossed the line between insolence and open challenge. A reckoning was inevitable. All that remained was a question of when. Haz'thur waited, ropes of drool dripping from his maw in anticipation of the clash. His claws flashing free, Zhara'shan ignited his thrusters... and dived towards the plaza.

Haz'thur laughed, knowing it wasn't fear that had driven away his rival. Despite his long millennia in the darkness, the talonmaster was still driven by *duty.* In his heart, the ancient monster was still a Space Marine.

ZETH CAUGHT THE momentary blur of shadows as a second ghoul was snatched from the bewildered crowd. It happened in an eye-blink, the work of a master. The third was slower and Zeth spied something manlike and impossibly huge.

Night Lord. The name slipped into his mind, redolent with promise. He didn't know if it was another gift from the Needle or a revelation from something deeper, but his heart sang to it. Recognising their game, recognising *them,* Zeth sank into a crouch beside the monolith and watched. The strikes weren't random. They were only taking the real crazies: berserk razers, fanatical darkscars, gibbering flesheaters... and anyone that ran for the gate. *Culling the weak.*

Glancing at his pack, Zeth winced. They were bunched together, just staring at the clouds! He needed to get them into cover, but he wasn't going to risk shouting for the sky-struck fools. This wasn't the time to get noticed, or distracted. Unwillingly, his eyes were drawn back to the Night Lords' game. *It was beautiful...*

* * *

As HE HOOKED another kill onto his shoulder spikes, Zhara'shan considered Haz'thur's challenge. It had been inevitable, yet it had surprised him. Had his talon forgotten that the mission always came first? *Had they fallen so far?* The Night Lords had entered the Long War bound by an oath to tear down the lie that was the Imperium, but watching his rapacious, shrieking brethren he wondered what bound them now.

Troubled, Zhara'shan's preternatural gaze wandered back to the youth he had spied hiding beside the monolith. It was a scrawny thing, its face bone white against lank black hair, but its stillness had caught his eye. Twice already he had spared it, convinced it wasn't hiding out of cowardice. No, there was no fear there, yet it was free of the rage or faith that so often blinded the fearless…

A brother whipped past him, hissing reproachfully. The talon was growing weary of the shadow play and their insolence incensed him. If Haz'thur took the lead now would they follow him? Surely their loyalty, no, their *fear* of the talonmaster hadn't waned so far? Bitterly he added Haz'thur's name to the personal harvest he would reap after this mission. Howling a command, he dropped from the cloud cover.

THE CROWD FELL silent as they spied the jagged black shapes emerging from the clouds. Spiralling above the plaza in swift arcs, their paths interweaving with arrogant precision, the flyers were inscribing something across the sky. Zeth watched it form and fade, over and again. It was just a phantom incarnated in the contrails of their jets, but the eightfold star was still potent. Zeth recoiled, torn between loathing and longing, struggling to ground himself. Time was running out and his pack was frozen in the killing ground…

Suddenly Zeth was running out into the open, shouting, 'Plan is on!' That got their attention, along with all the crazies and probably the Night Lords too… 'You want to live, go for the Needle!'

Unquestioning, Brox and Kert dashed towards him, but then Vivo sneered, 'You're crazy chief, Needle's a trap! We're going to the stars with the angels!' He was a rat but he had easy answers and the pack was frayed enough to listen. The hackles on the back of Zeth's neck were tingling in anticipation of rending claws. *He didn't have time for this…*

On impulse Zeth glared into Vivo's eyes, opening the shutters to the terrible dark country so recently revealed by the Needle. Vivo only caught a glimpse of the truth, but it shredded his mind in an instant. By the time he hit the ground he'd already died a thousand times.

FLOATING ABOVE THE plaza, Yehzod reeled as a spike of blacklight energy ricocheted through him. It was just an echo, but its lingering malice almost shattered his astral projection. Coldly subsuming confusion to curiosity, the sorcerer scanned the plaza. He had glimpsed a mind behind the attack, but the scene below was an impenetrable quagmire of psychic torment. Gauging the screaming, scrabbling animals, Yehzod felt the first stirrings of unease. Could there truly be such a mind amongst these wretches? *A mind that could focus the Black Star?*

ZETH STARED AT Vivo's corpse, confusion vying with horror vying with… joy? How had he done that? And why did he care when it had felt so good? *And why could he taste blood?*

Hearing the sudden murmur in the crowd, Zeth realised they were all tasting it. *The blood was in the rain.* Looking up, he saw the black rivulets pouring down from high above. Urgently he pulled Brox and Kert down into the shadow of the Needle, already knowing it was too late for the others.

Without warning the downpour exploded into a storm from hell. Glistening viscera, ragged limbs and unrecognisable raw fragments hailed down on the frantic mob as the hunters butchered their catch. With a chorus of hoots and harsh chirps they swept back and forth, showering the mob with gore as they spiralled ever lower. The ghouls were in turmoil, desperately ducking and diving to avoid the flyers, many slipping in the blood and tripping their neighbours.

Zeth saw a Night Lord glide low over the crowd, his clawed feet just skimming their heads. His helmet was carved into the visage of a snarling wolf, its lupine ears flaring into stylised bat wings, the eyes lambent with cold fire. As he swept over them he whispered, his harsh rasp somehow cutting through the chaos, *'We are the darkness between the stars... Die for us... We are the promise of murder in your hearts... Kill for us... We are the truth behind the lies... Kill or die...'*

It was like a trigger to some deep-rooted switch in their souls. First the razers went berserk, lashing out with crude clubs and cleavers, then the darkscars fell on unbelievers with their bone knives and the sane creeds fought back, shados and nailz and statiks all turning on each other in the name of True Night. And all the while the Night Lords circled above, taunting and tormenting, but only killing those who fled.

Watching his pack die, Zeth felt nothing.

ARMS OUTSTRETCHED, HAZ'THUR streaked between a pair of fleeing ghouls, neatly bisecting both at the waist, turning two into four. He spun, wondering how far their legs would run unburdened, but they just flopped over. This was poor sport and his blood sang to the tune of the rabid mob. Hearing the talonmaster finish his vainglorious speech Haz'thur knew it was time. Slavering with anticipation he jetted back into the clouds.

Watching his rival soar skyward, Zhara'shan felt his instincts prickle uneasily, but the newbloods demanded his attention. They fought with impressive ferocity but few promised any true depth to their darkness. Once again his thoughts turned to that strange, quiet ghoul. There had been something of the raptor vigil in its stillness and he wondered if it still lived. Intrigued, he flew towards the monolith.

ZETH SAW THE malevolent eight-pointed star reappear in the sky, blazing with fulfilment, glutted on the blood sacrifice of the ghouls. Recognising the moment, he chewed his lip, suddenly uncertain.

'We going to be okay, chief?' Brox asked, his eyes wide. The big ghoul had never been the sharpest player in the pack, but he'd always been loyal.

'Just stick with the plan.' Zeth said. 'Go. Both of you.' Nervously Brox and Kert ducked into the recesses of the Needle... and disappeared. Zeth knew this was the turning point. He could just slip away now and the Night Lords would never know. Come dawn he'd be King of the Spires.

But then the moment passed. It would never have been enough anyway. Zeth looked up and the wolf-helmed Nightlord was there.

THE GHOUL WAS looking straight at him. As Zhara'shan had soared towards the Needle its eyes had met his unerringly. *As if it had been waiting for him.* The strangeness had brought him to a standstill and now they took each other's measure, the mayhem around them forgotten. Warily, Zhara'shan wondered what its connection was with the monolith. *Was it another spawn of the Black Sun?*

Suddenly the ghoul's eyes flicked upwards, its warning coming a heartbeat before Zhara'shan heard the thrusters. He spun with a snarl and Haz'thur's clawed feet struck him squarely in the chest. The abomination's blistering dive tore the talonmaster from the sky, pounding him into the plaza with savage force. Three ghouls burst into bloody ruins beneath him and the rockcrete surface cracked wide open. Instinctively Zhara'shan rolled aside as Haz'thur's talons ripped towards him and the abomination crashed down onto the rockcrete.

His balance perfect, Haz'thur landed on his feet and spun after his rival, swinging down with those monstrous bone cleavers. Unable to recover, Zhara'shan could only roll and roll again, the shattered bones of his composite ribs tearing his chest like broken glass. A fraction too slow, he took a glancing blow to one of his shoulder pauldrons. The armour held, but it was enough to break the rhythm of his escape and Haz'thur was on him in an instant, a foot stamping down onto his chest and pinning him to the ground.

'Your Long War is a lie...' The abomination's voice was hoarse with pleasure, his drool spattering over the talonmaster's armour. 'And you were always blind to True Night!'

As the bone cleavers slashed down Zhara'shan ignited his jump pack. The explosive force tore him away from his rival, blasting him through the legs of the screaming throng. He gritted his teeth against the agony as he flashed along the rockcrete in a shower of sparks, the abused jump pack bucking and roaring under him like a living thing. Suddenly the exhaust jets spewed fire, scorching his armoured legs and leaving a wake of flame in his passing. Desperately he tried to cut the power, but the tortured machine-spirit was beyond tethering. Even as he fumbled for the locking clamps he knew it was too late.

Zhara'shan's bold manoeuvre had sent Haz'thur crashing to the ground, his legs swept from under him. As he leapt to his feet a crunching boom echoed across the plaza, followed a moment later by the vivid bloom of flames against the sky. His eyes glittering, Haz'thur threw back his head and bellowed his victory to the stars.

His joy was lanced by a stabbing agony in his thigh and he whirled around, but his attacker was already springing away, its black dagger glistening with Haz'thur's blood. Unbelievably it was just another ghoul, thinner than most and sickly pale. Glancing back, it flashed him a cold grin before ducking into the seething crowd.

With a bestial roar Haz'thur launched himself after his attacker, tearing into the throng like a primal tide of destruction, slicing and biting and crushing his way through the ghouls. Some tried to flee, others turned on him with their pitiful weapons, but all were reduced to shreds of meat and bone in his wake. And then he was through and his quarry was waiting for him.

It was less than twenty paces away, lurking beside the monolith, its eyes cold and calculating. Briefly a fading, rational part of Haz'thur's mind surged up through the rage, cautious and questioning. What was this creature? How could its feeble blade even scratch his armour, let alone pierce it? He was a god beside this worm, so how had it drawn blood?

As if sensing Haz'thur's doubt, the ghoul pointed at him, then slowly, deliberately ran a finger across its throat. And then it ducked into the shadow of the monolith and vanished. Gone in an eye blink.

Not a ghoul, but a ghost...

Hissing, Haz'thur leapt to the spot the creature had occupied only moments before, furiously sniffing for a scent, searching the dark whorls of the Needle for a huddled shape. *What trickery was this?*

And then he saw them, those cold grey eyes, peering at him through the iron web. *Inside the Needle!* Lightning fast, Haz'thur punched through the crevice, but the ghost was already gone, ducking away into the darkness. A gleam of admiration flashed through the rage as Haz'thur scanned the weave of the monolith. Yes, there were ragged gaps aplenty for a worm to crawl through, but what kind of fool would hide inside that killing machine? The answer surged back on the crest of his rage: *the kind that would taunt a raptor!*

Suddenly he was savaging the Needle. The iron was hard but brittle and it buckled rapidly beneath his bone cleavers.

THE CORE OF the Needle was a hollow vertical shaft. Zeth guessed it ran the whole length of the hive and maybe even beyond, but he'd only ever gone a few tiers deep. Scrambling down its gnarled guts, he heard the hunter ripping its way inside. Iron fragments tumbled past, rapidly lost in the abyss below and he shuddered, wondering whether a fall into that darkness would ever end.

But he wasn't going to fall.

He'd made this climb countless times over the years, finding gaps in the weave that led to other tiers of the hive. Of course they were all abandoned, but there'd been plenty to scavenge and he'd prepared well for this night.

With a final screech of tortured metal the Night Lord broke through and Zeth abandoned caution, speeding down the shaft. He glimpsed the others waiting below, crouched in a chamber on the other side of the web. He was almost there...

Suddenly something vast and dark plummeted past, the ferocity of its wake almost dislodging him. It struck the side of the shaft below with a violent clang and ricocheted away into the darkness. Glancing down, he saw a flare of light bloom in the depths. A heartbeat later the shaft reverberated with the roar of an engine and the light came streaking up.

LEAPING RECKLESSLY INTO the Needle, Haz'thur had dropped like a stone into the abyss beyond. *That warp-cursed ghost had tricked him!* Rocketing furiously back up the shaft he swiped at his quarry, missing by a hair's breadth as it slipped through another crawl hole. Furious, he jetted backwards and coiled into a huddled ball of spikes. Thrusters burning, he launched himself at the iron barrier.

THE CRASH OF the raptor's entry shook the rockcrete corridor, but the sprinting ghouls didn't look back. The shimmering glow-globes weren't the only things they'd planted along this stretch of tunnels. Over the years they'd turned the place into a death trap and one misstep would kill them as surely as their hunter's claws.

Leaping an almost invisible wire Zeth felt the panic rising in him. He'd planned for a better lead, but the raptor's sheer physical power had surprised him. Suddenly all the years of scheming and scavenging seemed pitiful, but he held onto the Needle's promise. *He would taste the stars...*

HAZ'THUR'S WILD CANNONBALL dive ripped through the web and carried him careening into the wall only thirty paces beyond. The impact pulverized the rockcrete and shook the whole chamber. Bellowing, he exploded from the ragged crater in a shower of debris, crashing down into a feral crouch. His head flicked about in rapid, avian jerks as he assessed the territory. Low ceiling, drab rockcrete walls threaded with pipes, passages branching off on all sides... Not a true tier then, just a service layer for the clockwork of the hive. It would be a maze of tight tunnels and cluttered chambers that would favour his prey and fight his bulk. *Clever little ghost.*

But he had their scent. There were three and they were close. Unable to jump, let alone fly in the confined warren, he skittered towards the exit... and the ground collapsed beneath his feet. Inhuman reflexes kicking in, he snagged the lip of the pit and leapt out, impelled by a jab of thrust. Peering back down he snarled at the nest of spikes jutting from the gloom. *A trap?* His ceramite armour would have crushed the pitiful spines like matchsticks, but the sheer arrogance of it affronted him. *Did the prey presume to hunt him?*

The traps came thick and fast after that, Haz'thur's furious pursuit triggering a new attack at every twist and turn of the tunnels. Mostly they were variants on the same themes; crude pitfalls, collapsing ceilings and tripwires that released spring-loaded spikes or swinging girders. Occasionally there was something unique, a shower of acid or a rigged laspistol, but all were the clumsy toys of a child playing at war. At first Haz'thur's instincts had compelled him to avoid the traps, but soon he was tripping them with scornful abandon, laughing as spikes shattered against his armour and dodging whirling debris with bravado.

By the time the prey came in sight his mood had grown almost sanguine and he was tempted to prolong the hunt. At thirty paces he teased them with a keening wail, enticing one of the three to glance back. Moments later the fool had impaled itself on a bed of nails. As he whipped past, Haz'thur beheaded the screaming wretch with a flick of the wrist. Predictably it hadn't been the ghost. No, the ghost was sly, but even so its life hung by a thread only twenty paces long...

DRENCHED IN SWEAT, his heart hammering wildly, Zeth knew they couldn't last much longer. Even Kert's slip-up hadn't slowed the hunter. When the fool had got himself spiked the dark thing inside Zeth had cheered, desperate for anything to delay those claws, but it hadn't made a damned bit of difference. Even so, that shadow was now eyeing Brox hungrily, looking for an angle to make him count...

The placid ghoul's breathing was steady beside Zeth's ragged gasps. Dim but strong, that was Brox. And so very loyal. The idiot could have pulled ahead long ago, but there he was, sticking shoulder to shoulder with Zeth despite the devil breathing down their backs.

Sacrifice the fool! Freeze him!

The thoughts lashed across Zeth's mind with a brutal logic that shocked him. The worst thing was he knew he could do it. All he had to do was reach out with his mind and *twist.* It would be so easy and it made such sense! But Brox was the last of his pack...

They swept round a corner and Zeth saw their destination looming just ahead. This was the endgame! They were so close, but so was the hunter...

Do it now!

And then they were bursting into the old generatorium storeroom, weaving through the heaped metal barrels, straining for the open hatchway on the far side. But then Zeth's heart sank in despair. They'd never get the blast door closed in time! From outside the storeroom they'd have to turn and *pull* it shut. It would take precious seconds they'd never have... but if someone just *pushed* it from the inside...

Zeth glanced at Brox and the cold thing inside him reared up.

Do it!

EXPLODING INTO THE storeroom Haz'thur saw the bigger animal suddenly turn on the ghost, thrusting it into the tunnel beyond. Excited by their conflict he stormed forward, the reek of promethium assaulting his finely tuned sense of smell. *Promethium?* He felt the tripwire break.

STAGGERING FROM THE storeroom Zeth glanced back and caught a glimpse of Brox's face. The big ghoul's expression was tranquil, empty. And then the hatch slammed shut and the concussion followed an instant later. It buckled the solid metal hatch and tore the ground from under Zeth's feet. Huddled in a ragged heap, he lay in the darkness long after the tremor had passed. Two thoughts hounded each other through his mind, vying for his soul: *I didn't... I did...*

HAZ'THUR AWOKE TO a world of raw pain. Every breath tore through his chest like a gust of broken glass and his nostrils twitched to the stench of his own charred flesh. His remaining eye had fixed on the maze of fissures in the ceiling above. There was significance to be found in that twisting conjunction of empty spaces. Besides, he couldn't move his neck, or anything else for that matter. Only the claws of his left foot still offered the ghost of a twitch. *The ghost...* The ghost had killed him. The same ghost that was looking down at him now with those cold, grey eyes. As it knelt over him something dark slithered behind the grey and suddenly he was gazing up into twin black suns. For the briefest instant he knew fear, and then the black thorn came down.

WHEN ZETH EMERGED from the Needle the sky was streaked with red and the plaza swam with it. The bodies were everywhere, razers and flesheaters and darkscars all alike in the unravelled simplicity of death. The survivors were gathered in a bewildered huddle, almost as ragged and bloody as the dead, their faces slack with the shock of just being alive.

The raptors were there too, but now they were still and silent. It was as if the sun's rays had petrified them where they stood, transforming them into dark statues. Their wolf-helmed leader crouched amongst them. His armour was a scorched wreck and his hunched posture spoke of barely contained agony, but he was alive. That was good, Zeth thought. He would need allies amongst them.

His eyes found the ones who would decide his fate. A faceless creature was skimming silently over the dead, the seething swathe of its robes never quite touching the ground. It was like a spectral carrion bird, seeking some arcane logic in the weave of the carnage. An armoured giant stalked silently by its side, the tapers of his sable cloak wet with the blood of trampled corpses.

Sorcerer and lord. Once again the words just slipped into Zeth's mind, along with an understanding that these ancient nightmares were not to be approached boldly. They would come to him in their own time. So Zeth waited, eyes fixed on the gore-spattered ground. And finally they came.

'Have we bled this world so dry?' The lord's voice was a desiccated whisper. 'So dry… that such a stunted creature can endure the harrowing?'

The sorcerer made no reply, but Zeth suddenly felt the barbed tendrils of its mind reaching out…

Digging into his soul… Tearing through the walls like paper… Seeing through to his edge…

Desperately Zeth brandished his sacrifice, 'A kill… a kill for True Night!' Hanging from his hand was the bloody rag of Haz'thur's flayed face.

With a smooth gesture the lord silenced the psychic assault and leant forward. His handsome, bloodless features might have been carved from white marble, but they were pooled with shadows and his eyes were a lustreless black.

'You claim to have killed a raptor?' No anger in that voice, just an ancient bitterness that was somehow worse. To answer with anything less than excellence would be fatal.

'He was… weak, lord.' Zeth breathed, waiting for death. The moments stretched into a dark eternity beneath that withering gaze. And then the ancient nodded.

'Yes, he was. And weakness is the only sin this galaxy truly despises.' The lord turned to the sorcerer. 'We will take this one.'

'It is dangerous.' The words were a hissing, electrical buzz.

'I would hope so, sorcerer'. There was the faintest trace of amusement in that bleak voice.

'Lord Vassaago, its essence has been tainted by... an element I am unable to quantify.'

Zeth fought down a wave of hatred for the faceless bastard. It had tasted the touch of the Needle on him and it was afraid, afraid of the power he would become...

'We are all tainted, Yehzod.' Zeth almost flinched at the acid in Vassaago's voice. 'It is the reason we must endure.'

'Lord, it is unpredictable.' Yehzod urged.

'We shall see...' Vassaago answered, turning his back on them.

Yes, you will, the Needle promised.

ONE HATE

Aaron Dembski-Bowden

I am the future of my Chapter.

My masters and mentors often tell me this. They say I, and those like me, hold the Chapter's soul in our hands. We wear the black, and we are the beating heart of a reborn brotherhood.

It is our duty to remember. We are charged to recall the traditions that came before the moment when our Chapter stood on the edge of extinction.

My name is Argo. In a Chapter with few remaining relics, I am blessed above my brothers in the tools of war in my possession.

My armour was born when the Imperium was born – repaired, amended and maintained in the centuries since by generations of warriors, slaves, servitors and serfs. My bolter roared on the battlefields of the Horus Heresy, and has been carried in the red-marked hands of thirty-seven Astartes since the day of its forging. Each of their names is etched into the dark iron of the weapon, along with the name of the world that claimed their lives. The eyes of my helm have stared out onto ten thousand wars, and seen a million of Mankind's foes die.

Around my neck is a gift from the Ecclesiarchy of Holy Terra: an aquila symbol of priceless worth and imbued with the warding secrets of a technology almost lost to time. My armour is black, for I am death itself. My helm is the skull of every man that died in every battle fought by my Chapter in the ten millennia since our founding.

More than that, my face is the victorious leer of the dying Emperor.

And why am I charged with this responsibility? Why do I wear the black?

Because I hate. I hate more than my brothers, and my hatred runs blacker, deeper, purer than theirs.

One hate stands above all others. One hate that burns in our blood and barks from the mouths of five hundred bolters when we stand together in war. It is a hatred with many names: the greenskin, the ork, the kine.

To us, they are simply the Enemy.

We are the Crimson Fists, the shield-hand of Dorn, and we have survived extinction when all others would have fallen into worthless memory. Our hatred takes us across the stars in service to the Throne.

And now it brings us to Syral.

SYRAL. A LONE orb around a diminutive sun, on the edge of Segmentum Tempestus.

The single celestial child of a red star that was taking thousands of years to die. The sun's waning would take thousands of years before its eventual expiration, and the planet it warmed was still of great use to the Imperium.

Syral was an agri-world, with the globe's landmasses given over to expansive and fertile continents of food-stuffs and livestock. Syral's great oceans were similarly plundered by Imperial need. Beneath their dark surface, the tides concealed hydroponics facilities the size of cities, harvesting the edible wealth of the depths. As a planet, Syral had but one colossal purpose: to export a system's worth of food ready for purchase by the worlds nearby that lacked such natural bounty. Syral fed three hive-worlds, from the spires of the rich to the slums of the destitute, as well as several Imperial Navy fleets and regiments of the Imperial Guard warring in nearby crusades.

From space, Syral was the blue-green of mankind's ancestral memory, as if drawn from an artist's imaginings of the impious ages of Old Terra. However, the face of a world can change a great deal in a year.

'The Fists are back.'

Lord General Ulviran looked at Major Dace, who had spoken those words. With his thin face, ice-blue eyes and aquiline nose, the lord general was a natural when it came to bestowing withering looks on those among his staff that disappointed him. He gave one of those glances to Dace now. The major looked away, suitably chastised.

The gunship sat idle, as it had for several minutes now, its landing stanchions and velocity thrusters still hissing with occasional jets of steam as they released flight pressure and settled into repose. Across the side of this midnight-blue vulture of a vessel, an engraved symbol stared back at the horde of Guardsmen that waited. A clenched fist, as red and dark as good wine.

The gunship's forward ramp lowered like a mouth opening. Ulviran was put in mind – as he always was when seeing an Astartes Thunderhawk – of a great steel bird of prey. When its forward ramp lowered, just beneath the cockpit window, the bird seemed to roar with the sound of whining hydraulics.

'I count four,' Major Dace said, making this his second most obvious observation that day. Four armoured forms, each more than a head taller than a normal man, tramped down the clanking ramp.

'Just four...' the major added a moment later. Ulviran would gladly have shot him, had he been able to think of a reason to do so. Not even a good reason, just a legal one. Dace was an asset on the battlefield, but at staff meetings his dullard observations were a tedium his fellow officers could easily do without.

The Astartes made no move to approach the crowd of Guardsmen. They stood as still as statues, monstrous bolters held to their eagle-emblazoned chests. Ulviran took stock of the situation. The Astartes were back, and it was not the time to stand around gawping. Control. The scene warranted control. Maybe there could be some dignity salvaged from this whole tawdry development. Having the Astartes arrive would be a cause for celebration right enough, but Ulviran recalled every single word in the missive he'd composed to Chapter Master Kantor of the Crimson Fists. Begging was the only word for it, really. He'd begged for aid, and here it was: deliverance once more. He was not a man who enjoyed resorting to begging. It had galled him even as he'd dictated the distress call.

Ulviran strode forward to meet the giants as they stood stone-still in the shadow of their avian gunship. He noted with unnoticeable displeasure that the heavy bolter turrets on the Thunderhawk's wing tips panned across the camp, as if seeking threats even amongst Imperial forces. Did the Fists not even consider the Guard capable of holding their own base camp secure against the enemy? In that moment, deliverance or not, the lord general hated their damned arrogance.

'Welcome back,' he said to the first of the Astartes, who was undoubtedly the commander of this small team.

The warrior looked at the lord general, his snarling visored helm turning down to regard the human. This close, no more than an arm's length from the towering warriors, Ulviran felt his gums ache from the pressuring hum of the squad's power armour. The whine of energy was more tactile than audible, making his eyes water and prickling the skin on the back of his neck. He swallowed as the Astartes made the sign of the aquila, the warrior's gauntleted hands forming the salute and banging against his armoured chest. Even the smallest of movements made their armour joints purr in a low mechanical snarl.

Ulviran returned the salute. His neck hurt a little, looking up like this, and he unwillingly flinched when the Astartes spoke.

'With all due respect,' the voice was a crackling, vox-distorted growl, far deeper than a normal man's, 'why are you addressing me?'

Ulviran hadn't expected this level of disrespect, nor this degree of informality. He was a lord general, after all. Planets lived and died by his tactical expertise.

The general took in the details of the warrior's armour. The suit was the blue of a starless midnight sky, trimmed in places with a bold red, nowhere more noticeable than the clenched fist on the warrior's shoulder pad. A scroll detailing oaths and matters of unknowable honour was draped from the warrior's other shoulder pad, moving slightly in the gentle wind. Hanging from a thick chain that had been made into a bandolier, oversized, mis-shapen skulls knocked quietly together as the Astartes moved. From the pronounced lower jaws and brutish bone structure, Ulviran knew they were the skulls of orks. In life, they'd been big orks, most likely leaders among their bestial kind. In death, they were impressive trophies.

This Astartes was clearly the leader of the squad. None of the others wore trophies to match.

'I am addressing you because I assumed you were in command.' He adopted the tone of one speaking to a small child, which his men would have found both laughable and insane had they heard. The thrill of authority over these giants rushed through the lord general's blood. He would, after all, brook no disrespect.

'Do I look like a brother-captain to you?' the Astartes asked, and Ulviran wondered if the warrior's vox-speakers made his voice into a growl, or if it was naturally that low.

Ulviran nodded in response to the question. He was determined not to be intimidated.

'To my eyes, yes, you do.'

'Well, I'm not.' Here the Astartes looked to his fellows. 'Not yet, anyway.' Ulviran heard something at the edge of his hearing – a series of quiet clicks coming from the helms of the armoured men. He assumed, quite correctly, that they were laughing with each other over a private vox-channel.

The Astartes draped in skulls, chains and scrolls detailing his many victories inclined his head at one of the others.

'He's the sergeant.'

Ulviran turned to face this next one, making the sign of the aquila once more.

Before the lord general could speak, this next Astartes – who was clad in a blood-coloured toga draped around his armour – shook his helmed head.

'No, lord general,' the Astartes intoned, his voice as much a mechanical rumble as the first one's had been. 'You do not address me, either.'

Ulviran's patience was reaching its end.

'Then who am I to address?'

The robed warrior nodded in the direction of the Thunderhawk, at the newest arrival striding down the ramp. This Astartes was clad in plate of charcoal-black, and even without much knowledge of Astartes technology it was clear to Ulviran that the dark suit of power armour was an antique, dating back centuries – probably even millennia. The black warrior's helmed face was a grinning skull, the red eye lenses lending it a daemonic cast as he looked left and right, surveying the landing site.

Ulviran swallowed, unaware of how his Adam's apple bobbed and betrayed his nervousness. *Throne,* he thought. *A Chaplain.*

The Astartes in the red toga offered the lord general a slight bow.

'You address him.'

IN PRIVATE, THEY discussed Syral. The Chaplain stalked around the large table with its map-covered surface. Here in the lord general's command room, aboard his personal Baneblade, *The Indomitable Will,* the human and the Astartes shared words away from the ears of others.

'We handed you this world four months ago.'

Those words chilled the lord general's blood. They were an insult, certainly, but they were also an unarguable truth.

'Circumstances change, Brother-Chaplain.' And they had. Ork reinforcements had come in flooding waves, washing the western hemisphere in a tide of greenskin invaders. The Imperium's easy victory, largely bought by the surgical strikes of the Crimson Fists four months before, was nothing more than a pleasant memory and a tale of what might have been. The Imperial Guard had been falling back ever since.

The Chaplain's vox-voice was edged by growls, as if the man spoke at an octave almost too low for words.

'You are losing Syral,' the Astartes said. His skullish face stared at the human across the room.

'I know better than to argue that assessment,' came the lord general's reply. 'I'd wager that I see it clearer than you, for I've been watching it happen for months.'

Ulviran watched as the Chaplain reached up to his helm and pulled the release catches on his armoured collar. With a serpentine hiss of venting pressure, the locks disengaged and the Astartes removed his skulled helmet, reverently lifting it then laying it on the table before him. Its red eyes were dimmed now the helm was detached from the armour's power supply, but they still glared at the lord general in dull accusation.

'I am not here to chastise you, lord general.'

Ulviran smiled to hear the warrior's true voice. It was deep and resonant, but with a gentility shaping the words. The Chaplain was, by the lord general's best guess, close to thirty years of age, but with the Astartes it was almost impossible to tell. He didn't even know for certain if they *did* age; he'd always taken the trope for granted that one determined a Space Marine's age by the scars on their flesh and the inscriptions etched into their armour.

Had this Astartes been allowed to grow as a normal man, he might have been considered handsome. Even as the product of intensive genetic enhancement since puberty, the Chaplain was a fair example of his kind. The Astartes was almost two heads taller than a normal man, with features and body mass to match, but Ulviran saw something undeniably human within the warrior's dark-blue eyes and the half-smile he wore.

The lord general liked him immediately. For Ulviran, who prided himself on being a fine reader of men, this was a rare development.

'Brother-Chaplain–'

'Argo,' he interrupted. 'My name is Argo.'

'As you wish. I must ask you, Argo, how did you respond so quickly to our...' he didn't want to say *to our plea*, '...to our request for reinforcement?'

Argo met his gaze. The half-smile left his face, and the warrior's eyes narrowed. The silence that followed the general's question bordered on becoming awkward.

'Just good fortune,' the Chaplain said at last, the smile returning. 'We were close to the system.'

'I see. And are you alone?'

The Chaplain spread his hands in beneficence. One gauntlet was the same coal black as the warrior's armour. The other, his left, was painted blood red in keeping with the traditions of his Chapter.

'I bring with me the brothers of Squad Demetrian, of the Fifth Battle Company.'

'Yourself and four others. Nothing more?'

'The Chapter serfs and servitors responsible for the flight and maintenance of our Thunderhawk.'

'No more Astartes.' It was a statement of resignation, not a question.

'As you say,' the Chaplain offered a shallow but sincere bow, 'no more Astartes.'

Ulviran was noticeably ill at ease. 'As much as I thank the Throne and your Chapter Master for any assistance the Fists offer, especially so quickly, I had hoped for a... bolder show of support.'

'Hope is the first step on the road to disappointment. Four months ago, we broke the Enemy's back here. I assume you recall the date.'

'I do. The men still speak of it. They call it Vengeance Night.'

'Very apt. We left the enemy reeling, lord general. We left them bloody, their armies shattered from our assaults across the globe. I was at the Siege of the Cantorial Palace. I was part of the strike force that destroyed the palace itself, and I was there when Brother Imrich of the Fifth took the head of Warlord Golgorrad in the battle amongst the smoking rubble. We are back, lord general, and I humbly suggest you be grateful for even the small blessing one squad of our Chapter represents.'

'I am grateful, to you and your Chapter Master.'

'Good. I apologise for any harshness in my tone. Now, let us talk of strategy.' The Chaplain pointed with his red hand at the largest map spread across the table. 'Southspire, the capital city, unless I am mistaken.'

'You are not.'

'And, according to the sensor sweeps made by my Thunderhawk as we broke orbit, the city – and the site of the Cantorial Palace at the city's heart – is once more in the hands of the enemy.'

'It is.'

Argo's blue eyes met Ulviran's, drilling into the officer with an unblinking lack of mercy.

'So when do we take it back?'

THE INTERIOR BAY of the Thunderhawk echoed with Argo's footfalls, his clanking tread ringing from the iron skin of the inert machinery stored there. Chapter serfs in robes of deep blue stepped aside, making the sign of the aquila as he passed. Argo nodded to each one in kind, whispering benedictions for them all. They thanked him and moved about the business of attending to the gunship's innards and readying the stored machinery. Argo's eyes raked along the heavy digging equipment stored in the hold, and his mood turned black.

Squad Demetrian was training. He heard them long before he saw them. Climbing a ladder to the next deck, Argo thumped the door release to the communal 'quarters', a room where Astartes remained strapped in flight seats when the gunship took to the skies. In the small usable space between the twin rows of seats, two of Squad Demetrian duelled in full armour.

The two warriors could not have been less alike. His armour draped in scrolls of his deeds, bone tokens of fallen foes, and the skulls of seven orks hanging from his chain bandolier, Imrich was a whirlwind of movement. Kicks, punches, elbow thrusts, headbutts – all thrown into a duel with shortswords, added between the moves of the clashing blades.

Opposing him was Toma, embodying pure economy of motion. Where Imrich's fury twinned with his skill, Toma's movements were calculated to the finest degree by a lightning mind that drove his vicious combat reflexes. His blade snapped into position to block and thrust in a silver blur, stopping precisely at each twist, never overbalancing, never overreaching, with Toma never giving ground.

'I'll wear you down, Deathwatch,' Imrich teased. Their gladius blades locked again, and the two helms glared at each other only half a metre apart.

Toma said nothing. Displayed on the polished iron of his unique shoulder pad was the stylised symbol of the Holy Inquisition. He always fought in silence. His recent return from three years in the specialist Ordo Xenos Deathwatch Chapter hadn't changed that.

The fight came to an end when Argo cleared his throat. Disengaging from one another, Imrich and Toma resheathed their blades.

'I had you, Deathwatch.' Imrich saluted his opponent with his clenched left fist against his heart.

'Sure you did, hero.' Toma's voice was toneless as he returned the gesture.

'I had you.'

'The day you have me is the day the Emperor rises from the Throne and dances all night long.'

Brother-Sergeant Demetrian silenced them both with a fist pounded against the metal wall.

'News, Brother-Chaplain?' the sergeant asked.

Argo removed his helm and gave them his half-smile. 'They think we're here in answer of a distress call.'

The squad looked at the Chaplain, awaiting further explanation. Now this had their interest up.

'You didn't tell them the truth,' said Demetrian. The veteran's scarred face was a map of battles fought across a hundred systems. Both his gauntlets were crimson; he'd served time in the Crusade Company among the best of the best, and on the knee of his armour, a Black Templar cross was proudly displayed. The Declates Crusade, when the Templars and the Fists broke ranks to fight in mixed units, was a point of great honour for both Chapters. Demetrian had been there. A roll of his honours was recorded in acid-etched lettering on a gold tablet in the Chapter's fortress-monastery back home on Rynn's World.

Argo nodded. 'I thought it best to retain the illusion of our compliance. The truth would breed animosity.'

'No surprise,' Demetrian's words were as clipped and to the point as ever. 'The plan remains the same?'

'We fight until the Cantorial Palace. Then we do the duty entrusted to us. I saw the maps of Southspire and the enemy's forces spread across the sector. A new warlord leads the enemy on the far side of the city, and the Guard ready for their last attempt at a big push. The city itself is flooded with roaming bands of foes.'

'Numbers?'

'Thousands within the city. Tens of thousands at the edge, where the warlord waits.'

'I like those odds,' Imrich said. They all heard the smile in his words, even from behind his helm.

Argo shook his head. 'This is not a war we can win without the Guard.'

Now Toma spoke up. He sat in one of the restraining seats, meticulously dismantling and cleaning the sacred bolter given to him by the Ordo Xenos during his tenure in the Inquisitorial kill-teams.

'Will the Guard win this war without us?'

Argo shrugged. 'We have our orders.'

Toma pressed on. 'And once we leave?'

'The Emperor protects,' the Chaplain replied.

Imrich's skulls rattled as he turned. 'So we flee a war that the Imperium is losing? I don't like the thought of running from the kine.'

'Duly noted, but Chapter Master Kantor was clear in his priorities,' Argo said. 'And you will do penance for your disrespect of the Enemy, Brother Imrich.'

It was a matter of small shame among some of the Crimson Fists that they referred to the greenskins as *kine*. On Rynn's World, another agri-world, it was slang for 'cattle'.

'Yes, Brother-Chaplain,' Imrich growled.

'Hate the inhuman, slaughter the impure, and praise the Emperor above all. But always respect the foe.'

'Yes, Brother-Chaplain.' Imrich wanted to insist Argo stopped quoting the litanies at him. Instead he bowed his head. He knew better than to apologise.

'When do we move out?' Demetrian cut in.

'Tomorrow night, the Guard will advance,' Argo said, as he held his golden aquila medallion in his red-fingered gauntlet. 'And we advance with them.'

DAWN FOUND ARGO in the cockpit of the Thunderhawk, still in his armour. He sat in one of the command thrones, his elbows on his knees, staring out of the window. He had not slept. He was Astartes. He barely needed sleep.

Toma came to him as he mused on the coming battle. The quiet warrior was a powerful credit to the squad, and Argo – who was over a century younger than the Deathwatch specialist – always welcomed his presence. He suspected it would not be long before the captain of the Fifth selected Toma for promotion into the Crusade Company, or to lead his own squad into the field of war.

'Another dawn, Brother-Chaplain.' Toma took the command throne next to Argo, sitting and holding his helm in his hands. The Deathwatch had aged him, Argo saw. New scars, faded from fast treatment but still noticeable, pitted the warrior's cheek and temple.

'Acid burns,' Argo said, gesturing with a gloved hand, his black one. 'The Deathwatch kept you busy.'

'I can't say,' Toma replied. His face was as expressive as stone.

'Can't or won't?' Argo asked, already knowing the answer.

'Both.'

'The Ordo Xenos keeps its secrets close.'

'It does.' Toma's expression was edged with thought as he replayed hazy recollections, little more than echoes, through his mind. Oaths had been sworn. Promises were made. Memories were torn from the mind by psyk-enhanced meditation and the ungentle scouring of arcane machinery.

It was the first time Argo had seen his fellow Fist's neutral mask slip, and he found it fascinating.

'We go to war today,' the Chaplain said. 'We are a poor portion of the Fifth's strength, but we are the Fifth nevertheless. In the fires of war, we are forged. And yet I sense a burden on your soul, brother.'

Toma nodded. This was why he had come.

'It's Vayne.'

BROTHER-APOTHECARY VAYNE was in the Thunderhawk's confined apothecarion, little more than an operating table and racks of monitoring equipment fastened to the small room's walls. Already prepared for the battle tonight, he was in full armour with one exception: his head was bare. The white-faced helm that marked him as an Apothecary rested on the surgery table, and this was the first thing Argo saw as he entered. The second thing was Vayne himself, adjusting data readouts on his arm-mounted narthecium. As Argo watched, several surgical spikes and knives snapped back into the bulky medical unit housed on Vayne's forearm.

Vayne eventually turned to the sound of thrumming power armour, though his enhanced senses would have detected the Chaplain's approach long before he came into the room.

'Argo,' he said in subdued greeting.

'Vayne,' the Chaplain nodded back.

The atmosphere between the two men was nothing short of ugly. Seven years before, they'd served together as novices in Nochlitan's Scout squad. Seven years since the final trials to become Astartes, when Argo had been chosen to wear the black, and Vayne the white.

A Chaplain and an Apothecary drawn from the same scout unit. Sergeant Nochlitan, who like Demetrian had served admirably in the Crusade Company among the

Chapter's elite, had been honoured by Chapter Master Kantor himself for honing such excellence in a novice squad.

With the Chapter still in its perilous rebuilding stage, the finest warriors of the Crimson Fists were often charged with the duty of training novice squads. It was no shame to step away from the First Company to the role of Scout-sergeant, and Nochlitan was one of the most respected.

Beyond a few scars, Argo looked no different. The same could not be said for the Apothecary. Half of Vayne's face was gone, replaced by cold, smooth steel shaped to resemble his features. Despite its artistry, the exquisite workmanship was clear evidence of a terrible wound that had almost been Vayne's death. Vayne's left eye, an augmetic lens of synthetic scarlet crystal, whirred in its circular socket as the Apothecary focused his gaze on the Chaplain.

'You're looking well,' he remarked. Argo didn't reply. He watched as Vayne limped around the surgical table, and considered the rest of the Apothecary's newly-restored body.

Daemon-fire had done this to Vayne, during the Cleansing of Chiaro two months before. Fresh from the victory on Syral and the destruction of the Cantorial Palace, the Crimson Fists had entered the warp for several weeks to reach Chiaro, answering a call for aid by the planetary governor. Mutant cults were spreading in the rotting industrial sectors of his world. A true purge was needed to stamp the problem out, after the local defence forces had failed to quell the matter.

The Fists had not failed. It took a month and was not without casualties, but their duty was done. The rest of the strike force returned to Rynn's World at the behest of Chapter Master Kantor. Argo and Squad Demetrian had returned to Syral aboard the support cruiser *Vigil*.

It had been a cold, quiet journey back to Syral. They were the only Astartes on board, except for a single

Apothecary from the Fifth Company that remained to preside over Vayne's injuries – and act in his stead if the younger man died.

Vayne had suffered as the servitors and his potential replacement rebuilt his body. He was almost certain to die, given the massive burns sustained and their initial refusal to heal. The Chapter would lose a gifted healer in a time when the Fists most desperately needed to reclaim and preserve their fighting strength. Had Vayne died, it would have been a true loss.

From shoulder to fingertips, his left arm was augmetic. It connected internally to the bionic sections of his spine and collarbone, purring in a smooth hiss of expensive augmentation that Argo's keen hearing could detect even underneath the background hum of their power armour. As with his left arm, so too was his left leg bionic – from hip to toes. The augmentations were still new, still untested in battle, and although Argo doubted a normal human could discern the minute inconsistencies in Vayne's gait and posture, to Astartes senses it registered as a subtle but noticeable hitch in his stride. A limp.

It was temporary, until the augmetics aligned with Vayne's body patterns and wholly fused with his biorhythms. The leg ended in a splayed claw of a foot for enhanced stability: a cross of blackened metal that connected to the well-armoured ankle joint and the heavy musculature of the bionic shin and calf above.

'Your attitude is beginning to create strain within your squad,' Argo began. 'I am told you are melancholic.'

Vayne scowled. His false eye hummed in its socket as it tried to conform to his facial expression.

'Brother-Sergeant Demetrian has said nothing.'

'You were saved because you have value to the Chapter. You stand in high regard for your skills. Why are you unbalanced by wounds which heal even as we speak?'

Vayne watched his own crimson left gauntlet close and open, repeating the motion several times. It was his bionic arm, and feeling was slow in returning.

'I trained a lifetime in my own body. Now I fight in someone else's.'

'It is still your body.'

'Not yet. There is acclimatisation to come.'

'Then you will acclimatise. There is no more to say.'

'You don't see? This is not false pathos, Argo. I was perfect before, made in the Emperor's image in accordance with his ancient and most sacred designs.'

'You still are.'

'No. I am a simulacrum.' He clenched his augmetic hand into a numb fist. 'I am the best imitation we are capable of creating. I am no longer perfect.'

'Our brothers in the Iron Hands would dispute that diagnosis.'

Vayne scoffed. 'Those uninspired slaves of the Mechanicum? They make war at the pace of toothless old men.'

'If you resort to insults against our brother Chapters, I will lose my temper as well as my patience.'

'My point is that I am no Iron Hand. And I have no wish to be some half-flesh imitation Astartes.'

'You will acclimatise,' Argo stepped forward, taking Vayne's helm from the table and looking down at the white faceplate.

'Even so, until then I am a liability to my brothers.'

Argo handed his friend the helmet and shook his head. 'You are petulant beyond my comprehension. Only in death does duty end. We are the Fists. We are the shield-hand of Dorn. We do not weep and cower from battle because of pain or fear or worries of what might yet be. We fight and die because we were made to fight and die.'

Vayne took the helm and smiled without humour. Half of his face didn't follow the expression.

'What amuses you?'

'You are blind, Argo. You may preserve the soul of our Chapter, but I preserve its body. I harvest the gene-seed of the fallen, and I ensure the wounded will fight again. So listen to me, *brother*. I fear nothing but allowing my failures to harm my brethren. I am not at peak performance, and I am unused to the wounds I still wear under this armour. That is the source of my unbalance.'

'You lose your own argument. You fear to let down your brothers because your battle skills are hindered for a short while. Vayne, you are harming your brothers far more with your withdrawn attitude and the bitterness leaking from your every word. You are eroding their trust in you, and destroying their confidence.'

Argo's battle-collar pulsed a single blip. He tensed his neck, activating the pearl-like vox-bead attached to his throat, which picked up the vibrations of his vocal chords.

'Brother-Chaplain Argo. Speak.'

'Brother-Chaplain,' it was Lord General Ulviran. 'I have a request to ask you and your warriors.'

'I will be with you shortly,' Argo said, and killed the link. The silence between Argo and Vayne returned.

'Your point is taken,' Vayne conceded. 'I will not allow my melancholy to taint my squad any longer.'

'That is all I demand.' Argo was already turning to leave.

'I remember a time when you could not make such demands of me, Argo.'

'I remember a time when I did not need to make them.'

THE FISTS SHED blood before the Guard's night-time advance. Under Ulviran's request, Argo and Demetrian led the squad into the shattered remains of the city's western sector.

In the minutes leading up to deployment, Argo had gathered the warriors together in the shadow of their

Thunderhawk. Dozens of Guardsmen around the camp looked on, dallying about their business while they watched the Astartes soldiers perform their rite. The Fists ignored them all.

With his gladius, Argo sliced the palms of each warrior's left hand. They, in turn, pressed their bleeding hands against the chest piece of the Fist next to them.

Imrich rested his hand on the embossed silver eagle decorating Toma's breastplate. The Larraman cells in his blood scabbed and sealed the gash quickly, but not before his palm left a dark smear on Toma's Imperial symbol.

'My life for you,' Imrich said, then removed his hand and fastened his helm. Toma was next, pressing his bleeding hand against Vayne's breastplate.

'My life for you,' the Deathwatch veteran said, before donning his own helm. Vayne forced a smile. He had to perform the rite with his remaining flesh hand, his right instead of his left, and did so without complaint.

When it came to the Chaplain's turn, Argo rested his hand on Demetrian's armour, as tradition necessitated the officiating Chaplain to honour the ranking officer.

'My life for you,' Argo said. A moment later, his senses were submerged in the audiovisual chaos of his battle helm. On the eye lens displays, he saw the flickering readouts of the squad's vital signs, communication runes, lists of vox-channels, sight-altering lens options, thermo-conditional and local atmospheric readouts, and a cluster of information pertaining to the myriad functions of his armour.

All of the information added up to one thing.

'Ready,' he voxed to the others, blink-clicking most of the lens displays into transparency.

'Ready,' they voxed back. They'd started walking then, loping strides that emitted a chorus of mechanical growls from their armour joints. The Guardsmen parted like a split sea as the Astartes neared them.

With blood on their Imperial eagles, the Crimson Fists went to war.

THAT HAD BEEN three hours ago. The Fists took a Guard Chimera troop transport to the city limits, and were advancing through the western edge of Southspire. It was a scouting run, and progress was predicted – by Lord General Ulviran – to be fast. Intelligence had pinned enemy resistance in this section of the city to be minimal. Only at the city's centre was resistance expected to pick up.

Intelligence had been wrong about that.

Argo crouched in the ruins of what had once been an Administratum building, where hundreds of barely-educated wage slaves typed their lives away into cogitators that amassed Syral's exportation data. Pressed against a wall half tumbled down months ago from Imperial Basilisk shelling, the Chaplain waited unmoving, listening to the thrum of his power armour and the sounds of several foes breathing nearby.

Roaming bands of greenskins claimed this part of the city. Squad Demetrian had abandoned the Chimera long before, in favour of stalking through the ruins and clearing a path for the Guard's advance tonight.

Argo heard the xenos trampling closer, around the corner. They muttered to each other in their guttural, swinish tongue. The Chaplain tasted bile in his mouth. Their inhumanity repelled him.

He heard the bestial things pause in their lazy search, heard them snuffing at the air and grunting. They had his scent, he was sure of it, and his blood ran hot as he clenched his short combat sword in one hand, his bolter in the other.

At his hip hung his deactivated crozius arcanum, the symbolic weapon of his role in the Chapter. Capped by an eagle-shaped maul fashioned from blackened adamantium, it was a fearsome bludgeon when sheathed in its crackling power field. Argo's crozius had belonged to Ancient Amentus, one of the first Crimson Fist Chaplains; a founder of the Chapter from when the primarch divided the Imperial Fists Legion ten millennia before. Upon an arm-length haft of dark metal, the inscription *Traitor's Bane* was written in High Gothic.

He treasured the relic weapon, which still felt unfamiliar in his fists even after seven years. Against detritus such as these greenskins, his gladius was more than enough to suffice. He would not let the filthy blood of weakling xenos mar an honourable weapon dating back to the Great Crusade.

The first of the creatures, alert now, came around the corner. In its fists was a collection of scrap that evidently served the greenskin as a firearm. Argo surged to his feet, superhuman reflexes enhanced even further by his armour, and before the ork could utter a sound, it was falling backwards with the hilt of the Chaplain's gladius protruding from its eye socket.

Argo rounded the corner to meet the others head-on and his bolter barked, spitting detonating shells into green flesh. Eleven of them. Each hulking figure was momentarily outlined by a flicker of light in his helm's vision, cycling through target locks. But eleven was too many, even for an Astartes. In a flashing moment of anger, Argo cursed himself for not listening carefully to their breathing and trying to discern their numbers. It was his failing, he knew. He'd acted in rage, and now it was going to kill him.

The brutish creatures ran at him even as they took fire, massive fists gripping jagged axes that were pieced together from vehicle parts and industrial machinery. Argo's bolter cut down three orks as his targeting reticule flitted between weak points in the greenskins' piecemeal armour.

'You dare exist in Mankind's galaxy!' Argo's bolter spat its last shell which destroyed an ork from the jaw up. He clamped the weapon to his thigh with its magnetic seal and threw his fist forward, shattering the forehead of the first greenskin to come in range. 'Die! Die knowing the Crimson Fists will cleanse the stars of your taint!'

Axes slashed towards him, which Argo weaved to avoid. A step back took him within reach of the first ork he'd felled, and he snatched up his gladius from the wretch's skull. Rivulets of dark blood slid along the silver blade, and the Astartes grinned behind his death's head mask.

'Come, alien filth. I am Argo, son of Rogal Dorn, and I am your death.' The mob of orks ran in and Argo met them, the primarch's name on his lips.

'Break left.'

The voice crackled over the vox and Argo obeyed instantly, throwing himself into a roll that scattered a dust cloud in the ruins of the building. He came up, blade in hand, just as the speaker joined him in the fight.

The midday sun flashed from Toma's iron shoulder guard as he hammered the greenskins from behind. His bolter disgorged a stream of shells that exploded on impact in bursts of clear, hissing liquid. As he fired one-handed, he plunged his gladius into the throat of the closest greenskin, giving it a savage twist to half-sever the creature's head. Four of the orks fell back, the horrendously potent acid from Toma's prized bolt rounds overriding even the orkish resilience to pain as it ate through their flesh like holy fire.

All of this happened before Argo's two hearts had time to beat twice.

The last two orks leapt at the Fists to die in futility. Toma impaled the first through the chest, shattered its face with a brutal headbutt, and fired a single bolt at point-blank range into the alien's temple. The skull gave way in a shower of gore as the explosive shell performed its sacred function. Gobbets of flesh and bone hissed as they span away, eaten by the mutagenic acid in Toma's Inquisition-sanctioned ammunition.

Argo grappled with the second ork, his gauntlets wrapped around the thing's throat as it broke its thick nails scrabbling at his armour. He bore the howling greenskin to the ground, his weighty armour crushing the life from its chest as he strangled it in trembling fists.

'Die...'

The ork's answer was to roar voicelessly, its red eyes burning with rage. The Astartes grinned in mimicry of his helm and leaned close to the thing's face. His voice was a whisper through his vox-speakers.

'I *hate* you.'

Toma stood to the side, reloading his bolter and scanning the ruins for more foes. Argo's skulled face pressed against the choking ork's forehead. Orkish sweat left dark smears against his bone-cream faceplate.

'This is the Emperor's galaxy.' With a final surge of effort, he squeezed with all his strength. Vertebrae popped and cracked under the pressure. 'Mankind's galaxy. *Our* galaxy. Know that, as your worthless life ends.'

'Brother-Chaplain...' Toma said.

Argo barely heard. He let the creature fall dead and rose to his feet, savouring the taste of copper, bitter and hot, on his tongue. His rage had not killed him, after all. The enemy lay dead in great numbers.

'Brother-Chaplain,' Toma repeated.

'What?' Argo unclasped his bolter, reloading it now with the proper litany to the machine-spirit within.

There was a moment when Argo was sure Toma would say something; chide him for letting his fury get the better of him and lead him into reckless combat. Despite the break with tradition and authority, Argo would have accepted the criticism from a warrior like Toma.

Toma said nothing, but the silence passing between the two Astartes was laden with meaning.

'Report,' Argo said to break the quiet.

'Imrich and Vayne report their section is clear now. Brother-Sergeant Demetrian reports the same.'

'Resistance?'

'Vayne and Demetrian described it as savage.'

'And Imrich?'

'He described it as thrilling.'

Argo nodded. He was running low on ammunition, and knew the others must be as well.

'Prepare for a withdrawal.'

As Toma voxed Argo's orders to the others, the young Chaplain looked out across the ruined city. Small by Imperial standards – large settlements were rare on an agri-world – yet the focus of so much destruction.

On the other side of Southspire, the new warlord waited with the bulk of his horde. And in the heart of the city, the broken remains of the Cantorial Palace: the Fists' true goal, surrounded by foes.

Argo's blood boiled as he spat a curse behind his mask. He wanted to press on. The palace was no more than a handful of hours away, but resistance from the roaming warbands was intense. With another squad of Astartes, just five more men, he'd have taken the chance. But alone, it was suicide.

'What's that noise?' Toma said.

Argo levelled his bolter. He'd heard it, too. Drums. The music of primitives, echoing across the city like the pounding heartbeat of an angry god.

'It's a warning.'

THE IMPERIAL GUARD advanced that night, and the weather turned bitter as if the heavens recognised the humans' intent.

Basilisks softened up the way ahead with relentless bombardments each hour. Ulviran was content to endure this halting advance, frequently cutting forward progress to establish another artillery barrage that took an age to set up. He pored over maps and holo-displays in his Baneblade's command room as Imperial guns pounded their own city into dust.

The big push consisted of the surviving elements of the Radimir Third Rifles, Seventh Irregulars and Ninth Armoured. These were the so-called 'Revenants', named for the many times Radimir had replaced entire regiments due to losses against the greenskins in Segmentum Tempestus. Rebirth at the precipice of extinction was a blessing familiar to the Crimson Fists, and the Chapter had fought well with the soldiers of Radimir countless times across the centuries.

Hundreds of Guardsmen clad in the gunmetal grey of the Radimir Revenants marched alongside rattling Sentinels in the vanguard of the assault, flanked by Leman Russ battle tanks in half a dozen variants. Radimir was close to being a forge world in terms of its armoured exports. No Revenant regiment ever went to war short of armour support.

The bulk of Ulviran's forces followed the vanguard: six thousand men including a detachment of storm-troopers serving as his ceremonial guard, riding alongside his Baneblade in eight black-painted Chimeras.

At the rear of this main force came the artillery: Griffons and Basilisks, their punishing guns stowed and locked until the next time Ulviran brought the column to a halt and ordered them to set up a shelling storm kilometres ahead.

Last of all came the rearguard, made of the lord general's veteran Guard squads interspersed with auxiliary units, medical transports and supply trucks.

The Fists' Thunderhawk gunship remained back at the abandoned base camp at the city's edge, ready to be summoned. For a short while, until Argo scattered them, Squad Demetrian marched in the vanguard of the force, forming the vicious tip of the Imperium's conquering blade. In scything rain and howling winds, as the elements battered down upon the miserable Imperial advance, the war to retake Southspire began. The Fists soon bled away into the night, leaving Argo alone.

Major Dace, who had been present in the Baneblade's command room when Argo reported the Fists' scouting run, couldn't resist voxing the Chaplain now. Argo's suit insulated him from the noise of the rain slashing against his ceramite armour, and he tensed his throat to activate his vox-bead as it chimed.

'Brother-Chaplain Argo. Speak.'

'This is Major Dace of the Revenants.' Argo smiled as he heard the voice. The ritual processes that had moulded his body like clay, forming him into an Astartes, had given him a memory close to eidetic. It was known by most imperial commanders who worked with Astartes that Space Marines possessed preternatural capacities for instant recollection.

'Have we met?' Argo asked with his half-smile in place. He didn't let his amusement leak into his voice. It had the desired effect; Dace's feathers were ruffled.

'I don't see your foretold resistance, Brother-Chaplain. All is quiet on the advance, is it not?'

'I can still hear the drums,' Argo noted. And he could, setting a distant rhythmic percussion to the thunder grinding across the sky.

'I can't,' Dace said.

'You are comfortably hidden in a tank, major.' Argo closed the link and added, 'And you are only human.'

The Fists had been killing greenskins their entire unnaturally long lives. Ulviran, no stranger to the orkish hordes himself, trusted Argo's belief that the drums pounded as a challenge to the Imperials. The new warlord, a curse upon his black heart, knew they were coming, and the drums of war beat to show he welcomed the coming bloodshed. The storm swallowed their noise now. Only the Astartes could make it out, and it was dimmed even to their senses.

'Ulviran to all units,' crackled the lord general's hourly message. 'Dig in for bombardment. Shelling to commence in thirty minutes.'

Argo bit back a curse. Too slow, much too slow. His thoughts were plagued by the Thunderhawk full of digging equipment back at the base.

'Brother-Chaplain?'

The communication rune that flashed on his reddish lens display was, thankfully, not Dace. Imrich's vital signs registered as almost a kilometre ahead.

'How goes the scouting, Brother Imrich?'

'Lord,' Imrich responded, speaking quietly and clearly. 'I've found the kine.'

'So have I, sir.' This was Vayne, a kilometre to the west.

'Contact,' voxed Demetrian. His readouts pinned him in the south.

Argo looked over his shoulder, at the procession of ocean-grey tanks with rain sluicing off their hulls.

'Numbers?' he asked them all over the squad's shared channel. The weather was banishing vox integrity, masking all the words in a haze of crackles and hisses.

'I count over a thousand, easily,' Vayne said. 'Perhaps two.'

'Same,' added Demetrian.

'I've got more. I've got lots more.' Imrich sounded overjoyed. But then, knowing Imrich, he probably was. 'Twice that number, I'm sure of it. If we hear from Toma,' Imrich added, 'we're in a world of trouble.'

The Deathwatch specialist had been sent to the south, stalking a good distance behind the rearguard.

The vox clicked live again. 'Brother-Chaplain, come in.' said Toma. The rest of his message was cut off by Imrich's delighted laughter.

With a cold feeling of metallic-tasting finality in his throat, Argo voxed the lord general.

Ulviran listened without hesitation. He ignored Dace's complaints and pulled the column into a still-advancing defensive spread that, admirably, took less than half an hour to form. No small feat for that many soldiers and vehicles. The organisational aspects of war were where Ulviran most prided himself. An orderly army was a victorious one. The faster orders were obeyed, the more men survived. It was a simple mathematic he liked, and had a talent for putting it into practice.

'The shelling,' Argo voxed to him, 'is doing nothing. The warlord has put significant force into the city against us, and the horde ahead is falling back to draw us in.'

Ulviran glared down at the hololithic display of the city projected onto the large table. His Baneblade rumbled as it rolled on.

'We're surrounded.'

'If we stop now, lord general, we will be. The pincers will close around us the moment we halt. If we push on at speed, we can make it to the Cantorial Palace and engage the forward elements before the rest of the noose can close around our throats.'

Ulviran liked that. Turn the ambush into an attack.

'Strike first, strike hard, and prepare to repel the rest of the attackers once the main force is crushed.' It sounded good. It sounded right. But...

'I am going purely on your word for this, Brother-Chaplain.'

'Good,' the Astartes replied, and ended the link.

'The Cantorial Palace?' voxed Demetrian.

'Yes. Squad, form up. We're taking the prize.'

THE CANTORIAL PALACE had been the seat of the planetary governor, and a masterpiece of gothic design; as skeletally, broodingly Imperial as would be expected.

All that remained was a series of shattered walls and a small mountain of rubble, where once battlements and ridged towers had risen around a central bastion. The previous greenskin warlord had claimed it as his lair, until the Crimson Fists had dissuaded him of the notion four months ago. Refuting his claim of ownership involved razing the building to the ground with infiltrating sappers, and even then, the gigantic xenos clad in its primitive power armour had survived to claw itself free from the smoking rubble.

Imrich had battled the warlord in the stone wreckage, finally taking its head after a long and bloody duel. He wore Warlord Golgorrad's skull on his bandolier, giving it pride of place on his chest.

The ork forces of this nameless new warlord evidently favoured the former site of battle. It was to be the anvil upon which the Imperial forces would be crushed by the flanking hordes.

Ulviran's army did not march sedately to a doom surrounded by foes. Time was of the essence, and the Revenants powered on to meet the larger force ahead. Men held to the side of speeding tanks and rode atop vehicle roofs. Within the hour, the Guard spilled with overwhelming force into the great plaza district where the Cantorial Palace's bones jutted from the ground.

The armoured fist of the Revenant advance crashed into the scattered greenskin lines. Rubble rained down as tanks unleashed the fury of their cannons, and a staccato chorus of heavy bolter fire filled the air between the thunder of main guns. Lacking entrenchments, the orks counter-charged the armoured column, finding walls of Imperial Guard coming to meet them. Las-fire sliced across the night, illuminating the battlefield like some hellish pre-dawn in scarlet sunlight.

The rain lashed down on troopers in cold-weather gear as they fired in disciplined ranks, and the orks still came on in a roaring wave that drowned out the sound of thunder above.

Imperial records came to know this battle as the Night of the Axe, when the Radimir regiments on Syral were decimated by the hordes of xenos creatures they faced. Losses stood at forty-six per cent, utterly damning Lord

General Ulviran's planned big push to face the new warlord that still lay in wait on the other side of the city. The Guard was bloody and beaten, and although thousands survived the assault, it was nowhere near enough to storm the warlord's position with any hope of success. The Radimir's one slim hope of survival on the kine-infested world – to strike the warlord down and cast the hordes into disarray – was gone. In turning the ambush into an attack of their own, the Guard had delayed their destruction but not avoided it.

However, for the purposes of the Crimson Fists, the Night of the Axe was neither the most critical juncture in the war for Syral, nor was it even recorded in their rolls of honour despite the harvest of lives reaped by Squad Demetrian of the Fifth Company.

The Fists, in true Astartes autonomy, had a sacred duty of their own to perform. This came to light the following morning, as the broken Guard made to move on from the scene of slaughter.

THE SECTOR WAS a mess of bloodshed and battle fallout. The corpses of thousands of orks and humans lay scattered over a square kilometre of annihilated urban terrain. The air thrummed with the growl of engines, frequently split by the cries of wounded men ringing out as they were tended by medics or died in agony, unfound among the charnel chaos that littered the ground.

Argo walked among the dead, gladius plunging down to end the lives of any greenskins that still drew breath. He listened to the general vox-channel as he performed his bloody work, making a mental note of casualties suffered by the Guard. He knew they were sure to be destroyed if they pressed on to face the warlord, just as surely as they'd be destroyed when the warlord's armies came hunting for them. He felt a moment of pity for the Guard. The Revenants were brave souls who'd always stood their ground in the face of the enemy. It was a shame to see them expire like this, in utter futility.

But the Fists would be long gone by then.

As he approached the edge of the colossal vista of rubble that made up the bones of the Cantorial Palace, he activated his vox and sent the signal he'd ached to send since his arrival. A single acknowledgement blip was the only answer he received, and the only answer he required.

Squad Demetrian stood a short distance from the lord general's Baneblade, honouring their wargear through daily prayer and muttered rituals. There they remained, ignoring the Guard all around, until thrusters shrieked in the sky above.

'What in the name of hell is that doing here?' Lord General Ulviran asked Major Dace as they looked up at the dark shape coming in to land with a howl of engines. The two officers left the cooling shadows of the command tank and approached the Astartes. Behind the warriors, throwing up a blizzard of dust, their Thunderhawk kissed the rubble-strewn ground and settled on its clawed stanchion feet.

'Are you leaving?' Ulviran demanded of Argo, aghast as he shouted above the cycling-down engines.

'No.'

'Then what–'

'Move aside, lord general,' the Chaplain said. 'We need room for our equipment. And if you would be so kind as to move your Baneblade, it would be appreciated.'

Dace, a short and rotund example of Radimir manhood, drew himself up to his unimpressive full height. 'We move out within the hour! You can't do… whatever it is you're doing.'

'Yes,' Argo said, 'I can.' His skullish helm glared down at the fat man. 'And if you try to stop me, I will kill you.'

To his credit, Dace did a fine job at appearing unmoved by the vox-growled threat.

'We have orders from Segmentum Command, and the Crimson Fists must abide by them.'

'That's an amusing fiction,' Argo smiled, knowing the humans couldn't see his expression. 'Feel free to entertain that fantasy as you get out of our way.'

Ulviran looked stricken, like he'd just taken a gut wound. He watched in mute sickness as servitors and robed serfs unloaded portable industrial equipment down the Thunderhawk's ramp.

'If you do not move aside,' Argo said with false patience in his voice, 'the Thunderhawk lander coming from orbit with more equipment will be forced to destroy your Baneblade to make room to land.'

'Equipment?' Dace was indignant. 'For what?'

It was Ulviran who answered. He'd seen the drills and clawed scoops on the machinery being unloaded.

'Digging...' The lord general's face was wrinkled in thought.

Argo favoured the officers with a bow. 'Yes. Digging. Now move aside, if you please.'

Defeated and confused, the two men backed away. Dace was red-faced and scowling, Ulviran subdued and voxing orders to make room for further Astartes landings.

When the Guard left just under an hour later, three Thunderhawks were nested in the ruins of the Cantorial Palace, each one freed of its cargo of servitors, serfs and machinery.

'They're heading west,' Imrich nodded towards the rolling Guard column.

'Then they'll die well,' the Chaplain snapped, and his hand cut through the air in a gesture to the work crews.

Drills ground into stone, scoops clawed piles of rubble aside, and the slaves of the Crimson Fists Chapter began to dig.

* * *

IT TOOK THREE days to make the first discovery.

By this time, the Guard was nearing the edge of Southspire, mere hours from their final encounter with the greenskin warlord. The Fists remained at the Cantorial Palace, silently admiring the Revenants' decision to die on the offensive, rather than retreat and die in their makeshift fort-camp.

Three days had passed since the Guard rolled out.

Three days of random sieges and petty assaults punctuating the sunlit hours and the long nights. Although the orks had been crushed in the area, wandering bands of savages still attacked the Crimson Fists' position. Each of the attempts made by the snorting, roaring mobs were met with torrents of heavy bolter fire from the grounded Thunderhawks and the seasoned killing prowess of Squad Demetrian as they maintained a perimeter vigil day and night, never resting, never sleeping.

On the evening of the third day, as the dull sun fell below the horizon, one of the serfs cried out. He'd found something, and the Astartes came running.

THE FIRST BOY was dead.

His scout's armour was largely intact, as was his body. Vayne was the one to lift the corpse from its rubble grave, treating it with all due honour as he laid it out on the ground by the first Thunderhawk. Argo came over once the examinations were complete to intone the Rite of Blessed Release. He knelt by the body, pressing his slit palm to the slain boy's forehead and leaving a smear of blood that mixed with the dirt on the child's dusty face.

'Novice Frael,' Vayne consulted his narthecium, tapping at the keypad as he examined the readout. 'Age thirteen, initial stages of implantation.'

'There's very little decay,' Argo observed in a soft voice.

'No. Blood and tissue samples indicate he died three or four days ago. My guess would be the day before we arrived.'

'Four months,' Argo whispered, looking back over the rubble. 'He was under there for *four months*, and we were three days too late. That...'

'What?' Vayne closed his narthecium and reset the data display. Surgical cutting tools snicked back into his bracer.

'That isn't... fair,' Argo finished. He knew how foolish the words sounded.

'If he'd been fully human,' Vayne said, 'he'd have died in the first two weeks. Thirst. Starvation. Trauma. It was a miracle his initial implantations even allowed him to survive this long. Almost sixteen weeks, Argo. That's worthy of the rolls of honour itself.'

They'd avoided discussing the odds up until now. It was a mission none of the squad expected to fulfil with anything approaching glory.

'Sixteen weeks.' Argo closed his eyes, though his helm stared at Vayne, its gaze unbroken.

'Even without the sus-an membrane,' Vayne was tapping keys on his narthecium bracer, 'our physiology will allow the slowing of the metabolism and the near-cessation of many bio-functions. It is still within the edge of prospective boundaries that an Astartes from the gene-seed of Rogal Dorn could survive the duration.'

Argo nodded. Full Astartes could survive, could *potentially* survive. That, however, wasn't the true issue. The Chaplain looked over his shoulder, where the corpse of the young novice lay.

'Kine,' snapped the vox. 'Kine at the south perimeter.'

Argo and Vayne were already running. 'That's penance for you, Imrich.'

'Yes, Brother-Chaplain. I'll do it right after we kill these whoreson aliens who've taken such umbrage at my trophies.'

THE SECOND BODY was discovered fifty metres away, two hours later. It was a dry husk, deep in waterless decay, and it took Vayne several minutes to identify the corpse as Novice Amadon, age fifteen, at the secondary stage of Astartes implantation.

'He's been dead for months,' Vayne said, without needing to point out the crushed ribcage and severed right leg. Scraps of scout armour still clung to the dry fleshy remnants. 'He was killed when the palace fell.'

The Chaplain was conducting the funerary rite on Novice Amadon when the first survivor was found.

'Argo,' the vox crackled live with Vayne's excited voice. 'Blood of the primarch, Argo, come over here now.'

Argo clenched his teeth. 'A moment, please.' He pressed his cut palm to the ruined corpse's skull.

'Argo, *now*.'

The Chaplain forced his twin hearts to slow in their beat as he suppressed his eagerness and finished the rite. Such things were a matter of tradition. Such things mattered, and the dead must be respected for their sacrifice. After what seemed an age, he rose to his feet and moved over to where Vayne and Demetrian were helping the survivor from the rubble.

His targeting reticule outlined the figure in a flash, indicating a failed lock-on. A runic symbol flashed onto his retinas. Gene-seed failsafe. Target denied.

The figure was bone-thin, on shaking legs. Argo's lens display conceded to a passive lock on the emaciated wraith, and at first all he saw was the digital displays of low-pulsing life signs under the figure's name. He couldn't believe anyone, even an Astartes, could be that weak and still live.

The name registered at last, a moment before Vayne and Demetrian brought the figure close enough to recognise. Hollow-cheeked, sunken-eyed and looking more dead than alive, the older Astartes grinned when he saw Argo. The Chaplain didn't miss the resemblance between the survivor's wasted face and his own skull helm.

'Who have you found?' Imrich voxed, sounding annoyed to be missing the discovery.

Argo tried to speak but couldn't form the words. It was Vayne who answered.

'Nochlitan. We found Scout-sergeant Nochlitan.'

The skeletal figure, the sergeant responsible for training both Argo and Vayne in the same squad, kept grinning as he took in the hulking form of Argo's black battle armour.

'Hello, my boy,' Nochlitan said, and his voice was strong despite a scratchy edge and the veteran's shivering limbs. 'You took your damn time.'

'We... We didn't know...'

'I can see why they made you a Chaplain with oratory like that.' The sergeant paused to cough, a dry rasp of a sound that brought blood to his lips. 'Now stop standing around slack-jawed and save the rest of my boys.'

THREE OF THEM had survived. Three of the ten.

It was enough to justify the mission – far more than enough. A single Fist novice would have justified the risk. For four months they had survived in the rubble, and they each emerged as wasted husks, life-signs barely flickering on Vayne's narthecium. Nochlitan was the only one with the power of speech remaining to him. The two novices, in their ruined armour, were little more than tangles of withered limbs, barely breathing, drifting in and out of silent delirium.

The squad had been entombed since the Cantorial Palace had fallen. Nochlitan's Scout squad were embattled in the undercroft as the explosives ticked towards detonation, and had been unable to escape the blast area.

Seven dead. Three alive. A small but blessed victory, torn from the jaws of catastrophe.

* * *

As the servitors stored the digging equipment and the serfs readied the Thunderhawks for orbital flight, Argo sat with Nochlitan in the modest apothecarion. Vayne tended to the two novices, neither one older than sixteen.

'Dorn's holy hand,' Nochlitan said, fixing the Chaplain with his grey eyes. 'What happened to Vayne?'

'A daemon.'

'Is it dead?'

'Of course it's dead.'

'Yes, of course. You see that one there?' Nochlitan waved a weak hand in the direction of the stretcher next to him. 'That's Novice Zefaray.'

Zefaray wheezed into a rebreather mask that covered half of his face. Lines of angry tissue marked his temples and neck, where veins stood out like lightning streaks.

Argo watched the boy's laboured breathing. Zefaray was the Scout squad's Epistolary candidate, marked by the Chapter Librarium for the power of his psychic gift.

'He will be greatly honoured by Chapter Master Kantor for this,' the Chaplain said.

'Damn right he will. Almost killed him, you know. Day and night, screaming into the warp and hoping one of the Librarium would hear. We were trapped close to one another. He would whisper and mutter, speaking of how he was riding a hundred minds to reach one we could trust so many systems away.'

Argo didn't know what to say. It was a psychic feat of incredible strength. When one of the Chapter's Epistolaries had reported the weak yet crazed contact, it had been all the incentive the Chapter's highest echelons had needed. A recovery operation was mounted immediately.

'Great things ahead for him,' Nochlitan grinned. 'Did you find my bolter, boy?'

They hadn't. It showed on Argo's face.

'Ah, well.' Nochlitan lay back on the stretcher, plugged into an array of tubes and wires. 'I'll miss that weapon, without a doubt. It was a fine gun. A fine gun. I killed a genestealer patriarch genus with that bolter. Tore its head clean off.'

'We'll be taking off in a few minutes. The *Vigil* waits in orbit. Once aboard, we make haste to Rynn's World as soon as we break away from Syral.'

Nochlitan sat up again, trembling and overtaxing his remaining strength as his glare speared Argo's eyes.

'You told me the Radimir were still here. Still advancing on this new warlord.'

'They are. They'll engage the enemy's main force this afternoon, if initial projections were correct.'

'You'd abandon the Revenants? Boy, what's wrong with you?'

'Please don't call me "boy", sir. Chapter Master Kantor–'

'Pedro Kantor, blessings upon my old friend, isn't here, my boy. You are. And by Dorn's holy hand, you want to face the Emperor one day knowing you ran from this fight?'

'The odds are... beyond overwhelming. Everything we came to achieve would be void if we die in this battle.'

Nochlitan grasped at Argo's bracer, clenching the smooth black ceramite in a thin-fingered claw that shook as if palsied.

'You are the future of this Chapter.' His grey eyes were the colour of summer storms. 'You shape the path these novices will one day walk.'

Argo rose to his feet, letting his mentor's hand slip from his arm, and left the room without a word.

THE THUNDERHAWK SCREAMED across the night sky, its downward thrusters kicking in as it hovered four hundred metres high. Its wing-mounted bolters aimed at the ground, barking in an unremitting stream. The servitors slaved to the weapons didn't even need to aim. They couldn't miss the horde below: a sea of green skin and chattering weapons, ringing a diminished cluster of grey.

The Revenants' last stand.

The guns cut out after a minute, autoloaders cycling but not opening fire again. On the ground, the armoured divisions of the Radimir kept up their onslaught against the ork host in the city's ruins, and Ulviran watched the Crimson Fist gunship as it stayed aloft, out of enemy fire range.

'It's the Fists,' Dace said, and Ulviran smiled to himself at the man's painfully obvious statement. *Good old Dace. No better man to die with.*

'We did well, Dace. Almost reached that bastard warlord, eh?'

'We did fine, sir.' The major was still looking up at the sky, ignoring the war hammering around him.

'So what are the Fists doing, exactly?' the lord general asked. 'My eyes aren't what they once were.'

'They're…'

ARGO'S LENS DISPLAYS registered the altitude as he fell. The ground soared up fast in his red-tinted vision, and he clutched his sword and bolter tightly, blink-clicking the propulsion icon at the edge of his sight. The weighty jump pack on his back fired in a roaring kick, slowing his descent, but he still landed with jarring force ahead of the others.

He hit the ground running and his weapons sang. Left and right, he slashed his gladius into flesh and fired a relentless stream from his bolter, clearing a space around him in the thick of the churning orkish tide.

Toma was next, thudding to the ground and repeating Argo's lethal sprint. Then Demetrian, then Vayne. Imrich was last, much to his gall. The others, whirling and killing, heard his curses as they started without him.

Twenty metres ahead of them through the ocean of writhing orkish flesh, unmistakeable in salvaged armour that swelled his form to the size of an Astartes Dreadnought, was the greenskin warlord.

Imrich landed and opened up his bolter, running for the brute.

'He's mine!' he voxed to the others. 'That skull is mine!'

In two gauntleted fists, one red, one black, the ancient weapon *Traitor's Bane* was wreathed in coruscating waves of sparking force. The relic mace smashed aside three orks in a single swing, sending their broken forms to the ground still twitching with energy.

'No.' Argo stopped screaming the Litanies of Hate, drawing breath to reply to Imrich and the squad behind him.

'The kine lord is *mine*.'

ABOUT THE AUTHORS

DARREN COX

Living in the deep south USA, Darren Cox works for the United States Space and Rocket Centre managing their international operations. When he's not travelling or chained to his desk he spends his free time following his numerous addictions: tabletop RPGs (including running his own custom written Inquisitor 40K, D20 game), completing his first, full length novel and haunting the weight stacks of his local gym in the wee hours of the night – just to name a few...

'And They Shall Know No Fear...' is his first published work.

AARON DEMBSKI-BOWDEN

Aaron Dembski-Bowden is a British author with his beginnings in the videogame and RPG industries. He was the Senior Writer on the million-selling MMO *Age of Conan: Hyborian Adventures*. He's been a deeply entrenched fan of Warhammer 40,000 ever since he first ruined his copy of *Space Crusade* by painting the models with all the skill expected of an overexcited nine-year-old. He lives and works in York, UK. His hobbies generally revolve around reading anything within reach, and helping people spell his surname.

PETER FEHERVARI

As a full-time television editor, Peter Fehervari's life is an eternity of cuts and mixes and the dreams of thirsting producers. In this deathless state he has cut promos for overlords ranging from Russell T. Davies to Stephen Poliakoff, but none have been as fearsome as the taskmasters of the Black Library. When off-duty he frequents caves, abandoned churches and the occasional haunted asylum in pursuit of guerrilla filmmaking. He has been accused of being a fictional character, but insists he is strange but true. 'Nightfall' is his first published story in this reality.

RICHARD FORD

Richard Ford hails from deepest darkest West Yorkshire, a veritable hotbed of literary talent including the likes of Chris Moyles and Marco Pierre White. He currently works as a writer and editor, though has a chequered work history, which includes sheep rustling and road testing Jack Russell terriers.

He has previously appeared in the Warhammer anthology, *The Cold Hand of Betrayal*, and his first novel, *The Dragons of Lencia*, is currently available through roleplaying and miniature game producer Mongoose Publishing.

NICK KYME

Nick Kyme hails from Grimsby, a small town on the east coast of England. Nick moved to Nottingham in 2003 to work on White Dwarf magazine as a Layout Designer. Since then, he has made the switch to the Black Library's hallowed halls as an editor and has been involved in a multitude of diverse projects. His writing credits include several published short stories, background books and novels.

You can catch up with Nick and read about all of his other published works at his website:
www.nickkyme.com

GRAHAM MCNEILL

Hailing from Scotland, Graham McNeill worked for over six years as a Games Developer in Games Workshop's Design Studio before taking the plunge to become a full-time writer. In addition to many previous novels, including bestsellers *False Gods* and *Fulgrim*, Graham has written a host of SF and Fantasy stories and comics. Graham lives and works in Nottingham and

you can keep up to date with where he'll be and what he's working on by visiting his website.
Join the ranks of the 4th Company at
www.graham-mcneill.com

DYLAN OWEN
In his youth, Dylan Owen roamed England as an itinerant scholar of history and archaeology until settling in Nottingham, where he worked for seven years in Games Workshop's book production department. He now ekes out a living as a freelancer, and has begun to forge a career as a wordsmith. When not dreaming of the forests and mountains of his native Wales, he routinely gets beaten in Scrabble by his wife, Kimberly.

STEVE PARKER
Born and raised in Edinburgh, Scotland, Steve Parker now lives and works in Tokyo, Japan. As a video-game writer/designer, he has worked on titles for various platforms. In 2005, his short fiction started appearing in American SF/fantasy/horror magazines. In 2006, his story 'The Falls of Marakross' was published in the Black Library's *Tales from the Dark Millennium* anthology. His first novel, *Rebel Winter*, was published in 2007. Aside from writing, his interests include weight-training, non-traditional martial arts and wildlife conservation.
Read all about Steve's other works at
www.red-stevie.com

CHRIS ROBERSON
Chris Roberson's novels include *Set the Seas on Fire, Here, There & Everywhere, The Voyage of Night Shining White* and *Paragaea: A Planetary Romance,* and he is the editor of the anthology *Adventure Vol. 1*. Roberson has been a finalist for the World Fantasy Award for Short Fiction, twice for the John W. Campbell Award for Best

New Writer, and twice for the Sidewise Award for Best Alternate History Short Form (winning in 2004 with his story 'O One'). He runs the independent press Monkeybrain Books with his partner. For more about Chris see his website: *www.chrisroberson.net*

GAV THORPE

Prior to becoming a freelance writer, Gav Thorpe worked for Games Workshop as lead background designer, overseeing and contributing to the Warhammer and Warhammer 40,000 worlds. He has written numerous novels and short stories set in the fictional worlds of Games Workshop, including the Time of Legends 'The Sundering' series, the seminal Dark Angels novel *Descent of Angels*, and the *Last Chancers Omnibus*. He lives in Nottingham, UK, with his mechanical hamster, Dennis. Read Gav's blog at: *mechanicalhamster.wordpress.com*

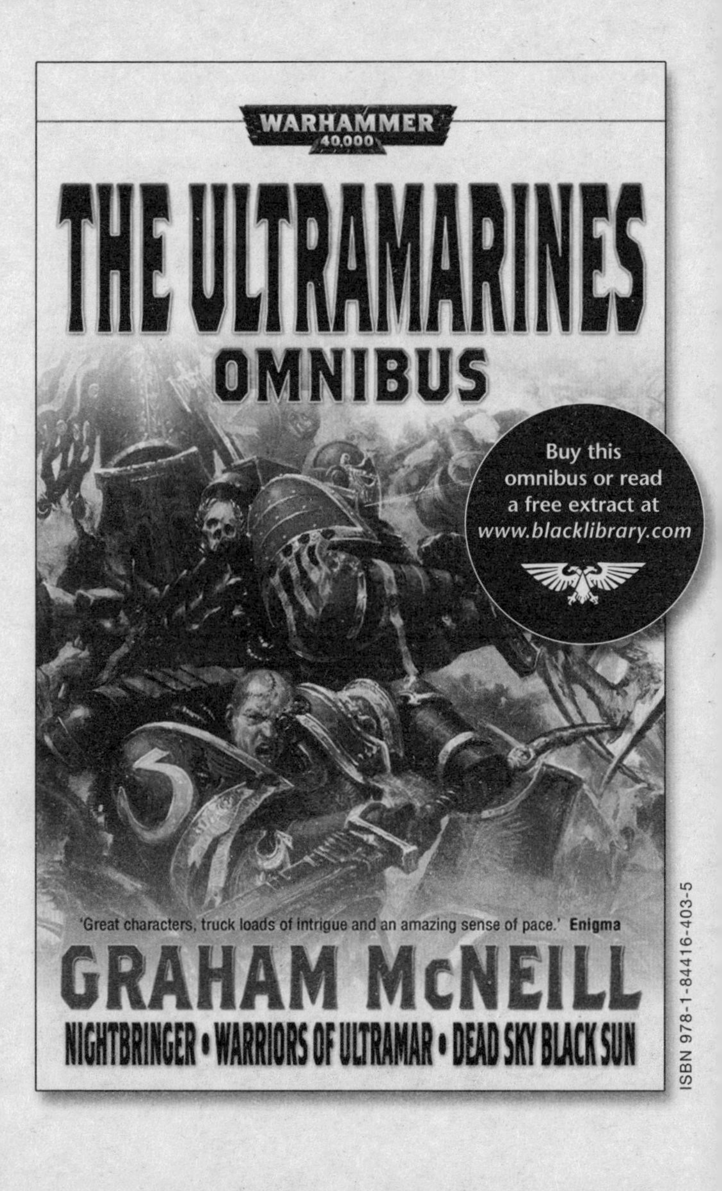
WARHAMMER 40,000
THE ULTRAMARINES
OMNIBUS
Buy this omnibus or read a free extract at www.blacklibrary.com
'Great characters, truck loads of intrigue and an amazing sense of pace.' Enigma
GRAHAM McNEILL
NIGHTBRINGER • WARRIORS OF ULTRAMAR • DEAD SKY BLACK SUN
ISBN 978-1-84416-403-5

WARHAMMER 40,000

THE BLOOD ANGELS OMNIBUS

This omnibus contains the novels Deus Encarmine and Deus Sanguinius

'War-torn tales of loyalty and honour.' – SFX

JAMES SWALLOW

ISBN 978-1-84416-559-9

WARHAMMER 40,000

DAWN OF WAR

BLOOD RAVENS

THE DAWN OF WAR OMNIBUS

Contains the novels Dawn of War, Dawn of War: Ascension and Dawn of War: Tempest

C S GOTO

ISBN 978-1-84416-535-3